THE CURSED GUARD

SOUTHERN STAR TRILOGY BOOK THREE

By K.J. Taylor

Published by Shooting Star Press

http://www.shootingstar.pub

1st edition 2019
This edition 2023

National Library of Australia Cataloguing-in-Publication entry:

Taylor, K.J. (Katie Jill) 1986–

Fantasy—Fiction
The Silent Guard/K.J. Taylor
Speculative fiction--Young adult fiction.
A823.4

Cover design by Sabrina RG Raven

ISBN-13 - 978-1-925821-96-3

Shooting Star

Acknowledgments
Editor: Jessica Stewart

Contents

Acknowledgments ....- 5 -

The Void ....- 1 -

Chapter One - The Cursed Guard...........................- 3 -

Chapter Two - Apprehension.................................- 5 -

Chapter Three - Cursed Eagleholm........................- 19 -

Chapter Four - Lying in Wait ....- 28 -

Chapter Five - Nightmares ....- 44 -

Chapter Six - Eternal Darkness.............................- 59 -

Chapter Seven - Kraego Supreme..........................- 68 -

Chapter Eight - Hope...- 80 -

Chapter Nine - Prince Caradoc's Lessons................- 94 -

Chapter Ten - Seeing .... - 110 -

Chapter Eleven - Negotiations.............................. - 118 -

Chapter Twelve - The Battle for Eagleholm................ - 129 -

Chapter Thirteen - Peace.................................... - 147 -

Chapter Fourteen - The Night God's Punishment....... - 157 -

Chapter Fifteen - Life .... - 171 -

Chapter Sixteen - A Knife in the Back.................... - 189 -

Chapter Seventeen - The Last Redguard .... - 202 -

Chapter Eighteen - Freedom................................ - 212 -

The Scholar.. - 224 -

Other Books By K.J. Taylor .... - 241 -

Also Published By Black Phoenix............................ - 242 -

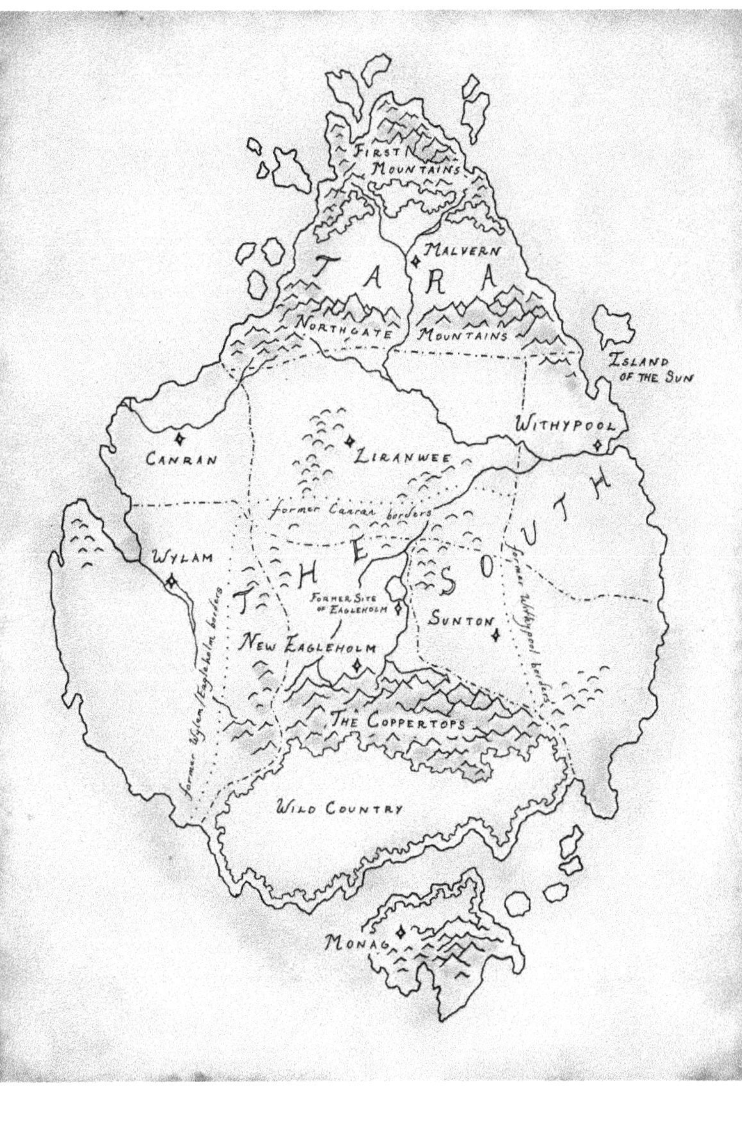

FIRST
MOUNTAINS
MALVERN
T A R A
NORTHGATE
MOUNTAINS
ISLAND
OF THE SUN
WITHYPOOL
CANRAN
LIRANWEE
former Canran borders
T H E   S O U T H
WYLAM
former Withypool borders
FORMER SITE
OF EAGLEHOLM
SUNTON
NEW EAGLEHOLM
former Wylam/Eagleholm borders
THE COPPERTOPS
WILD COUNTRY
MONAG

The Void

Arenadd Taranisäii, former King of the North, lay curled up on his side in the darkness and sobbed softly. 'Stop it…please make it stop…'

The Night God stood over him, her single eye pitiless. You can beg harder than that, Arenadd.

Another savage blast of pain went through him, and Arenadd cried out weakly. 'Stop it!'

More pain racked his body and he convulsed at her feet, eyes bulging like a wounded animal. But he did not beg for mercy again – that was what she wanted, and he wouldn't give it to her.

Finally it stopped, and Arenadd slumped back down, breathing harshly. 'It wasn't my fault,' he said in a thin voice. 'I didn't…'

Rise.

Arenadd stood up. 'It wasn't my fault, Master,' he said again, staring at his boots. 'I swear.'

She stared at him, cold and indifferent as the void all about, and then abruptly turned away from him without a word.

Arenadd breathed out slowly – it was over. For now.

He turned his back on her and wrapped his arms around his thin chest, hugging himself for comfort, and there inside his robe he felt the presence of a precious treasure, safely tucked away. So far his master had shown no sign of suspecting he had it, and it remained with him, strengthening him every moment, as if it wanted to lend him its help. In that sense it was a friend to him here in this nightmare place.

Arenadd smiled – a wide, pained, crazed smile. 'Such a small thing,' he whispered to himself. 'But so strong and fierce.'

He laughed in a broken kind of way and waved a hand across the darkness in front of him, fingers spread. A window opened up, bringing a touch of light with it, and he saw a man he was very familiar with by now. A Southerner, tall and wide-shouldered with red hair. Once he had been heavy with muscle, but now he had begun to look gaunt and ill, and his eyes had gone from honest brown to empty and lightless black, like Arenadd's own. He was in a room, standing beside a fat and balding middle-aged Southerner, looking down on someone else. While he spoke, he rubbed the raw red scar on his throat with his thumb. He did that a lot, Arenadd had noticed.

He wondered if it still hurt. Certainly, it had changed the sound of his voice.

Elsewhere in the crumbling old Eyrie tower, Arenadd saw a woman kneeling in prayer, and her words whispered into his ears. That made him smile a little. She was praying to him, asking for guidance and protection. She believed in him. Yes…Despite everything, people believed in him and spoke his name with hope – and that gave him hope in return.

And he saw others. So many others, living out their mortal lives. So much fear and uncertainty ruled over Cymria now. And yet most people would have every reason to believe the war was over. King Caedmon had done exactly as he said he would do, and the South was his.

Only one part of it had escaped his reach, and that was the tiny, eccentric Monag Island and the handful of refugees now hiding on it. But they wouldn't stay there much longer. They couldn't.

Arenadd turned his attention back to the man with the red hair. 'You can win this if you try, Red,' he whispered. 'Use it. Use the power…Be the Shadow That Walks. Save me from this place…'

Chapter One

The Cursed Guard

Red looked towards the bed. 'Who is he?'

'He was out of it, but he woke up just now,' said Ranulf. 'Says his name's Ridley.'

Red hurried past him – he knew that name! But he barely recognised its owner any more.

Last time Red met him, Ridley had been a guard like himself. He had lived in Canran, which was north-west of Red's old home city, Liranwee, and had patrolled along with his brother Tarn. He hadn't been as powerfully built as Red, but he'd been a strong man, well-muscled from training, and with the natural command of an experienced guard.

Now he was thin and sick-looking, and patches of his hair had fallen out. His eyes were sunken, open but dull. When they turned on Red, their owner cringed and shuddered on his pillows.

'Ridley,' said Red, trying to hide his shock. 'It's me, Red. Don't get up.'

Ridley hadn't tried. He was trembling. 'You're dead,' he mumbled. 'We're all dead. My…'

Red reached out to try and reassure him, but stopped himself. His hands were cold now, and not likely to make anyone feel better. 'It's all right,' he said. 'Yer safe. An' you ain't dead. Ridley, what happened to the others? Do they need help? You gotta tell me, so I can get to them in time.'

Ridley's eyes closed. 'New…New Eagleholm. Went there t'meet you. Too late. All gone. Northerners got us. Senna, Tarn, everyone. My…my son…'

'You what?' said Red. 'Your son? You ain't got a son.'

'Do,' said Ridley. His words were so mumbled they were almost unintelligible, but he went on. 'Senna, me … had a baby. Shouldn't have. They've got her, and him. Had me. Let me go.'

'They let you go?' Ranulf interrupted. 'Why?'

'You!' Ridley's eyes snapped open and fixed on Red. He

coughed. 'He sent me t'find you, Captain. Told me to say…to come find you, an' say…they're all at New Eagleholm. He's there. He's got my son. He's waiting. For you. Said that. Said he's waiting for you.'

'Who is?' asked Red, who already knew the answer but dreaded hearing it.

'Morgan,' Ridley muttered, and closed his eyes again.

Red let him rest. 'Morgan. That son of a bitch. He's never gonna leave me be.'

'It's a trap,' said Ranulf. 'Gotta be. He wants you, Red. He knows if he catches you, it's all over for us.'

'I know,' said Red. 'But we can't just leave New Eagleholm in their hands. Anyhow…'

And anyhow, he didn't care that it was a trap, because Morgan would be there.

His lifeless black eyes narrowed. Morgan the spy. The liar. The backstabbing traitor. The one who had framed Red for his own crimes, and nearly gotten him killed by his own city. The one who took him to his King as a prisoner and presided over his torture. The one who poisoned the wells in Canran and killed half the population. The one who helped his King destroy Withypool and send most of its people to Amoran in chains.

Red had vowed to resist his urge to kill, but with Morgan he wouldn't. With Morgan, he would go to the ends of the earth just to see the life leave the Northerner's eyes. With Morgan, he would give into every savage fantasy. He'd tear the man limb from limb and love every moment of it. He'd…

Red realised that the others were looking at him with slightly nervous expressions.

'I'm going there,' he said finally. 'We're all going. We'll take the city, an' while we're at it I'll find Morgan. I'll get our people out of his clutches, an' this baby too. An' then I'll kill the son of a bitch, an' take time about it too.'

Nobody argued. Everyone knew what Morgan had done.

But afterwards Red recalled what he had said, and the vicious pleasure he had felt, and wanted to vomit.

Chapter Two

Apprehension

Eagleholm, Morgan thought, was a cursed city. Not just New Eagleholm, but old Eagleholm as well.

Everyone in Cymria, Northerner or Southerner, knew what had happened to Old Eagleholm. Once it had been one of the richest cities in the country, with a large territory around it. But it had made the mistake of allowing a Northerner to join its Eyrie as a griffiner. A griffiner who had been murdered by Southerners, only to rise again as the first Shadow That Walks. Arenadd Taranisäii, founder of the Kingdom of Tara, once the leader of all Northerners. He had committed many massacres and destroyed many Southerner strongholds in his time, but his first act had been to destroy Old Eagleholm. He had the Eyrie and murdered many of the people inside it. The city had descended into anarchy, and its neighbouring Eyries had invaded, seizing huge chunks of its lands until almost nothing was left, and finally destroying the last of the city in pointless fighting over a prize that was rapidly crumbling.

After that there was almost nothing left of Eagleholm's lands, and the mountain it had been built on became a heap of rubble haunted by a few starving survivors. Now, that mountain was called Dead Mountain, but a few survivors lingered on. They had found a leader, Lady Liantha, and left to go further south and found a new home. A new Eagleholm.

Morgan smiled a thin, joyless smile. New Eagleholm. A new hope for the last inhabitants of the old city. But then they had made the same mistake their predecessors had made: they had crossed the wrong Northerner. And they had paid the same price.

Morgan was a Taranisäii as well, though only by adoption. He had been chasing Red and Kraego on his adopted father's orders, intent on eliminating the pair of them before they could do any more harm. It had been a futile hope. Morgan was no fighter, and his partner Echo was clever but nowhere near powerful enough to kill a griffin like Kraego, even with the help of a second, stronger griffin who had followed them with her own partner.

Red had captured Morgan and he and Kraego had dragged him to New Eagleholm and handed him over to their friend Liantha, to be interrogated. It was just what Morgan had done to Red once upon a time but, like Red, he had escaped.

Or so he had thought.

Morgan stood on the balcony of the Eyrie Master's quarters, and looked out over the city he hated. He had thought he was escaping, but he had fled straight into the clutches of a mob. The people of New Eagleholm hated nothing more than a Northerner.

He shuddered slightly, but then relaxed and let himself feel the throbbing of his injuries. They had healed as much as they ever would, but he would never lose the limp, or the weakness in his right arm. Time might erase the scars from his face, but he wasn't going to fool himself about that. There was no time left for him.

Behind him, in his stolen quarters, he heard the baby crying. The Southerner brat wouldn't give him any rest, and no wonder. Its mother was locked up in a cell under the Eyrie, and its father was probably dead. Nobody had fed it all day.

Morgan didn't even turn around. He stayed where he was, still as death, and looked down on New Eagleholm. He had conquered it with a group of other griffiners – not that it was much of a prize. Only partly built, with a tiny population of lowlifes. Most of them had fled into the wilderness with their so-called Eyrie Mistress when they realised they had no chance of saving their city.

Still…Morgan could see that New Eagleholm might have stood a chance of being a good city one day. The streets were well laid-out, with the larger, important buildings at the centre near the Eyrie, and the houses neatly arranged inside the city walls. Clearly, someone had properly planned it all out and probably used markers to show where everything should go – stakes to show the corners of buildings. Morgan could only imagine it.

He found himself thinking of Malvern, in the North, where he'd grown up. He had been born in the poorest part of the city, the son of a petty criminal who had been hanged for burglary when Morgan was only small. His elder brother, Henwas, had chosen to follow in their father's footsteps, but much more effectively. He had become a professional fraud and liar, who stole by trickery and impersonation. The skills he'd learnt doing that had served him very well after he was finally arrested – King Caedmon, just a fugitive trying to win his throne at the time, had decided to employ him as a spy.

Morgan smiled again, fondly this time. His witty and resourceful brother had gone from thief to a hero of the North. There was a statue of him in Malvern now, put up by Caedmon. But heroics, as Henwas had often said, got people killed – and they had. Henwas had helped Caedmon win his throne, but had died in the process.

But Caedmon hadn't forgotten his sacrifice, and after the civil war was over he had gone to his friend's birthplace. He had found Morgan there and formally adopted him as his own son, and it wasn't long before Morgan had the chance to prove he was as skilled as his brother when it came to lying and the art of disguise.

And now, he thought, it had come to this. He had followed his brother, and would go on following him…all the way to the end. At least that was what he had promised himself, but now he faced it at last the fear had taken hold of him. It was in him now, chewing away at him like a termite.

He tried to push it away. It was absurd. He had come so close to death here; he shouldn't still be afraid. But he was.

Morgan finally turned and went back inside. His new bride, Lady Arwydd, had just entered. He gave her a long, lingering look before he said anything, trying to convince himself that there was a slight bulge under her dress. It was too early to be certain if she was pregnant, but he hoped that she was. The path he was on would be hard for her as well as him, and she should have something left of him after it was all over.

'Morgan.' She came to him, and hugged him.

He hugged her back before he let her go. 'What was that for?'

'You looked so sad.'

'Did I?' Morgan smiled. 'I was thinking about you.'

'That's not very comforting!' Arwydd smiled back, but it quickly faded. 'Morgan, you don't have to do this.'

'Yes I do,' he said sharply. 'You know I do. You know what this man is capable of, and you know what he's threatened to do. We can't kill him, so we have to do whatever else we can.'

'But this?' said Arwydd. 'Morgan, this is…evil. And if you can't do it—,'

'Even if we succeed, the outcome will be the same,' said Morgan.

'I'm going to die.' The fear lurched in him as he said it, but he stayed outwardly calm. 'There's no point in lying to ourselves about that,' he added, seeing her expression. 'We both know what happens to someone who tries to attack the Shadow That Walks. He'll kill me. I just have to hope that it'll be quick.'

'But—,' Arwydd began.

'You're going to say I don't have to put myself in this situation,' Morgan interrupted. 'But you know I do. It has to be me. You know what happened between us. He wants revenge, and he'd go to the ends of the earth to get it. He probably knows this is a trap, but he'll come anyway because he won't be able to help himself. Even just the baby and his friends might not be enough to bring him here. But I will be.'

'But how can you want to die?' Arwydd pleaded. 'You almost died before – it was a miracle you didn't.'

'I know,' said Morgan. 'The Night God spared me for a reason. So I could do this one last thing. For our people, and our King, and for her.'

'But how do you know it's for her?' asked Arwydd. 'He's the Shadow That Walks. He belongs to her.'

'He's a Southerner,' Morgan snapped.

'He's the Shadow That Walks,' Arwydd repeated. 'What if that's what the Night God wanted? What if she doesn't want us here in the South – that could be why she chose one of them. Don't you understand, Morgan? You're not just flirting with death: you're flirting with damnation. The Night God sends her enemies to the void.'

'You sound like one of those heretics from Malvern,' Morgan growled. 'Worshipping the Shadow That Walks like a god, thanks to that traitor priestess. Are you going to run off and join this Southerner too?'

'What—? No! I mean…Morgan, don't.'

'I'm sorry.' Morgan relented and reached out to touch her hair. 'Sorry. I'm just…'

'You're afraid,' she said softly.

'Yes. Yes, I'm afraid. I…' Morgan turned away, wrestling with himself. He couldn't tell her about the thoughts that had been going through his mind. If he did, his doubts might become too strong and stop him from doing what he had to.

Arwydd came to his side and gently took his hand in hers. 'What is it? Tell me.'

It was too late. Morgan tried to stop himself, but he couldn't, and his fears came tumbling out of him. 'I'm afraid,' he repeated. 'You're right, Arwydd. I can't help but think about it. What if he is the real Shadow That Walks? I mean…we've all heard the stories. And this whole thing is a gamble. I'm willing to die for our people, but if we're wrong…'

'You could die for nothing,' said Arwydd.

'But what else can I do?' asked Morgan.

She pulled his hand towards her, and laid it on the small swelling between her hips. 'Live,' she said. 'For me and your child.'

Morgan kept his hand there, and said nothing.

Arwydd looked into his scarred face, and she could see the gleam in his eyes. She knew that what had happened to him here had nearly broken him. For a long time he had been on the edges of sanity and, even now, she was sometimes afraid that she was going to lose him. But there was nothing mad about what he had said. He was afraid, just as he should be.

She clutched his hand, and wondered if she should tell him the truth. But would that persuade him to change his mind, or just make him angry? She had been hesitating over that for a long time now. But he already looked as if he guessed part of the truth.

Arwydd was a shadow worshipper. She was one of the heretics from Malvern. The apprentice priestess, Teressa, had converted her to join her cult which worshipped the Shadow That Walked as a god. Now, with the coming of the new Shadow That Walked, Teressa had led her fellow worshippers out of Malvern to join him – Southerner or no Southerner. And if Arwydd had been in Malvern to hear the word, she may well have decided to go with them.

But she loved Morgan, and how could she abandon him to join this man who had nearly been the death of him?

'He's not our enemy,' she murmured, almost without meaning to.

Morgan looked irritated.

'He's not an enemy to Northerners,' said Arwydd. 'He went to Malvern himself to rescue Teressa. She's one of us.'

'She's a traitor,' said Morgan.

'She's a Northerner,' said Arwydd. 'He's not an enemy to

Northerners, just the King.'

'That's enough, Arwydd,' said Morgan. 'He's a Southerner, and he's our enemy, and I don't care about what the Night God thinks. He has to be stopped, and I'll do it even if I die for it.'

After that, Arwydd didn't dare say anything else. But later, when she went to pray alone, she found herself reliving the strange dream that had come to her before the conquest of New Eagleholm. She had seen the face of the great Arenadd, and seen it change to another face. The face of a Southerner with red hair. And it had given her that message that she whispered to herself now as she had many times before.

'…Serve the Shadow That Walks.'

*

Back in Monag, Red's followers were preparing to leave. Lady Liantha had been asked to take charge since their goal was to recapture her city, and she had organised everyone into groups and begun the tedious process of sending them back to the mainland. Since Monag only owned two ships, it wasn't possible for everyone to leave together, but Liantha, together with Red, Isleen, former guard commander Talmon, and others with experience and leadership skills, had made a plan that seemed viable. The attacking force would separate into two halves and, rather than slog through the thick forest that covered a good part of the southernmost end of the continent, they would travel around the continent and land on the east and west coasts. From there they would march upward and inward, going around the mountains. The griffiners would keep them in touch with each other until they met up at New Eagleholm. It would be a long march, but most likely faster than trying to drag their weapons and armour through dense undergrowth and then climb through a mountain range which may well still be occupied by hostile wild griffins.

But Red was going in first. He'd explained that to the others, and resisted all efforts to persuade him otherwise.

'They've got some of ours locked up,' he insisted. 'We can't let them be used as hostages, or get them caught up in the fighting. Kraego an' me will go in first an' get them out of there.'

'But what if—?' Liantha began.

'Relax, we've done it half a dozen times before,' said Red. He hadn't told anyone about Ridley's message; he didn't need to have them all in his face reminding him that it was a trap.

As the fastest travellers, he and Kraego would move back and forth between the two armies to keep an eye on them, and enter Eagleholm once they were in position and ready to strike. Everything would have to be properly timed but Red wasn't expecting the occupiers of New Eagleholm to put up much of a fight. Once they had seen himself and Kraego, plenty of them would be too frightened to do much. Some might even turn traitor. Others had already done it, after all.

The Northerners who had betrayed their King to come and follow him were coming too. Seeing their own people fighting on his side would help to demoralise the enemy, and anyway, Red wanted them to prove they were serious about following him.

Many of them were unhappy about the idea of fighting their own people, but none had argued; they had turned traitor in the first place because they believed he was the avatar of the Night God – holy, and therefore always right. Red didn't like it much, but followers were followers.

While the ships were being manned with the first two groups to go, Red went to see Teressa.

The heretic priestess was in her thirties, and as a priestess in training had converted many to follow her. Given her upbringing, worshipping things must have been second nature to her anyway. But she must have been good at it; many of the people she had converted to join her cult were griffiners, some very high-placed in Malvern's Eyrie.

Red expected to find her praying, and he was right: she was in her temporary quarters with her grey-feathered partner Orak, holding the prayer stone she had made and murmuring over it.

Red didn't interrupt her; he stayed in the doorway and waited. It took longer than he had expected, but nowadays he had discovered a new ability to stand still for long periods without getting tired or bored.

He watched Orak shifting about and occasionally nibbling at a loose feather. Teressa had said that when she first met him, the purple-eyed griffin had been a cripple with a twisted foreleg. But when he and his new partner had gone to Amoran in search of Kraego, he had touched the massive skull of a dead serpent god and been healed.

So Teressa had claimed. Red hadn't seen it, but he had been there, and had felt the invisible blast of force from the skull that had knocked everyone over, himself included. He wouldn't be seeing it again; by now it must be back in Erebus with its rightful owners, but it had shown him that there were stranger things in the world than he had ever suspected.

He watched Teressa as well. She was older than him, but he'd always thought she was much more naïve in some ways than a woman of her age should be. Her black hair was long, and like most Northerners she was tall and had narrow shoulders and hips. She wore the silver robe of a priestess, even though she had only ever been an apprentice and now would never be welcome back at the Temple where she had once lived.

Red's fellow Southerners didn't like her much, of course – not just because she was a Northerner, but because she was a traitor and everyone knew that traitors weren't to be trusted, even by those who had benefitted from the betrayal. Her fellow Northerner traitors, though, seemed to adore her, and Red…Red liked her. He liked her more than he'd admitted to her, or anyone, in fact.

She had come all the way to Amoran, looking for himself and Kraego, and had shown a lot of courage in doing so. She believed that her loyalty belonged to Arenadd, not his successor Caedmon, and she believed that finding Red and following him was what Arenadd wanted. Since then she had never let her loyalty waver, and had risked her life more than once for him.

But that wasn't why Red liked her. The thing he liked her for was what she showed when she turned around and saw him there – or, rather, what she did not show.

She smiled. 'Red. Hello.'

Red smiled back. 'Prayin' for good luck?'

'Aye, I am,' she said. She came towards him while she spoke in her lilting Northern accent, and touched him lightly on the arm. 'I decided I wouldn't pray so much after…well, I decided not to. But sometimes prayer is what everyone needs. I know all ye Southerners went to yer own Temple to pray a few days back, and that's what ye should be doing now. I felt the same need, but there's no Temple here for me.' She patted her pocket where the prayer stone sat, and smiled. 'I carry my Temple with me wherever I go.'

Red chuckled roughly. 'A portable temple, eh? It's a good idea. I was thinkin' we should talk a bit before we head off. Want to go for a walk?'

'I'd be honoured,' said Teressa. 'Orak?'

The grey griffin stirred. 'I shall follow you, in case there is danger.' He had become very protective of his partner, not just because she was surrounded by potentially hostile Southerners, but also because she had nearly been killed in Malvern and that had made him nervous. He looked at Red. 'Where is Kraego?'

'Not far,' said Red. 'He'll probably join us once we go outside. C'mon, Teressa.'

The two of them left together, walking down the inside of the Eyrie towards the ground floor.

'Y'know, us Southerners have portable Temples too,' said Red. 'Never seen one, but I've heard the priests keep these mini altars made out of wood, an' a special tent an' everything all packed up ready. So when one of our armies goes out in the field a priest goes along, an' brings all of that so he can set up a temporary Temple whenever they make camp. Soldiers got a lot to pray about, an' someone's gotta do the rites for the dead.'

Teressa fell into step beside him. 'That's a good idea. Our people haven't had Temples at all for very long though. We worshipped in the open air until Arenadd took Malvern and made Saeddryn High Priestess. She built the first Temple. Ye saw it yerself.'

'I did.' Red nodded grimly – Teressa had been arrested for blasphemy and nearly used as the sacrifice for the Blood Moon. Red had rescued her, and accidentally performed the sacrifice himself by stabbing the new High Priestess to death over the altar.

'It's a shame ye couldn't see it properly,' said Teressa. 'It's a beautiful place. I grew up in it.' She looked sad. 'I knew I was going to miss it when I left.'

'Just like I miss Liranwee,' Red sighed. 'But before you had Temples, you had them stone circles, right?'

'We did, and we built one inside the Temple as well,' said Teressa. 'The real ones are much smaller, though.'

'It'd be easy to make a stone circle while you was travelling,' Red joked. 'If you didn't mind about it bein' tiny.'

Teressa smiled. 'I know for a fact that Saeddryn did just that after she became the Shadow That Walks.'

'How d'you know?' asked Red.

'She told me.'

Red stopped and stared at her. 'What? She told you? You mean you met her?'

'Aye, I did,' said Teressa. 'She came to Malvern, ye see, after the half-breed had her killed and the Mighty Skandar brought her back the way he had done for Arenadd. She snuck in just as ye did, and persuaded people to join her side, and Caedmon's. Of course since she'd been High Priestess, we priestesses were some of the first she spoke to. I was already worshipping Arenadd in secret, but I didn't see what I could do to help her. I was afraid of what might happen to me. But—,' she smiled again, with open pride. 'But I can say this now. There have been three Shadows That Walk in all of recorded history, and I've met all of them. The first blessed me, the second inspired me, and the third led me.'

Red had to smile back. 'It's no wonder you got people t'follow you when you can come up with that sort of thing on the spot!'

Teressa laughed. 'I've always had a knack for it. If we Northerners had holy books, I could try and write one.'

'Maybe you should,' said Red.

They reached the bottom of the Eyrie and passed out into the open air, setting out in no particular direction.

'Now then,' Teressa said unexpectedly. 'Why did ye come to see me?'

The question caught him by surprise, and he stumbled a little before he came up with an answer. 'I wanted to go over the plan with you an' make sure you had it all down. After all, you're gonna be leading the other Northerners.'

'Ye want me to fight?' Teressa sounded surprised.

'Well, no,' Red said awkwardly. 'You ain't trained for it. But you'll be leadin' them from the back, like. You know, inspiring them. We both know yer good at that!'

'I'll do my best,' said Teressa. 'But…'

'But what?'

She looked nervous. 'There's something I wanted to tell ye. I've been thinking of it since ye rescued me from Malvern, but—,'

Red tensed slightly. 'But?'

'Never mind. Ye see, I got myself into trouble there,' said Teressa. 'I got caught, I needed to be saved like some fragile little princess out of a story. I was a coward.'

'Stop that,' said Red. 'Don't you dare call yerself a coward. For gods' sakes, Teressa. I've been locked up too. I was nearly killed by my own people as well. My best friend Ranulf, my old partner, hauled me off to prison! An' I'm the one who got sold to Amoran like a piece of meat. There's nothing cowardly about bein' overpowered.'

'But ye got yerself out of all that!' said Teressa. 'Nobody rescued ye.'

'It was all luck,' Red said dismissively. 'Anyway, I'm a fighter. You ain't.'

Teressa did not look reassured. 'That's the point, Red. That's what I mean. I've done all I can for ye so far by finding ye in Amoran and bringing the others to follow ye. But now I want to do more. What ye need now are fighters.'

'You mean you want to be a fighter now?' said Red, nonplussed.

'I do,' said Teressa. 'I let ye down before, and I want to make up for it.'

Red shook his head – this woman was unbelievable.

Teressa saw him do it, and got the wrong idea. 'What, ye don't think I can fight?' she snapped. 'I'm a Northerner, remember? Every Northerner is a warrior at heart, that's what we're all told when we're little. Be a carter or a baker or a stableboy, but underneath ye are a warrior, and ye can always call on it when ye need to.' She stuck her chin out fiercely.

Red forced himself not to laugh at her. 'That ain't what I meant! I'm just amazed.'

'By what?' asked Teressa, still defensive.

'By you!' said Red. He gave her an admiring look. 'I can't believe you reckon you're a coward after all the things you've done.'

'Well…' Teressa looked pleasantly embarrassed.

Red decided to go ahead and tell her. It could only be helpful to her to know it. 'You know what I like about you?' he said.

'What?' She listened intently.

They were walking through Monag's only town now, and Red waved an arm to indicate everyone in it. 'There's so many people here on this island with us,' he said. 'An' out of all of them, you're the only one who never looks scared of me. Even the other worshippers what came back here with you are scared, but you ain't.

You've only ever looked scared of me once since I've known you, an' that was when I was about to kill you in Amoran.' He paused. 'An' that was when I was alive.'

Teressa blushed. 'Well, that was – I mean…'

'Are you afraid of me?' asked Red, unable to stop himself.

'No,' said Teressa.

'Why not?'

'Because I know yer on my side,' she said. 'I knew it before ye saved my life.'

'Everyone else here knows it too, but that doesn't change things,' said Red. He sighed. 'I can see it in all of them. Even Liantha, who I've known since I was a boy. Even Ranulf. They try an' act normal, but all the time there's this…I dunno, hesitation. I can always see it. I…' he trailed off.

'What?' asked Teressa.

'I can smell fear,' said Red. 'Sense it, kind of. It's like I'm always searching for it now. I can't help it. It's there on everyone, like a shadow. But not you. Never with you. So I'm damned if I'm ever calling you a coward, Teressa.'

They walked in silence for a little while.

'Do ye know,' said Teressa, 'I think that's the nicest thing anyone's ever said to me.'

'You're welcome,' said Red. 'But if you really want to try yer hand at fighting, go ahead. Just stay close to Orak so he can protect you.'

'I agree,' Orak said unexpectedly. He flexed his healed foreclaw. 'I am a griffin, and we too are born to fight. I have never had the strength before now, but now I do, and I am ready.' He hissed. 'I did not want to be left out of this fight for Eagleholm, and I shall not be. If you wish to fight, Teressa, come and fight beside me. As your master has said, I shall protect you.'

'Settled, then,' said Red. 'An' once I've gotten the others out of the city, I'll come back to help out. I'll find you an' stay close by in case you need me.'

'No,' said Teressa, with sudden ferocity.

Red blinked. 'What?'

'Don't help me. I want to show I can do this,' said the Northerner. 'Don't ye see what I meant? I want to show I'm strong by fighting without needing help or protection except from Orak. He's my partner. But I'm not so precious that I need protection, and ye are too important to waste time watching over me. Let me fight alone, and if I die, so be it.'

Red looked at her with open astonishment. 'Seriously?'

'Yes,' said Teressa. She smiled. 'Trust me.'

'I will, then,' said Red. 'If that's what you want. But you don't have to die to prove you can fight.'

'I'm not planning to,' said Teressa. She softened. 'I'm sorry.'

'It's fine,' said Red. 'I just don't want you to go doing something you shouldn't for the sake of pride. 'Cause trust me – once you've been a slave you know how cheap pride really is.'

'I understand,' said Teressa.

'It will be fine,' said Orak. 'I have never fought either, so we shall prove ourselves together.'

'Yeah…' Red shifted uneasily. 'Teressa, listen. There's somethin' else I wanted to say, an' it's important.'

'Yes?'

'If anything happens to me,' he said. 'If I'm caught, or lost or somethin'…'

'Yes?' said Teressa.

'If that happens, Liantha will be in charge,' said Red. 'I've told her that. Isleen an' Alaric will help her out. But without me, I can't promise you an' the other Northerners will be safe. You'll have nothing to follow. So if that happens, you should go. Get yerselves out of this mess before things turn ugly. Don't try an' fight for a lost cause. Just take the others an' go.'

Teressa looked grim. 'No, Red,' she said.

'Yes, Teressa. I don't want any of you to die just because——,'

'No,' she said again. She stopped walking and faced him without fear. 'We're Northerners. We don't run away. If something does happen to ye, then this is what I'll do, and ye have it on my honour as a woman of the North. If ye are lost then I won't rest. I won't stop. I'll do everything in my power to find ye and bring ye back. And I will not run.'

There was so much vehemence in her face and voice, and so much determination, that Red didn't dare argue. But in that moment he found himself fighting down a very different urge. Just then, while she faced him so proudly, he wanted to reach out and touch her.

He didn't move.

'All right then,' he said softly, and afterwards, for the rest of that day, and the rest of that week, and long after that, he couldn't help but feel honoured, and humbled, that he had ever been able to inspire such powerful loyalty in anyone.

It made him wonder whether it would be better to avoid whatever trap Morgan had waiting for him, but something stronger pulled him onward. Because however much he dreaded the thought of leaving Teressa behind, if something did happen to him, he could not fight the urge that had been in him ever since he had been brought back to life. It was a hunger even stronger than the endless desire to kill, and one he knew had always driven the Shadow That Walks – revenge.

Chapter Three

Cursed Eagleholm

The march to Eagleholm went off more smoothly than Red had expected; as planned the two ships each made several trips, until both halves of the army were ashore. Red and Kraego went last, once Red had taken time to thank Lady Merca, the eccentric Monag Eyrie Mistress, and promised her that her help wouldn't be forgotten after the war was over.

'I don't mind it so long as ya don't come back eating all the produce!' was all the old lady had to say by way of reply.

There weren't many young griffiners in Monag but, out of those, a handful had decided to join up with Red's army. They helped make his already mixed group even more motley with their odd woollen clothes and peculiar accents. The people of Monag had been all but cut off from the mainland for a long time and, up until he had gone there himself, Red hadn't even known there was anyone living on the half wild island, which some people referred to as "The Isle of Hags" for reasons no-one seemed to remember – old stories about witches, maybe.

He and Kraego didn't take a ship, but flew to the mainland together. It wasn't far to go, and even though Kraego had more growing to do and would ultimately become even larger than he was now, he was already a powerful flier.

Red enjoyed the sensation of flying with his partner again. It was good, too, to be alone together again. Talking in the air wasn't really practical, but that was all right. Just being with Kraego was pleasant enough. The two of them had always been close – or as close as anyone really could be with a creature as unemotional as a griffin. They'd grown up together, more or less; when Red was a boy he had been there to witness Kraego's hatching, and since the griffin chick hadn't had any siblings Red had been something of a brother to him. They'd played together, and travelled together until they had to part ways, and neither of them had forgotten the other.

But now it was different. Kraego wasn't dead, but he could still use the shadows as Red did, and when Red was near him he could sense the power inside the giant griffin. Everyone could sense the dark power in himself, and in Kraego as well, and it made them uneasy. For Red, though, it made him feel good. Kraego's presence soothed him and reminded him that he wasn't alone.

Once they reached the mainland, Kraego landed on the beach to rest. Griffins weren't made to fly long distances, and needed to stop every so often, especially if they were carrying someone.

Red slid off his back and walked around on the sand to stretch his legs. 'Are we gonna use the shadows to get to the others fast?'

'Yes.' Kraego stretched luxuriously, like a cat, finishing with a shake of his wings and a flick of his tail. 'It is good that we can do it together now.'

'Yeah.' Kraego had taken them both through the shadows before, when Red was still alive, but living people weren't meant to be in the shadows. It sapped their life force and could make them ill or even kill them.

'We shall take New Eagleholm, and do it easily,' said Kraego, confident as always. 'I have no fear of this griffin Eck-hoo who rules it now. He is cunning, but weak.'

'Yeah, well, I'd say the same about Morgan but that doesn't mean I'm lookin' forward to meeting him again,' said Red. 'I got a bad feeling about it, Kraego.'

'Why?' the griffin asked tersely. 'You are Kraeai kran ae. No mortal human can kill you.'

'But they can still hurt me,' said Red. 'I don't trust that Morgan. He wouldn't try an' lure me in if he didn't have somethin' up his sleeve.'

'If you are worried about this trap he must have prepared, then use the shadows,' said Kraego. 'Stay hidden and kill him from behind, before he has the chance to even know you are there.'

'Yeah.' Red had already planned to do that. 'I'm sure it'll be fine.'

'And I shall be there,' said Kraego. He stretched again. 'Once we have taken Eagleholm, I think we should move on quickly, before our enemies have the chance to strike back.'

'Agreed,' said Red. 'If the King's still in Liranwee, that's where we should go. It's a straight shot from New Eagleholm.'

'We shall go there and steal his son as planned,' said Kraego. 'Then we will have a hostage and we can force Shar's human to surrender.'

Red nodded. They had long ago decided that it would be best to strike at whatever city the King was in – most likely Liranwee, which he had decided to make his new capital. The quicker this was over, the better.

But first…Eagleholm.

Red felt a shiver of cold anticipation move over his skin. 'Let's get goin',' he said.

*

After that he and Kraego were constantly on the move, travelling back and forth from group to group, keeping an eye on everyone, bringing messages and scouting out the land ahead. They used the shadows, which allowed them to travel unseen and much faster than anyone else, and with them and other, ordinary griffins helping, the journey passed without any major problems and faster than they had first thought.

Finally, after several weeks of marching, they were on the open plains around New Eagleholm, with the Coppertop Mountains behind them and the city within a day's march. Red, Kraego, and the other leaders of the resistance came together for a last meeting the night before the advance on the city began.

Talmon, the former commander of Liranwee's city guard, had been put in charge of one half of the army with Ranulf, Elthan, and several other former guards as his immediate subordinates. The other army was commanded by Lady Liantha, backed up by a group of other experienced guards, with Isleen and Alaric as advisors. Teressa and the Northerners were with this group.

All of them were at the meeting, which took place in a small camp Red had put up for them, and all listened while Red spoke first.

'I don't like this,' he said. 'It's too quiet. Kraego an' me scouted out the city as you know, an' there's hardly anyone there. Foot troops an' a handful of griffiners, an' that's it. I think they're tryin' to get us off our guard. Make us think it's gonna be an easy victory.'

'But it will be, if that's all we're up against,' said Talmon. 'We outnumber them, and most likely the Southerners left in the city will help us once they realise what's going on. Unless they're hiding more troops in the mountains?'

Red shook his head. 'We thought of that, an' we searched 'em. There's nothing. They've got no backup, nobody nearby to come running when they need it. I dunno what they're playing at.'

'Maybe they're overconfident,' said Liantha. 'Assuming that since they had an easy victory when they took the city, there isn't any serious resistance in these parts. They could be excused for thinking it.'

'That could be true,' said Isleen. 'This Morgan is a spy, not a military commander.'

Red frowned while he thought it over. 'It could be that. But there's another possibility.'

'What's that, Captain?' asked Talmon.

'That it's a trap,' said Red.

'But we've already established that they don't have anyone lying in wait,' said Talmon. 'What sort of trap could it be if it isn't that?' He was a middle-aged man, wiry and lined with experience, and he wore his grey hair very short. He frowned as he spoke.

'I think it's a trap for me,' said Red. 'See, it's a hard truth, but in the end, I'm the most dangerous enemy they've got. I ain't just the leader, I'm the Shadow That Walks. It's in their best interests to get rid of me first, and fast. I think they've set this up so I'll see it an' think it'll be easy. So I'll charge in without thinking, trying to get to Morgan. They might even think I'll try an' take the city all by myself. An' then…well, then there'll be something waiting for me inside. There's no way of knowing what, but it could be they're hoping to take me prisoner.'

'Hah,' said Talmon. 'That's a futile hope. Even if they succeed, we'll take the city and get you out of there in no time.'

'Yeah, and I've got no intention of lettin' myself get caught,' said Red. 'Three times was enough.'

The others chuckled.

'I've thought it over, an' I still want to go in first,' said Red. 'I gotta get our people out to safety so they don't get caught up in this.'

'And will you go after Morgan?' Talmon asked. 'You want to, don't you?'

'Yeah,' said Red.

'Then do it,' said Talmon, with unexpected fierceness. 'That man deserves whatever you've dreamt up for him, and he's a dangerous enemy. Kill him, Captain.'

'You can count on it,' Red said grimly.

'So we're going to stay with our original plan?' asked Liantha.

'Yeah,' said Red. 'But with one change. Just to be on the safe side.'

They all leaned forward to listen.

'Just in case this is a trap, I'm gonna take a couple of people with me,' said Red. 'To help out, or go back for help if anything happens.'

'That's good thinking,' Talmon nodded. 'Who did you have in mind?'

'They shall have to be partnered,' said Kraego. 'We have decided that one Southerner and one Northerner would be best.'

'But they've got to be volunteers,' Red added. 'This is gonna be dangerous, an' I don't want anyone coming unless they're ready for it.'

'Seerae and I should go,' Liantha said immediately. 'It's our city.' She glanced at her partner, who rasped agreement.

'And I'll go,' said Teressa.

'Two women?' said Talmon. 'Neither of them fighters?'

'This ain't about fighting,' said Red. 'It's about stealth. Liantha an' Seerae know the city, an' Teressa knows me, an' I can trust her not to panic. If there's fighting to be done, I'll do it.' He paused to mull it over. 'All right, I got an idea. Liantha, Seerae – how about you two hide out in the city? I'll nip in first an' find a good spot. I'm thinkin' it's gonna be pretty quiet with most of your people already out of there. Then Teressa an' me go into the Eyrie. I can disappear if I need to, an' she can pass herself off as one of them. We'll get into the prison an' get our mates out of there, an' we'll get them to you. Meanwhile everyone else will be lying low in the trees just here, like we've already planned. Liantha, once you've got our lads with you, you'll be ready to strike the first blow. They're all guards like me, an' they know how to fight. Get the gates open – Teressa an' Orak can help with that. Then our troops can get in, an' we'll take 'em down hard an' fast. In the meantime, me an' Kraego will go straight to the Eyrie. We'll take out Morgan an' anyone else in there who gets in our way. Shouldn't be too hard. How's that sound?'

The others listened, and murmured amongst themselves while they thought it over.

'How will we signal to the others?' asked Liantha.

'I shall do that,' said Seerae. She hissed. 'This Eck-hoo is the leader of the ones who took my city from me. To win back my territory, I must fight him. I will signal the beginning of the attack when I challenge him.'

'Perfect,' said Red. A griffin's challenge shriek was one of the most intimidating sounds in the world, and would be just the thing to frighten the enemy. It also carried a very long way. 'Anyone else got any suggestions?'

There were a few minor details to smooth out, but nothing serious. Everyone seemed happy with the plan. Only Seerae looked uneasy.

'Remember, black griffin,' she hissed at Kraego, who was her own half-brother. 'This territory is mine, and you must leave it to me to win back. If you kill Eck-hoo, I shall challenge you.'

'And then you will die,' Kraego said coolly.

'But I shall challenge you even so,' said Seerae. 'My territory has been taken from me once, and you will not take it a second time.'

'Are you afraid?' the giant griffin mocked.

'I fear nothing.'

'Kraego,' Red warned.

His partner flicked his tail dismissively. 'Do not be afraid, Seerae. I have no interest in this little territory, and Eck-hoo is not a worthy opponent to me. I shall drive him out of his Eyrie and into your talons.'

'Then what griffin is worthy to fight you?' Seerae hissed back. 'Shar? She has defeated you once already, and she is barely half your size! Remember that before you mock me.'

Kraego lurched forward and snapped his beak at her, making her start away from him. 'She will not defeat me again,' he snarled. 'We will meet again, and when we do, she will die. And if you speak to me this way again, so will you.'

Everyone there, griffins included, had backed off. Red and Liantha stayed nearby, both hesitating over whether to try and restrain their partners. But, thankfully, Seerae finally backed off.

'When this fight is done, I shall stay in my territory,' she said. 'You must go, and you will not be welcome back.'

'Seerae—,' Liantha began.

'Say nothing!' her partner snapped. 'This is not your concern, human. My brother will not come back to my territory, or I will attack him.'

'All right,' Red stepped in. 'Kraego, stop it. We're on the same side, remember?'

'A griffin is on no side but his own,' said Kraego.

'Yeah, an' that's why you lot never built a civilisation,' said Red. 'An' why you've nearly died out in the wild.'

Several people gasped.

Kraego said nothing. He reared back, and slammed Red into the ground with his talons.

Red fell hard, but was up in an instant. 'Don't you dare!'

Kraego snarled at him. 'Speak to me with respect or I shall make you suffer, Kraeai kran ae.'

Red could see there was no point in arguing with him. 'I ain't scared of you, Kraego,' he said. 'Now stop it an' let's just forget about this. We've got enough enemies without fighting each other.'

'Your human is right, Kraego,' said Orak. 'Save your arguments for later.'

Kraego still looked angry but, thankfully, he calmed down. 'Very well. We will forget this, and prepare to fight. Seerae, keep your human close and sharpen your talons. We may argue over territories later.'

After that things settled down, and everyone there looked relieved. The humans still looked a little shaken up, but Red quickly smoothed things over by moving on with the discussion as if nothing had happened.

'So Teressa, are you right with how everything's shaping up?' he asked.

The Northerner looked slightly paler than usual. 'Er, aye. I mean, yes. I had to bluff things out in Malvern before I was caught. I can do it again. I can try to order the guards away from the prison, or ye can kill them.' She laughed nervously.

'We could try that first, an' if it doesn't work I'll kill them,' said Red, deliberately speaking as calmly as possible despite his damaged voice. 'I got a bit of a soft spot for guards, even if they're working for the enemy.'

Talmon grinned, which was unusual for him. 'It's a tough job, but someone's got to do it. But everyone knows when the enemy attacks, us guards are always the first to get it.'

'Damn right,' said Red.

A bit of humour, however black, was just what everyone needed, and they finished their discussion in a lighter mood. By the end, everything had been sorted out to Red's satisfaction. The attack was ready to go ahead that evening.

But afterwards, when the leaders parted ways to go back to their separate groups, now within walking distance of each other but poised to attack the city from both sides at once, Red went after Liantha.

'Listen, I'm real sorry about that,' he said – having waited until both griffins were out of earshot. 'I think Kraego's nervous.'

Liantha twisted a lock of her dark blonde hair between her fingers. 'I was going to apologise too,' she said. 'But I had a feeling something like this would happen. Seerae's afraid of Kraego. He's younger than her, and much stronger, and now she's lost her territory she feels…well, more or less the same as how I feel. Humiliated. And afraid. It makes people irrational, so why not griffins?'

'Yeah, well, Kraego's got no territory at all,' said Red. 'Never has. He's always been a little nervy around other griffins. But he reckons he's a cut above everyone else because he's so big, an'…well, 'cause he's black.'

'Griffish arrogance,' Liantha sighed. 'It's always been a problem for griffiners like us, hasn't it? I mean, they say it drives us to do great things because no griffin is ever content unless they're pursuing some ambition, but it's destroyed plenty of us. My father Roland used to say it destroyed Old Eagleholm.'

'Really?' said Red. 'I thought it was Arenadd who did that.'

'Yes, but…' Liantha looked uneasy at the mention of his name. 'But Roland was there, you see. He knew everyone involved. You know Arenadd only died because he was betrayed, and it was another griffiner who betrayed him. Lord Rannagon, Master of Law. He was one of Roland's friends. Most people assumed that Rannagon only betrayed Arenadd because he didn't like having a Northerner in the Eyrie. But Roland told me he never thought that made sense. Plenty of people didn't like Arenadd, and some wanted him dead, but Rannagon had been one of his biggest supporters. So why did he suddenly turn on him?'

'His griffin told him to?' Red guessed.

'Exactly,' said Liantha. 'Hardly anyone knows that, but I do. Roland said that the day before he died, Rannagon spoke to him and told him something awful. Apparently, his partner Shoa forced him to betray Arenadd. She threatened to kill his son if he didn't do what she wanted, and he believed her. Nobody will ever know why she did it, but whatever it was, she turned on her partner and that was why he died.'

Red rubbed his head. 'Really? Dear gods.' He didn't know what else to say. He'd never imagined that a griffin could or would do that to their own partner.

'They can do it, if they want to,' said Liantha. 'Don't ever forget that, Red. Most of the time, a griffin trusts her partner's judgement, but if she really wants to, she can force you to obey her. You know they don't have any real morals. And they'll turn on each other over an insult. You saw the proof of that today.'

'So Seerae's decided, has she?' said Red, his heart sinking. 'Your people won't help us any more after this?'

'Maybe,' said Liantha. 'She might change her mind. I'll try and persuade her. But if she won't, then there's not a lot I can do. I'm sorry, Red.'

'An' we won't be able to stay here after the fight,' said Red. He'd been counting on that. Eagleholm would have been a good stronghold now that Monag was behind them.

'Not you,' said Liantha. 'The others, probably, if they're polite.'

'Well, I guess that's better than nothing,' said Red. 'Let's worry about it later.' He gave her a reassuring smile. 'Don't worry, Liantha. No matter about griffins arguing – we'll get your city back.'

She smiled back, and moved closer to give him a quick hug. 'I trust you, Red.'

He hugged her back. 'An' I trust you.'

Chapter Four

Lying in Wait

Not long after the meeting was over, Red, Teressa and Liantha left the rest of the group to eat a quick meal and sharpen their weapons, and set out with their partners to begin the first part of the plan. Since it was almost impossible for a griffin to fly into an occupied city, they would need to use stealth to enter it without being attacked.

Fortunately, in their earlier scouting Red and Kraego had found a likely entry-point: a side gate which was just large enough for a griffin to enter by. The two of them went in first, using the shadows to slip in over the walls, and land down in the city. Its streets were almost completely deserted, and there was only a tiny flock of griffins circling above.

'Right,' Red whispered once they were safely hidden in the shelter of an abandoned warehouse. 'I'll go on ahead an' see if the gate's guarded. Wait here.'

Kraego huffed softly, and settled down while Red walked silently off towards the wall.

He kept to the edges of the streets, walking as casually as he could and ready to use the shadows if he needed to. But there wasn't much chance of being spotted: he saw only two people on the short walk to the city wall, both Southerners like himself, and neither one spared him a glance. There weren't even any guards around.

Red reached the gate, and to his amazement it wasn't guarded. Were the Northerners really that unprepared for an attack?

He didn't waste any time puzzling over it, and quickly and quietly lifted the wooden bars that held the gate shut. It swung open without much noise – like the rest of the city it was very new.

Orak and Seerae had crept to the base of the wall using the dim evening light for cover, and were waiting outside, tensely pressed up against the stonework. The moment the gate opened, they padded through it with their partners close beside them.

All four of them looked to Red once he had closed the gate. He gestured silently at them to follow.

He and Kraego had already picked out the warehouse as a good hiding place for Liantha and Seerae. Red led them straight to it now, scouting ahead along the way to make sure nobody would see the two griffins.

They reached it without a hitch. Kraego had levered the large front door open with his beak and talons, and Liantha and Seerae crept inside first.

'All right,' said Red, once they were safe. 'First part of the plan's over. Liantha, you an' Seerae wait here but be on the alert. If anyone comes in here, grab 'em. If they're one of us, tell them who you are an' get them on our side. If they ain't…kill them.'

'Understood,' Liantha said grimly. She looked as if she would be more than happy to kill one of the Northerners who had stolen her city.

Red started to tell Teressa and Orak to follow him, but he hesitated and turned back to Liantha. 'Good luck,' he added. 'An' also…'

'Yes?'

'If something goes wrong, stick to the plan,' said Red. 'If I'm lost somehow, you're in charge. Trust Talmon an' the rest, an' protect Teressa an' the other Northerners. They'll need it if I ain't there.'

'I understand,' said Liantha. She came forward to hug him again, tentatively. 'Just don't let anything go wrong, Red. We can't lose you.'

'I'll do my best,' he promised. 'You just look after yerself, all right?'

'I will.'

'Right, I'm off,' said Red, letting go of her. 'I'll see you later, right? Now, Teressa – let's go.'

He gave Liantha a last comforting smile, and left.

Outside, he turned to Teressa. 'You an' Orak, just walk along like nothin's unusual. You live here, right? Me an' Kraego will use the shadows. You won't see us, but we'll be nearby.'

'If we are attacked, I shall kill our attackers,' Orak vowed. 'Even if they are your people, Kraeai kran ae.'

'Try not to,' said Red. 'Now let's go.'

He went to Kraego's side, and the two of them slipped into the shadows. From there, they followed Teressa and Orak as they started to walk towards the Eyrie, sometimes going ahead to scout things out, sometimes returning to check on their friends. So far, everything was going smoothly.

Red moved in absolute silence, unseen, his presence marked by nothing but an eerie chill to anyone who came too close. He felt as if he were gliding rather than walking, each step flowing into the next. Here, in the shadows, colours were muted, but everything else was intensified. He heard every sound, and saw every movement. His nose filled with scents. Wood. Mud. Ox manure. Bread from a bakery the next street over. But none of these scents was as important as the smell of living things. Whenever someone came close to his hiding place, his senses would scream at him and a little jolt would go through his body. He would smell their sweat, their breath, their blood. He could hear the faint thudding of their hearts, and noticed how the sound sped up slightly as they felt the inexplicable fear of the presence of the Shadow That Walked.

His instincts made him want to follow them, to stalk them like a cat after a mouse. The murderous impulses rose up in his mind. Here, in the shadows, they were harder to ignore.

He distracted himself by watching Teressa instead. She seemed to be coping quite well; strolling down the street by Orak's side as if this wasn't anything unusual. She was just another griffiner, taking in the sights of the city that her leader had conquered. She had shed her usual silver priestess' robe in favour of an ordinary griffiner's outfit: a thick woollen tunic and leggings reinforced with leather, of the sort even wealthy griffiners wore. With griffins, hardwearing was best.

The few people she passed were Southerners – the few inhabitants of Eagleholm who had stayed behind after the city was overrun. They cast hateful looks at the Northerner as she passed, but with Orak there none of them dared attack. No doubt plenty of them had already died for that.

To his surprise, Red found that he didn't have much sympathy for them. They'd been brave enough to form a mob and try to murder Morgan when he'd been here by himself, but in the face of an army they'd surrendered almost without a fight. Red was determined to fight for his fellow Southerners, but cowards had always disgusted him.

Soon enough, he, Kraego, Teressa and Orak had reached the Eyrie. It was an elegant building, made from the reddish coloured stone that gave the Coppertop Mountains their name, and like all

Eyries it was flat-topped and peppered with large arched openings for griffins to enter by. It had a pleasingly clean rounded shape, and the stones were well cut. Liantha's people had done good work, and hadn't even had the teams of Northerner slaves that had built all the oldest Eyries in Cymria. It reminded Red of the Eyrie in Liranwee, which had also been built by free men – himself among them.

He smiled to himself, a little sadly. His old life as a free, living man in Liranwee, felt as if it had been a hundred years ago. And it was sadder to realise that, even if he freed his old home, he would never have that life again. He would never be alive again, and he couldn't go back to the simple life of a city guard. Nor would he ever be able to stay among living people; he hadn't changed his mind about that.

Red brought himself back to the present. He could mope about the future later. For now, there was work to do.

He and Kraego lurked around at the base of the Eyrie tower until Teressa and Orak arrived.

'All right,' he whispered. 'Kraego an' Orak, you'll have to stay here. They don't make prison corridors wide enough for griffins. Teressa, you're with me.'

'I shall wait here,' Kraego promised. 'If enemies chase you, lead them to me and I shall deal with them.'

'And so shall I,' said Orak. 'Teressa, remember – while I cannot be with you, your leader must protect you.'

Teressa had brought a sickle with her. It was the traditional weapon of Northerners, and she touched its handle now. 'I understand. Don't worry, Orak.'

'He's right,' said Red. 'No heroics, Teressa. There's no shame in letting your mates help you out in a fight.'

'Yes, yes,' she hissed back, impatient and edgy with nerves. 'Understood. Now let's go before I change my mind!'

Red grinned, and slipped back into the shadows.

Apparently alone, Teressa went in through the open door at the bottom of the Eyrie. Inside was a great round room, with a ramp that led up inside the building in a spiral shape, and a barred door which led to the prison which housed all of Eagleholm's prisoners. Usually there would be a second prison out in the city for less important prisoners, but Liantha had explained that, so far, one had not been built and all prisoners went to the cells under the Eyrie regardless of who they were and what they had done.

There was a pair of guards standing on the other side of the door, alert and suspicious. When Teressa approached they noticed her clothing and stood to attention. 'Milady,' said one. 'What can we do for ye?' He was a native Northerner with an accent similar to Teressa's, but thicker.

Teressa hesitated nervously before replying. 'I've come from Morgan,' she said. 'He wants to see ye.'

The guard frowned. 'What, me in person?'

'No,' said Teressa. 'I mean he said he wanted to talk to whoever was guarding the prison.'

The guard looked unhappy – apparently, he thought he was in some kind of trouble. 'Did he say why?'

'No, but he didn't look happy,' said Teressa, who was intelligent enough to pick up on the man's unease and take advantage of it. 'I don't think he'd be pleased if he was kept waiting,' she added. 'So ye should hurry up.'

'All right, but we'll need to fetch replacements,' said the second guard, speaking for the first time.

Teressa glanced at the hidden Red. 'Well…hurry up then,' she said.

The second guard left, but his friend stayed behind. 'I didn't do something wrong did I?' he asked.

'I don't know,' said Teressa. 'Ye'd better hope not.'

Red watched them both. Teressa had done fairly well so far – at least she'd gotten one guard away from the door, even if he'd be back soon with two more guards. Red wondered quickly what he should do – go in now while there was only one, and risk having him raise the alarm before he could be silenced, or wait until the door opened and have four men to deal with instead of one. He could handle four of them, of course, but one might escape and bring more.

In the end, the thought that he didn't want Teressa to get caught up in a skirmish made up Red's mind.

He moved forward, silent and unseen, while Teressa exchanged small talk with the guard, finding room to be surprised. In his old life as a guard he'd never had the opportunity to speak to a griffiner, and if he had he would have been expected to be far more respectful. This man, on the other hand, was talking to Teressa as if she was his equal. Was this how it always was with Northerners? Were they just not used to having other Northerners as their superiors?

Amazed that he could be this calm when he was this close to a fight, Red made his move. Still hidden, he wrapped his hands around the bars in the door, tensed, and pulled with all his might.

The door resisted for only a moment, before it started to shudder and creak. Red put his boots against the wall on either side, and gave it one last brutal wrench. There was a loud cracking noise, and the entire door broke away from its lock and hinges. Teressa darted out of the way, and before the guard on the other side could do more than freeze in shock, Red hurled the door aside and lunged forward out of the shadows.

He had intended to knock the man down, maybe put him out of commission for a little while, but the moment his hands found the guard's throat, it was too late. The murderous impulse grabbed hold of him, and before he could blink he had broken the man's neck and thrown him aside after the door.

Teressa saw him fall, and yelped in fright.

Red tried to breathe deeply and calm down, but he couldn't. His whole body trembled lightly, and his breath came fast and shallow. He wanted to laugh. 'Wait here,' he growled. 'I'll be back.'

He went down into the prison, and immediately ran into the second guard with two of his comrades. He hadn't gone back into the shadows, and they saw him at once.

Red drew his sword before they had recovered from their surprise, and charged without a word or a sound, and after that…after that…

After that there was only blood, and screams, and a horrible laugh that rose up over the sounds of death. A harsh, cold laugh, a laugh full of sickening excitement.

Red was dimly aware of what he was doing, and even thought he could resist it, but he didn't try. Happiness filled him.

No, even that was too weak a word. Ecstasy. He moved like a dancer, infinitely graceful but full of savage strength, his sword hacking down all those who stood in his way. When anyone got past that, his hand found them. Arms snapped, necks broke, skulls caved in. Everyone who tried to attack him died, fast and violently. When the survivors saw sense and tried to run, he chased them down and killed them one by one.

In far too little time, every guard in the prison was dead. But the thrill and the urge were still there in Red. There had to be more people to kill. He should go up into the rest of the building, and kill there as well, yes…

Some vague recollection came to him that he was supposed to be opening a cell or something. Oh yes…he could smell living blood in the cell nearest to him. There were more people to kill here.

He wrenched the door open with his bare hands, and saw a group of people in front of him. They weren't armed, but what did that matter? It would just making killing them easier—

'Red?'

Red hesitated.

'Red, is that you?'

Red.

The sound of his name got through to him, and he stopped and shook his head dazedly. 'What…?'

His vision cleared, and with a shock, he realised that he knew the people in front of him. But they were looking at him with expressions of absolute horror. Why, though?

'Holy Gryphus,' one of them said in a low voice. 'That can't be…'

Red realised that he was breathing hard and that his whole body was hunched and ready to spring forward. Slowly, he straightened up and let himself relax. He felt his face relax as well, and realised that he had been smiling. But it must have been the kind of smile that put terror into a man's heart.

His sword was dripping with blood. So was his arm up to the elbow. He hastily sheathed the weapon, and rubbed his face with his other hand to wake himself up. 'Lads?' he managed.

'Lads an' one lass,' said a rough but shaky voice from the cell in front of him.

Red peered at them all. It was them, or most of them. The group who called themselves the Last Guards. Senna, and Tarn, and Asple the brewer, and about twenty others. Red and Kraego had rescued them from Canran, and they had sworn to follow him and help him free the South. He had put Senna in charge, and now here she was.

I almost killed them, he realised. *I was gonna…*

'Come with me,' he said roughly. 'I'm gettin' you all out of here. Hurry up!'

They followed him without any further prompting, though several of them still looked unnerved. Red knew why, now that he'd come to his senses again. They'd seen him in the middle of a killing frenzy, covered in blood and most likely with a crazed smile on his face. Not exactly the kind of man you would want rescuing you.

Red pushed the thought away, and led them out into the corridor. It was full of corpses. 'All right,' he said, trying to ignore the sight. 'Head up into the Eyrie an' you'll find my friend Teressa waiting. She's a Northerner, but she's on our side. I'm gonna check an' see if there's anyone else in here what needs rescuing.'

'Yes, sir,' said Senna. 'I'll see yer later.' She sounded as strong as anyone could under the circumstances, and Red gave her a grateful look. Trust her to bring back some kind of sanity in all this.

He let them go, and headed off to check the other cells. He was surprised by how quickly he'd calmed down. But as he clambered over the corpses in his way, he felt a low and awful revulsion swim in his stomach. He saw the dead strewn about, and found that he vaguely remembered killing them. It was like waking up after a night of drinking: the memories were muddled and vague, but they were there, and in this case they were horrible.

He tried not to think about it. In the end, killing them was probably for the best. He could have tried locking them up or some such thing, but some would have escaped. Now they wouldn't be able to report what had happened, and by the time anyone found the carnage it would be too late.

But none of these rational thoughts changed the cold, hard facts: he had killed them, in some cases when they were trying to run away, and he had enjoyed it more than he remembered enjoying anything in his whole life. The nightmare he had had that night in Monag had come true.

He had seen himself standing with the others, his predecessors, bloodstained and leering, and all of them had chanted the words to him, which danced through his head now as he checked the cells.

You are the shadow that comes in the night, you are the fear that lurks in their hearts, you are the Shadow That Walks.

Red found an occupied cell, and pulled the door open with unnatural strength. Inside was a single Southerner, who eyed him nervously. 'What's going on?'

'You're free,' Red said briefly. 'That's what goin' on. Head up out of here an' join up with the others. I don't care what you did.'

The man didn't need any further prompting, but he didn't look very happy about squeezing past Red to go up out of the prison to where the others waited.

Red found a few other prisoners, mostly just single Southerners probably locked up for resisting or doing something else the city's new rulers deemed a crime. In the last cell he checked, though, he found a Northerner.

The man backed off. 'Who are ye?'

'Your lucky day,' said Red. 'What're you doing in here?'

'They caught me with a Southern woman,' said the man. 'Are ye here to kill me?'

'No, I'm settin' you free,' said Red.

'Yer a Southerner.'

'I'm the Shadow That Walks,' Red growled, and left the prison.

Outside, the others were waiting.

Teressa hurried to meet him. 'There ye are. What happened?'

'I lost control,' Red said honestly. 'It's not a pretty sight down there. But I didn't kill any of ours. Now, let's get everyone out of here. Did you tell Senna what's goin' on?'

'Aye, I did,' said Teressa.

'After Tarn stopped me thumpin' her one on instinct,' the burly woman put in.

'Then there's nothin' else to talk about,' said Red. 'Let's go.'

'Wait.' For the first time Senna showed real unease, and Red tensed, expecting her to say something about the massacre in the prison. But what she actually said was, 'Red, they've got my baby. Morgan took him. Took Ridley too, but I dunno…'

'It's all right,' said Red. 'Ridley got away. We found him; that's why we're here. Once I've got you to Liantha, Kraego an' me are going back. We'll get your kid out of there.'

'Kraego's here?'

'Yeah, he's outside with Orak. Now hurry up! We'll talk later.'

None of them needed any further prompting. They hurried out of the building, and sure enough Kraego and Orak were still there, the latter shifting restlessly.

'You have them all?' Kraego said the moment Red emerged.

'Yeah, so let's get on,' said Red.

It was nearly night-time by now, and without a proper city guard there was nobody to light the street lamps. The group of escapees hurried out into the city under cover of darkness, with Red and Kraego to lead the way. As a black griffin, Kraego could see very well in the dark. So could Red.

They got to the warehouse where Liantha and Seerae were waiting. All was still quiet.

'Thank Gryphus!' said Liantha. 'I was worried.'

'Did anything happen while we were gone?' asked Red.

'No, nothing. We kept watch, but nobody came in here.'

'Good. Now,' Red turned to Senna and the others, 'you lot stick with Liantha. You're gonna help her get the gates open. Kraego an' me are going back to the Eyrie. We'll see you later.'

'Good luck,' said Liantha.

'And you,' Red nodded back, and made for the door where Kraego was waiting impatiently.

'Save my baby, Red,' Senna called after him. 'Please—,'

'I will.'

Red didn't pause any longer. Any moment the dead prison guards could be discovered, so the sooner he and Kraego dealt with Morgan, the better.

Outside, Red climbed onto Kraego's back. The black griffin took off without a word, flying up and over the city. He didn't even bother to use the shadows – in the dark he was almost invisible anyway. Together, the dark man and the dark griffin made for New Eagleholm's Eyrie. They were so intent on their goal that neither of them noticed Teressa and Orak follow.

*

Kraego flew straight to the top of the Eyrie, where he landed. 'We shall come at them from above,' he said. 'That is the best way to attack any griffin. If I wished to kill Eck-hoo I would go in through the entrance to his nest and surprise him there, but if we come from the other side he will be driven out into the open air for Seerae to attack.'

'An' by then, Morgan'll be dead already,' said Red.

Kraego didn't wait to reply, and slunk off towards the opening in the roof that led into the building. Red followed.

Inside the Eyrie was well-lit, with fine lamps hanging on the walls at intervals. The ramp that led down inside the Eyrie was very large

– in other words, griffin-sized – and well-carpeted, with tapestries and animal hides hanging on the walls. There didn't seem to be anyone around but Red and Kraego used the shadows wherever they could, just in case.

They didn't have far to go. Morgan had occupied Liantha's old quarters, which were on the top floor of the Eyrie as Eyrie Masters' quarters always were. They were also very large, occupying most of that floor, but divided up, separated by a wall with a large archway covered by curtains. On the other side of that, Red remembered, was Liantha's old bedroom. The room in front of him, though, was an audience chamber with a platform for the ruling griffin to sit and a chair for guests.

It was deserted, but brightly lit, with extra torches placed in iron stands. Clearly, Morgan was expecting him and wanted there to be as few shadows as possible.

Red hesitated for a moment in the audience chamber. He could hear something up ahead. A baby crying.

'That's where he'll be,' he said aloud. 'I'd better nip on ahead an' make sure there's no nasty surprises.'

'Be careful,' Kraego warned.

Red nodded briefly, and slipped on over to the curtains. He peered through them, careful not to let himself show.

Beyond them was Liantha's bedroom, as expected, nicely furnished but not overly luxurious. New Eagleholm was not a wealthy city. There was a bed over by one wall, and a fireplace, and the floor was covered by thick animal hides. Near the fire, there was a table and, on it, the baby was in a basket, still crying.

Red might have pulled back then, or gone into the shadows to investigate further, but then he saw something that put icy cold hatred into his now-silent heart.

Morgan.

The Northerner was standing with his back to him, near the fireplace, apparently deep in thought, and it was the sight of him that put an end to any rational planning for Red.

The moment he laid eyes on the Northerner, the moment he smelled the man's hot blood, the hate consumed him. Memories flooded into his mind. Morgan, sneering at him as he lay under his partner Echo's talons. Morgan, standing over him and ordering a guard to hit him in the face with a wooden club. Morgan, fleeing like a coward after the destruction of Canran.

'Morgan,' Red hissed.

The Northerner turned, and Red immediately slipped forward into the room. It was just as well-lit as the audience chamber, but there were enough shadows to hide him, and he vanished before Morgan saw him.

But the spy had already guessed that he was there. He turned, his back to the fire, and Red saw his pale, nervous face. In anyone else that might have made him feel some sympathy, but not here. Not now. Now it only fuelled his hate, and made him forget all else.

He forgot about Morgan's cunning. He forgot that this was a trap. He forgot the baby. All he remembered now was that this was his enemy. And now he had him at his mercy and there was nothing to do but to torment him just as he had longed to, and bring him to the edge of terror before finally slaughtering him like the vermin he was.

'Morgan,' Red said again, and now his voice was low and cruel.

Morgan shivered. 'It's you, isn't it?' he said. 'You've come for me.'

Red laughed a vicious, hollow laugh, and then he started to chant – pacing around Morgan all the while to make his voice sound as if it came from everywhere at once. 'I am the shadow that comes in the night...'

Morgan groaned, and took a step backward.

'...I am the fear the lurks in your heart...'

'Stop that,' Morgan murmured.

'I am darkness.'

'Stop it!'

'I am death.'

'Stop it!'

'I am the Shadow That Walks,' Red spat, and he could taste the fear. It was delicious.

'Stop it!' Morgan shouted again. 'Please...'

Red left the shadows, and confronted him. 'Hello, Morgan,' he said menacingly.

Morgan stared at him. 'Holy Night God, it's true,' he said. 'It's you. You're really...'

'Yeah,' said Red. 'Bad news for you, you backstabbing son of a bitch. I said I'd kill you one day, didn't I? I said it to yer face. An' a

Redguard always keeps his word.'

'A Redguard doesn't murder people,' said Morgan. 'Does he? I'm not armed and I won't attack you.'

'The Shadow That Walks does,' Red snarled.

'But you're a Redguard,' Morgan persisted, with astonishing courage. 'You're a Redguard, not a filthy blackrobe like me. Aren't you? You always said you were a man of honour.'

'But you ain't,' said Red.

'No,' said Morgan. 'I'm not. But I'll tell you what else I'm not – I'm not stupid, and I don't want to die.' He took a step away from the table, and gestured at the crying baby on it. 'Take the brat. Go on. Take it, take your friends, and take the city. I won't try and stop you.'

Red hesitated. 'What?'

'You heard me. My King ordered me to lay a trap for you, but I can see now that it's not going to work. And anyway…' Morgan gave Red a slow look. 'You're the Shadow That Walks. You're the Night God's servant, aren't you?'

'Maybe,' said Red. He had started to feel irritated. Even now, it felt as if Morgan had the upper hand on him. But how? What was he up to?

'Then as one of the Night God's people, I can't stand against you,' said Morgan. 'It would be blasphemy. My wife reminded me of that. I lured you here because I had a trap ready for you, but now I see you, I…I can't make myself do it. So here's the deal.'

'Oh yeah?' Red folded his arms.

'Let me go,' said Morgan. 'I'll take Arwydd and go back to my King. In return, you can have Eagleholm. It's worthless anyway.'

'Why should I let you live?' Red demanded. 'After what you did?'

'And what about what you did?' asked Morgan. 'I saw the men down in the prison. You stabbed half of them in the back. And now you're prepared to kill an unarmed man? I'm disappointed in you, Kearney Redguard.'

Red hesitated.

'You're the Shadow That Walks, but you don't want to be, do you?' Morgan asked keenly. 'You still think you can be the man of honour you were before. You want to bring murderers like me to justice, not become one. Because if you don't have your honour any more, what do you have? I knew you in Liranwee. You wanted to make the Redguard family name honourable again. Wipe away the memory of your uncle Bran the Betrayer. Well guess what? Killing me now won't do that. It'll put a stain on that name that nothing will ever erase, because after you there won't be any more Redguards. You're the last one. Why not show the world you can be better than your uncle, who betrayed his whole race for the sake of a filthy Northerner?'

'An' what about you?' asked Red, unable to stop himself from listening to the Northerner's calm words.

'I, on the other hand, am more than happy to run away like a coward. I'm a spy, not a heroic guard like you.' Morgan smiled thinly. 'Guards stay at their posts and die to protect their cities. Spies backstab and run away, just as you said. Let's both stick to what we're good at, shall we?'

Finally, painfully, Red relaxed. 'Fine.'

Even Morgan looked surprised. 'You'll take my offer?'

'Yes. Now piss off before I change my mind.'

Morgan breathed a deep sigh of relief. 'Thank-you, Red. You're a good man.'

'An' you ain't.'

'But I'm going to be a father,' said Morgan. 'That's something worth living for.'

'Yeah,' said Red. 'I s'pose it would be. Now shut up and get lost.'

'All right—,' Morgan took a step forward and suddenly tensed. 'Wait – no!'

Too late, Red heard movement off to his left. Too late, he sensed the other presence in the room. He turned sharply, reaching for his sword, and saw the figure appear from behind the curtain and lunge towards him.

'Stop!' Morgan shouted, but too late.

The gaunt, bland-faced woman slipped out from her hiding place. There was a hot branding iron in her hands, and as Red turned, ready to kill her, she calmly stepped forward and thrust.

Red saw her, and had a brief glimpse of something glowing yellow and orange, before it hit him hard in the face and the world exploded in white-hot agony.

He screamed – not the normal pained shout of an injured man, but a loud, piercing shriek. Clutching at his face, still screaming, he lashed out blindly with one big hand.

The woman who had attacked him was too close for him to miss. His fist hit her in the face, and she went down with a loud crash and did not move again.

Red turned around, stumbling, and reached out. 'Help…Kraego!'

Hands caught him by the arm. 'Captain…Captain Redguard. Let me help you…'

Red lashed out blindly. 'Get away from me! You son of a bitch!'

'I'm sorry!' Morgan's voice came to him through a haze of agony. 'Captain, I'm so sorry, I didn't mean…I thought she would hear me and realise—,' his words cut off as Red hit him in the face, and he stumbled away with a muffled swearword.

A screech came from behind him, and he heard a loud tearing and a crash as the curtain came down. Kraego.

Red turned towards where he thought his partner was, and called out to him. 'Kraego! Get him! Kill the bastard! He's—,' he stumbled sideways and nearly fell.

After that everything dissolved into a confusion of sound and motion. He heard Morgan shouting something in griffish, Kraego's scream of rage, a crash somewhere. The baby was crying, somewhere, beneath it all.

Confused, Red tried to feel his way towards the table. He had to get the baby out of here, even if he couldn't see it.

He felt a great rush of air as a griffin charged past him – Kraego, it had to be – and he followed the sound of the child's wails until he walked into the table. He fumbled around until his bloodstained hands found the basket, and clumsily lifted the baby out. Then, moving slowly for fear of falling and hurting his tiny burden, he clumsily made his way to the nearest wall and crouched down there. He couldn't go anywhere now; he'd have to wait until Kraego got back.

And then, quite suddenly, there was silence. Kraego was gone, and so was Morgan. The baby had stopped crying, and he was alone with his pain.

The first searing agony was over, and now it had settled into a steady throb, but something told him that this was only the first, vague hint of real pain to come.

Tentatively, Red reached up to try and touch his injury. He expected it to hurt and it did, but nowhere near as badly as he had thought it would. His fingers brushed against something that felt like charred meat. There was a huge patch of it, from his forehead to his nose.

His eyes were gone.

For the briefest moment, Red tried to convince himself that they were still there. Maybe his eyelids had been sealed shut by the burn. Maybe they'd be able to open again after they'd healed a bit. But from the way the pain went, stabbing into his eye sockets, he knew it was all a lie. That woman, whoever she was, had hit him hard and accurately. His eyes had been burnt out of his face.

It wouldn't kill him. Fire couldn't kill the Shadow That Walked. He would still live forever. But now, it would be in darkness.

Quietly, knowing nobody was there to see him now, Red lowered his head over the baby and started to sob.

Chapter Five

Nightmares

Teressa and Orak had hung back from entering the Eyrie, neither one wanting to get in the way of Red and Kraego. But when Orak saw Echo, the spotted griffin who was Morgan's partner, come flying out of the building with Kraego in pursuit, he immediately made for the opening the two griffins had used. He landed there, on the protruding ledge, and leaned to one side, forcing Teressa off his back. Then, without a word, he took off and went after Kraego.

Teressa stood and watched him go, not quite sure what to do, but then the horrible thought crossed her mind that if Morgan had escaped, that could mean something had happened to Red. Had her fellow Northerner sprung his trap, whatever it was, and used it to make his escape like the coward he was?

Forgetting her own safety, Teressa drew her sickle and hurried through the nest and into the Eyrie Master's bedroom. Most of the furniture had been knocked over, and there were talon marks on the floor.

Teressa stood in the doorway for an instant, seeing the body on the floor before she realised that she could hear something. It sounded like a human voice, but…

She saw Red, sitting hunched in the corner and holding onto something, and had already walked halfway across the room towards him before she realised that he was doing something she had never imagined. The Shadow That Walked was crying.

'Red,' Teressa said softly, seeing the bundle in his arms and thinking, with sudden horror, that maybe the baby had died in the struggle.

Red lifted his head, and she bit back a strangled cry.

The upper half of the big Southerner's face was…gone.

In its place, where his eyes and the bridge of his nose should have been, there was now nothing but a patch of charred, raw flesh.

'No.' Teressa dropped her sickle and ran to his side. 'Red!'

Red's ugly, hacking sobs had stopped, and now he groped blindly towards her. 'Teressa? Is that Teressa?'

She crouched beside him and took his hand in both of hers. 'Yes, Red. It's me. Oh gods…what happened?'

Red pulled his hand away, and indicated the baby cradled in his free arm. 'Teressa, is the baby all right?'

'Red—,'

'Is the baby all right?' Red repeated. 'I can't hear it.'

Teressa reached down to touch the baby's face. It looked very pale. 'He's alive,' she said. 'But he doesn't look well.'

'Here.' Red held the infant up towards her. 'Take him. He shouldn't be this close to me. It's bad for him.'

Teressa took the baby. 'Red, who did this? Did Morgan—?'

Red made a sound that might have been a sob, or a cough. 'I had him. I had him. I could've…but he…'

'It was a trap,' Teressa said bleakly. 'Wasn't it?'

'Never thought anything could…he kept me talking. Thought he could appeal to the Redguard sense of honour. Got me to say I'd let him go, an' then his friend comes at me with a…something hot. Hit me in the face. Think it was a poker or something.'

'Red, what were ye thinking?' said Teressa, half reproachfully and half in despair. 'Ye know what he is. Ye knew it was a trap.'

'I killed all those men in the prison,' said Red. 'With some it was a fair fight, with some it was murder. They were running away an' I killed them anyway. Morgan was right. I don't wanna be a murderer. He wasn't armed. He just wanted to live.' Red made that half-sobbing sound again. 'So did I once. So did…' he wrapped his arms around himself and started to shake.

Moving carefully, Teressa put the baby down and reached out to pull Red towards her. He resisted briefly, but she persisted, and pressed him against herself. He gave in and held her back, and started to sob again. 'Teressa, what'm I gonna do? I can't lead…I can't do shit like this. I'm blind! What sort of…There wasn't even any…My first bloody fight an' this happens. I thought…'

Teressa wanted to say something to comfort him, but she didn't. Sometimes, she knew, it was best to say nothing. Sometimes, it was better to let someone talk.

'Thought I could be a good man,' Red mumbled. 'Even with this. But it's all nonsense. There's no honour here no more. All I want to do is kill. Can't help it. I should thank Morgan,' he added with a twisted half laugh. 'Can't kill nobody now unless you put 'em in my hands for me.'

He was cold in Teressa's arms, but she didn't let go. 'Stop,' she said softly. 'Red, stop. Don't.'

He quieted. 'Sorry. I'm scared. Can't help it.'

'If I were stupid I'd have said ye weren't afraid of anything,' said Teressa. 'But only fools fear nothing. That's an old saying in the North.'

'Well I am a fool,' said Red, with the slightest hint of humour. 'We both know that now.'

'But not a coward,' said Teressa. 'And ye are a man of honour. Ye let Morgan go instead of listening to the part of ye that wanted revenge no matter what.'

'I feel real great about that, sure,' said Red, but at least he said it with a kind of smile, however unpleasant it looked on a face without eyes.

'Now,' said Teressa in her most soothing voice – a voice she'd learnt to use in her training for the priesthood. 'Let's get ye out of here and find this baby's mother. I think he needs feeding.'

'Yeah, sure,' said Red. He sounded relieved.

Teressa helped him to his feet, and left him there for a moment while she retrieved her sickle. Then, awkwardly carrying the baby with one arm and leading Red with the other, she took them out of the room.

Her touch seemed to have revived the baby, who started to whimper but, thankfully, didn't cry.

Red heard it. 'Always wanted kids,' he grunted. 'I should've done something about that when I was alive.'

'Priestesses aren't supposed to have children,' said Teressa.

'Celibate, are you?' said Red, clearly glad to have a distraction.

'Not quite,' said Teressa. 'Careful, we're going through the door now. It's not a religious rule really. We just have too much to do every day to have time for children. High Priestess Saeddryn had two of her own, mind ye. A son and a daughter. She named the daughter, and her husband named the son. It's a Northern tradition some people still follow.'

'Oh yeah?' said Red.

'Aye!' Teressa smiled. 'The daughter was Arddryn, after her mother. She died in the war. The son was named after his grandfather. Caedmon.'

'King Caedmon,' Red muttered.

'Yes. He had to fight for it, though. Laela Half-Breed didn't give up easily. But she was Arenadd's daughter. These things run in families, so it seems.'

'Who were your parents, then?' asked Red. They were making slow progress, and there was nobody outside.

'Don't know,' said Teressa, whose arm was already starting to ache. 'I'm an orphan. All I know is my parents were slaves from the South. That's why my name isn't so Northern. Arenadd's lover, Skade, brought me back to him with the others. That was when I met him.'

'What'd he want with a slave girl?' asked Red.

'Oh, they showed me to him,' said Teressa. 'The people who were looking after me. They told him how I was an orphan and the last one left who hadn't been adopted. I don't know why, but he took pity on me. He blessed me. I was the only one he ever did that for. I was only five years old, but I remember it so clearly.'

'So that's why you love him so much,' said Red.

'Aye, but sometimes…' Teressa sighed wistfully. 'Sometimes I wish I had parents. I suppose he was the closest thing I had to a father, even though I never saw him again.'

Red winced at the pain in his face, and reached out clumsily to squeeze her shoulder. 'If it's any comfort, I'm an orphan too. My mum died when I was little. She was Finna Redguard. Branton Redguard's sister. My dad was Danthirk. He was all I had until I was fourteen. Then one day he went to the Eyrie for a meeting, an' never came back.'

'So odd that ye and I would meet,' said Teressa, trying to sound light. 'Isn't it?'

'Lots of things are,' said Red. 'Teressa, are you sure we're all right here? Morgan's still got lackeys in here an' I don't reckon I could handle them anymore.'

'It's fine,' said Teressa. 'If we run into anyone, I'll deal with them.'

She expected Red to protest, but to her surprise he didn't. Maybe he was too far gone to think of it.

'Show them ye are the Shadow That Walks,' she said. 'They're Northerners. Once they know it they won't touch ye.'

'Right,' Red mumbled.

Teressa glanced at him, and cringed at the sight of his wound. The more she looked at it, the worse it seemed. She couldn't even imagine how much it must hurt, and didn't want to try. But Red wouldn't succumb to the agony he must be feeling. Not her Red.

For a while, though, he started to look as if he were weakening. He stopped talking, and his head drooped.

Teressa started to panic slightly – if he lost consciousness she wouldn't be able to carry him; he was twice her weight. But he was still the Shadow That Walked. Surely he would have the strength.

Then, quite unexpectedly, he spoke again. 'Teressa.' His voice, damaged as it was, sounded soft and sleepy. 'Want to…'

'What is it?'

'Wanted to tell you,' Red mumbled.

'Tell me what?' She had to keep him talking, so he would stay awake.

'When I saw Arenadd in the Temple,' he said. 'After the— the priestess…'

'Ye came to save me and killed the High Priestess,' Teressa prompted. 'Her blood went on the altar and ye had a vision of Arenadd because that counted as the sacrifice.'

'Meant to meet the Night God,' said Red. 'She wouldn't come. Arenadd said…he said…'

'What did he say?'

'"Thank you,"' said Red.

'It's all right,' said Teressa. 'What did he say?'

'No, "Thank you",' said Red, sounding a little more awake now. 'That's what he said. Thanked me.'

'For what?'

'Saving you,' said Red. He sagged, and Teressa had to struggle to pull him upright again.

'Red, don't!' she said. 'Stay awake! I can't carry ye out of here by myself.'

'What are you doing?' a voice shouted suddenly.

Teressa turned, and fear hit her. A Northerner had come around the corner from below them, and now he was coming towards them, hand on his sickle.

He stopped briefly, and puzzlement showed on his face as he took in what he was seeing. A Northern woman, helping a wounded Southerner, with a baby cradled in one arm.

'What in the gods' names?' said the man.

Anger and despair gripped Teressa. Stupidly, she let go of Red and put herself between him and the intruder. 'Stay back!' she said in her loudest, most commanding voice.

'What for?' asked the Northerner, who was well dressed and looked like a griffiner. 'He's not going to do any harm in that condition. Who are you?'

'My name is Teressa,' Teressa said recklessly. She raised her free arm in a dramatic gesture, just as she had seen the High Priestess do in Malvern's Moon Temple. 'I am the High Priestess of the Shadow Worshippers.' She looked at him, hoping he would be impressed.

'You're a bloody lunatic is what you are,' said the man. 'What are you doing here anyway? Didn't you get the order? Morgan says we have to leave, and fast, before the Southerners get here. Who's this half-faced bastard?'

'This is Kearney Redguard, the Shadow That Walks,' said Teressa. 'My master, and yer own.'

The man looked past her at the half-conscious Red. 'You're crazy, and I don't have time for this,' he said. 'I'm off to find my partner and get out while the going's good. Stay here if you like, but his mates will gut you when they find you.'

He pushed past the infuriated Teressa, and went on his way.

'Damn it!' Teressa swore. She looked back at Red.

He gasped a laugh. 'Nice work.'

Teressa went to help him up again. 'Don't make fun of me, Red.'

'I'm not. You got rid of him, an' that's all that matters.'

Muttering irritably, Teressa helped him on down the inside of the Eyrie. They didn't meet anyone else. Her fellow Northerners were leaving, just as the one they'd met had said.

'Guess Morgan was telling the truth,' Red said when she told him. He stumbled again, and groaned. 'Does this bloody tower have a bottom?'

'We're getting there,' said Teressa.

But they never did reach it. When they were about halfway down the building, past most of the griffiner quarters, they heard the sound of running feet. Teressa tensed herself for a fight, but then a gang of Southerners came rushing up the ramp towards them. They saw Red and Teressa, halted, and she heard several of them groan.

'Oh shit,' said a voice, and a burly woman shoved to the front.

'Senna,' said Teressa.

Senna had been looking at Red, but now she saw the baby, and reached out frantically to take him. He stirred in her arms and peered up at her, and she groaned softly. 'Thank Gryphus.'

Red didn't move. He stayed by Teressa, unsteady on his feet, and turned his head blindly. 'Senna? Is that you?'

'It is, Red.' She reached out to touch his arm. 'Godsdamnit, Red, what happened to you?'

'A branding iron or a poker or something,' he said. 'Is anyone else here?'

'We're all here, Captain,' said Tarn.

'Good.' Red's head drooped again. 'They're leaving. The Northerners. Running away. Morgan…'

'We saw him,' said Asple. 'That son of a bitch. He flew off with that griffin of his, the one with the spots. Red, did he——?'

'No,' said Red. 'It was someone else. Some woman. I killed her. Let's…Is the city taken?'

'More or less,' said Senna, who had freed one breast and was feeding her baby without any embarrassment. 'We got the gate open an' our lads are in the city. We've got the bastards outnumbered.'

'Then let's get Red into the infirmary or something,' Teressa interrupted. 'He needs rest, and healing.'

'Hah, yeah,' Red laughed weakly. 'Need it like crazy.'

'We don't know where it is, but Liantha will,' said Tarn. 'She'll be here soon. On foot, though. Seerae went after Morgan with Kraego an' that other griffin.'

'Orak,' said Teressa, finally finding the space to be worried about her partner.

'Yeah, the grey one.'

'Let's just get Red to a regular bed for now,' said Senna.

The others agreed, and Red didn't protest. With the others' help, Teressa was able to get him into the nearest bedroom and lay him down on the bed without much trouble.

'Bring Liantha here once she's back,' said Red, and finally passed out.

Teressa stood by the bed with some of the others who'd stayed rather than join the others in hunting down any Northerners who might have remained, and looked down at her leader. He lay on his back, breathing slowly and, without eyes, the only hint that he was unconscious was the stillness that had come over him. For now, at least, he could hide away from what had happened.

'That poor bastard,' Senna said softly.

Teressa hadn't taken her eyes off him. 'I'll stay here with him. Ye should go and help the others.'

'You go,' Senna told her fellows. 'I won't be much use with a baby on my arm, so I'll stay here an' guard the door. Tarn, you stay with me.'

They nodded quickly and left without any discussion.

Teressa smiled tentatively at the other woman. She didn't look like any woman she had ever met, and was burly even for a Southerner. 'Ye sound like Red when he gives orders.'

Senna didn't smile. 'Yeah, I know whatcha thinking,' she said. 'What's a woman doing playing at bein' a guard.'

'What? That's not what I meant!'

'Women ain't allowed to be guards in the South,' said Senna. 'But my dad trained me up anyway 'cause he didn't get no sons. Never got the chance to try an' join up – Canran got sacked by the likes of you the day I got there.'

'I had nothing to do with that,' said Teressa. 'I'm on yer side.'

'Whatever,' Senna said ungraciously, and went off with Tarn to keep watch.

Teressa stayed where she was, and reached out tentatively to take Red's hand in hers. 'I'm so sorry,' she said in an undertone. 'But I won't leave ye. No matter what.'

*

Red was unconscious, but he wasn't alone.

He felt himself descend into darkness as soon as he lay down – a darkness even deeper than the blindness that had taken him. But it was a darkness he already knew far too well. It was icy cold, utterly empty, a blackness more absolute than night, or blindness.

The void.

He found himself wandering in it, though there was nowhere to go and nowhere to turn that didn't look exactly the same as everywhere else. Frightened, he started to run, thinking that there had to be something, some way out, some light in this emptiness.

But there was nothing. He may as well have been running on the spot. He was lost.

And then, the voice began to whisper to him.

Lost.

Red froze and then turned, trying to find it.

Alone.

'Who is that?' he yelled.

Forsaken by his god.

'Where are you?'

But when hope is gone and life is over, I am here, the voice whispered.

Red stood still. 'I can't see you because I'm blind,' he said.

Even here, said the voice. It was a woman's voice, soft and icy.

'Who are you, then?' asked Red. 'Am I awake?'

More awake than you have ever been before, said the voice. *Listen to me, Kearney Redguard. You need help. Guidance. Now, I am here to give it.*

Red didn't dare move. 'Are you—? Are you the Night God?'

Yes.

He stood there a moment, trying to take it in. The voice he heard didn't sound how he imagined she would sound. He had expected something cruel and savage, like the murderous feelings that had filled him when he became the Shadow That Walked. But this voice, though cold, was gentle and comforting. Like a mother.

All men need gods. And now yours has turned his back on you, as he does on all those who are dead.

'He wouldn't help me,' said Red, despite himself. There was something about this voice that made him want to speak, something so understanding that it felt as if only the truth mattered here. 'His temples hurt me.'

That is because you are dead. And the dead belong not to him, but to me.

Red tried to think, but it was hard, with her quiet voice all around him. The sound of it seemed to reach into his mind.

'I don't belong to you,' he managed. 'I belong to me.'

She laughed. *Even those who will not worship still belong to the gods. Now that you do not have Gryphus any more, you are lost. Now, you need me.*

'Why?'

Because without me, you are damned.

Red turned around again, still hoping vainly to see her. 'I reckoned I was damned anyway.'

By him, perhaps, but not by me. Shall I restore your vision, so you may look upon my glory?

'Yes,' Red blurted. He couldn't help himself.

See me, then.

Light appeared in the void, and she came with it. A woman, a Northerner. She wore nothing but a light silver mantle that draped over her shoulders and left most of her body bare. One of her eyes was as black as the void. The other was the full moon, somehow set into her pale, impassive face.

Red saw her, and an overwhelming urge came over him to kneel, to bow, to prostrate himself.

Kneel, the Night God commanded, as if she could sense his thoughts. *I am your god, Kearney Redguard, Shadow That Walks.*

Red hesitated, and was about to obey, but then he saw something else. It was easy to miss with her there, so brilliant in front of him, but they weren't alone.

There, standing beside and just a little behind her, was a man. He looked surprisingly ordinary considering the place, but he was a man Red knew.

He was tall and gaunt with a pointed chin-beard and long, curly black hair. He was shrouded in a black robe that hid everything except his boots, hands and head.

Arenadd Taranisäii. The Night God's servant.

Arenadd hadn't moved or spoken, but his eyes were on Red. He looked just as impassive as his master, but that stare did not waver, and when Red looked back he started to feel as if the dead Northerner was trying to tell him something.

The Night God saw what he was looking at. *Pay no attention to him. My servant will not interfere.*

Arenadd said nothing, but he did not look away.

It was enough to strip away some of Red's awe, and bring him to his senses. 'What d'you want from me?' he asked the Night God. 'Why am I here?'

Because I am here to help you. Now there is no other chance for you.

'Because I've lost Gryphus?'

The Night God made a gesture, and suddenly she was gone. Darkness closed over Red's eyes.

Eternal darkness, the god whispered. *That is what your world will be, Kearney. And for you, there can be no escape. You cannot take your own life, and nor can you grow old and die. You shall live forever, without sight.*

Red shuddered. 'I know.'

But with me, there is hope. Sight suddenly came back, and she was right there where she had been before.

'Hope?' Red repeated in spite of himself.

Yes. I am your only hope now.

'You can give me my eyes back?'

Yes.

Red glanced at Arenadd again. The Northerner looked back, outwardly calm, but the more Red looked, the more he thought he could detect something there. But what?

He looked back at the Night God. 'Why would you do that?' he asked. 'Why help me? I'm a Southerner.'

You are dead, she reminded him. *In death, race is irrelevant. Come to me, Kearney. Be with me. Love me, and I shall love you. Then your eyes will be opened, inside and out.*

Red hesitated.

I know what you have planned. You mean to leave. Once this war of yours has been fought, you plan to flee from Cymria and spend your eternity alone. But in the future I see for you, you are not alone. She smiled, as if she were indeed seeing some glorious future that he could not. *Do you honestly think that you can force yourself to hide forever? That loneliness will not force you to return? And then what shall you become? I have known one other who did the same. He travelled the world alone, always hiding his true nature, never staying long in one place. But in the end, he returned. He came back to me, and in my wisdom, I found the path for him. Only then did he become great.*

'You mean him?' asked Red, pointing at Arenadd.

No. Arenadd was wise enough to accept me into his heart almost at once. And you have seen the glory that was his.

'He's trapped in the void,' Red dared to say. 'You killed him.'

Glory was his until he turned against me, said the Night God, with a hint of anger. *Did you not say yourself that traitors must be punished? Enough of him. Admit to yourself that your plan will not work, Kearney. You cannot hide from who you are. You have no choice but to accept the truth.* She held out a hand to him. *You are the Shadow That Walks. You are my creature. Once you have accepted me, I shall give you back your eyes and show you the way to greatness, and there will be no name more honoured than yours.*

'But...' Red trailed off, still looking at Arenadd. The god's words were lulling, compelling, hypnotic, but Arenadd's stare was distracting him. And now, when Red looked closer, he finally saw what it was that had been disturbing him.

It was subtle, but there was a tightness to Arenadd's mouth, and the slightest twitch of his hands. He was hiding it very well, but the Night God's servant was afraid.

But of what?

Red looked at the Night God again, and knew what she was offering, behind the soothing words. 'You'll give me my sight back if I serve you,' he said. 'Like he did.'

I shall give you my guidance.

'You'll command me,' said Red. 'What d'you want me to do?'

What is right.

'Which is?' Red persisted, not liking her indirectness.

My people need you, said the Night God. *They are losing their way, and must have the Shadow That Walks to help them.*

'Just tell me,' said Red, finally deciding to take control of the situation if he could. 'I ain't gonna agree to a damn thing until you tell me what it is I'd be doing.'

You shall go to the King, and offer him your help, said the Night God. *The war will end quickly after that. You will tell the King that I have commanded that you shall rule beside him. He will lead my people, and you will lead your own. Together, you will see Cymria prosper.*

It caught Red by surprise. 'You mean you don't want me to kill all the other Southerners?'

No. They will live beside my own people, in their proper place. They will worship me, and be ruled by my people.

'But they want to rule themselves,' said Red. 'And worship Gryphus.'

You shall rule them, said the Night God. *Once the two races are united under yourself and Caedmon, acting in my name, you will be ready to strike. Amoran will fall, and Erebus, and every country will be united in the worship of me.*

Red stared at her. 'What? You want to——? The whole world? Worshipping you?'

Only then will there be no more war, said the Night God. *Think of that, Kearney Redguard. Think of the glory will be in your family name then, when the last of your line will be the one to bring peace to all men.*

'But Gryphus——,'

Do not lie to yourself more, the Night God warned. *You kept your loyalty with Gryphus, and he abandoned you and will not hear you. Shall I tell you the truth behind his great lie?*

'All right,' Red said cautiously.

Like all your people you were told that a good, loyal and faithful Southerner goes to the golden meadows when his life is over, said the Night God. *To be reunited with his loved ones. You were all of those things, Kearney. Now you are dead, but where is this meadow? Where are your dead parents, welcoming you to join them in blissful eternity?*

'I…' Red didn't know what to say.

Now you see the lie which Gryphus tells. There are no golden meadows. There is no joyous reunion. The dead come to me, and only me, and Gryphus does not care.

'That's not true!'

It is true, she said coldly. *And the only thing that can be done with truth is to accept it.*

Unable to look at her anymore, Red returned his gaze to Arenadd. The Northerner caught his eye, and shook his head grimly.

Red watched him in desperation. What did that mean? Was he saying that his master was telling the truth?

Decide, and decide now, said the Night God sharply. *You are the last hope for your people. Accept me and do what must be done, or turn away from me and live the life of a blinded nothing while your home crumbles, knowing that you could have saved it but failed.*

Red wavered. What could he do? He did not trust the Night God but still, he knew that what she had said was true. Without his sight, he wouldn't be able to lead anyone. He wouldn't be able to fight. And then he would be forced to spend the rest of his immortal existence unable to see, stumbling around in the dark forever.

But if he obeyed the Night God, he could save his people, maybe. Maybe…

Or…he looked away from her, as another possibility occurred to him. He could lie. He could pretend to agree, so she would give him his eyes back, but then…

No. He couldn't do that. One look at Arenadd was enough to remind him of what happened to people who betrayed the god of death.

Arenadd…

Red saw him, and stopped his frantic internal debate. Now, at last, Arenadd was moving.

Safely behind his master, where she could not see what he was doing, he had lifted one arm and was doing something odd. He gripped the black cloth of his robe, and tugged at it, as if urging Red to look at it.

He did, but couldn't understand why. What was so special about it?

Arenadd tugged on the robe again, and mouthed something, some frantic word. Red couldn't make it out, but he kept his eyes on the cloth where Arenadd's slender fingers pulled at it. Blackness. Was that it?

Arenadd shook his head and pulled at the robe with both hands, still mouthing that word. Red strained to see the shape of it on the other man's lips, but it evaded him.

He looked at the robe again instead.

Speak, the Night God prompted.

Red wasn't listening now. Arenadd had gone still again, but he obviously hoped that his message had gotten across. But what was it?

The robe. The black robe. It was what had given rise to the old racial slur against Northerners: blackrobe. It was an insult, because once most of the Northerners in Cymria had worn them. Now it was what their King wore, but back then it had been a mark of shame. After all, it was the uniform of a—

Red started, and finally the word Arenadd had mouthed at him became clear.

Speak! the Night God said again. *Choose. Choose wisely.*

Red spoke. 'Slave,' he said softly.

The Night God only stared at him.

But now Red knew what Arenadd had been trying to tell him, and he said the word again more loudly. 'Slave,' he said. 'A slave. That's what I'd be. Your slave.'

A faithful follower, she corrected.

'A slave,' Red repeated. He started to back away from her, and his voice became accusing. 'I'd be your slave! You liar! Holy Gryphus, I can't believe I almost fell for your bullshit. I've been a slave already, an' I'm damned if I'll do it again. You reckon I want to end up like him?' he pointed at Arenadd. 'I do what you want, an' the moment I won't, you do that to me. Bring me here to live in the void forever. After everyone hates me an' wants to see it happen.'

'Ouch,' Arenadd muttered.

How dare you? the Night God roared, her smooth exterior suddenly breaking down. *I am your god, and I will not be spoken to like that!*

'You ain't my god!' Red yelled back. 'You're a lyin' bitch. If Gryphus doesn't want me no more, then I've got no god. I'd rather be damned then have anything to do with you.'

Then go, the Night God hissed. *You will not see me again. Go and live out your tortured existence, but always remember how you threw away your only chance at redemption.*

'Kiss my arse,' Red suggested.

Arenadd burst into a peal of cold, snickering laughter.

The Night God snarled at him, and vanished.

Arenadd stayed behind, and for a fraction of an instant a look of intense relief crossed his face.

'You were tryin' to help me,' said Red. 'Weren't you?'

Arenadd smiled ever so faintly. He slowly raised his hand – and there on the back behind the knuckles – there was a brand scar just like Red's own.

'Nothing is more important than freedom, brother,' he said. 'Nothing. Don't let it go, not for anything, not for—'

He vanished.

Chapter Six

Eternal Darkness

Thanks to Morgan's rapid retreat along with most of his followers, which must have been planned beforehand, the retaking of New Eagleholm was as easy as the Southerners had hoped. Seerae returned to her Eyrie soon enough, and found Liantha waiting with the other leaders. Orak and Kraego came with her, but Kraego had scarcely entered the building before advancing on Liantha.

'Where is Red?' he demanded. 'Where is my human?'

'In the infirmary,' she said. 'Teressa's with him. He's hurt, Kraego.'

'Take me to him. Now.'

Liantha quickly assigned one of her officials to show him the way, but the black griffin loped on ahead with Orak close behind. He caught Red's scent well before they reached the infirmary, and followed it straight inside. It was a large room with many beds, and Kraego went to the one where his human waited, completely ignoring Teressa as she came forward to meet Orak.

Red lay on his back, with a bandage covering half of his face. Kraego crouched to sniff at him. He gave off the cold, metallic smell that he had had ever since Kraego had resurrected him, but under that there was an ugly taint of burnt meat. It made Kraego hiss.

He looked up quickly at Teressa. 'What is his injury? I did not stop to see, but went to chase down Eck-hoo.'

She answered him, but hesitantly. 'It's his eyes. He's been blinded, Kraego.'

'No!' Kraego advanced on her. 'Tell me that is not true!'

Teressa backed off, while Orak quietly moved ready to defend her if he had to. 'I'm sorry,' she said. 'It's true. Morgan had someone lying in wait. She hit him with something in the face – some kind of branding iron or something. His eyes were burnt out. The healer already had a look at him. They're just gone. There's nothing but destroyed flesh left.'

Kraego turned back to look at Red. 'No! No, this cannot be!'

But it was. There was no reason for the human to lie to him. His partner was crippled.

'I do not believe it,' Kraego said furiously. 'He will heal. He is Kraeai kran ae.'

'I hope so,' said Teressa. 'It's said that the Shadow That Walks can recover from any injury. But…'

'But what?' Kraego glared at her.

'The great Arenadd's fingers were broken,' she explained. 'Crushed. The Southerners tortured him. Afterwards they healed, but they didn't heal properly. They were always twisted and crooked. He couldn't use his hand any more. I saw it myself when I met him. Red's burn will heal, but there's no certainty his eyes will grow back.'

'They will,' said Kraego.

'You must think now, Kraego,' Orak said suddenly. 'With your human injured, it is you who are our leader now.'

'Red said that Liantha—,' Teressa began.

'I do not follow Seerae's human,' said Orak. 'She may lead the other humans here, but our griffins follow you, Kraego. It is now you who must decide what to do while your human cannot be there to help you.'

Kraego listened – the grey griffin was right. 'I must think,' he agreed. 'I must act. Do not be afraid, Orak. I am more cunning than any other griffin.'

'I know it,' said Orak. 'Decide.'

Kraego paced around the bed where Red lay comatose, his tail swishing. He knew that he was more intelligent than other griffins, but he still wasn't used to planning. That was for humans to do. Automatically, therefore, he started to think over the plan that Red had made, and chose it as a matter of course.

'I will go to Liranwee,' he said. 'And I will go alone. I will find this human pup, Caradoc, and I will steal him and bring him here.'

'Ereska will try to stop you,' Orak warned.

'Then I shall kill her,' said Kraego. 'I wish to challenge Shar as well, but…that must wait.' He had some vague notion that Red had said that, but couldn't remember why.

'Do it, then,' said Orak. 'The human pup will be less valuable without a partner, but his father will do anything to have him back.'

'What about Morgan?' asked Teressa. 'Did he get away?'

'Yes.' Kraego huffed irritably. 'Eck-hoo is small, but fast in the air. Seerae is not pleased, but that is no concern of mine.'

'Good,' said Teressa.

Kraego gave her another glare. 'Why is it good, human?'

'Because if Morgan gets back to his King, he'll tell him that Red has been blinded,' said Teressa. 'It'll make him think his son is out of danger. He'll be less careful.'

Kraego clicked his beak thoughtfully. It was easy to forget how clever humans could be, but this was a reminder. 'Yes,' he said. 'That is true. Perhaps I should wait a little while so that he has the chance to reach his goal before I follow him. After all, I have been fighting and I need food and rest. But I should not stay long. Seerae will be pleased that my human is wounded, and may take the chance to provoke me again.'

'A fight between the two of you would not be good,' said Orak.

Kraego bristled. 'Why, do you think that I could lose?'

'No, you would win, and then there would be one less follower for you,' the grey griffin flattered.

It worked. 'That is true,' said Kraego. 'To kill her would be beneath me. Go now – I must sleep by my human's side. When morning comes, I will leave.'

He lay down without waiting for a reply, and put his gaze on Red, where it stayed. It was not good that he would have to leave his human unprotected while he was gone, but Red was still strong. Anyway, he would make Orak and his human stay behind to guard him, just in case. He could trust Orak to do as he was told.

Kraego had no fear for the future. He trusted his strength and his power, and there was no possibility in his mind that the plan could fail. The human pup would be his, and after that, victory would somehow follow. He, Kraego, would be the supreme griffin of the South.

There was no doubt about that, either.

*

Pain was waiting for Red when he woke up. It lay in wait while he was unconscious, and he felt it creeping back as he returned to his body, like a stalking griffin. When he tried to open his eyes, it lunged.

He convulsed on the bed, gripping the blankets so hard they tore. A moment later he went still, breathing harshly. His whole face felt as if it was on fire.

Unable to move, not knowing what to do, he lay back and clenched his fists until the pain gradually subsided.

'Red.' Another hand touched one of his, and he relaxed as he realised there had been someone saying his name the whole time.

'Who's…that?' he mumbled. His lips felt swollen.

'It's Teressa. Are ye in pain?'

The pain rose again, and his jaw clenched. 'No, feels – great,' he gritted out through his teeth.

'Do ye want to sleep again?' she asked quickly. 'I can give ye something…'

Red almost said yes – he wanted to shout yes – but an image of the Night God flashed up in his mind, and he shook his head sharply. 'No.'

'Are ye sure?' Teressa persisted. 'We've been keeping ye asleep for a while…the healer thought it was best.'

Red made himself lie still, and breathed deeply, trying to calm himself down. 'How…long?'

'Two days.'

'Right.' The pain was fading again now, and he felt stronger. Had he really been out of it for that long? It had felt like a long time, but two days? 'Where's the healer?' he wondered.

'Asleep in the next room,' said Teressa. 'I can go and get him, if ye like.'

'Sleepin' on the job?' Red gasped, with an attempt at humour. 'I should…kick his arse for that.'

'It's the middle of the night.'

'Oh.' Red shuddered slightly. 'Can't tell.' He reached up towards his face, and his fingers touched bandages. The pain flared up immediately.

Teressa's invisible hands gently pulled his own away. 'Don't touch it.'

Red obeyed. 'Is it—?'

'It's getting better,' said Teressa. 'That's probably why it hurts more now than it did before.'

'Better?' Red repeated, hardly daring to believe it. 'Healing up?'

'Aye. I saw it last time the healer changed the bandage. It was…awful for a while.' He thought he could hear her grimacing at the memory.

'But getting better?' he prompted.

'It took a while,' she said. 'The…dead stuff fell away first.'

Red pulled a face, and groaned at the pain that caused. 'Don't tell me that!'

'Sorry. But then the healer said there was healthy flesh underneath, and now that's healing up.'

'My eyes,' Red said urgently.

She hesitated before replying. 'I'm sorry. There's nothing there. The sockets are healing, but it's all…scar, the healer said. The pain will stop, but…'

Red heaved a long, weary sigh. 'Knew it. Damn her.'

'Well, she's paid the price for what she did,' said Teressa.

'What?' Red turned his head towards where he thought she was.

'She's dead. We found her body.'

He lay there for a little while, trying to figure out what in the world the Northerner was talking about. How could the Night God be dead?

'Who's dead?' he asked eventually.

'The woman who did this to ye,' said Teressa, sounding puzzled. 'Ye killed her in Liantha's audience chamber. Remember? We knew it was ye who did it – her neck was broken so badly her head had just about come off.'

'Oh.' Red had completely forgotten about Morgan's blank-faced accomplice. He quickly forgot her again as he remembered the vision of the Night God. 'Don't let me sleep,' he said urgently. 'Keep me awake.'

'It's all right,' said Teressa. 'Ye're badly hurt, Red – ye need plenty of rest to get better.'

'Hah,' Red coughed a laugh. 'Never gonna be better an' we both know it. Don't let me sleep, Teressa.'

'Why?'

'Because she's there,' he said. 'Waiting. Might try again.'

Teressa held his hand in one of hers, and reached up with the other to touch him lightly on what was left of his forehead. 'Who's waiting, Red?'

'The Night God. Tempting me.' He was starting to babble again, confused by pain and darkness. 'Wants me to be hers. Says she'll give me back my eyes. Nearly said yes, but he – he stopped me. He's…I saw it. Saw it in his eyes. He's…he's frightened, Teressa. He's scared to death. But…'

'But what? Who is he?'

Red wanted to cry, and then remembered he could never do that again. 'She said if I was hers I'd see again. Inside and out. Without her, I'll be in darkness. Eternal darkness. But he didn't want it. Slave. That's what he said, an' he's scared. But I saw somethin' else too. Saw the truth about him. He's hiding it, pretending like he doesn't care, but—'

Teressa held him, and he stilled. 'What is it?' she asked.

'He hates her,' Red whispered. 'He hates the Night God. He's stuck with her, an' he hates her. That's why he wanted me to stay away, so she wouldn't win. He warned me away from her. He was so afraid I'd say yes. He tried not to show it, but I could see.'

'Who?' asked Teressa, though she must have guessed by now. 'Who was afraid?'

Red relaxed against her – she was warm and alive, and the touch of her took away some of his own fear, though he could feel unconsciousness rising up again in his exhausted mind, the void dragging at him, pulling him down, bringing him back. 'Arenadd,' he whispered, and sank back into darkness.

*

Arenadd…

The man who had once been King of the North turned. 'Yes, master?'

The Night God stood taller than him, and there was no expression on her face, but he knew her well enough to sense that she was troubled. *You must act now*, she said.

Arenadd tensed. 'Act how? Are you sending me somewhere?' He imagined that his heart beat faster in a mixture of fear and wild hope, but he had no heart to beat at all now, and never would again.

He will not be in our reach for much longer, the god of death whispered. *Soon he will be strong enough to stay in the living world.*

'And?' said Arenadd, though he could guess what she wanted. Trying to irritate her was the only real outlet he had now.

You must go to him. He will not listen to me, but he may trust you more.

'What, me?' Arenadd said in mocking tones. 'Well of course. Oh, of course he'd trust me. I'm only the Dark Lord Arenadd, the worst enemy of his entire race. The man who dragged his whole beloved family down into the mud. The one who gave his uncle Bran the

"Betrayer" title. Oh yes, our blessed Captain Redguard would trust me to the ends of the earth.'

Nevertheless, you must go, said the Night God. *Speak with him.* She smiled thinly. *You are a persuasive man, Arenadd. Reason with him.*

'Tempt him, you mean,' said Arenadd. 'It won't work, Master. Even if he listens to me, he doesn't trust you. You're the problem here, no matter what either of us says.'

Do not speak to me that way.

'Think about it from his point of view,' Arenadd went on, ignoring her. 'He's been raised his whole life to hate the both of us. You're the god of death who only deluded Northerners worship, and I'm a mass murderer and a power hungry monster. For the gods'— for your sake, think about it. Because if you do, you'll realise that this little ruse of yours won't work.'

The Night God smiled humourlessly. *Despair has always been your greatest weakness, Arenadd.*

'And arrogance has always been yours,' he spat back. 'You tried to tempt him, you tried to threaten him, and it didn't work. Admit it to yourself and move on.'

The Night God stared at him for a moment, and he wondered if he had gone too far. She obviously did not want to trust him, but she was not an entirely self-willed being. She had some ability to make her own choices, but in many things she was overruled by the will and beliefs of her people. They adored – in some cases worshipped – him, and trusted him absolutely, and so their god was influenced to trust him as well despite all the times he had tried to get in her way.

But too much back-talk could still make her angry, and she had made him suffer for it more than once.

But then, to his surprise, she answered calmly. *And if we do not take this chance, then what shall we do? I cannot have this, Arenadd. His existence is the ultimate blasphemy against me. The Shadow That Walks cannot exist without obedience to me! My people are becoming confused…they believe he obeys me when he does not. They will begin to think that I am against them, and if they are not united by one goal they will fail.*

She sounded about as impassive as always, but Arenadd knew her well enough to hear the hint of desperation in her voice. He gave nothing away, but internally, he smirked.

He walked away from her, back turned as if he were leaving,

letting her linger over her fears. Yes, fears – he knew she was afraid. This Southerner who had her power frightened her very much, though he couldn't tell exactly why. But now she was afraid, and desperate, it was time.

He turned around suddenly. 'I have an idea.'

Speak.

Arenadd smiled a cold, cruel smile. 'I know what to do, master. I've been thinking about it for a while, and it all makes sense. It'll work.'

Yes? He had her attention now.

'I can't help you. But I know someone who can.' Arenadd paused for effect, and for a moment his mind went back to those days, so long ago, when he had stood in the Council Chamber of Malvern's Eyrie and spoken to his council. They had argued and debated over every important decision, but when King Arenadd spoke, everyone listened. And now, he had that same keen attention from a god. It was glorious. 'We can't control him,' he continued. 'Therefore, the only option is to kill him.'

But unless he gives me his soul, I cannot touch him, said the Night God.

'Indeed,' said Arenadd, with a hint of sourness. 'You can't kill him. But I know someone who can.'

And who is that?

Arenadd told her.

No, the Night God said at once. *I cannot. I will not lower myself…*

'But he can help us,' said Arenadd. 'It's in his interests to do so. Besides, you don't have to speak to him yourself. Send me. I'll soon bring him around.'

No, she said again.

'At least consider it,' said Arenadd. 'But just remember – the longer you hesitate, the more damage this Southerner will do. Not just to our people, but to you. You said yourself they're getting confused, and some of them have even joined him. And if he kills the King…'

The Night God hesitated. *I do not like it, but I will think it over. I will resort to this only if no other way is open to me.* She gave Arenadd a slow, calculating look. *You persuade me well, Arenadd. You have not forgotten your old talents.*

He smiled the same thin, humourless smile that she had given him. 'You can depend on me to do that, master. I'm a politician. And a complete bastard, which helps. You can't afford to have much empathy in my position.'

Nevertheless, said the Night God. *We shall not give in. Madness could be our salvation.* A look of anger and callous cruelty showed in her single eye. *I cannot kill him, but I shall punish him for his insolence. I will torment him until he begs me to forgive him, or until madness takes him.*

'You're an inspiration to us all, master,' Arenadd muttered, but she had already turned away from him – too late to see the look of absolute hatred that briefly flitted across her servant's cold, angular face.

Chapter Seven

Kraego Supreme

By the time Red woke up and spoke to Teressa, and well before he succumbed to the agony of nightmare visions which the Night God sent him, Kraego was long gone.

He had waited out the day after the capture of Eagleholm with bad grace; doing nothing wasn't something many griffins enjoyed, and he was itching to fly. But he forced himself to wait, following Orak and Teressa's advice. He ate plenty, slept and groomed, and hissed at Seerae when she came by with her human. His half-sister gave little away, but it was obvious enough to him that she was taking a great deal of pleasure from his human's blinding. She hadn't forgiven him for his insults, and though she had too much sense to try and fight him she knew that all partnered griffins were most vulnerable where their humans were concerned.

Kraego suspected that she had ambitions of taking over his role as master of the griffins in the army, which was not much of a leap to make, nor even unusual; humble griffins were not common, and, like him, she had been raised by Senneck, who had passed on her ambitious nature to her offspring.

Normally, a griffin who wanted to take over would do so by trying to remove their rival, which in this case was himself. But if Seerae couldn't kill him, she might try and attack his human. If Red was somehow removed, Kraego would lose the right to lead. He would be disgraced, and most likely driven away to live in the wild.

But Kraego had no fear of Seerae, not for himself or for his human. Her own human was too loyal to help her, and Orak had promised to keep watch. Besides, Red was immortal.

Still…Seerae had to be watched, and Kraego, able to do some thinking while he flew northward, determined that if she caused too much trouble he would kill her. She would be an easy victim. Her human would not be the leader of New Eagleholm's humans after that, but no matter; someone else would rise to take her place. It was all the same to Kraego.

For now, it was time to carry out Red's plan and see to it that Shar and her human would not dare to attack. With the pup of Shar's human in Kraego's clutches, her human would not allow any attack for fear of his offspring's life.

Kraego stopped to rest and groom, and hissed contemptuously to himself. Humans were such stupid, weak creatures. It was so ridiculous that this King Caedmon placed so much importance on the life of his single, puny young. If it died, it would be easy to have another. And besides, it was shameful that he should only have one. Any male worth his life should consider it a matter of pride to pair with many females and father many offspring. Kraego himself had already mated with several females, and his virility was proven. He had no need to stay nearby and trouble himself over the lives of his chicks. A chick that needed protection from both parents was weak, and should die anyway.

Well, this human Caedmon would soon pay the price for his foolishness. With his pup stolen, he would look weak in front of his fellows. A male who did not have young was beneath contempt.

Kraego found himself looking forward with pleasure to the task ahead of him. It would be easy. He was a dark griffin, and could use the shadows to surprise his intended victim. But beyond that, he was a griffin. A predator. It was in his nature to stalk and capture prey. The only difficult part would be stopping himself from killing it. Humans were so fragile, and the youngsters in particular, that he might do so by accident.

No, no…Kraego shook out his feathers before taking to the air again. He would not fail. If the pup died, he would say he had done it deliberately. Griffins did not make mistakes.

He flew on at a leisurely pace, not using the shadows. There was no hurry, and he had to ensure that Eck-hoo reached Liranwee before himself.

Kraego's great, black shadow rippled over the trees beneath him. Where it touched, birds flew up in shrieking flocks. Every creature below knew that there was a dark griffin above, and Kraego imagined their fear going out ahead of him to infest the hearts of those in his path. He thought of the griffins and humans in the city that had once been Red's home. Once they had heard Eck-hoo's news, they would think that they were safe. Kraeai kran ae was blinded, and harmless.

Such stupidity. Every creature feared Kraeai kran ae, but they had far more to fear than a mere human, immortal or not. In their arrogance, they would forget that there was another being to fear. Kraego the dark griffin was coming.

*

King Caedmon listened to Morgan's report, stony-faced. If he felt any satisfaction at the news of Red's blinding, he didn't show it.

Nearby, close to his partner Ereska, Prince Caradoc listened with open horror. 'They burnt out his eyes?' he repeated.

Morgan winced. 'Yes. He must be completely blind now, Sire. I'm certain of it.'

Caedmon nodded curtly. 'Understood. You've done well, Morgan. Honestly, I...I didn't think I would ever see you again.'

'Neither did I,' said Morgan.

'But...' Caedmon sighed. 'I hardly like to say this after all you've done, but I have to ask – Morgan, why didn't you finish it? You had him blinded. Why didn't you bring him here to me as planned? Did something happen?'

Morgan's answer came slowly and reluctantly. 'I...no, Sire. I could have done it.'

'Then why didn't you?'

The spy looked away.

Caedmon frowned. Tall and thin, wearing a robe and a pointed chin-beard, he looked very much like his cousin Arenadd. But his voice was gentle as he reached out to touch his adopted son on the shoulder. 'It's all right. I won't blame you if you were afraid. I know what it's like when you see him. I was afraid myself.'

Morgan must have known how rare it was for his King to admit to fear. 'I was afraid,' he admitted.

'But he was blind,' said Caedmon. 'Surely that would have made him far less dangerous.'

'That's not what I was afraid of.' Morgan finally looked his King in the face. 'Sire, I'm sorry. I wasn't afraid that he would kill me – I went there expecting it to happen. I thought I was resigned to it, and I swear to you – I'm willing to die for you if I have to. But I wasn't afraid of death. I was afraid of damnation.'

'What? You mean the Night God—?'

'Sire...Caedmon, he's the Shadow That Walks,' said Morgan.

'We all know what that means. What if the Night God did send him? What if he's following her? I know he said he isn't, but why would she choose him if she didn't want this to happen? If that's true, then if we fight against him, we fight against her.'

'Morgan, for the love of gods!' Caedmon thundered. 'This is nonsense! Why on earth would the Night God be against me? Against us? She wanted us to invade the South – isn't that why she sent my mother back to make me King? Isn't that why Arenadd had to be removed – because he refused?'

'But what if she changed her mind?' Morgan persisted.

'The Night God doesn't change her mind,' said Caedmon. 'My mother told me that herself, and she'd spoken to her. Are you going to argue with that?'

'It's a matter for the priestesses to decide—,' Morgan began.

'My mother was a priestess,' said Caedmon. 'She was High Priestess. She was the Shadow That Walks. Who would know the god's mind better than her? Morgan, this Southerner is a nothing. An accident. He doesn't follow any god. All he wants is to send us back out of his land.'

'Then maybe that's what we should do,' said Morgan.

'What?' Caedmon's eyes narrowed dangerously. 'What did you say?'

'You heard me,' Morgan said boldly. 'If you ask me, this invasion was a mistake. We're out of our home territory here, and we're stretched too thin trying to manage it all. We both know that. Northerners belong in the North. And besides—,'

'Besides what?' Caedmon's voice had gone low and quiet, which was far more frightening than when he shouted. In the corner, Caradoc nervously pressed himself against Ereska's warm flank.

'And besides, don't you realise what we've done?' said Morgan. 'We've lowered ourselves. We hate the Southerners because of what they did to us all those years ago, and we all know what that was. Invasion. Slavery. Rule by foreigners. We fought them off and drove them out, so we could be free to govern ourselves. We thought we were better than them. Isn't that what Arenadd taught us? But now look at us. Look what we've done. We haven't made ourselves as bad as them – we've made ourselves worse, because we've shown that we didn't learn a damn thing from what happened to our people.'

'Oh yes?' said Caedmon. 'And what's the alternative? Staying in Malvern and waiting for them to come after us? Letting them come back through those mountains to take back what used to be theirs? You know why we had to do this, Morgan. We've both known since we were children. It's us or them. If we hadn't struck first, it would have been only a matter of time. And now, thanks to your cowardice, that Southern scum is still out there. And what if he gets better? Well? Did you think of that? The Shadow That Walks can heal from anything. What if his eyes grow back? And then he'll come back here. You know what he threatened to do to my son, and to you.'

'But only if we didn't leave!' said Morgan. Both of them were shouting now, and Caradoc had put his hands firmly over his ears. 'He gave us an ultimatum, don't you remember? Leave or Caradoc dies. If—,'

'It's too late for that, and you know it. He gave us a time limit. We didn't take it.'

'Then if your son dies, you'll only have yourself to blame,' said Morgan.

Caedmon started forward, and hit him hard in the face. Morgan went down with a yelp of surprise, and Caradoc bit back a shout. Immediately, Echo stepped forward angrily to protect his human.

Shar put herself in the way. 'Enough!' the red griffin snapped. 'Back down, Eck-hoo, or I shall hurt you.'

The smaller griffin obeyed, angry and resentful but not daring to challenge her.

Morgan stood up. His nose was bleeding, but he acted as if he couldn't feel it. 'I'm sorry, Sire.'

'Go,' Caedmon said shortly. 'You get your wish, Morgan. Go home. I'm sending you back to Malvern and you can stay there until I change my mind.'

Morgan hesitated. 'Sire, I—,'

'What?' Caedmon asked sharply.

'I want to stay here,' said Morgan. 'To protect you. I swore I wouldn't—,'

'I have enough protection,' said Caedmon. 'Go back to Malvern. Your wife can go with you. You wanted to go home, so go. Don't argue with me, Morgan.'

Morgan stared at his boots. 'As you say, Sire.'

'Shar—,' Echo began.

'Say nothing,' Shar rasped back. 'My human has decided, and I agree. We cannot have traitors fighting for us, or those who insult us.'

'It's fine, Echo,' Morgan muttered. But before he left the room, he turned back and pointed accusingly at Caradoc. 'Think about it, Sire. What's more important to you: this damned city, or your son's life?'

Caedmon did not reply, and Morgan and Echo left together without another word.

After they had gone, Caedmon sat down. He was breathing hard. 'Damn him.'

Caradoc waited a little while, but finally decided to go to him and touch his father on the arm. 'Is Morgan going to be in trouble?'

'He already is,' said Caedmon. He looked up at his son's troubled face, and smiled at last. 'Come here.'

Caradoc climbed onto his father's lap. 'He was very rude. That's why you sent him away, isn't it?'

'No. Rudeness I can live with. He's been compromised.'

'What does that mean?'

'It means that he doesn't believe in what we're doing any more,' said Caedmon. 'If there's too much doubt in someone's mind, they'll make mistakes. They'll hesitate. Doubtful people can ruin everything. Sometimes they even turn traitor.'

'Morgan wouldn't do that!'

'No, I don't believe he would. Even after that little spat he still wanted to stay. I don't like to send him away, but it's for his own good. Anyway…'

'Anyway what?' asked Caradoc.

'Anyway, I need him,' said Caedmon. 'All our people do. If anything happens to you and I, Caradoc, Morgan will be King. It's best he stays in the North – hopefully he'll be safer there.'

'What about Captain Redguard?' asked Caradoc. 'Will he always be blind?'

'I hope so,' said Caedmon.

'But that's horrible!'

'I know it is, but it's for the best. For your safety.'

Caradoc said nothing, but inside his wishes had not changed. All he wanted – all he had wanted since Red had visited and made his threats – was to go home. But if he said that, he would only make his father angry again. He nodded unhappily instead.

'Anyway,' Caedmon went on, 'Now we know he's been rendered harmless, and we know where he is too. Morgan did well.' He gently let Caradoc down off his lap, and stood up. 'We have to act, and fast. We'll send troops to New Eagleholm immediately, and see to it that they do what our predecessor Arenadd did to the old Eagleholm.' He shook his head. 'That Southerner is as big of an idiot as I suspected, keeping all his strength in one place and then letting people get to us with information about where it is and how many of them there are. Once New Eagleholm has been crushed, we'll have destroyed the last of them for good. Most likely we'll capture him in the process, and it doesn't even matter that we don't know how to kill him. He can rot in a cell under his own home Eyrie for the rest of eternity, or we'll sink him to the bottom of the sea.' He snorted. 'Invincible my arse.'

*

After Shar and his father had left, Caradoc stayed with Ereska. He didn't like it when his father talked that way; his face would go hard and cruel and his voice sounded cold. It always made him uneasy.

'Everything's all better now, isn't it?' he said to his partner, desperate for some kind of reassurance.

Unfortunately, asking a griffin for comfort was rarely a good idea. 'No,' she said. 'It will not be better until Kraeai kran ae is no longer able to be a threat of any kind, and his followers are crushed.'

Caradoc's shoulders sagged. 'I just want it to be better,' he said plaintively.

'Well then, make it better,' the yellow griffin said impatiently.

Caradoc looked glumly at her. 'I'm going to go and pray again.'

'No,' said Ereska. 'I do not like it when you go into that little room. I cannot follow you in there.'

'Then…then I'll go up on the roof,' said Caradoc. 'And pray to the moon.'

'Very well,' said Ereska. 'I will be able to guard you there. But do not expect your god to protect you. I tell you again, Caradoc, these gods do not exist.'

'Yes they do! Father says—,'

Boy and griffin headed up through the tower together, still bickering. Caradoc had tried to explain why it was obvious that the gods existed, but Ereska wouldn't listen. She never liked being told she was wrong. Neither did Shar, or any other griffin. His father had said it was because they were too arrogant to listen.

Caradoc kept trying anyway, because everyone knew that life was meaningless without the gods.

It was twilight outside, and the sky had turned a beautiful shade of pale purple, with hints of red on the horizon where the last of the sunset had not quite faded. Caradoc stepped up into the open on the Eyrie tower's flat roof, and happily breathed in the cool evening air. It was not as cold here as it was in Malvern, and the land was greener. His father had said that was why Southerners were fat and Northerners thin – the South had more sun, and therefore more food.

Above the moon had already begun to glow brightly, but before Caradoc settled down to pray he walked around the rooftop and looked down at the city of Liranwee. It was a new city, he had been told. The Southerners had fought amongst themselves for years, before Caradoc was born. They'd destroyed the city they were all trying to take for themselves, but two new ones had been founded: Sunton, and Liranwee. Liranwee was in the middle of the country, and not too far from the Northgate Mountains, which Northerners called Y Castell. That was why King Caedmon had decided to make it the new centre of his government. From here, he would rule not just the North, but the entire continent.

Caradoc had to admit that he liked Liranwee. It wasn't like Malvern, where he had been born. Houses in the North had very tall, peaked roofs to stop snow piling up on them. Here, though, they were flatter. Some had thatch on them, others had tiles. Smoke drifted up from the chimneys.

Below that, he could see people walking through the streets, and sometimes a griffin swaggering along. There were a lot of Northerners down there, and some of them had already taken houses and found new jobs. They were trying to live alongside the Southerners who were still here. There had been some fighting and so on, but his father had worked very hard to keep things peaceful. Now, from up here, it all looked nice to Caradoc – like any other city he had seen, with everyone going around doing whatever they had to do.

He could see a few bare patches in the city, though – places where buildings had been destroyed when the city was captured. In one of those places, a new building was being made and a great dome was already taking shape. A Moon Temple, where the Night God would be worshipped once it was ready. The Southerners were helping to build it, so maybe they didn't mind. They had to be pleased that their new ruler hadn't destroyed their Sun Temple or told them they couldn't worship their own god, which was what the Southerners had once done when they ruled the North.

There would be equality here, his father had said.

Caradoc nodded to himself, liking the thought. If it weren't for Captain Redguard, this would be a nice place to live. Everyone could be happy here. But Captain Redguard didn't want Caradoc here, or his father, or any Northerners. This was his home, and he wanted it back.

Caradoc frowned, and turned away to look back up at the moon as he remembered why he was here. He needed to pray again, and remind the Night God to protect everyone he cared about.

That was when he realised that Ereska hadn't moved since they had arrived. Nor was she anywhere near him.

Caradoc looked around, alarmed, and realised that she had been standing near the entrance that led back inside, crouched low and scarcely moving except for the slow twitching of her tail.

Standing in front of her, blocking the way back, was a giant, black griffin.

Caradoc stood there, utterly bewildered. He had never seen this griffin before.

It was male, and huge – bigger even than Ereska, who was already large for a griffin. His feathered forequarters were pitch black, and his furry hindquarters were pale brown tipped with silver. His eyes were icy blue.

Confused, Caradoc went to Ereska's side. 'What's going on?' he asked. 'Who's this?' He looked around while he spoke, but couldn't see a human partner anywhere. Was this griffin alone?

The black griffin took a step towards Ereska. 'Do not flee,' he said. His voice was deep and growling. 'If you do, I shall chase you and you will die. Do not attack, or you will also die.'

Ereska had not moved. 'Stay away from my human, Kraego.'

'Then you know who I am?' said the black griffin. 'That is good.'

'All griffins know the name of Kraego, son of Skandar,' said

Ereska. 'I know why you have come.'

'Then you were a fool,' said Kraego. 'If you guessed that I was coming, you should have kept your human in places I could not reach. But now it is too late. Stand aside. I will take him now.'

Caradoc grabbed Ereska by the wing. 'No! Ereska, make him go away!'

She hissed at Kraego. 'You will not hurt him.'

'No,' said Kraego. 'I am not here for that. But if you try to fight me, your human will be caught up in the struggle and may die.'

Ereska looked quickly at Caradoc and then, slowly, rose up out of her angry posture. 'Speak to me, Kraego,' she said softly. 'Tell me who you are. Tell me about your strength.'

Seeing her newly passive posture, Kraego relaxed slightly. 'I am the mightiest griffin in Cymria,' he bragged. 'My human is Kraeai kran ae. Immortal.'

'But not here with you?' said Ereska.

'He waits with his followers for me to return,' said Kraego. 'I did not need his help to steal this human pup.'

'Is he strong?' asked Ereska.

'The strongest,' said Kraego. 'I have seen him bend steel, and break the necks of his enemies with his bare hands. He is a mighty leader of humans, and his mind is the most cunning. Together, he and I shall take this land from Shar. If you stand in my way, you shall die.'

Ereska moved closer to Caradoc. 'I see the truth in what you have said, but I cannot allow you to take my human. Your own has threatened to murder him.'

'A lie,' said Kraego. 'Dead, the pup is no use. Alive, he is a hostage. My human only wished to frighten Shar's.'

Caradoc moaned softly, but didn't dare speak. He had to trust in Ereska to know what to do now; he himself had no chance.

Ereska was silent for a while, and she shifted on her big paws. She looked as if she was thinking.

Finally, she said, 'I cannot trust you to tell the truth. Nor do I trust you to leave my human unharmed. I will not allow you to take him.'

'Then you will die,' said Kraego, who did not look surprised. 'Move away from the human and fight me.'

'No,' said Ereska.

'Flee, and I shall chase you down,' Kraego warned. 'I do not wish to harm the pup, but I will not hesitate if you force me. I am the dark griffin, and you cannot escape me.'

'No,' Ereska said again. 'Kraego.' She lowered her voice to a purr – a griffin's persuading voice. 'I have known that you were coming, with your human or alone. I have thought this over for many days, and I have made plans of my own. I knew that I could not fight you and hope to win. Nor am I foolish enough to think that I can escape you. I know the power of the dark griffin.'

'Then give me your human,' said Kraego. 'It is your only choice.'

'I will not,' said Ereska. She flicked her tail, swishing the feathers on the stonework beneath her. 'I have ambitions, Kraego, and to reach them, I will not need Shar. I only need my human. Therefore, my human and I will go with you.'

'No!' Caradoc exclaimed. 'Ereska—!'

'You would betray Shar?' said Kraego.

'To protect my human, I shall,' said Ereska. 'I will bring him to your human, and stay beside him. Once we are there, we shall talk and you and I shall make an agreement that benefits us both.'

'You are bold, to do this,' Kraego observed. Both griffins were ignoring Caradoc's horrified expression. 'Shar will want your skull in her talons.'

'It is in my best interests, and those of my human,' Ereska said blandly. 'The past has shown that a griffin who allies herself with the dark griffin always triumphs. You are now my leader, Kraego, and I submit to you.'

With that, she bent her forelegs and lowered her head to the other griffin, in a gesture of respect and obedience.

'Then it is good,' said Kraego. 'Come, Ereska.'

Caradoc didn't know what to do. He couldn't accept what had just happened. He stared at Ereska, wide-eyed. 'You can't!'

'I must,' said Ereska. She lay down on her belly. 'Climb onto my back, and quickly. We must go.'

'But—,'

'Come!' Ereska said again. 'And come now, or I will carry you in my talons like prey, and that is no way for a prince to travel.'

'Listen to your partner, human pup,' Kraego hissed.

Panic-stricken, Caradoc broke and ran. But Kraego was still standing in front of the only way back into the tower. He was trapped.

'Help!' he shouted. 'Somebody help!'

Ereska hissed in irritation. She stood up and bounded after him.

In moments she had him cornered. 'Be silent!' she rasped at him, and when he kept shouting she snatched him up in one huge forepaw and brought him back.

'Little fool,' said Kraego. 'Ereska – fly South, to New Eagleholm. I shall fly behind you. If you betray me, then you and your human will both die.'

Ereska rasped her agreement and took off, with Caradoc dangling from her talons.

He tried to break free, despite the danger, and shouted again for someone to help him, but it was already too late. If anyone heard him, they would never reach him in time.

Ereska flew away out of the city, due south, with Kraego close behind – carrying her own partner straight into the clutches of his enemies.

Chapter Eight

Hope

'How is he?' The moment Kraego arrived back at New Eagleholm, he confronted Teressa with the demand.

Bleary eyed, Teressa looked past him at the yellow griffin and the trembling Northern child. 'Is that who I think it is?'

'Answer me!' Kraego snapped. 'How is my human?'

'Not well,' said Teressa. 'Ye'd better come and see for yerself. Who's the griffin?'

'I am Ereska,' said the yellow griffin. 'And this is my human, Prince Caradoc of Malvern. You will treat him with respect, human.'

Teressa shook her head. 'Ye brought the Prince and his partner?'

'She follows me now,' said Kraego. 'Where is Orak?'

'With Red. We've both been watching over him.' Teressa shifted uneasily. 'We should wait until Seerae gets here. She'll want to know what's happened.'

Kraego snorted, but they didn't have to wait long before Seerae and Liantha came running.

'What is this?' Seerae demanded. 'What griffin are you who comes into my territory?'

Ereska eyed the smaller griffin haughtily. 'I am Ereska, and my human is Prince Caradoc. What griffin are you?'

'I am Seerae, and this is my Eyrie,' she retorted. 'How dare you come here and not show me the proper respect?'

'I give respect to none but my leader, and that is Kraego,' said Ereska.

Seerae reared up angrily. 'Leave my territory at once!'

'Seerae, stop!' Liantha exclaimed.

Her partner wasn't listening, but thankfully the situation was quickly defused by Kraego. 'Ereska, this is not my territory but Seerae's,' he said. 'We cannot stay unless we recognise that.'

Ereska huffed, and gave a perfunctory dip of the head. 'I come without designs on your mates or food,' she said, speaking the customary promises without any sincerity at all.

Seerae accepted it, but clearly did not like it, and stood there looking angry and uneasy while Kraego explained what had happened.

'So we have the Prince, and his partner as well,' Liantha said afterwards, trying to calm things down. She looked at Caradoc, and frowned. 'Oh, you poor thing – look at him, he's terrified. Teressa, why don't you look after him? He might prefer to be with another Northerner.'

Ereska eyed them both suspiciously. 'I will not be parted from him. Who are you?'

Teressa came closer, bowing respectfully to Caradoc. 'Hello,' she said, addressing him in her kindest voice. 'My name's Teressa. I'm a priestess. It's an honour to meet ye, Prince.'

To everyone's surprise, Caradoc snapped back. 'You're a traitor! Teressa the Traitor, that's what everyone calls you. Stay away from me!'

Teressa smiled thinly. 'So I've been given a title? That's flattering. Listen, Prince – I know ye must be afraid, but I swear that we're not going to hurt ye.'

'Liar!' he shouted. 'I know what you're going to do! Your leader said he was going to cut me to pieces!'

'He was lying,' said Teressa. 'He'd never hurt a child.'

Caradoc was carrying a miniature sickle, clearly scaled down for his use. He pulled it out of his belt and pointed it at them all in turn. 'Let me go,' he said. 'Send me back to my father. I order you!'

Liantha chuckled. 'He sounds like a tiny Eyrie Master.'

'I'm not an Eyrie Master. I'm a prince!'

'A very brave one, too,' said Teressa. 'Don't worry; we're going to send a message to yer father, telling him yer safe. Ye can sign it so he knows it's true.'

'I want to write to him,' said Caradoc.

'Ye can,' said Teressa. 'Now, come along with us and we'll give ye somewhere nice and warm to rest.'

Caradoc looked angry and afraid, but with Ereska forcing him along he didn't try and argue further – maybe he valued his dignity too highly to make them drag him away kicking and screaming, which another child would probably have done.

'He's got a mouth on him, hasn't he?' Teressa murmured to Liantha, which made the Southerner smile.

'Take me to my human,' Kraego cut in. 'I must see him.'

'Of course,' said Teressa. She rubbed her eyes and stifled a yawn – it had been days since she had slept properly.

She fought past her tiredness and led Kraego to the infirmary where Red now lay.

He was the only one in there – there were other wounded and sick, but none of them could be kept in the same room as him. There was something about Red's presence that made sick people worse. He lay alone, with a blanket over him. He was on his back, unmoving and scarcely breathing.

Orak was lying curled up like a dog beside the bed, apparently asleep – but his eyes snapped open the moment Teressa and Kraego came in.

The grey griffin stood up. 'Kraego. It is good to see you. Did you succeed?'

'I have succeeded, and succeeded mightily,' Kraego boasted. 'I have brought the human pup here. I have also brought his partner, Ereska, who has seen sense and agreed to follow me.'

'She has turned on Shar?'

'Yes. She has realised that I am the more powerful griffin and that my victory is assured.' Kraego went straight to the bed, and bent to sniff at Red. Red's eyes were still bandaged, and he did not stir at his partner's touch.

Teressa came to stand at the head of the bed. 'I think he's awake, but he won't move,' she said.

Kraego looked up at her. 'Why? Has he healed?'

'Some of the way. The burnt flesh is gone, but he's still eyeless. But it's not just that.'

'Then what is it?' asked Kraego.

Teressa looked troubled. 'For a long time, we thought he was going mad. He'd be lucid sometimes – I think that was when he was awake. He spoke to me a few times, but he rambled; he was confused. Then, other times, he…raved. Screamed, sometimes. Pleaded to be left alone. It was as if there was someone else there, someone nobody could see except him. Someone torturing him, or saying things he couldn't bear to hear.'

'His brain is wounded?' Kraego suggested.

'I don't think so. When he was awake the first time he said something about the Night God. I think it could have been her. She must be angry with him, and it's said that she torments heretics with nightmares.'

'But there is no more madness now,' said Kraego, looking at the motionless Red.

'No…after a while it was as if he just decided to let go,' said Teressa. 'Now he won't move or say anything. He won't eat. But like I said, I don't think he's unconscious. I think he's just…given up.'

'He cannot do that!' said Kraego.

'I'm sorry, but it looks as if he has,' said Teressa. 'Nobody can get through to him anymore. He believes he's lost everything he had to hope for. That's more or less what he said last time he spoke. A man can only take so much before he breaks.'

'No,' said Kraego. 'I will not allow this.' He put his head down, close to Red, and spoke – loudly, and with command in his harsh griffin's voice. 'Kearney Redguard! I am your partner, and I demand that you wake. Speak to me. Hear me.'

Red stirred slightly, but otherwise did not react.

'I have done as you wished,' said Kraego. 'I have captured the human pup. His partner is now my follower, and she has told me that your enemy, Morgan, has been sent back to Malvern in disgrace because he did not take you prisoner as he was told.'

Red's hand twitched. Maybe he was listening, but he didn't reply.

'Maybe he needs someone to talk to him,' Teressa murmured. 'That could help him bring himself back to us. I've started to wonder if maybe he just doesn't believe anything's real any more.' She groaned, and her head drooped. 'By Arenadd, I'm so tired…'

'Go then, and sleep,' said Orak, with unexpected gentleness. 'Kraego and I shall watch over him.'

Teressa nodded vaguely, and stumbled over to the next bed along. She had been fighting off tiredness for a long while now, but now that she had finally confessed her fears to someone she had lost the last of her desire to stay awake. Sleep would mean escaping from her troubles for a while, at least.

She thought of praying before she went to sleep, but quickly found out that she was even more tired than she had thought: she fell asleep as soon as her head hit the pillow. Mercifully, her own sleep was dreamless.

*

Teressa slept for a long time, happily oblivious to Red's comatose form and to New Eagleholm's Council Chamber, where Liantha and the others were discussing what their next move should be now that the King was certain to send troops their way.

When she woke up, it was into the kind of luxurious half-wakefulness that comes to the very tired after a long-needed sleep; the kind that left her aware but not wanting to move. She felt blissfully warm and drowsy.

In moments like these, with the body at rest, the mind would become surprisingly clear, and Teressa found herself thinking with a swiftness that would normally be much harder, with fewer thoughts swirling around to distract her.

Something had to be done, and soon. So far she hadn't told anyone except Liantha about Red's condition. She had simply said that he was resting, and healing well, and shouldn't be disturbed. She had discussed it with Liantha, and the Eyrie Mistress had agreed that it was the sensible thing to do. Best not to worry people unnecessarily. Right now everyone needed to focus on carrying out the next stage of their plan, which now needed revising.

The trouble was that without Red, there was no single leader of the resistance. Liantha was supposed to be in charge, as he had instructed, but she did not have any of Red's fighting skill or military experience, and most thought she was too naïve. Nor were the other griffins willing to bow to Seerae. It was Kraego they wanted to follow, but without Red, he couldn't make any proper decisions.

They needed Red back, and soon. This was no time for their leadership to be in disarray, but it was. How could Teressa get that through to him? She could tell him, but would he be listening? Or had he truly lost his mind?

Lying there and thinking through all this with a kind of paradoxical ease, Teressa decided that she had to get help. She couldn't handle this on her own; she needed advice. She needed to talk to someone who knew him better than she did.

But who?

She finally settled on a few names, and wearily got up to go and check on Red.

She found him unchanged. Kraego was gone – probably off trying to bully the council – but Orak was still there. Her partner was asleep, and she didn't try and wake him. She went off to look for the people who might be able to help, and found them soon enough.

The first was easy to locate: Isleen, former Eyrie Mistress of Liranwee. Red had an uneasy relationship with her – after all, he blamed her for the murder of his father, and she was most probably guilty of it. But despite that he had a kind of odd loyalty to her, since she had once been his Eyrie Mistress.

Teressa found the pudgy, dull-faced woman sitting in her room with her equally dumpy and dull looking lover, Alaric. She eyed them both with some caution before announcing herself.

Isleen looked equally cautious. 'Teressa. Hello. What can I do for you?'

Alaric had already stood up. 'Is the Captain any better?'

'Some,' said Teressa. She coughed. 'I…uh…I came here because I thought ye could help.'

'How?' Alaric asked at once. 'We'll do whatever we can.'

'Agreed,' Isleen nodded.

Teressa tentatively explained the situation, finishing with, 'I think it would help him to hear familiar voices. If he's confused, it could bring him to his senses. If he's just given up, like I think he has, then maybe ye could give him something to hope for.'

Isleen paused, and then nodded slowly. 'Yes…I think there's something I could do for him. I'll come now.'

'I was hoping Talmon could come as well,' said Teressa. 'But he's probably in the Council Chamber.'

'He will be, but I can go and fetch him,' said Alaric. 'We know Red respects him a lot, and he's a guard as well, so there's that.'

Teressa smiled at him. Alaric was smarter than he looked.

'In the meantime, I'll go with you,' Isleen said in a businesslike way. 'Alaric – you bring Talmon and come and meet us.'

'I will.' Alaric hurried off, ungainly but determined.

*

Isleen and Teressa headed back to the infirmary together, and along the way Isleen asked more questions about Red's condition – sounding like the Eyrie Mistress she had once been. Teressa eyed her with pity; her partner Arak had been dead for some time, and without him Isleen would never rule an Eyrie again.

'If he's given up, as you say, then I think I can help,' said Isleen. 'There's something I…well, there's something I can tell him.'

'It can't hurt to try,' said Teressa, noticing the other woman's grim expression.

'Indeed it can't,' Isleen said shortly.

When they got into the infirmary, Isleen went straight to Red's side. Like everyone else who had seen him in this state she tried to talk to him, and gently shook him by the shoulder, but nothing worked.

'Ye see?' Teressa said sadly.

'All right.' Isleen found a chair and brought it over to the bed, where she sat down on it. 'I'll speak to him. Even if he can't hear me, I should say it. I should have said it long ago, but I never had the courage.' She was murmuring now, apparently speaking half to herself and not caring if Teressa was listening.

Even so, Teressa moved politely away – but couldn't stop herself staying within earshot. What could the bland, shut-in former Eyrie Mistress have to confess that was so important?

'Captain Redguard,' Isleen began, leaning down towards him. 'It's me, Lady Isleen. I've come to tell you something important.'

Red moved slightly, as he generally did when someone spoke to him. Teressa hoped he was listening.

'All your life, you've worried about your honour,' said Isleen. 'You've wanted nothing but to win back the respect of the Redguard family name, and that's because you believed it was tainted. So did everyone. Your uncle, Bran the Betrayer, was the one who tainted it. He was a guardsman like you, and he betrayed his city to a Northerner. And that Northerner destroyed the city. Everyone knows that story. Your uncle Bran was put on trial in Withypool for it, and even though he was acquitted, everyone knew he was guilty. He was Bran the Betrayer forever after that. He went into exile, and was never seen again.'

Teressa, listening in, shook her head sadly. She knew this story – Red had told it to her himself.

'But there's something I want you to know,' Isleen continued. 'Something I should have told you a long time ago. I was there, Captain. I was there in Withypool. I was apprenticed to the Master of Law there, and it was me who helped in your uncle's arrest. I was there for his trial, and I visited him in prison. And when your father Danthirk came to talk to him there, I was listening. I heard everything.'

While she spoke, Alaric and Talmon arrived. They came over to join her, saying nothing, and waited while she talked. On the bed, Red was stirring. His mouth moved silently.

'Your uncle was innocent,' Isleen said strongly. 'He never betrayed Old Eagleholm. And the only reason he was ever accused of it is because someone lied. A griffiner called Anyon lost his partner in the Eagleholm fire, and nearly lost his life as well. It drove him mad. He wanted revenge on the man who had done it to him, but nobody could get to him anymore. So he blamed it on your uncle Bran instead. He bribed others to lie for him, and tried to manipulate the trial so that he would be found guilty and executed.'

Red was definitely stirring now. His hands opened and closed on the blanket beside him.

'Everyone turned on him,' Isleen continued. 'Even his own sister – your mother. The only one who stood by him was your father. Anyon tried to bribe him as well, but your father wouldn't let him. He visited your uncle in prison and told him the truth, but no-one else would listen to him. Bran was forced to fight for his freedom in the ring. He won.'

'It's true,' Talmon spoke up suddenly. 'Captain, it's true. It's me, Talmon. I was there.'

'And so was I,' Alaric added. 'I was there with the Master of Law. I saw the trial as well. I knew it was rigged, but what was I to do? I was only an apprentice, and nobody would listen to me. They wanted your uncle Bran to be guilty.'

'I was a guard,' said Talmon. 'Working at the fighting pits. I saw your uncle fight the wild griffin to prove he was innocent. He was a brave man, and a strong one – strong like you, Captain. He fought that wild griffin, and he killed it.'

'But afterwards, he was so disgusted by what he'd seen griffiners do that he left,' said Alaric. 'He chose exile rather than stay. I heard that from the Master of Law.'

'So you see,' said Isleen. 'There's no shame. Your family name was never tainted. It was all a lie. Your uncle stayed true to his city even when everyone in it had turned on him. I heard him say so with my own ears. He said that he never betrayed his city – he betrayed his friend Arenadd. He chose duty over friendship. He regretted it, as you can imagine. But I never saw anyone braver or truer than him.'

She fell silent, and everyone there watched.

Slowly, Red coughed and mumbled. 'Bran…'

'Captain Branton Redguard,' Alaric corrected. 'A relative to be proud of, if you ask me.' He smiled.

'There's something else,' said Isleen. 'And I don't want to say it here with other people listening, but I will. You saved my life twice, Captain, and I owe this to you, even if you never forgive me. You deserve to know it.'

Everyone looked at her in surprise.

'You were right,' Isleen said. She looked depressed, but she set her jaw and forged on. 'Your father Danthirk was never a traitor either. I know the word was sent out that he tried to stage a coup and take over Liranwee's Eyrie, but it was a lie. A lie I put about. I killed him, Kearney. I had your father murdered. He wanted to be Eyrie Master, but Arak and I were determined to rule the city. So we assassinated him and his partner. Then, afterwards, we lied to protect ourselves. I know you never believed it, but you deserve to hear me confess it.' She paused. 'I am not a good woman, Captain. I never have been. That same year I tried to assassinate Kraego's father as well, because I wanted to take over the North. But now you see how I'm punished for that. I tried to take more than I had, and lost everything. You were right, Captain. It was my fault that Caedmon took the throne. We could have made peace with the Northerners, as Kullervo wanted, but my meddling ruined everything.' She shook her head. 'So you see, there's no shame in your family name. If there's any shame, it's on me. Not on your uncle, nor your father, and never on you.'

Isleen had nothing more to confess, and now she fell silent and sat there, hunched and miserable. Alaric quietly put a hand on her shoulder to comfort her, but everyone was looking at Red.

Finally, he moved. Finally, he spoke.

'You bitch,' he mumbled, and went silent again.

*

He said nothing more after that, but it left Teressa feeling much happier. He'd spoken, and that meant they had finally gotten through to him. And at least now he knew the truth, and she knew how much that must mean to him.

Isleen left with Alaric, looking more miserable than Teressa had ever seen her, though Alaric murmured to her to comfort her. Talmon left as well, eyeing his former Eyrie Mistress with distaste.

Only Teressa stayed.

She sat down on the chair Isleen had left, and held Red's hand. 'It must have been painful, but at least ye know,' she said. 'That's got to count for something.'

Red said nothing, and Teressa sighed.

'Listen,' she said. 'I know how hard this is. I can't even imagine what ye were going through before, but this has to stop. Ye have to wake up. We need ye. Blind or not, we need ye. And if ye don't wake up soon and lead us again, we could be in big trouble.'

'Why?' Red's voice was low, but clear.

Teressa froze, and then leaned in close. 'What is it, Red? Why what?'

'Why stay?'

'Why stay with ye?' said Teressa. 'I'm starting to wonder the same thing.'

He coughed a laugh. 'Been here this whole time. Never left. Why?'

'I thought it was obvious,' said Teressa. 'I'm trying to look after ye.'

Red said nothing, but this time it felt as if he was waiting for something.

'Everyone's worried about ye,' said Teressa. 'Especially me.'

Still, he waited.

'What, do ye want a confession from me as well?' asked Teressa, trying to sound light, though the tension in her was painful.

'I can hear it,' Red said unexpectedly.

'Hear what?'

He reached out clumsily, and found her heart. 'This. It's going like crazy.'

'Ye seem better,' said Teressa, trying to ignore the remark.

'I've been thinking,' said Red.

'About what?'

'Lots of things. Wondering if I could make myself die by willing it hard enough. It didn't work.'

'Don't do that,' Teressa said sternly. 'Giving up is what cowards do.'

'Yeah,' Red grunted. 'That's true. Tempting sometimes, though.

Heard you crying,' he added unexpectedly. 'Before.'

Teressa flushed. 'I was upset!'

Red groped towards her, and she reached out in return. Once he found her hand, he gripped it. 'Thought it wasn't real,' he said. 'I couldn't tell…been hearing a lot of things these days.'

'So that's why ye wouldn't answer,' said Teressa. She felt the coldness in his hand, but never wanted to let go. 'I thought ye'd just given up.'

'I had,' said Red. 'Couldn't tell what was real and what wasn't. I figured it was better if I just didn't answer anything anymore. But…I think it's gone now.'

'Were ye dreaming?' asked Teressa.

'I dunno,' said Red. 'I'm blind. I couldn't tell when I was awake. But I saw things…'

'But I don't think ye want to tell me what they were,' Teressa said gently.

'Saw death,' Red mumbled. 'Saw you dead. Saw everyone. Killed in all different ways. An' every time it was my fault somehow. Mostly it was because I killed you. Heard voices too. Sometimes yours. Sometimes her.'

Teressa gripped his hand more tightly. 'The Night God?'

'Yeah. She's real angry with me, Tress. She said things…awful things. Said I wasn't Kearney Redguard no more, never again. I'm a monster now, she said, and—,'

He was starting to ramble again, and Teressa touched his face and gently shushed him. His voice trailed off, and he relaxed.

'But ye didn't listen to her,' Teressa reminded him. 'Ye told me that before all this. Ye wouldn't be controlled by her. That's why she's so angry.'

'Yeah. But I could've had my eyes back…' Red sighed.

'But ye would have been a slave,' said Teressa. 'That's what Arenadd tried to tell ye.'

'But you only followed me in the first place because you reckoned I was followin' her,' said Red.

'No I didn't. I decided to follow ye because ye were the Shadow That Walks. And now, I'd follow ye even if ye were nothing but an ordinary man.'

Red smiled for the first time in days. 'Why?'

'Because I believe in what yer trying to do,' said Teressa. 'And I believe in ye. Ye asked me before why I wasn't afraid of ye,' she added. 'It's because I can't help but think of ye as a man. Before I thought of ye as the Shadow That Walks, but now yer a man to me first.'

'Fancy that,' Red muttered, but she could hear the quietness in his voice.

Teressa could feel her heart still beating frantically, and it was worse because she knew he could hear it. Living hearts always caught the attention of the Shadow That Walked. 'I do,' she insisted.

Red went silent for a while, and then asked the question she had hoped he wouldn't. 'I can still hear your heart goin' like mad,' he said. 'What are you so scared of? Can't be this blind sod right here, can it?'

'I'm not afraid,' Teressa lied.

'Yeah you are. Don't say you ain't. I can practically smell it. It's creepy, but I can.'

She hesitated for a long moment, wrestling with herself as she had done several times over the painful days that had passed. Should she tell him?

Most of her said she shouldn't. There were so many reasons why she shouldn't say it, and she wanted to mock herself for the part that said it would somehow help. And anyway, it wasn't proper. It would be…disrespectful to say it.

'Go on,' said Red. 'I won't bite.'

His voice was as gentle as it could be nowadays, and Teressa found herself pretending that he already knew what she wanted to say, and that he too wanted to hear it.

But she still didn't say it. She tried, but the words stuck in her throat.

Instead she reached out to touch his forehead again, and ran her fingers lightly over the bandage that still covered most of his face. 'I remember yer eyes,' she said. 'So clearly.'

'Black,' Red mumbled.

'No.' Teressa leaned in close, unable to stop herself. 'They were brown.'

And she kissed him, lightly, on the bandage where those eyes had once been.

'Don't,' said Red.

The word felt like a blow to her heart. She pulled back

immediately. 'I'm sorry! I…'

'I know it.' She had tried to pull her hand out of his, but he wouldn't let go. 'I knew that's what you were thinking,' he said.

'How?' Teressa wanted to cry.

'Because I ain't half as stupid as I look,' said Red. His voice was rough, but not angry. 'You've been here this whole time because you wanted to look after me. You always have. You've always been there for me, Teressa, since the moment I turned into this. An' now with all this nervousness when you know me so well an' I know you ain't scared of me.' He laughed a cold humourless laugh. 'True love's kiss fixes everything, right?'

Now Teressa really did start crying. 'How could ye be so cruel?'

'Because I'm dead.' He still hadn't let go of her hand, and when she tried to pull away again his grip hurt. 'Listen, girl,' he said, 'don't do this to yerself. Just don't. You'll die if I touch you, an' you know it. The Shadow That Walks can't love like a real man. This road you wanna go down leads to nowhere but pain for the both of us. So let it go, Teressa. Let it go now, before it's too late to turn back. Find yourself another man – one who's alive, an' not a bloody Southerner.'

Teressa stopped struggling. 'I can't.'

'Yeah you can. You're good looking an' brave an' kind, an'—,' Red broke off abruptly, and went on a moment later. 'There's lots of men who'd count themselves lucky to have you.'

'But I don't want them,' said Teressa. 'I want ye.'

'I said don't.' Red finally let go of her hand. 'Drop it, Teressa. Spare yourself the suffering, an' spare me too. I've got enough blood on my hands.'

Teressa couldn't bear to stay a moment longer. She turned and rushed out of the room.

*

Once she had gone, Red stayed there for some time, lying on his back with his hand still outstretched. In his chest, his dead heart ached.

'Damn fool woman,' he mumbled through the lump in his throat. It was weak and silly, but he felt halfway to crying himself.

He reached up and dug his fingers painfully into the raw flesh where his eyes had been. 'Stop that, you great lump,' he told himself.

'You can't cry – you ain't got nothing left for making tears.'

But he still wanted to cry. For Teressa's hopeless wishes, and for himself as well. Once he had thought he knew how cruel life could be – but now he knew the truth of it. All the tragedies he had ever suffered in his life, or his non-life as it was now, had been nothing compared to what could and did happen. To what had happened. And not just to himself, though his life had turned into one tragedy after another. Now it had left him here, blind and wallowing in self-pity while Teressa probably went to find a place to cry, and so many out there were suffering because…

Red coughed around the obstruction in his throat, and pulled himself together. Teressa was right. Enough was enough. He had to get up. Blinded or not, he had to do something.

With a rough, angry motion, he tore the blanket off himself and got out of bed – slowly and stumblingly. He felt weak from lack of exercise, and he wondered how he was going to go anywhere without someone to guide him.

But while he stood there in thought, the memory flashed across his mind. Of course! The shadows. They had always made him feel stronger; maybe they could help him now.

Even unable to see them, he slid into them without effort – and gasped.

He could see! Here, in the shadows, he could see!

It was faint and wavering, but he could make out the shapes of things from here, and as he stood there, hidden away in this world of cold blackness that only he and Kraego could reach, he felt new strength pouring into him. The shadows were healing him, giving him back his energy.

Red wanted to laugh. Outside of the shadows he might still be a cripple, but here…here he could see. Here, he could still fight. There was still a chance after all.

With that knowledge, all of his despair left him, and was replaced by a cold and calculating determination – the same determination that drove him to stalk and kill his enemies, the kind that he imagined must fill the mind of a predatory animal. And that was what he was now – a predator. The world's deadliest predator.

Smiling savagely, head low, Red stalked away to find his council. It was time to plan.

Chapter Nine

Prince Caradoc's Lessons

Red didn't waste any time on ceremony when he reached the Eyrie's Council Chamber. He hadn't seen it before his blinding, but in his mind's eye it looked like all the others he had seen – a big, round room with raised seating where people could watch the Council members debate. They would stand in a ring, with the ruling Eyrie Master or Mistress in the centre. From the shadows he had a vague impression of something like that, but the people there stood out far more than such background details. Every one of them stood out like a beacon to his strange new senses, stirring the bloodthirsty impulses that lurked in his mind.

He pushed them aside yet again, and lingered in the shadows for a moment longer, listening to the discussion before announcing himself.

'Talking ain't acting,' he said brusquely as he emerged. 'Let's make some decisions.'

The moment he showed himself, the wavering images vanished and he was blind again – but he could hear their voices loudly and clearly.

'Captain Redguard!' Isleen's voice.

'Thank gods.' That sounded like Talmon.

Someone moved closer to him – he felt the air move, and to his surprise he heard Teressa's quiet voice. 'I'm glad to see ye back, Red.'

Red reached out and clumsily patted her shoulder. 'I'd say the same, but it'd be in bad taste. Where's—?'

But Kraego was already there. The griffin's great, warm shape appeared beside him; he was amazed to notice how he sensed it when they hadn't actually touched. A moment later, though, the griffin's beak nudged at his back.

'I have been waiting for you.'

Red touched his partner's soft feathers. 'Been tryin' to bully this lot along too, I'll bet.'

'They listen to me, but all agreed that you must make the plans,'

Kraego rumbled.

'You're the smart one out of the two of us, but thanks,' said Red.

He brushed off his council's attempts at asking after his health, and let Kraego lead him to what he guessed must be the centre of the room. The Eyrie Master's spot. He heard an irritated huff which sounded like Seerae. She couldn't be pleased to see her brother taking her rightful spot, but she would just have to put up with it. There were bigger things at stake than her pride.

'Now then,' Red began. 'Is everyone here?'

'They are, Captain,' said Isleen.

'Good. First up, I'm fine. I mean…better. Can't see, but it'd take more than that to put paid to me, even if I was alive.'

'We knew you'd get better,' Alaric's voice piped up.

Red smiled to himself. Ever since he'd given up storytelling, the pudgy former griffiner had become a lot bolder.

'You shall be better,' Kraego said loudly, apparently intending to make it an announcement rather than a reassurance. 'You are the Shadow That Walks, and cannot be crippled this way. Your eyes shall return.'

'That'd be nice, but in the meantime I'll stick with talking,' said Red. 'I still got my tongue at least.'

His audience chuckled – mostly, he suspected, with relief.

'Enough of that,' Red interrupted. 'Let's get on. I know what the score is: we've got the Prince, an' his partner too. Where are they?'

'Locked up in one of the rooms,' said Talmon. 'Ereska is guarding the Prince, but Orak is there too in case she turns on us.'

'Good,' said Red. 'The kid ain't hurt, is he?'

'No,' said Teressa. 'I saw him myself. He's angry and scared, but fine.'

Red turned his head towards her while she spoke. She sounded quiet, and perhaps a little shaky, but steady enough. He smiled again, forgetting people could see it. She was stronger than she seemed. She would get over him, and the sooner the better.

He was surprised to find that the idea upset him, and the smile vanished at once.

'Right,' he went on hastily. 'I'm gonna go visit him once we're done here. In fact, from now on, he's gonna stay with me.'

The others murmured.

'Why?' asked Liantha.

'I'm a guard, right?' said Red. 'I can keep an eye on him. So to speak. But more important than that, I'm gonna…influence him.'

'You what?' said Talmon.

'He's only a boy,' said Red. 'Boys need teaching. I'm gonna teach him.'

'Teach him what?' Isleen, sounding puzzled.

'About…us,' said Red. 'I'm gonna try an' show him that he's wrong about us Southerners. I want him to learn that we're people too. His dad will have been filling his ear with nonsense about how we're all power hungry an' cruel. An' stupid,' he added sourly. 'Which some of us are, sure, but so what? The kid needs to learn that we're as human as his lot.'

'What on earth will that accomplish?' asked Isleen.

'He's gonna be King some day, right?' said Red. 'Personally, I'd prefer a King who doesn't think we need conquering. I know it's a stretch, but if I can get the boy on our side…'

'It won't work,' Teressa said flatly. 'Why would he listen to ye?'

'You did,' said Red.

They all went quiet.

'I don't know why this is necessary,' Isleen said eventually. 'I thought we were going to drive the Northerners back past the Northgates and leave it at that. And besides, wouldn't it make more sense to, well…dispose of him? Once we've used him against his father he won't be needed any more. Alive, he would be a danger to us.'

'It would make more sense to keep him,' Talmon put in. 'Send his father home and keep the boy as insurance to make certain he doesn't come back.'

'That would be better,' said Liantha. 'I've been in favour of that idea right from the beginning, as you know.'

'Perhaps, but I don't trust them,' Isleen said grimly. 'It seems like a reasonable chance, I agree, but don't forget that these are Taranisäiis we're dealing with. They won't listen to reason; their hatred of us is far too strong. If we keep the boy, he would be nothing but trouble. Either his father would refuse to keep the peace, or he himself would declare war on us the moment he was old enough. I wouldn't be surprised if he found a way to turn our own people on us.'

'Don't be ridiculous,' said Liantha. 'You're attributing divine powers to him, Isleen.'

'Even so,' said Isleen. 'You and I both know that you can't trust a Northerner. They're traitors by nature, and a Taranisäii doubly so.'

'Obviously I agree—,' Liantha began.

'Excuse me,' Teressa snapped. 'In case ye haven't forgotten, I'm standing right here.'

'Exactly!' Liantha snapped back. 'Captain, why is this traitor even on our council?'

'Shut up,' Red growled. 'All of you. Liantha, Isleen – apologise.'

'But—,' Isleen began.

'Do it, or I'll bang yer heads together,' said Red. 'I might be blind, but I'm betting I can manage it.'

'Fine. I'm sorry, Teressa. I got…well, it was unfair.' Isleen didn't sound very sincere.

'And you, Liantha,' said Red.

'Sorry,' she muttered.

'But I stand by what I said about Taranisäiis,' Isleen resumed. 'If you ask me, we would all be better off with the boy and his father dead.'

'A dead enemy is no longer a threat,' Kraego agreed.

'Yeah,' Red murmured to himself, but he wasn't really listening any more. He reached up absently and rubbed the raw flesh under the bandages on his face. It had started to itch horribly.

Everyone there went quiet, waiting for him to speak.

Red went silent for a long moment, thinking deeply. Thoughts and ideas that had swum through his mind during his time of semi-consciousness rose tantalisingly to the surface, and he let them spread out and grow larger. But they hadn't only come to him then, he knew. They had been with him for his entire adult life, planted there by a man he had loved like a father.

He thought of that man now, and smiled sadly to himself.

The young Red had lost his father at fourteen, but only days afterwards someone had come into his life and changed it forever. Kullervo Taranisäii. Half man, half griffin, the only son of Arenadd Taranisäii. But that wasn't what Red remembered about him. Being Arenadd's son had troubled Kullervo, but he had never let it define his life. He had turned his back on the gods who tempted him, and gone his own way. The ideas he had preached to others came from himself. When Red first heard them they had seemed bizarre, radical, impossible…but he had never forgotten them, and now, after his blinding, when everything seemed hopeless, they had returned. And, while he retreated from the Night God's torments, they had given him hope.

He spoke now, slowly and carefully, as if the words might break if he said them too harshly. Even now, a part of him said it was insane. The others wouldn't believe it, or if they did it wouldn't work. It was ludicrous.

'I've been…thinking a lot about all of this,' he said. 'An' I've got an idea about it. It feels impossible, but, thing is…it feels right. So I'm gonna say it now. Laugh if you want, but listen.'

'We're listening, Captain,' said Isleen.

'Thing is,' said Red. 'Thing is…we could kill them. We could kill the King, an' his son. If we wanted, we could chase them back to the North. We could follow them, just like we did centuries ago. We could take the North like we did then, put things back the way they were before. If we wanted, we could kill the lot of 'em. Make Cymria belong to Southerners an' nobody else. I know that's what some people want,' he added, looking towards where he thought Isleen was.

'It would put an end to any more wars between us,' Isleen admitted. 'If the Northerners were kept down properly this time—'

Teressa gave a half-strangled cry of outrage.

'No it wouldn't!' Red said loudly. 'It wouldn't, Isleen, an' that's the thing. Don't you get it? Ain't you seen the truth of it?'

'No, I'm afraid I don't "get it", Captain,' Isleen said frostily. 'Please do enlighten me.'

'I will,' said Red. He turned his head to give the impression that he was looking at everyone. 'I've seen the truth of it. The Northerners didn't come here because they wanted our land – they came here because they were afraid of us. They've always been afraid. I lived in Liranwee – you all know that – an' all my life we were told that one day, any day, the Northerners might come through the Northgates. An' if they ever did, we'd be the first ones they'd hit. Everyone grew up hearin' horror stories about it. Our parents told us when we were kids. Eat yer beans, or the Northerners will come an' get you. They'll come through them mountains they'd say, an' they'll kill us all. They hate us.'

'And that's exactly what they did,' Isleen growled. 'I saw it with my own eyes.'

'So did I,' said Red. He could almost feel Teressa's anger, and now he turned and pointed in her general direction. 'Teressa,' he said. 'It's your turn.'

'My turn to what?' she snapped. Clearly, she wasn't enjoying any of this.

'When you was little, what did people tell you about us?' said Red. 'What were us Southerners to you?'

'They said ye were arrogant and cruel,' Teressa said coldly. She raised her voice, clearly wanting to insult the other members of the council. 'They said if we weren't careful, then one day ye'd come through the mountains and take the North back. And then it would be slavery again, and not being allowed to worship our own god, or speak our own language, or even carry weapons. We'd go back to being vassals in our own land. And we believed it because it really did happen. One of the priestesses who raised me had scars on her neck from the collar, and whip marks on her back, and a brand burnt into the back of her hand.'

Red folded his arms. 'An' now you see it,' he said. 'Right?'

'No, I don't,' said Liantha. 'All I see is you making us angry with each other.'

Red shook his head impatiently. 'An' I thought I was stupid. Don't you get it?' He raised his voice. 'Any of you? This war ain't about power, it's about fear. We're afraid of them an' they're afraid of us. That's why they attacked us, an' that's why we're talking about killing the lot of 'em now. It's because we're afraid of what might happen if we don't. Fear makes people hate each other.'

'Yes, very insightful, Captain,' said Isleen. 'But I really don't see how this is relevant.'

'It's relevant because if we kill them all, or try an' use fear to end this, it won't end,' said Red. 'It'll keep on going forever. Sooner or later they'll find a reason to attack us again, or we'll find a reason to attack them. If it ain't us, it'll be our children, or our children's children.'

'Well then, what's the alternative?' said Talmon.

'Peace,' said Red. 'Peace that ain't based on fear. Peace what's based on understanding. That's why we need the Prince on our side, because if he becomes King an' he's on our side because he trusts us—,'

'Oh, come on!' Liantha exclaimed. 'Captain, this is ridiculous. Do you really think you can end centuries of hatred just by—,'

'No, I can't,' said Red. 'But I can damn well make a start. I know about fear, all right?' he added. 'I'm bloody terrifying. That's why this happened.' He pulled the bandage off his face, and heard some of them groan or swear when they saw the ugly mess that had once been his eyes.

'She's right,' said Isleen. 'I can understand what you're trying to say, but it won't work. They don't want to listen, and they won't.'

'You didn't think this idea was so mad last time you heard it,' said Red. 'I should know – I was there. I brought him to you.'

'I'm sorry?' said Isleen. 'Brought who?'

'This ain't my idea,' said Red. 'It came from someone else, an' he taught it to me. He believed it could work, didn't he? An' when he said it, you listened. Everyone did. Well, he's dead now, because his plan failed. He never saw his dream come true. But by Gryphus I'll have a go at making it happen now.'

'Who came up with it, Red?' asked Teressa.

Red smiled sadly. 'His name was Kullervo Taranisäii. The one Arenadd wanted you to find, Tress.'

Silence fell again. Red guessed that everyone was thinking. They must all think he was mad, or be wondering what had happened to the military leader who had been full of murderous plans of revenge.

'I've turned my back on revenge,' he said aloud. 'It was revenge that cost me my eyes. Revenge breeds revenge.'

As he said that, the part of him that was dark and dead and full of hate screamed in protest, but he fought it away. That part wasn't him. That part belonged to the Night God, and he had sworn that he would never succumb to her.

Arenadd had followed the path of revenge, and Red had seen what had happened to him. So had Saeddryn, and she too had met a cruel end. Well, their fates would not be in vain. They were a warning and a lesson to him. Captain Kearney Redguard would be a lot of things, but he would not join them.

'So it'll be peace instead,' he said loudly, thinking of the Night God's rage at those words. 'Peace between North an' South. We'll fight the King until he surrenders, an' then we'll give him our terms.'

'And what if he doesn't surrender?' said Liantha. 'I wouldn't be surprised if he chose death. And if we kill him, his son will never forgive us.'

'Oh, he will,' Red said grimly. 'I told you – I'm bloody terrifying. If anyone can make someone surrender, it's me. An' just wait an' see how he feels when I do it without any eyes.'

'Shar's human will tremble before us,' Kraego hissed.

'Yeah, but I won't kill him,' said Red. 'I'd like to, but I won't.'

He said it firmly, and he meant it – but even so, the fear did not leave him. He could defeat the King in combat, even blinded, but he would need to use the shadows to do it. And that would make it harder than ever to control the impulse to kill. He'd lost control of that impulse before, and during a battle it would be certain to happen again. And if he did lose control, and kill Caedmon the way he so badly wanted to, then everything would be lost.

*

Prince Caradoc had been never been so frightened – not even when he had been kidnapped once before. But after a day of imprisonment, his fear had quickly turned to anger.

He was in the hands of his enemies, and that was frightening. But Ereska's betrayal had made him angry.

She was here, now, with that other griffin, the grey one called Orak. They left him alone, but neither one would let him leave. He was in griffiner quarters, so of course there was a griffin's nesting chamber next door with an opening for flying, but Ereska wouldn't take him away as he kept asking her to. The door that led into the Eyrie's interior was locked, and guarded outside. He was trapped.

He refused to touch the food they gave him, in case it was poisoned, and sat on the bed, where he glared at Ereska and tried to think of ways he could escape. He had to get out of here, and go back to his father before it was too late. He knew that Captain Redguard was blind now, but that didn't matter; he was the Shadow That Walked, and everyone knew that made him nearly invincible. Caradoc didn't believe the promises he'd been given that he wouldn't be hurt. He'd heard the Captain with his own ears, and knew that any time now he'd carry out his threats. He'd cut Caradoc to pieces just as he'd promised.

Caradoc had already searched the room for something he could use as a weapon, but there was nothing. They hadn't given him a knife with his food, either. But anyway, he couldn't fight the Shadow

That Walked; nobody could.

He'd tried everything to persuade Ereska to help him, but that hadn't worked either.

That only left him one choice: escape by himself.

He sat and looked sullenly at his partner who had become his guard, and thought of ways he could get away. Obviously he couldn't fly out, so he would have to try and get through the door into the Eyrie. Then he would have to try and sneak out into the city, and then get through that into the countryside. He'd have to try and walk back from there.

It was scary to think of, but he knew he had to do it. If he didn't, he would die.

Caradoc felt his heart thumping. Part of him just wanted to do nothing. A little voice kept telling him that if he stayed where he was, then his father would come and rescue him. But he had to ignore that voice. His father might not make it in time, and anyway, just sitting here waiting to be saved would be cowardly. Taranisäiis weren't cowards, he reminded himself. They didn't cry, and they never gave up.

Meanwhile, Ereska and Orak were talking. Caradoc listened, hoping they might say something that would help him.

'I am not afraid of Shar's anger,' Ereska boasted. 'I am larger and stronger than her. I shall see her dead, and take her place as master of the North.'

'And what if Kraego wishes to do this himself?' said Orak.

'He will be master of the South,' said Ereska. 'I will rule the North as his ally. That is the price for my help. If not, then once I have killed Shar, the Unpartnered will destroy Kraego at my command. But I have no wish to do this.'

'Why? He is no friend of yours.'

'He impresses me,' said Ereska. 'If I must kill him, I shall, but first I intend to have him as my own. I have not mated before, and Kraego will be a worthy male to be my first. I shall have his young, and they will be my pride.'

'Do not mock me,' Orak hissed. 'I am as worthy a male as Kraego.'

'You are strong and healthy enough,' Ereska admitted. 'Perhaps I shall have you once I have had Kraego.'

'If we did not have to stay here and watch over your human, I would have you now,' said Orak.

'I would allow you to fight me for the right,' said Ereska. 'But that cannot be now.'

Caradoc knew exactly what they were talking about, and he grimaced. Griffins were disgusting sometimes.

He thought sadly about Ceinwen, the girl who would be his wife when they were older. She was back in Malvern, and maybe he would never see her again. He didn't know her very well, but his father had explained that he had to marry as soon as he was big enough to have children, so that the Taranisäii family didn't die out.

He thought of his father, too, and felt sure that he must be very angry. Once he knew what Ereska had done, he might kill her. But now he would just be angry at Captain Redguard. He would come here and fight him to get Caradoc back. But…

Caradoc's eyes ached with tears. If his father tried to fight the Shadow That Walked, he would die. But he would do it anyway, because he wanted to save Caradoc.

Caradoc breathed deeply, fighting back the urge to cry. He couldn't let that happen. He had to escape and go back to his father, before it was too late.

He let his anger rise, so it would make him stronger, and got off the bed to go and look at the door again. He tried the handle – it was still locked, of course, and when he put his ear to it he could hear the faint sound of someone standing outside.

If he wanted to get out, then he would have to wait until the door opened – but if he just ran for it as soon as it did, then whoever opened it would grab him.

Caradoc thought fast, and finally decided that he should hide when the door opened. Then, when they came looking for him, he would run past them and out the door.

He liked that idea, and looked around the room for a hiding place. He could go under the bed, but he might not be able to get out fast enough.

Instead, he went to look at the wardrobe. Maybe he could stuff himself inside it.

He opened the door. There were some clothes inside, hanging on hooks, but it was mostly empty. He should be able to fit in easily.

Caradoc checked to see if Ereska was watching. She was, but she didn't do anything to stop him, so he climbed into the wardrobe and pulled the door shut as far as he could.

He settled down to wait in the semi-darkness, listening intently and watching through the crack, ready to move the moment the door handle turned.

Nothing happened.

Time dragged on, and Caradoc quickly started to get bored. He inspected the door minutely, still not daring to move, but it wasn't very interesting to look at. Being made for griffins to fit through it was very big, and would open slowly. It shouldn't be hard to get past anyone standing in the doorway.

If only someone would come.

Caradoc waited tensely.

And waited.

And waited.

And still nothing happened.

He prayed under his breath to the Night God, asking for her help. It helped to make him feel braver.

Eventually, though, boredom won through. Caradoc burst angrily out of the wardrobe, and stomped around the room to ease his tingling legs. This was stupid. He couldn't stay in the wardrobe all the time.

He explored the room instead, trying out other hiding places, and eventually decided to go back to the wardrobe the moment he heard anyone outside. That would be better.

'You should eat and rest,' Ereska said suddenly. 'You are exhausting yourself.'

'Shut up,' Caradoc snapped back. 'I'm not talking to you anymore. You're a traitor.'

'I did what I had to do, for your protection,' she said. 'If I had not agreed to follow Kraego, then you and I would be dead now.'

'I'd rather be dead than here!' Caradoc retorted.

'Then you are a fool,' said Ereska. 'Almost any fate is better than death. Do not be afraid, Caradoc. You will be free soon enough, and you will be King.'

'I don't want to be King,' said Caradoc. 'I just want to go back to Father.'

Ereska yawned, and didn't reply, which made Caradoc even angrier with her.

He went back to his patrolling.

Unfortunately his bad temper distracted him, and when he heard the door handle turn it took him completely by surprise. He gasped and ran to the wardrobe, but before he had climbed in the door had already opened.

Fatally, Caradoc hesitated.

An instant later the door closed, but by then he already knew it was too late. He had felt the coldness in the air, the prickling on the back of his neck, and a deep, animal sense of fear. A sense he remembered all too well.

Caradoc turned and saw him standing there, large as life: the big, powerful Southerner, his red hair and beard now all raggedy and wild. His eyes were bandaged and his skin was pale, and the part of his face that Caradoc could see was gaunt.

'No!' Caradoc backed away for an instant but then, stupidly, even though the door was closed, he ran – straight at the terrifying figure of the Shadow That Walked. Panic-stricken, he charged at him and started to hit him as hard as he could.

The big Southerner didn't move. He stayed right where he was and let Caradoc hit him.

The Prince's fists bounced harmlessly off the man's stomach, but he kept on anyway. Eventually, he realised that he was sobbing – great, loud, pathetic sobs, like a little boy. 'Leave – me alone!' he shouted. 'You stupid Southerner!'

Finally, the Shadow That Walked reached down and pushed him back. 'Stop that.' His voice was low and growling, just as Caradoc remembered.

Caradoc tried to push back. 'Don't touch me!' he wailed.

'I take it you remember yer old pal Captain Redguard,' said Red.

Caradoc was definitely crying now. Seeing sense, he backed off and stumbled into the bed. 'Please!' he said. 'Please don't hurt me. I just want to go home, I just…'

Red came towards him. 'Sssh. It's all right. Stop crying.'

Caradoc, though, cried harder. 'I don't want to die.'

'Neither did I.' Red looked blindly over towards the griffins. 'Orak? Ereska? I heard you were here. I can smell you.'

'We are here,' said Ereska. She stood up. 'Stop frightening my human, Kraeai kran ae. I was promised that he would not be harmed.'

'He won't be,' said Red. 'That's what I'm here to tell him. I figured he'd believe it if he heard it straight from me. I'm just here to talk.'

Ereska stayed where she was. 'You are still blind.'

'Yeah.'

'Kraego told me that you would recover,' said Ereska. 'He swore it.'

'Never mind about it for now,' said Red. 'I'm just here to talk to the boy. Tell you what – why don't you stay close by? He'll feel safer if you're there. That way, if I try anything on, you can knock me back. I can tell you a whack from a griffin will be enough to put a stop to me for a bit.'

Caradoc tried to stop crying, but he took great gulps of air while he spoke. 'I don't – trust her; she's a – traitor. Stay – away from me!'

'Shush. That's enough.' Red crouched, and reached out towards him. 'Lemme help you up.'

Caradoc was too afraid to refuse. He sat there for a moment, and then took Red's hand. It was big and callused, just as he remembered, but it lifted him up gently.

'There, now,' said Red. 'Why don't you sit down?'

Caradoc did, but soon started to sob again. 'You're going to kill me now, aren't you? Like you said you would.'

'No,' said Red. 'I know I said I would, but I lied.'

'No you didn't! You're lying now! You're going to c— cut me to pieces!'

'I'm not,' said Red. 'If I were I'd have done it already. I don't believe in wasting time. I actually came here to check up on you. You ain't hurt, are you? You're gonna have to tell me – I can't see you no more.'

'I'm fine,' Caradoc snapped. 'Let me go. I want to go back to my father.'

'You will,' said Red. 'He's coming here right now.'

'He'll get me away from you,' said Caradoc.

'I'll give you back to him,' said Red. 'That's a promise. Redguards always keep their promises. I gave you back before, didn't I? Didn't hurt you then. I could've, but I didn't. I let you go.'

Caradoc finally went silent, and glared at him.

'I bet you're glaring, but I can't see it,' said Red. 'Now then, I'm here for a reason, an' that reason is because I want to talk.'

Caradoc said nothing, but some of his fear started to subside.

The man in front of him was the same one who had threatened to kill him, but he didn't look like he was going to. He sat very still, not moving around much the way normal people did, and his bandaged eyes were creepy, but he talked like an ordinary person. He was speaking to Caradoc as if he wasn't a child, but another grown-up.

'I'm gonna let you go,' said Red. 'But first I've got some things to tell you, an' all you've got to do is listen.'

'Why?' asked Caradoc.

'Because I want you to stop being scared of me,' said Red. 'I want you to understand. So I'm gonna tell you some things, an' if you'll just listen, everything could get better for us.'

'All right,' Caradoc said cautiously.

*

Red hesitated for a moment, knowing the risk he was taking. But he'd sworn to try it, and he had to keep going. It was too late to turn back now. Kullervo had told him that understanding was the key to friendship, and that made this necessary.

So he took a deep breath, and talked.

He sat down on the bed with Caradoc, and told him everything – all his secrets. He told him about the history of the Redguard family, and about his own eventful life. He told him about Liranwee, about the Hangman and the guards. He told him about Morgan's betrayal, and his framing and imprisonment. He told him about his travels with Kullervo as a boy, and those with Kraego as an adult. He told him about the Last Guards, about slavery in Amoran, and Lady Ahamay's killing of the Emperor. He told him about his death and resurrection, and Kullervo's passing. He told him about the return, and about the taking of Eagleholm – leaving out any mention of Monag, just in case. He told him about Teressa, as well, and her own journey. He told him about his blinding. But most of all he told him about what it was like being the Shadow That Walked; the fear, and the horror of what he had watched himself becoming. He told him about how it felt to know he could never be a father, or truly belong to the world of the living. And, finally, surprising himself, he told him about Teressa's declaration of love.

'She thinks she's in love with me, an' maybe she is. An' I think that I…care about her too. But I can't tell her that. It's cruel enough for her as it is. I know what happens to people who try an' love the

Shadow That Walks. It's all pain.'

Caradoc listened. Cautiously at first, then with suspicion, but after a while he started to ask questions, and then settled into rapt attention. His questions became deeper and more sympathetic, especially when Red talked about the agony of being the walking dead. All of his fear had vanished.

The telling took a long time, but neither of them moved much, and when Red had finally finished, he found he had nothing left to say.

Caradoc, meanwhile, had unconsciously moved closer during the story, and now he finally spoke up. 'That's so awful what happened to you,' he said.

'It's been a hard time,' Red agreed. 'So much for a quiet life, I s'pose.'

'Did you really talk to Arenadd?'

'Yeah. More than once.' Red had described the visions, but hadn't said anything about Teressa's attempt to resurrect her idol. That, at least, was better kept secret.

'What was he like?'

'He reminded me of your dad,' said Red. 'All…commanding, I guess. You could tell he'd been a leader. You could tell he'd suffered too. But he's nastier than your dad. Your dad's got love in him, see. I could see it all over his face when he thought you were in danger. But Arenadd's got nothing. He's full of hate an' anger. Can't tell whose side he's on, but I pity whoever he's against.'

'You were really brave,' said Caradoc. 'Father said so too, after you got out of prison. So did Morgan. Did it hurt?' he added. 'When you lost your eyes?'

Red touched the wound – it was itching again. 'Worse than anything I've ever felt before,' he said honestly.

'I don't think Morgan wanted it,' said Caradoc. 'He looked upset when he told us. Why did you tell me all that?'

'Because I figured if you saw me as a human being it'd help,' said Red. 'An' trust me, I might be dead, but I can still get scared, an' feel pain, an' care about people. It was the same when I was alive. Us Southerners aren't so different as you think we are. We were all afraid of Arenadd, an' we're afraid of your dad as well. More so now he's done all this.'

'We had to do that!' Caradoc said sharply. 'You Southerners

would have come to kill us.'

'But we didn't.' Red stood up. 'Did we?'

'You would've,' said Caradoc.

'Maybe, but we'll never know now, will we? Anyhow…I reckon it's time you got some rest. You did some good listening there – I just hope I didn't give you nightmares.'

'I'm not scared,' said Caradoc.

'I hope not,' said Red. 'But I am, an' that's the honest truth.'

Chapter Ten

Seeing

The first step had been taken, and Red went to work with a new sense of optimism. He wasn't under any illusions about the situation, of course. He knew that there would have to be war before there could be peace, and to begin with there was still the question of whether the King's army could be defeated. The human soldiers might be outnumbered, now that most of them had been spread out to postings in the conquered cities, but there were still the Unpartnered, and so far they had never been defeated in combat. That said, they wouldn't fight without their leader, so if Kraego could defeat Shar, they would be out of the picture.

In the meantime, preparations had to be made, and during Red's absence his followers had not been idle. Scouts had been sent out to take stock of the army that was coming their way – Northerners all, followers of Teressa. One of them had even gone so far as to make contact with a friend in the King's ranks, and had come back with useful information.

'They're coming all right,' he reported. 'Every man and griffin who was with the King in Liranwee, and the King himself is leading them. The word is that he's half mad over losing his son, which is why he didn't have the sense to send a subordinate to lead them. He's sworn to take your head off with his own hands, Captain, and burn the rest of you.'

'Fat chance,' was all Red said, much to the amusement of his listeners.

In the meantime, others had been sent out as messengers to the Southerners in the occupied cities. It was unlikely that many of them would come, with their leaders subjugated and constantly watched by the King's most loyal followers, but there was always a chance.

Now, it was left to Red to organise the defences with the help of Liantha, Talmon, and others with the necessary experience.

'The trouble is we ain't got too many griffins,' Red lamented. 'Everyone knows you need griffins to fight griffins. But we'll do our best.'

Fortunately, as former commander of Liranwee's guards, Talmon knew a few things about how to build a particular type of seige weapon: giant wall-mounted crossbows that could shoot down a griffin by launching spears the size of small tree-trunks. Red put him in charge of a squad of craftsmen to build as many as possible. Meanwhile others were set to distributing weapons and making more.

New Eagleholm armed itself.

Isleen and Alaric worked together to organise people and see to it that orders were carried out properly. Neither of them were fighters, but Red had heard that Alaric had acquired a sword and spent a lot of time practising, apparently still hoping he could be like his imaginary alter-ego, Alaric the Dashing. Nobody had the heart to laugh at him for it, least of all Red, who had plenty of experience with vain hopes himself.

Teressa remained in charge of her fellow Northerners, all of whom were reluctant to fight. Instead, knowing that their loyalty belonged to Red first and foremost, Teressa suggested that they be assigned to protect him. They might not be prepared to fight other Northerners, but they would see off anyone who tried to attack the man they still saw as Arenadd's rightful successor. Teressa herself insisted that she be among them, despite the distance that had come between herself and Red.

Neither of them had mentioned the conversation they had had, but both of them knew the other was thinking of it. Neither of them spoke, because neither of them knew what to say, and a great, aching void of silence appeared and widened, and hurt.

But, once Teressa had quietly declared her intention of staying by him during the battle, he silently vowed that he would do everything in his power to protect her.

As for Red, his job was to do everything, more or less. He went from group to group, talking to people, asking questions and making sure that everyone knew he was there, up and about and ready to do whatever they needed him to.

But he spent most of his free time with Caradoc.

He talked to the boy most evenings, unable to feel any particular tiredness despite all the work he did each day, and before long Caradoc was ready to talk as well. The boy told him stories in return, about his own life, and Red knew what a sign of trust that was. His plan was working.

After a few days and several conversations in which Red made a point of telling the truth, and treating the boy with respect, Caradoc stopped showing any fear of him. Before much longer he was willing to share his own secrets, and Red listened – again, with respect.

Around this time he started letting the boy walk around outside his room, as long as he stayed by Red the whole time. Red took him to meet people – other Southerners, but Teressa as well. He had instructed all of them to be open with him, and friendly as well. They did as they were told. Caradoc talked to Isleen, asking her questions about her life. He talked to Alaric, and the pudgy storyteller – with some embarrassment – shared some of his imaginary tales. Teressa talked to him, and this time he listened politely while she told him about her journey to find Red, and confirmed Red's own version – though like him she said nothing about Flell, his rival for the throne, whom she had delivered safely to Amoran and her now-dead grandfather the Emperor.

Caradoc, finding no threat from anyone in the Eyrie and seeing only respect from his fellow Northerners – who bowed to him and called him "Prince" – quickly became confident there, and even started trying to order people about. Red gently put a stop to that, explaining that he wasn't in charge here, but Caradoc wasn't particularly upset about it.

Only one thing bothered Red now, and it wasn't Caradoc. It was his eyes.

His injury had never really healed, but continued to ache and itch. Sometimes the pain became agonising again, and he had to go into the shadows to soothe it. He'd been using the shadows a lot since getting out of bed, partly because it made him feel better but also because he thought he should teach himself how to move around, guided by the vague images he could see from there.

He took to practising alone at night, in the training yard once intended for the city guard. There were some archery butts and straw dummies there, so he made use of both and did his best to look innocent in the morning when people complained about the damage. He'd never really gotten the hang of holding back in a fight.

It took a while to get the hang of it – his substitute vision was so attuned to the beating hearts of living things that it was hard to make out inanimate objects. He supposed that would just make the actual fighting easier.

But the more he practised, the more he used the shadows, the more his wound started to bother him. It was fine in the shadows; never better, in fact. But when he left them, it would itch and ache worse than ever.

Could it be a trick of the Night God, he wondered? To make him spend more time in the shadows and therefore become more dangerous? It was the sort of underhanded thing she might try. But if he didn't use the shadows, he'd be useless.

Finally, albeit reluctantly, he went to see the man who was Liantha's Master of Healing.

'I know you said it was healing clean, but I think you should take another look at it,' he explained. 'It's been driving me nuts. Shouldn't it have stopped hurting by now?'

'In an ordinary person, no,' the healer said frankly. 'An ordinary person would probably have died. If they hadn't, they'd still heal far more slowly than you. You're healing insanely fast, but still normally. By now I would have expected the scar to have finished forming. Mind you, these things often keep bothering us long after they've supposedly healed. Some wounds never stop hurting.'

'It doesn't hurt so much as it just itches,' said Red. 'I thought it might be infected.'

'Let me have a look, then.'

Red pulled the bandage off, and sat still while the healer inspected the wound. He prodded at it and murmured to himself.

'Well?' Red said immediately. 'What's it look like?'

'It's not infected,' said the healer. 'A lot of the time, itching just means it's healing.'

'Is it still healing?'

'Yes, but…it looks a little odd.'

'Oh yeah, how?'

The healer carefully touched the wound again. 'There's no scar. There is some scarring, around the edges, but in the middle here…'

'Still all burnt?'

'No. There's raw flesh there, but it's not wounded. It looks brand new. Healthy. It wasn't there before. Your…eye sockets are exposed now. Before they'd been sealed over.'

'Well?' Red said impatiently.

'There's something in them, and it's not flesh,' said the healer. 'It's something else. I can't really tell what…It's messy. But there's definitely something in there.'

'What's left of my eyes, I'd guess,' said Red.

'No. Your eyes were gone,' the healer said frankly. 'The burn completely destroyed them and the remains sloughed away with the other dead flesh. This is something that wasn't there before.'

Red froze. 'Something growing?'

'Maybe. I mean, I can't really tell…'

But Red wasn't listening any more. He'd been given a hope, and he latched onto it at once. And now he realised that using the shadows was making it happen, he resolved to use them more than ever.

He started immediately, full of a grim determination to see what would happen, hardly daring to hope that it could be true. He stopped walking normally to places, instead sliding through the shadows like a ghost. He trained all night, every night. Sometimes he wouldn't even leave the shadows to talk to people, but would stay there and let his voice come out of nowhere. People complained, but he ignored it. What did it matter?

And the more he used the shadows, the more it happened. His empty eyesockets itched and ached, but bit by bit the feeling lessened. He checked it obsessively, and after a few weeks of almost constantly staying in the shadows he felt the skin around his eyes heal. New flesh grew over the bone, and fresh skin covered it. The upper part of the bridge of his nose grew back as well. And that was not all.

Red's eyes grew back. Slowly, painfully, but steadily, they healed. Thin, fragile orbs formed and then thickened, while the lids and lashes grew over them. His eyebrows sprouted, all rough and carrot-coloured like his hair.

At first his new eyes were useless, but he took the bandage off for the last time and people exclaimed in astonishment when they saw what was underneath.

'Eyes!' Isleen said. 'They're rather whitened, but they're definitely there.'

Red didn't need telling twice. He could feel them, turn them in their sockets, even if they were still blind. That, he knew, would come later.

And when, at last, his sight returned, he knew who he wanted to show first.

He returned to his quarters at dawn, after a night of training. Kraego was in his nest, still asleep, but Red gently nudged him awake.

The black griffin got up at once, hissing a threat before he recognised his partner.

'Red. What is it?'

Red had put the bandage back on, but now he slowly pulled it off, and looked straight at Kraego for the first time in two months.

The black grifffin filled his vision, huge and hulking and glossy with health, staring back at him with his own icy blue eyes.

'You've grown,' Red said softly. 'I can see it.'

Kraego came towards him. 'I knew it,' he said. 'I knew that you would recover.'

'You were right,' said Red. 'See? See?' He started to laugh. 'I see you! My gods, I can see!' He darted forward impulsively, and hugged his partner around the leg.

Kraego huffed and pressed his great feathery chest against his partner. 'Yes, Red. You have fought your wound and you have won, as I knew you would. Now every griffin and human will know that you are truly unstoppable.'

'Holy Gryphus.' Red rubbed his new eyes. 'I hate being the Shadow That Walks, but I'm damn glad about it now.'

'And so you should be grateful for the power I gave you,' said Kraego.

'Right now, I am,' said Red. 'Thank you, Kraego. Thank you so much. An' to think I was so desperate that I—,'

Realisation finally hit him, and he froze.

'Oh my gods,' he said softly. 'Oh dear gods.'

Kraego pulled back to look at him. 'What is it?'

Red scarcely heard him. 'Oh my gods,' he said again. 'I don't believe it. That bitch. That unbelievable, lying bitch!'

'Who is this?' said Kraego. 'Who lied?'

Red was shaking with rage. 'I don't believe it! That – the Night God! She told me if I didn't follow her I'd be blind forever, an' now look what's happened!'

'She lied,' said Kraego.

'Damn right she lied! Oh my gods.' Red took a deep breath. 'She knew this was gonna happen! She knew that sooner or later my eyes'd grow back, so she took her chance to try an' get me on her side. But it was all a trick. She was never gonna give me a damn thing!'

'She would have used you, as she wished to use me,' said Kraego.

'Oh my gods.' Red couldn't stop saying it.

And then, on a mad impulse, he turned away from Kraego. He knelt, bowed his head, and prayed – but not to the gods.

'Arenadd,' he said. 'Arenadd, thank you. Thank you. Thank you so much. My gods. If I could…if I could do anything for you, I would. I swear I would. Thank you a thousand times. I nearly lost. I nearly fell into her clutches, an' I would have if you hadn't warned me. Thank you. I'll tell Teressa. I'll tell her everything, I'll tell her she was right about you. You are on my side.'

*

In the void, Arenadd heard his words and whispered a reply he knew the other would not hear.

'Your side?'

And he laughed like one gone mad.

*

The news of Red's restored eyesight spread like wildfire through the Eyrie. Red, resisting the temptation to stay in the shadows and savour the feeling it still gave him, went around normally and visited everyone so they could see the story was true. People greeted the news with joy and excitement, and Red enjoyed it. It was such a wonderful feeling to have something genuinely good to celebrate – something that hadn't hurt anyone.

He knew Teressa would want to be one of the first to see the proof, so she was one of the first people he went to visit.

'By gods it's good to see you again,' he told her with a smile.

Teressa looked at him with wonder, and came closer to touch his face. He let her reach up and brush his new eyes with her fingertips. 'By Arenadd, it's true,' she said.

'It is, so it is,' said Red, playfully imitating Lady Merca's bizarre accent.

'Thank gods,' said Teressa. 'I'm so…well, I'm glad.'

Red smiled again, but then turned serious. 'There's somethin' I gotta tell you.'

She tensed. 'What is it?'

He grimaced internally when he realised he'd given her the wrong idea, but quickly plunged on and told her about what Arenadd's intervention meant.

She listened with growing astonishment. 'But how could that be true?'

'I don't know, but it's got to be,' said Red. 'He's against her. He hates her, an' he's trying to stop her. He's on our side, Teressa, just like you thought.'

Teressa shook her head in disbelief. 'Incredible.'

'Well then, I'm sorry for doubtin' you before,' said Red. 'It looks like you were right all along when you prayed to him. I prayed to him myself once I realised. An' frankly, it made more sense than prayin' to the gods, because now we know for certain that there is someone on the other side who's watching out for us.'

'Aye, there is.' And, caught up in the excitement of the moment, Teressa hugged him and he hugged her back.

It felt good.

Chapter Eleven

Negotiations

Some months after this, when New Eagleholm was as prepared as it would ever be for the coming fight, the King and his army finally came in sight. In the meantime, a few Southern griffiners had dared to leave their home Eyries to answer Red and Kraego's call for support. They did something to increase the number of griffins on his side, but Kraego knew they would not come close to matching the Unpartnered. No, Kraego knew what would decide this battle, and he discussed it with one of his newest followers: Ereska.

Now that her human no longer wanted to escape – and stood no chance of succeeding if he ever tried – Ereska felt safe enough to leave him with Red and go to spend time with Kraego. Her fears for her human's safety had been calmed.

'Kraego, we must plan,' she told him, her voice a low purr.

'We must,' Kraego agreed. 'Now that you and I may speak freely and the humans have made their plans, it is time for us to form our own. But it will not be difficult.'

'No,' said Ereska. 'It will not.'

They had gone out into the city, neither willing to go any further away from their partners, and padded through the streets together. Here, they would not be disturbed by any humans who could understand them, but in any case they were using the faster, more complex form of their language, which few humans could follow easily.

'You and I have both made our choices,' Kraego said tersely. 'My human and I will rid this land of our enemies. Then, we shall rule it together. The other Eyrie masters will bow their heads to me. I will make Liranwee my home Eyrie, but it will be the foremost, and the rest shall pay tribute.'

'And I shall be your ally in the North,' said Ereska. 'It will be my territory. I will not bow my head to you, but be your equal – a ruler in my own territory, which will be separate.'

'Yes, in return for your help,' said Kraego. 'I have the sense not to think that I can rule North and South together. But for us both to triumph, Shar will not be needed.'

'That is true,' said Ereska. 'I have considered this already, before I agreed to come to you. Now Shar will not welcome me back, and I do not expect it. For us to succeed, we must kill her.'

'Once I would have objected to this, but your plan pleases me,' said Kraego. 'Shar killed my father and took his place by treachery. I will now do the same to her. You and I shall strike at once, as partners in battle. Shar will not be able to fight us both.'

'But what of her human?' asked Ereska. 'Alive, he will be in my own human's way.'

'I have thought this, but my own human has said he must live,' said Kraego. 'So that they may plan together for our glorious future. It will not matter. Without Shar, he will not be able to lead the other humans again. Beside that, you have said that he wishes for his son to take his place. Once Shar is dead, he will stand aside for him.'

'Then that will be good,' said Ereska. 'I have no fear of him. If he chooses to try and revenge himself on me for my treachery, I will kill him.'

'That will be the best way,' Kraego agreed. 'Now that we have made our decision, it is time to sharpen our talons.'

'Soon.' Ereska moved closer to him. 'But first I must have something from you, Kraego.'

'You wish to have me?' Kraego asked with amusement. 'I guessed that.'

'Yes.' Ereska began to purr. 'Come closer, and speak of our glorious future again. Then, together, we will make a part of it.'

'You speak well,' said Kraego. 'It pleases me. You are a fine, strong female, Ereska.'

'And you are the strongest male,' said Ereska. 'Together, we shall rule Cymria. One day, our young will fight for that same right.'

'So they shall,' said Kraego. 'Come. We will fly together.'

Their business concluded, the two griffins took off together without any further discussion. They flew the mating flight, chasing each other over the city and showing off their strength. Then, once they had landed on top of the Eyrie roof, they paired. Their mating was violent and savage, like their natures. Like all males, Kraego was barbed, and Ereska screamed and attacked him the moment they had parted. But soon enough she came back, purring her satisfaction and asking for more.

Like all griffins they stayed together for the next few days before abruptly losing interest, but Ereska was content. She had had the most powerful male griffin in Cymria, and that was enough of a triumph to keep her happy for now.

Later on she would pair with Orak as well, as he had suggested – but only once she was certain that she was already pregnant.

The yellow griffin slept in her nest, beside the room where Caradoc rested. Soon Shar would be dead and power would belong to Ereska, and then she would return home to lay Kraego's eggs. It would be a glorious future indeed.

*

The King's army arrived about a week after Kraego and Ereska's pairing, and when Red first saw it with his new eyes he was surprised.

'I didn't think there'd be so many,' he said.

But there were. He stood up on the Eyrie roof with Kraego, and looked down on what, from this height, looked more like a great mass of swarming ants than an army.

Hundreds of Northern soldiers, all in neat ranks, drew up out of arrow-range and began to make camp, while around them the Unpartnered came down to land. There were more of them than Red had expected, even though he had seen them more than once.

'They will not want to fight once Shar is dead,' Kraego said carelessly. 'This time I will see it done.'

Red glanced at him. It was true that Kraego had grown since their first meeting. The griffin was still young as griffins went – not much older than nine, if he remembered rightly. Fully mature for a griffin, but not yet as big as he would be at about fifteen, which was when most griffins reached full size. Even so, he was big – bigger than any other griffin in New Eagleholm, and probably bigger than any of the Unpartnered as well. He had grown stronger, most definitely, and more experienced in fighting. Shar had defeated him last time they fought, but by now, maybe, they would be a better match.

'You could use your magic on her,' Red suggested, knowing the rumours that the power of the dark griffin could kill hundreds in one go.

'No,' said Kraego. 'It would weaken me and I would be vulnerable, and besides I must defeat her with physical strength to truly be the victor.'

'Whatever.' Red shrugged; he wasn't about to try and make sense of a griffin's mind, especially now.

He had guessed that the King wouldn't attack right away, and he was soon proven right: while the army was still making camp a solitary white flag went up, indicating that they wanted to talk.

'Righto.' Red nodded to himself. The King would have received the letters which Caradoc had written for him, assuring his father that he was fine.

A moment later Shar appeared as well. While the Unpartnered and the other griffins were ground-bound, the red griffin took to the air and circled over her camp, calling out a message which Red and Kraego could easily hear.

'Kraego! Kraego, come to me! Our humans must speak!'

'Damn right they should,' said Red. 'I guess we'd better go.'

'Agreed,' said Kraego. 'Come, now.'

'Wait. We should take someone with us. Call for Orak, will you? An' call Ereska as well. I think it's best if we let Caedmon see his son face to face. It's better than just taking our word for it.'

'That would be best,' said Kraego, and Red clapped his hands over his ears while his partner screeched for his fellow griffins to come to him.

Orak and Ereska were nearby, and they arrived shortly with their partners.

'Are we taking me back to my father?' Caradoc asked hopefully.

'Yeah, we are,' said Red. 'We reckon now he's here you should go see him. You'll have to stay with us, but you can visit him so he knows you're all right.'

The boy nodded eagerly and climbed onto Ereska's back the moment she lay down to let him up.

'Ye want us to come too?' Teressa asked.

'Yeah,' said Red. 'I reckon it'll be good if he sees us together. Shows him I've got Northerner friends. Anyway, you're persuasive, Tress.' He looked fondly at her, and she smiled back, shyly.

'Right, let's go,' said Red.

'I will call first,' said Kraego, and screeched a message back to Shar. 'Shar! I come now, with my human and two of my followers!'

He called the message a few more times, but Shar soon understood and screeched back. It was time to go.

Red and Teressa mounted up, and together the three griffins flew down towards the Northerners' camp.

Despite himself, Red winced when he saw them up close. There had to be at least three thousand, men and women, all well armed. They were lightly armoured – the Northern fighting style relied on speed and agility rather than brute strength, and anyway, they valued courage. Their simple tents had been erected in neat rows, and the King's triple-spiral banner fluttered everywhere. The Unpartnered were all over the place, many lying down between the tents. They wore the splashes of red dye on their feathers that marked them out as a group, so they could fight more effectively against other griffins and not attack each other by mistake. Red saw them kneading the ground with their talons or rubbing their beaks in arrogant anticipation while their human comrades sharpened their weapons.

Clearly, this was not an army that would go down easily.

King Caedmon's personal tent had been put up in the middle of the camp, and Shar was waiting outside.

Up close the red griffin looked bigger than he remembered. She wasn't as big as Kraego, but she was lean and tough, her head and flanks scarred. She was missing a talon on one forepaw – bitten off by the Mighty Skandar himself in the battle in which she had defeated him, so Kraego had told him. Her feathers were an attractive russet colour, and her eyes were narrow as she sized up the three intruders.

'Ereska,' she hissed. 'You will pay for your treachery.'

'I went with them to protect my human,' Ereska replied without a hint of remorse.

'I have humiliated you, Shar,' said Kraego. 'I have taken your human's pup, and won Ereska's loyalty. And this grey one here, Orak, was once from your Eyrie. Now, he too serves me.'

'We shall see,' said Shar. 'Come into this nest now, and meet with my human. He and your own human must talk.'

It was a very large tent, which was just as well. The three griffins filed in, with their humans, and Shar followed close behind. Inside some simple furniture had been set up – a table, a bed, and a couple of chests for clothes.

Caedmon was there, alone. He wore the black robe and the crown of kingship, and on the surface he was as neat and calm as always, but Red thought he looked haggard and red around the eyes.

The moment Caradoc entered the tent, he broke away from the group and ran to his father.

Caedmon, for once forgetting dignity, grabbed his son in a fierce embrace. 'Caradoc, thank the Night God…'

Caradoc held his father tightly. 'I'm so sorry! I tried…'

Caedmon let him go. 'Caradoc, are you all right? Did they hurt you?'

'No,' Caradoc sniffled a little. 'They were nice. They took good care of me and they promised I could go back to you soon.'

Caedmon looked up at Red, and stood up, keeping his son close by. 'So here you are, Southerner,' he said. 'And you're looking a lot healthier than I expected.'

'Yeah,' said Red. 'Turns out the Shadow That Walks can grow a new pair of eyes. Who would've thought? As for you, I'm surprised you ain't got more protection. Shouldn't there be some guards?'

'Why bother?' said Caedmon. 'They wouldn't be able to stop you. I'd just be wasting their lives. I'm not stupid, Captain.'

'I never thought you were,' said Red. 'That's why I'm hoping we can talk this out.'

'You stole my son,' Caedmon said icily. 'Talk won't get you far, Southerner.'

'You say "Southerner" like it's a bad thing,' said Red. 'I could've killed him, Caedmon. You know I could've. I could kill you, too. Right here an' now. I could kill the pair of you with my bare hands before either of you made a sound. Ain't that so?'

'Maybe,' said Caedmon. 'But I assume you've come here to offer me some kind of deal?'

'Yeah, I have,' said Red. 'But first – this is Kraego, my partner. An' this is Teressa an' her own partner Orak. They're…friends of mine.'

'Oh yes?' Caedmon gave Teressa a filthy look. 'You must be Teressa the traitor priestess I've heard about.'

'The one who stayed faithful to the great Arenadd, unlike ye,' Teressa threw back.

Caedmon glared. 'How dare you come here and say that to me when you've betrayed your whole people?'

'Ye are one traitor talking to another, then,' said Teressa. 'Ye tried to have Arenadd killed when he was still here. Everyone knows it. Ye murdered his daughter and rightful heir and stole her throne.'

'All right, that's enough,' Red interrupted. 'We're not here to trade insults. Now listen, Caedmon – here's my offer.'

'Make it,' Caedmon said tersely.

'We'll give you back your son,' said Red. 'And we'll end this right here and now, if you make us a promise.'

'And what promise is that?'

'That you'll leave,' said Red. 'You'll take your friends an' go back North, and promise never to come back. In return you get your son back, and a promise from us that we'll leave you alone. We'll let you live in peace, an' forget this ever happened.'

Silence followed.

'Is that it?' Caedmon said at last.

'Yeah,' said Red. 'That's about the shape of it.'

Caedmon laughed in his face. 'You're an even bigger fool than I thought if you think I'll accept that. You're in no position to make treaties on behalf of the entire South.'

'No I ain't,' said Red. 'I'm speakin' for Liranwee, and we're the city closest to the North. That's why we were the first ones you attacked. Make a treaty with us, an' you'll never be able to invade the South again without violating it, will you?' He glanced over at Kraego. 'I wasn't always a griffiner, you know that. I was a guard. I reckon, at heart, I still am. Once this is over I'll go back to Liranwee an' I'll guard those mountains. I'll see to it that you don't come back through them, an' in return I'll make sure none of us goes bothering you. I'll guard the North and the South.'

'Oh yes?' said Caedmon. 'You think you can hold back the entire South?'

'I'll do my best, but if you sign this treaty then I'll help you,' said Red. 'We'll make treaties with the other cities as well.'

'And have you talked to any of them?' asked Caedmon, with a sardonic edge to his voice that said he already knew the answer was no.

'No,' said Red. 'Can't very well do that, can I? They've got no way of making their own decisions anymore, not with you holding 'em hostage. I reckon they'd be more than happy to sign in return for getting their positions back.'

Caemon said nothing. He looked as if he were thinking deeply.

'We can put it behind us,' Red added. 'We can stop being afraid of each other, an' move on. Make our country better for everyone.'

'Hmph. Those are fine words from the Shadow That Walks,' said Caedmon. 'But you're right. I do want peace, and there was peace before you came along. You're the one perpetuating this, not me.'

'Well I don't know what "perpetuating" means, but you're still lyin',' said Red. 'You started this, not me. I just wanted to be a guard. You're the one who wanted to be King of Cymria. This never would've happened if you'd just left us alone.'

'If we left you alone?' said Caedmon. 'As I recall, it was your people who invaded us first. Centuries of oppression don't just fade away, Captain. As King it's my duty to protect my people, and I promised them I would ensure that the South would never again be a threat to us.'

'But we weren't threatening you!' said Red. 'You drove us out, an' we left you alone for nearly thirty years. Look, can we just stop this? I'm trying to make you an offer here so that nobody else has to die.'

'I'm sorry, but I can't trust any offers that you make, Captain,' said Caedmon. 'You are, after all, a Southerner, and I'm a Northerner, and there's never going to be any trust between us.'

'Be careful, Sire,' Teressa warned. 'Lord Redguard gave ye a chance before and ye threw it back in his face. How many more do ye think he'll give ye? Say no again and he'll have no choice but to kill ye, and none of us want that.'

'We don't,' said Red. 'You started this, Sire, an' only you can end it. I'm just giving you the opportunity.'

Caedmon hesitated ever so briefly, and in that moment, Caradoc spoke up.

'He's right, Father,' he said. 'You said you didn't want to fight any more. The Captain doesn't either. Can't we just go home?'

Caedmon patted his son's shoulder. 'It's all right, Caradoc. We'll go back to Liranwee together after this is over.'

'I don't mean Liranwee,' said Caradoc. 'I want to go back to Malvern. That's where we live.'

'Caradoc, I've told you before. Liranwee is where we live now.'

'No it isn't. That's the Captain's home and we stole it. Please, Father. Just say yes and we can go back to our home. We're Northerners. We should be in the North.'

Caedmon glared up at Red. 'What have you been telling him?'

Red shrugged. 'I told him about everything that's happened to me. Showed him I could be honest with him. In the end, he decided to be honest with me. He said he'd been wanting to go home for a good while but thought you'd be angry if he said so. I told him when he saw you he should just say it because you should always be honest with people you care about. Anyway…he's got the right idea, Sire. You should listen.'

'Enough!' Caedmon snapped. 'Be quiet. The answer is no, Southerner. I don't trust you, and I won't accept any offers you make me. This will be over once we've dealt with you and your rabble, and not before.'

Red sighed and shrugged again. 'See you on the battlefield, then. An' once my hands are around your neck, you'll be wishing you'd had more sense. Caradoc, get over here. We're going back to the Eyrie.'

'No.' Caradoc clutched at his father's hand. 'I won't go with you.'

'All right, then,' Red growled. 'Then here's the deal. You come here right now, or I'll go over there an' punch Daddy in the face an' drag you back.'

Caedmon took a step back. 'Leave him alone, Captain. He stays with me.'

'Sorry, mate, but you had your chance to get him back an' you didn't take it.' Red had had enough of arguing, and when Caedmon still refused to let go of his son he growled, strode forward, and snatched the boy.

'No!' Caedmon lurched forward, pulled out a dagger, and stabbed Red through the chest.

Red roared and punched his enemy hard in the chest. Caedmon went staggering to the ground, and Red gave him a spiteful kick before throwing the protesting Caradoc over his shoulder and unhurriedly returning to his friends.

'All right, let's get goin',' he said, passing Caradoc back to Ereska.

The little group wasted no time. They left the tent together, pushing past Shar, who did not try to stop them. The moment they were in the open they were free to fly back to the Eyrie.

By the time Red set foot back on the Eyrie roof, he was grimacing. He pulled the dagger out of his body and slapped a hand over the wound. 'Argh. Stupid son of a bitch.'

Teressa was already at his side. 'What should I do?'

'Alaric,' said Red through gritted teeth. 'Go an' get Alaric.'

Teressa looked surprised, but she ran off without asking any questions. Once she had gone, Red turned to Ereska.

'Right then,' he said. 'We don't want the boy hurt in the fighting, so we'll keep him underground. He oughta be safe there. You can stay with him an' keep an eye on him. I don't reckon they'll risk firebombing us, though, knowing he's with us.'

'They will not,' said Ereska. 'But I will not stay to guard my human. I must be with Kraego.'

'We have agreed on this,' said Kraego.

'All right,' said Red. 'I gotta talk with Alaric, but we'll get Teressa to help find a safe spot. Down in the storerooms, I reckon.'

'Don't you dare lock me up again!' Caradoc shouted. 'You promised I could go free!'

'You will, but first we got a little battle to fight,' said Red. 'Blame your dad for that, not me.'

Teressa returned at this point, followed by a panting Alaric. 'You asked for me, Captain?' he said.

'That's right, but first—,' Red beckoned Teressa over. 'Tress, take our little friend here underground an' find a good place to lock him up where he'll be safe. Take a couple of guards along to keep an eye on him – Northerners, preferably. They'd be less likely to want to hurt him.'

Caradoc knew better than to argue, and he seemed to like Teressa. He went with her, looking sulky but resigned.

'Good luck, boy,' Red called after him. 'I'll see you later. Maybe.' He turned to Alaric. 'Now then. I got a job for you.'

Alaric peered at him, his bad eyesight giving him a permanent squint. 'Me? Are you sure, Captain?'

'Yeah, I am,' said Red. 'You're handy with words, right?'

'Well, I wouldn't say…' Alaric mumbled.

'An' also, back when you were a griffiner, you were apprenticed to the Master of Law in Withypool,' said Red.

'Yes, I was. After Isleen went on to help found Liranwee, I was close to being made the new Master.' Alaric said this with a touch of pride.

'Perfect,' said Red. 'Then here's what I want you to do. You're gonna write something for me, an' you're gonna start now.'

'It would be my pleasure, Captain,' said Alaric. 'What do you want me to write?'

'A peace treaty.'

The little man looked shocked. 'But Teressa said the King rejected your offer!'

'Yeah, so he's forfeited his chance to help pick the terms,' said Red. 'Now you're gonna write one without his help. This one will be all about our terms, an' maybe once the fighting's done the King will change his mind about signing it. D'you think you can do it?'

'I do,' said Alaric. 'And I'll get Isleen to help me. But you'll have to give us an outline so we know what you're after. We can dress it up in the proper language, but you have to give us the terms you want us to put down.'

Red smiled to himself – he'd never heard Alaric sound so businesslike before, or sound like a man who wasn't out of his depth. 'All right,' he said. 'I've got other things to do, but you come with me first an' I'll give you an idea of what I'm after. It's pretty straightforward.'

'I'm listening, Captain.'

'A peace treaty?' Kraego interrupted. 'This is foolish. Shar's human has rejected us. Now the only choice is to kill them both.'

Ereska moved closer to him, and rubbed her head against his shoulder. 'No, Kraego. Listen to your human. He has not been wrong before. Stay here with me, and we will keep watch and prepare for our attack.'

Orak had gone with Teressa, but now Kraego looked towards Red.

'Go, my human,' he said. 'And I will see you later. Soon we will be ready to fight.'

Red was already deep in discussion with Alaric. 'Gotcha,' he said absently, and went inside to find his council.

Once they had gone, Kraego looked to Ereska. 'Are you ready to do what we have agreed?'

'I am. Fight well, Kraego. We will fly together again.' Ereska flew away, leaving Kraego to watch as she made for the camp where Shar waited, ready to begin.

Chapter Twelve

The Battle for Eagleholm

Ereska knew what she had to do, and she told herself that she felt no fear, but as she flew back to Shar's camp she could not hide it from herself. She knew very well that if her plan failed, it would cost her her life. But if she wanted to please Kraego and therefore own the North, it had to be done.

She knew that it would be a fatal mistake to underestimate Shar. The red griffin may be smaller than Kraego, and more lightly built than herself, but she was a powerful fighter. She had, after all, defeated the Mighty Skandar himself, and until then the giant griffin had never lost a fight and most had believed he was invincible. But Shar had defeated him, and wounded him badly before driving him away. He had flown off to die somewhere alone, and Shar had won Malvern and the loyalty of the Unpartnered. Ereska had only been a youngster then, but every griffin in the North knew the story.

Now, Ereska's own glory would come from the defeat of Shar. But it had to be done cautiously.

The Unpartnered saw her coming, and a large number of them flew up to intercept her. Ereska did not try and fight them, but let them force her to land on the open ground between the city walls and Shar's camp.

The moment she was grounded, three large griffins landed on top of her. She went down under them, frightened and angry but ignoring her instinct to fight back.

'I am here to speak with Shar!' she screeched.

A male Unpartnered latched his talons onto her neck. 'Are you unpartnered?' he demanded.

'No!' Ereska choked. 'My human is Prince Caradoc, son of Shar's human. I am here to speak with Shar. Bring her to me.'

'We know your name, Ereska,' said a second griffin. 'You have chosen to go with Kraego, whose human is a Southerner. You are now Shar's enemy and ours.'

'I went to protect my human,' said Ereska. 'I am here to help

Shar.'

The third unpartnered griffin hissed. 'It would be good to kill you, but Shar will want to do this herself. I will call for her.'

He did, but Shar had already noticed that something was going on. She arrived moments later, angrily ruffling her wings. She snarled when she saw Ereska. 'So you have come back, yellow griffin. Did you wish to die, then?'

'I have come to offer my help,' said Ereska.

The Unpartnered let her go, and she stood up – but took care to lower her head in submission while she waited for Shar's reply.

It was scathing. 'You think I will believe you?'

'I did what I must, for my human's protection,' said Ereska. 'Kraego warned me that if I did not do as he said, he would kill me and my human would have died in the fight. If I had tried to flee, he would have hunted me down. I was not fool enough to think I could fight or escape him.'

'But now you have fled from him,' said Shar.

'In desperation, I have,' said Ereska. 'They have locked my human away, and I was not allowed to be with him. Only Kraego's defeat will allow me to have him back.'

'But mine would do the same for you,' said Shar.

'I am not a fool,' Ereska repeated. 'Kraego cannot hope to defeat you. The Unpartnered will tear him to shreds the moment he tries to challenge you.'

'They cannot do that if he uses the shadows,' said Shar. 'That is in his power.'

'He will not do that,' said Ereska. 'It would be weak to rely on magic to fight you. The Mighty Skandar did not use his power. His son will also try to win by brute strength. I know that you have already defeated him when he tried to win that way. You will do it again. Kraego is young and arrogant. He believes he can defeat you alone, but he cannot, and he does not have enough allies.'

Shar was silent for a while. 'Then what will you do?' she asked.

'I will fight beside you, to win back my human,' said Ereska. 'When the city is taken, I will go with the Unpartnered to attack the Eyrie, and take him back.'

'You are lying,' said Shar.

'I have only seen sense,' Ereska insisted. 'I cannot fight against you. My human cannot become King after yours if he is his father's enemy. Where his loyalty lies, so does mine.'

Shar considered this for a moment, and then turned away. 'I will speak with my human. You will stay here.'

Ereska stayed obediently where she was, and groomed herself to hide her nervousness. The worst of the danger was over, at least. Now Ereska would have to hope that Shar's human would speak out on her behalf. He was cunning even for a human, and she had seen how difficult he was to persuade many times already, but hopefully he would be more easily manipulated because she was partnered to his son. If not…then the outcome could well still be her death.

After a while Shar returned, and this time she had her human with her.

'Shar tells me you've offered to get me my son back,' he said tersely.

'I have,' said Ereska. 'I will help the Unpartnered to capture the Eyrie, and I will kill all those who try to stop me.'

'No,' said Caedmon. 'I can't allow that. It would be too dangerous for him, and they may have put him somewhere you can't reach. If you want to help him, then stay here with us. Once the Southerners have been defeated, we can force them to give him back.'

'My human is right,' said Shar. 'We will win by killing Kraego. But for this, I do not need help. I will defeat him as I defeated him before, and this time I will not allow him to escape. Ereska, you may join the Unpartnered. If you turn on us again, they will kill you.'

Ereska had no choice but to accept. 'We will win this battle together,' she vowed.

'Go with them,' Shar ordered the three Unpartnered who had stayed to keep watch over her.

Ereska was a griffin, and it was much easier for her to conceal her emotions than it would be for a human. But inside, she burned with triumph. Shar had been fooled, and for that, she would die.

*

Caedmon spent the last moments before the fight began alone in his tent, while Shar stayed outside – keeping an eye on Ereska and preparing the Unpartnered for the first assault.

He had meant to pray, but though he managed a brief appeal to the Night God, his mind refused to stay focused on her. Instead, of all things, he found himself thinking about Laela the half-breed, the woman who had stolen his throne and murdered his entire family.

Those had been desperate days for Caedmon. His family gone, with a tiny handful of allies, he had faced odds that looked impossible. Even with the help of his mother Saeddryn, the last Shadow That Walked, he had suffered defeat after defeat, failure after failure. More than once – though he had never admitted it to anyone – he had thought of giving up. Laela had had all the advantages, and almost supernatural luck. Even Saeddryn had been unable to remove her. Somehow, the half-breed had evaded her at every turn.

But Caedmon had not given up. He had refused to turn his back on his duty to his people. While Laela betrayed them all by allying herself with Southerners and marrying an Amorani, he had seen how she would soon bring the downfall of the North, and known that he was the only one who could stop it.

Everyone else had failed. His followers had died or betrayed him, and even Saeddryn had been killed. The half-breed's allies had captured and tortured her, and finally killed her. The woman Caedmon had loved had been slaughtered in front of him, along with his unborn child. In the end, all he had left was Shar and himself. A man and a griffin, against an entire country.

But even then he had stood firm. He was a Taranisäii, and he had refused to lie down and die. He had stood up one last time, and this time the North had stood with him, and Laela the half-breed had finally fallen.

Now, sitting alone in his tent, Caedmon thought back to his enemy's death, and his expression turned grim.

He had wanted to take Laela alive, so she could be tried for her crimes against the North, but by the time he reached her she was already dying. Childbirth had all but killed her, and he had found her on her deathbed, with her child lying still and cold in its cradle. His last rival for the throne, dead.

In the North, when a woman died in childbirth, or gave birth to a dead child, it was sometimes referred to as "the Night God's punishment". She was the god of death, and if a pregnant woman betrayed her, she would punish that woman by killing her child. Caedmon had made certain that every man and woman in the North knew what had happened, and the High Priestess of the time had remarked on how fitting it was.

But that wasn't what had killed Laela the half-breed. She had still been alive when Caedmon confronted her, and when he found her, she had spoken to him. He remembered it as if it were yesterday.

'…once I was an ordinary peasant girl what couldn't read. I never thought nothin' about ruling, or hurtin' anyone. I just wanted a place in the world. Half-breeds don't get them easy. But once they put that crown on my head…What do yeh think's gonna happen to you, Caedmon? How many people're you gonna kill?'

He remembered it all – the coarse peasant's accent, the icy blue stare, and then that smile – that horrible, knowing smile she had smiled at him as she drank the poison that killed her in moments.

'…how many people will you kill? Maybe you'll just go mad.'

Caedmon shivered. In spite of everything, even though Laela had never been anything to him but an enemy, he couldn't let go of what she had said to him that day. How many people had he killed so far? Had he gone mad? Was this madness, after all?

No. He shook himself – it was too late for doubts. He had to stay strong, and lead his people into battle this one last time. It wasn't over yet.

He grimaced. Everything would have been so simple, if it weren't for that one thing. This man, this Captain Redguard. He was the one thing that had gone wrong, the thing that should never have happened. His very existence should have been impossible. Caedmon hadn't wanted to even accept it at first, but now he knew he had to, and he could not shake the fear it put into him.

Now, at last, he did pray. He turned away to face the little altar that had been set up in his tent. It was a simple block of stone supporting a slab of white marble, which had been carved with the stylised figure of a woman. She had been depicted with only a few etched lines – one eye was a black gemstone, and the other was a disc of mother-of-pearl. The cuts had been inlaid with silver, and the mouth was an impassive line.

Caedmon knelt, and cut himself with the copper knife that sat on the altar before smearing a little drop of blood at the carving's feet. 'With this offering of true Northern blood, I call to you,' he recited, and then bowed his head. 'Night God,' he murmured. 'Guide me. Protect me. I will give up my life for my people, if I have to. But I ask you now – let me live long enough to take my son back, and lead my people to a final victory over the Southerners. Everything I do, I do in your holy name. My life is yours, my faith is yours, and my victories are all for your greater glory. I swear it. But…' He nearly stopped there, as the word slipped out of him, but it was too late. He had said it. He hesitated for a long moment before he went on. His mother had taught him that the gods understood that every mortal had doubts, and that the Night God wouldn't condemn him for being honest.

'But I don't understand,' he said. 'I want to understand, but I can't. Why did you give your power to a Southerner? Why is he fighting for them instead of us? I thought…but I know he's the Shadow That Walks. I can nearly smell it on him. The Shadow That Walks is supposed to be our friend, not our enemy, so why…? Morgan thinks it's a sign that you want us to stop. He refused to take the man prisoner, because he was afraid of your anger. I wouldn't listen to him, but now…' Caedmon looked up into the carving's face. 'I just want to be certain. I want to know that I'm doing what you want me to do. I would never go against you, Night God. Never. But I want to be certain. I need a sign. This man, the Southerner – he told me he doesn't serve you, but how could that be? You made him. I thought…'

He trailed off and turned away, shaking his head. Questioning his god wouldn't help him now, but at least he had finally said most of what had been troubling him. The Night God would understand that. But he felt guilty as he left the altar – as guilty as if he had lied to her. But how could he say that part out loud, and admit the unthinkable?

I feel betrayed, he thought – the words he wished he could say aloud, but didn't dare. *I feel betrayed by you, Night God. I feel as if you've abandoned me.*

He felt slightly better for admitting it to himself, even if he couldn't say it to her.

Caedmon squared his shoulders, and put his fears aside. It was time to go. The last battle for the South was about to begin.

*

Outside the tent, Shar was waiting for her partner.

'I am ready to begin,' she said when he came to her side. 'Have your followers been given their orders?'

'Yes,' Caedmon nodded. 'The Southerner will come after me, so we'll see to it that I'm surrounded by as many men as possible. They'll have nets – with luck we'll be able to capture him. He's the only real danger we're facing here – him and Kraego.'

'Leave the black griffin to me,' Shar said curtly. 'I will challenge him now, and once he is dead, his human will be far less of a threat.'

'Agreed,' said Caedmon. 'But…' he moved closer to her, and put a hand on her scarred shoulder, 'be careful, Shar.'

'Do not be afraid for me,' said Shar. 'I have killed a dark griffin before, and today I will do it again. Ereska!'

Nearby, surrounded by several Unpartnered, the yellow griffin looked up.

'You will stay by my human,' said Shar. 'And help to capture Kraeai kran ae. Fail, and I will kill you.'

'I will do this,' said Ereska. 'Your human will be under my protection, Shar. Kraeai kran ae will fall under my talons.'

'Now…' Shar turned away dismissively to look up at the city walls. 'I see Kraego.'

The black griffin had appeared in the sky over New Eagleholm, and as they watched he flew down to land on the wall over the main gates. Even at this distance, he looked huge as he raised his head to screech.

'Shar!' The red griffin's name echoed out over the plain where the armies of the North waited. 'SHAR! I am Kraego, son of Skandar, and I challenge you! Fight me now, and prove your strength against me. Show the Unpartnered that you are the greatest griffin in Cymria! Fight me now, Shar! Fight me to the death!'

Shar reared up and screamed back. 'Fight me, Kraego! Fight me now, and die!'

With that she took to the air with several powerful blows of her wings, while the Unpartnered called her name. Those in the air came in to land, clearing the way for her, and in the city the few griffins fighting for the Southerners came to perch on the walls where they would be able to watch the battle.

Kraego took off, screeching his own name, and flew up to meet Shar. He was larger than her, but she was faster and more experienced, and she had already beaten him once before. Caedmon reminded himself of that. Now, just as it had been on the day he took Malvern, it was all up to Shar.

*

Shar flew easily, circling over the campsite that was her territory for now, and waited for Kraego to come to her. She climbed for height while she waited, knowing that the griffin who attacked from above had the advantage. If she could reach a great enough height before Kraego reached her, he would be forced to come at her from below – straight into her talons. It was what he had done in Withypool, and it had lost him the fight. She had caught him by the wing and damaged it, and sent him straight to the ground – defeated and humiliated.

But Kraego must have learnt his lesson from that, because he didn't come straight at her as he had done then. He kept his distance and flew higher, clearly planning to attack from the same height as her – or higher if he could.

Shar, seeing that, came at him while she was still above him. Kraego did not retreat, not wanting to show any sign of weakness. He beat his wings hard, climbing towards her, but it was less easy for him, with his heavier body. Shar, seeing her opportunity, folded her own wings tightly against her body and dived straight at him, aiming for his vulnerable neck and head.

Just as before, Kraego made no attempt to avoid her attack. He came on, screeching mindlessly at her, and Shar felt controlled and savage triumph clutch hold of her. He hadn't learnt anything after all; he was just as reckless as she remembered.

She narrowed her eyes and opened her beak wide, and spread her talons, ready to strike.

But an instant before she reached him – just as she thrust forward with both forelegs, Kraego suddenly twisted in midair. Pulling his wings in tight to his sides, he rolled over onto his back, and struck.

The curving tip of his beak hit Shar in the soft place on her underjaw, and tore it open. In the same moment, Kraego's talons struck her from both sides simultaneously, and ripped down through her shoulders.

Shar's front paws, still outstretched to hit the back of his neck, hit Kraego in the chest instead, and curled backward, hooking themselves into the flesh.

Kraego let go of Shar, but as he pulled away her talons dragged through his body and left rows of ragged slashes on either side of his chest.

Kraego screamed and rolled away from her, his wings reopening to catch him. If Shar had not been injured she would have come after him immediately, but as it was she pulled away too, and for a few moments both of them flapped erratically in a circle around each other, both gasping slightly as their wounds began to bleed.

Shar could feel hot blood streaming down her neck, and knew that the injury under her beak was serious. Before long it would weaken her badly, and she had to strike now, before it was too late.

She lunged, catching Kraego by surprise. This time, her beak caught him on the side of the neck, just behind the angle of the jaw. She knew that a large blood vessel sat just there, and she had killed that way before.

But Kraego twisted his head away before she could open it, and his beak snapped shut over hers, pinning it closed. While Shar tried to pull it free, the black griffin's talons came up and kicked at her, trying to catch her in the throat. She blocked him with her own, and for a while the two of them struggled, spinning around each other, caught in a bizarre, bloody dance in the air.

Even now, Shar wasn't afraid. Her talons closed around Kraego's throat, and she kept them there, pressing with all her might, hoping to destroy his windpipe.

It nearly worked, and it would have worked, if it hadn't left her right side unprotected. Kraego's front paws hit her in the neck simultaneously, and as she pulled back in shock he suddenly let go of her beak and bit her on the left foreleg.

Shar hung from his grip, flailing at him with her wings and her free front leg, but she couldn't balance herself like this. Both of them started to fall from the sky, neither one able to fly in this position, but it lasted long enough for Kraego.

He thrust his talons into Shar's chest and throat and ruthlessly bit down on her leg, working his way forward until he had it at the back of his beak, where his bite was the most powerful, and bit again, as hard as he could.

Shar felt the crunch in her leg as the bone shattered, and then Kraego let her go.

She nearly fell to her death, but her wings were undamaged and she only just managed to save herself. She made no more attempts to attack her enemy, but flew in a slow, raggled circle, bleeding and shocked.

Kraego flew over her, and screamed his victory to the sky. 'I am mighty! I am Kraego! I am the dark griffin! I have defeated you, Shar!'

And everywhere, on the city walls and in the camp, the other griffins called back.

'Kraego! Mighty Kraego!'

The only griffin who did not call out was Shar. She flew for the ground, knowing that Kraego could strike her down from behind at any moment, but in too much pain to care.

But Kraego didn't come after her. He stayed in the sky, savouring his triumph, and let Shar go.

She flew clumsily back down to her human's tent, and tried to land there – but her broken leg crumpled under her and she fell onto her chest.

Caedmon watched in horror and shouted her name, but he had too much sense to try and go to her. In this state, she would almost certainly attack him without a moment's thought.

Shar tried to get up, but couldn't. Her leg refused to support her weight, and she had lost too much blood to try for long. She slumped onto her belly and stayed there, her breathing fast and ragged.

'Shar!' Caedmon called again.

Shar stilled. 'Come, human,' she gasped.

He ran to her, followed by a pair of humans carrying bandages. 'Shar…'

Shar looked up at him through hazy eyes. 'We have lost, Caedmon,' she said. 'Do not…'

Caedmon snatched a bag of healing things from one of his two followers, and pressed a pad of cloth from it against one of her injuries to soak up the blood. 'It'll be all right, Shar,' he said. 'You'll be fine.'

'No,' Shar groaned. 'Do not heal me. I am defeated, and I will die rather than live with my shame.'

'No, Shar,' said Caedmon. 'No…'

Her eyes had closed. 'Do not surrender,' she said. 'Fight on, Caedmon. Fight on…'

'Forever,' he said. 'Shar…'

But Shar had said all she had to say. She let herself slide away from him into darkness, not caring what happened to herself any more, or even to him. It was all over.

From above, she heard Kraego calling to his new followers.

'Kill them!' he screeched. 'Kill the humans that follow Shar's human! I command you!'

The battle for Eagleholm began.

*

Red had seen it all. He doubted anyone would have spotted him from below, but he had stood up on on the wall over the gate with Kraego, and watched Shar's defeat.

The moment he saw the red griffin go down, he turned and ran down the steps and into the street just behind the gate. There, the others had gathered. All his human followers, armed and ready. When they saw Red, they stood taller and waited for him to speak.

Red took up position just in front of the gate, facing them all. 'Now,' he said. 'Now's the time. Today we fight together. But before we go, we have to remember one thing. We're not fighting for ourselves, an' we're not fighting for revenge. We're fighting for the future. For our children, an' their children. For Cymria. And if a man surrenders, let him go. We're here to defeat them, not kill them. As for me, I'm going to the King, and I'm gonna fight him myself, but I won't kill him either. He's going to surrender to me, and then he'll help me end the war.'

Nobody spoke. He saw the men and women in the front line – Senna, Ranulf, Talmon, Liantha – all clutching their weapons, all white-faced but determined. Beside them were the Northerners Teressa had brought – Lord Anfri his wife Lady Lowri, and more than twenty others, most of them griffiners. At their head was Teressa, with Orak by her side. She wore her silver priestess' robe and carried her sickle, and her face was set and determined.

Now, as if she and Red had agreed on it beforehand, she came to his side.

'Some of us are fighting our own people today,' she said. 'But we're doing it in the name of the Night God, and in the name of Arenadd. Caedmon must be defeated. We will put a stop to this madness of his, and stop our people from disgracing themselves by becoming tyrants and occupiers. Stay with me, and have faith in the great Arenadd. Remember that before he disappeared he was against the invasion of the South. His council urged him to do it, but he refused – for years he refused. What we do today is what he wanted. So if ye feel like a traitor, remember that. Remember Arenadd.'

Lord Anfri raised his sickle. 'In King Arenadd's holy name!' he roared.

Around him his fellow Northerners did the same.

'For Arenadd! For the great Arenadd!'

'For the South!' the Southerners shouted. 'For Lord Redguard!'

'Now!' Red turned, and lifted the bar holding the gates shut with his bare hands, even though it was the length of a tree. He shoved one gate open, and Teressa pushed the other, and together they led the march out of Eagleholm.

Outside, a terrible scene awaited. The Unpartnered had followed Kraego's command without a moment's hesitation, and attacked their former allies, with only the partnered griffins there to fight back against them. But they were outnumbered, and many had retreated to try and protect their humans.

Red's whole body trembled inwardly as the violence in him screamed at him to be unleashed, but he led his people out of the city and waited until they had formed into an orderly rank before he gave the word.

'Attack!'

He charged.

Behind him Teressa charged as well, and the others, but Red forgot about them in a moment. The killing urge closed over his mind, and he hurled himself forward, leaving the others behind.

He had dressed as a guard, in his old leather breastplate and bracers, with the red tunic of an Old Eagleholm guardsman underneath, and a steel helmet covering his head. His medal swung against his breastplate as he ran, shining like a tiny sun, but there was no light in Red's heart.

The King's armies came to meet his own, charging out from among their tents, but there was no sign of the King himself.

When they saw Red coming, almost none of them tried to attack him. They parted, charging past and around him to engage his followers. But some of them did come for him.

They died.

Red scarcely even wasted his time with them. He had brought

his father's old sword with him – a short guard sword, made for stabbing rather than slashing. When anyone got in his way he cut them down and ran on, not even noticing the wounds that soon opened up on his arms and shoulders, or the bleeding cut on his neck.

Screams and shouts filled his ears, blood splashed over his face, and he felt the killing madness start to take control.

No, he thought.

Yes, the darkness in him whispered.

He reached the tents of the army and effortlessly fought on, and the sickening joy of it rushed through him like hot blood.

A woman came at him, thrusting a spear towards him. He cut the wooden handle in half with a single blow of his sword, and stabbed her in the face so hard his sword impaled her through the skull. He wrenched it out, and killed a man who tried to attack him from behind with a single brutal blow of his free hand. He was speeding up now, his mind starting to fall away from him in pieces as the excitement of killing seized control with terrible ease.

Kill everyone, he thought. *I can…*

'Red!'

He turned around sharply, raising his sword, and saw a Northerner running towards him, armed with a sickle. He growled and stepped forward to kill her.

'Red!'

As he raised the sword, he saw the silver robe and recognised the voice, and sanity came back.

'Teressa,' he rasped.

There was blood on Teressa's robe, but she looked unhurt. 'Red,' she said again, sharply. 'Stop.'

Red stopped, and quickly looked around. His followers had come into the camp, and everywhere fighting had broken out. The Unpartnered charged through the tents, killing anyone who got in their way, and his fellow Southerners ran with them, their faces alight with the lust for revenge.

'Come on,' said Teressa. 'That's enough. We have to find the King.'

'Yeah.' Red wiped the blood off his face, and jogged away towards the centre of the camp. He grimaced as he ran. More killing. More losing control. He'd known it would happen here, of course, but Teressa was right; it had to stop.

Teressa drew level with him. 'I honestly thought ye were going to kill me for a moment there,' she said.

'Maybe I would have if I hadn't recognised you,' Red said honestly. 'Stay close, Teressa. You're the only one who can pull me out of it again. Don't let me kill the King.'

'I won't,' she promised. 'Now let's find him.'

Caedmon wasn't hard to find. He had stayed by his tent, with his personal bodyguard, and so far nobody else had reached him. Shar lay outside the tent's entrance, scarcely breathing, and Caedmon knelt beside her, cradling her head in silence. Ereska stood nearby, watching the sky, but Caedmon himself looked as if he were completely unaware of anything but Shar.

When his bodyguards saw Red coming, they drew up in front of their master and readied their weapons. All of them were carrying nets.

Red stopped. 'Caedmon!' he shouted, ignoring the guards altogether. 'I ain't here to kill anyone. It's over. Surrender.'

Caedmon did not move.

'Surrender!' Red said again. 'Surrender an' it can be all over.'

Caedmon did not look up. 'Do it,' he said softly. 'Now.'

His guards attacked – but not with their weapons. As Red stood back, raising his sword to defend himself, they stepped in quickly and threw their nets. Red dodged them, and when one snarled itself around his leg he reached down and pulled it apart without any effort at all.

'Stop it, Caedmon!' he shouted. 'It's not gonna work!'

The guards closed in, pointing their spears at him.

Red stood firm, pushing Teressa behind him. He could feel the bloodlust rising inside him again. 'Caedmon!' he said. 'Stop this now. Call them off or I'll kill them all. An' then I'll kill you too.'

But Caedmon said nothing.

Red roared – a half scream, half bellow of pure rage and despair. He lunged forward, sword raised, and threw himself onto the spears pointed at him. One of them knocked his helmet off, and the others embedded themselves in his armour, but he didn't feel them at all. He grabbed the first guard around the throat with one hand and stabbed him to death with a quick thrust of his sword. Two others caught him by the arm, but he whirled around and struck them down.

Incredibly, the surviving guards did not run away. They attacked him from both sides simultaneously, ignoring Teressa altogether.

She moved back, knowing how suicidal it would be to try and intervene, and watched in grim silence as Red slaughtered every single one of them with a look of terrible joy on his face.

When the last one had fallen, he didn't hesitate. He advanced on the King, snarling, bloodstained sword ready in his hand.

Caedmon saw him coming and stumbled away, making no effort to try and protect himself.

'Red!' Teressa shouted. 'Stop! Don't kill him!'

But it was too late. Red couldn't hear her any more. All he saw in front of him was his enemy. Caedmon, who had had him locked up and humiliated. Caedmon, who had sold him into slavery in Amoran. Caedmon, who had invaded his home city and taken away everything he had ever cared about. Caedmon, who had sent him to his death.

Red's black eyes narrowed, and the ghastly excitement in him doubled. Now, at last, it was time. Now, he could finally have his revenge. He saw the fear on the face of his enemy, and savoured it. Now…

But then, as he stepped past Shar, a sharp and terrible pain shot through his leg.

He cried out and staggered sideways, but couldn't get away.

Shar's beak had closed around his ankle. 'You will…not…harm my human,' she gasped.

Red snarled and raised his sword to kill the wounded griffin, but her delay had been long enough.

'Red, stop! Don't!'

But it was not Teressa's voice.

Red turned, confused and distracted, and astonishment banished the hatred inside him.

'What—?' he began.

A small figure came running through the tents – small, weak, alone, but determined.

Caradoc.

The boy hesitated for just an instant, taking in the bodies and the dying form of Shar, before his gaze settled on Caedmon.

'Father!' he shouted, and ran towards him.

Teressa tried to stop him, but Caradoc was a boy trying to save his father that day, and desperation gave him a speed he would never normally have had. He avoided her without even looking at her, and ran at Red, shouting his name.

'Red, don't!' he said. 'You promised!'

Red wrenched his leg out of Shar's grip. 'Caradoc—,'

Caradoc ran to him, and grabbed hold of the big Southerner's sword-hand, trying to pull the weapon out of it. 'You said you wouldn't hurt him,' he said. 'You promised!'

The sound of the boy's voice dragged Red back to reality. He started, and threw the sword down. 'Caradoc,' he said. 'I…Caradoc, it's all right. It's fine.' He turned to look at Caedmon. 'It's fine…'

Caradoc smiled at him. 'Thank you,' he said.

Caedmon knelt, and reached out towards his son. 'Caradoc,' he said. 'Come here.'

Caradoc hurried towards him, but then hesitated. 'Ereska!'

The yellow griffin loped forward. 'I am here for you, my human.'

Caradoc ran into his father's arms, and Ereska stood by as the two of them embraced fiercely.

Red, keeping his distance, watched them and felt ashamed.

'I nearly…' he mumbled.

'But ye didn't,' said Teressa, coming to his side. 'Ye didn't.'

A faint thump came from behind them – but it was only Kraego. The giant griffin came to join his partner, bloodied but alive, and full of triumph.

'We have won,' he said. 'Shar is dead.'

They looked over at the red griffin, and saw that he was right. Her final effort to save her human had been the last thing she ever did in life.

'Surrender,' said Red. 'Do it now, Caedmon, before all your followers are dead.'

Caedmon looked up at him through bloodshot eyes. 'Yes,' he muttered, looking away with a shameful expression. 'It's over. I surrender. Tell them, Kraego.'

Kraego lifted his head to the sky. 'Shar's human surrenders!' he screamed. 'Stop now! It is over!'

Ereska joined him, screaming his message for all to hear.

Almost immediately, the Unpartnered stopped fighting. They flew back to New Eagleholm and stayed there, settling down to lick their wounds. The human fighters, seeing them leave, knew what it meant and lowered their weapons. It was over.

'Now.' Caedmon stood up and walked towards Red, leaving Caradoc under Ereska's protection. He faced the big Southerner for a moment, breathing hard through his nose, and then pulled his sickle from his belt and threw it down at his feet. 'You win, Captain,' he said bitterly. 'The war is over. I'll take my people back to Malvern, and if it's not too late I'll sign this peace treaty you've offered.'

'Agreed.' Red held out a hand. 'Peace.'

Caedmon linked fingers with him, tugged briefly and then let go. 'Peace.'

'Then it is agreed?' Kraego asked suddenly. 'The war is finished?'

'Yes,' said Red. 'It's over.'

Caedmon turned away, and went back to stand by his son. 'Thank you,' he said quietly. 'For sparing my life, and for protecting my son.'

'It wasn't easy,' said Red.

Caradoc smiled. 'But now everything's all right,' he said. 'Isn't it, Ereska?'

The yellow griffin moved slowly away from him. 'No,' she said. 'But it will be.'

She rose up without an instant's warning, raised her talons, and struck Caedmon down with a single, brutal blow.

Everyone froze.

'No!' Caradoc screamed.

Caedmon fell without a sound, crushed into the ground by the yellow griffin's talons. Ereska did not strike him again. She pulled her talons free and moved away, staring silently at Kraego. He stared back, motionless and silent.

Red ran to Caedmon's side, and together he and Caradoc lifted the King's shoulders up out of the mud and rested him on Red's arm.

Caedmon stirred and reached out to clutch at his son's hand. Ereska's talons had torn through his ribcage, and his breathing was weak and rasping.

'Caradoc,' he whispered.

Caradoc sobbed. 'No,' he said. 'No, this…don't, please don't!'

Caedmon's eyes closed. 'No,' he whispered. 'I…deserved it. Betrayal…wins…betrayal.'

He said nothing more after that, and though Teressa came over and tried to help tend to his wound, there was nothing any of them could do. He breathed on for a time, eyelids fluttering, his lips moving sometimes as he tried to speak. Blood trickled out of the side of his mouth, and he coughed weakly. It was the last sound he ever made.

'An Unpartnered did this,' Kraego said quietly. 'Shar's human surrendered as he died. That is what we all saw.'

Caradoc looked up at Ereska. 'How…how could you?' he screamed.

'I have done nothing,' said the yellow griffin. 'It was an Unpartnered that did this. That is what you will say, Caradoc.'

He stood up and came at her, trying to hit her. 'Murderer! Murderer!'

Ereska did not flinch. 'You and I will make an alliance with the South,' she said. 'I will protect you for all our lives, Caradoc.' She looked up at Kraego, griffin to griffin, and added softly, 'Long live the King.'

Chapter Thirteen

Peace

Red said nothing afterwards. The two armies which had fought each other for New Eagleholm quietly regrouped after the battle had ended, both sides too shocked to do anything but look after their wounded and gather up the dead. Hundreds had died, and hundreds more had been wounded. But it was over. All over.

The surviving generals gathered at Caedmon's tent, and a dull silence settled when they saw what waited for them. Shar lay dead, and not far away Captain Redguard sat, holding onto the King's body while his son huddled nearby in the arms of Teressa the priestess. Kraego, Orak and Ereska sat on their haunches behind the three humans, silently guarding them.

Red heard the accusing shouts from the Northerners when they saw the King dead, and he raised his head to answer them.

'He was killed by an Unpartnered,' he said. 'We found him dying.'

'Yes,' Teressa muttered. 'We came too late. He surrendered before he died.'

Caradoc said nothing at all. He looked too beaten for tears. But when his father's generals came for him, he stood up and went to them with surprising strength.

'The war's over,' he said softly. 'I'm going to sign the treaty with Captain Redguard. I'm…' He looked back at his father's body. 'I'm the King now, and that's what I want to do.'

'There will be no more war between North and South,' Ereska rumbled. 'Shar's mad plan has been ended. We will make our peace with the Eyries of the South, and then we will go home to Malvern.'

Red gently laid Caedmon's body down, and stood up. 'Ereska is right,' he said firmly. 'The King is dead. The war's over. Now it's time to make peace.' He gestured back at the city. 'I'll take my followers back into New Eagleholm, and you can rebuild your camp here. But all of you—,' he indicated Caedmon's generals, 'and the Prince can come back to the Eyrie. We'll give you anything you need in the way of medicine and food, while we organise the treaty. I left my best man writing it before I came out here.'

'What about my father?' Caradoc asked in a shaky voice. 'We can't leave him.'

'No, we can't,' said Red. 'He's got to go back to Malvern. That's what he wanted. We'll burn Shar, and her ashes can go with him. They'll want to rest together.'

Teressa bowed her head to Caradoc. 'I may have left the temple, but I'm still a priestess,' she said. 'I'll say the rites for him now if ye would like me to, Sire.'

Caradoc nodded. 'Say them,' he said. 'I want everyone to stay and listen.'

Not even the Southerners there had the heart to say no. They waited while a group of Caedmon's former followers went forward to lay the King's body out beside that of his partner, and then stood by, heads bowed, while Teressa recited the funeral rites.

'Night God,' she intoned. 'Ye have taken our great King Caedmon to be with ye, to walk the silver fields with every true Northerner who has gone before him. His blood has been offered up to ye, as he laid his life down in yer holy name.'

Lies, Red thought. All of it. Every damn word is a lie.

But he listened anyway, head bowed in respect. While he listened, a strange thought came to him.

Nobody ever said them for me, he realised. *I died, but nobody said the rites.*

He sighed, and waited while Teressa spoke on, asking the Night God to take special care of this man's soul because he had been a true and faithful Northerner all his life, and had earned his place beside her. The thought of that filled Red with despair.

He had seen a man who stood by the Night God's side. A true and faithful Northerner, no less. A great man, loved by his people. He had looked into that man's face, and had seen the face of a man whose very self had been torn out of him in pieces. That, he knew, was the only reward the Night God could give.

But he looked at the people around him, and saw the faith and hope on the faces of the Northerners, and on Teressa as well, and knew that he would never have the heart to say so. How could he take that hope away from them? He couldn't, and he wouldn't. It would be his secret. His, and Arenadd's.

*

Alone in the void, the Night God heard, and saw.

Beside her, Arenadd saw as well. 'You waited too long, master,' he said.

She turned sharply to him. *It is time*, she said. *Go now, Arenadd. Go to him. The Southerner must be destroyed.*

Arenadd's face did not betray a single hint of whatever was going on behind it. 'Yes, master,' he said quietly. 'I understand.'

He waited until she had opened the way for him and then slipped away, out of the darkness and into the light.

*

Red returned to the New Eagleholm Eyrie with Kraego and the others, including Teressa, Caradoc, and the generals whom the boy now commanded. There, the visitors were given temporary quarters, and Red and the others had time to take stock.

The Northerner army had had the greater numbers, but had suffered the heaviest losses thanks to the Unpartnered. The Southerners had suffered badly as well, but not as badly as Red had feared.

But there had been deaths.

Ranulf was dead, and so were several of the Last Guards. Talmon had survived, but his sword-arm had been badly broken and he would probably not be able to fight again. Liantha and Seerae were still alive and not badly wounded, but Lord Anfri the Northerner had been killed along with his partner, and his wife Lowri was so badly injured that she would probably join him soon enough.

Isleen and Alaric, though, had not taken part in the battle, and so they were fine. By the time Red and the others returned to the Eyrie, Alaric had finished drawing up the peace treaty with Isleen's help, and once everyone had taken some time to rest and have their wounds tended to, they were ready to sign it.

They didn't straight away though. First, Red wanted to go through it with Liantha and the others, and make sure that it was everything he needed it to be. And first, he wanted to speak to Kraego.

'You planned it, didn't you?' he asked the black griffin, once they were behind closed doors. 'You planned it all with Ereska.'

'No,' said Kraego. 'I won Ereska's allegiance, but we had agreed that she would help me to defeat Shar. I expected her to strike a blow from behind and weaken her, but she did not. As it was, I did not need the help.'

'I saw her look at you,' said Red. 'She told you she was going to kill Caedmon.'

'She did not,' said Kraego. 'I have no reason to lie to you. Ereska told me nothing. She wanted her human to become the master of the North, but Caedmon did not need to die for that to happen. If he had become unpartnered instead, he would still have been forced to stand aside. Ereska made her own decision.'

'Well she's stabbed herself in the foot,' Red muttered. 'Caradoc will never trust her again. He'll hate her from now on.'

'But he will have no choice,' said Kraego. 'The other humans will not follow a leader who allowed his partner to kill his father. They will think he had some part in it. For the sake of his power, he will be forced to stay silent.'

'It's hideous,' said Red. 'That poor kid. He's far too young to be King.'

'But now that he is,' said Kraego, 'the advantage is with us. Caradoc is too young to outsmart us, but his word is final. Ereska has agreed to our plan, and so has he. There will be nothing to stop this treaty from being made.'

'Yeah,' said Red. 'I s'pose.' He made for the door. 'I'd better go have a word with Liantha.'

*

He met up with Liantha and the rest of his surviving council in the Eyrie Council Chamber, as usual. Liantha and Seerae took the lead, both clearly anxious to reclaim their control over the city.

'I've inspected the treaty,' said Liantha. 'And it looks fine to me. A mutual agreement between Liranwee and Malvern that the North will not invade Liranwee and that, in return, Liranwee will see to it that no other Eyrie tries to invade through the Northgates. Alaric did well.'

'That's good,' said Red. 'Now since Isleen an' me are speaking on behalf of Liranwee, we'll be the ones to sign it.'

'Agreed, but who will lead Liranwee once the Northerners have left?' asked Isleen. 'I note that wasn't included in the treaty, as per your instructions. It only said "Liranwee's appointed leader—,"'

'Yeah,' said Red. 'Once this is done with, you an' I will go back to Liranwee and form a new Council there. Then that Council will choose a new Eyrie Master, same as always.'

'That seems fair,' said Isleen. 'And now you, Liantha, can instruct Alaric and myself on how to draw up a second treaty for New Eagleholm.'

'Yes,' said Liantha. 'But I have a better idea.'

'Yes?' said Red.

She paused. 'I suggest that we all return to Liranwee together, once our treaty is signed. From there, the boy can send out orders for all the Eyrie Masters and Mistresses in the South to come to the city. We can hold a great council of Eyrie rulers in Liranwee, and negotiate treaties with each one. But first the Liranwee treaty can be signed here, and the New Eagleholm treaty as well. We can lead by example.'

Red listened, and then nodded. 'Good. That's a great idea, Liantha. I'm all for it. What d'you all think?'

The rest of the council looked thoughtful, and murmured their own agreement.

'But for myself, I would suggest that we offer some more stringent terms than what has been put forward in this draft of the Liranwee treaty,' said Isleen. 'I wanted to discuss this with you first, Captain…but I would say that it would not be unreasonable, considering that the Northerners rejected all our attempts to negotiate and forced us to fight them here, to demand some kind of recompense for the damage they've caused. Tribute, perhaps, or favourable trade taxes, assuming we can agree on free trade between our Eyries?'

'I agree,' said Liantha. 'We could invade the North if we wanted, and they should not be allowed to forget that.'

'No,' said Red.

'Half the population of your city was slaughtered, Captain,' Liantha said coldly. 'I don't think some form of repayment would be unreasonable.'

'The Liranwee treaty stays the way it is,' said Red. 'We're not gonna ask them for anything except that they leave us alone. But we will open trading with the North. And—,' he glanced at Teressa. 'As for repopulating the city, I've had a think about that. We're gonna give permission for Northerners to live in Liranwee. As equals.'

The councillors all looked outraged.

'Absolutely not!' said Isleen. 'You're speaking madness, Captain. Do you honestly think that after what happened, our people will be happy with an arrangement of this sort? There would be civil unrest, probably rioting…'

'We'll deal with that,' said Red. 'With a good strong city guard.' He nodded to Talmon. 'It's gotta happen, Isleen. It's not just the leaders like us who have to learn to work together – ordinary people have to do it too. They can complain if they want, but if they break the law, they'll be punished for it.'

'He's right!' Teressa said loudly, cutting across the complaints. 'I can't go back to the North,' she said. 'And I don't want to either. There's nothing for me there. I'm going to live in Liranwee, and I won't live there as anyone's subordinate. I'm a griffiner, and I'll be equal to any of you, and I'm sure my friends here agree.'

The other Northerners nodded.

'We helped you win today,' one man said. 'All we want in return is a new home. If Lord Redguard here will let us live in Liranwee, then we will, and we'll work with you to restore the city to its former glory.'

'And I suggest you do the same in New Eagleholm,' said Red. 'I'll say the same to the other Eyrie Masters when we meet them. That's how we'll end it for good. Treaties don't last forever. But if you grew up with a family of Northerners next door, and your kids play with Northerner kids in the street, and maybe you're even married to a Northerner, you won't want to invade their homeland, will you?'

The council erupted. The Southerners pushed forward, shouting their objections, while the Northerners stepped back, gathering around Red and protesting loudly. The griffins started to snarl and hiss.

'Enough!' Seerae finally screeched. 'Stop this! You are in my Eyrie, and you will be silent and listen to me.'

The shouting died down.

'Thank you,' said Liantha. She looked to Red. 'That's enough for now. It's been a long day and we're all tired. If you're happy with your treaty, you can go ahead and sign it today if you choose. In the meantime, my friends and I will discuss the terms of our own and set Alaric and Isleen to writing it. As for your…little idea for Liranwee…we can discuss it there with the other Eyrie Masters who, let us not forget, have far more experience in governing than either of us. Let them give us their advice.'

'Right.' Red nodded. 'Meeting over. Let's go and rest, and we'll worry about it later, as you said. In the meantime, let's just be happy the fighting's over.'

The council broke up, many of them casting angry or suspicious looks at each other.

Once they had left, Teressa moved close to Red and touched him on the arm. 'Thank ye,' she said in an undertone. 'That was brave of ye, standing up to them like that.'

'I knew they wouldn't like it,' said Red. 'But it had to be said. They won't listen to me forever.'

'No, they won't,' said Teressa. 'I don't think they even listened today. I don't know if this will work, Red, I really don't.'

'Well, what's the alternative?' he asked. 'Like you said, you can't go back to Malvern.'

'I could, if Caradoc lets me,' said Teressa. 'But I don't want to. This is our country, isn't it? We fought for it together. It's not much to ask for my friends and I to live wherever we choose.'

'Yeah,' said Red. 'Exactly. But I dunno about Southerners living in the North. Maybe that'll have to be something for another time. But we've got Caradoc on our side, an' that's the main thing for now.'

*

Back in the Council Chamber, Liantha and her fellow New Eagleholm councillors had stayed. They were only a small council, but they were still the proper rulers of the city, and they gathered around their leader now and waited for her to speak. She had led them out of the ruins of Old Eagleholm, and brought them here to make a new life, and they trusted her absolutely.

'He's insane,' she said now. 'He's a brave man, but he's no politician. These wild ideas of his will get him into trouble sooner or later.'

'I agree,' said one of her friends. 'Noble principles don't win wars, or run governments.'

'Well, it's his city,' said another. 'If he wants to let Liranwee descend into anarchy, so be it. We've done our part, and we've won our city back, and that's what's important for now.'

'I won't have Northerners living here,' the Master of Building said flatly. 'I built this city, and I'll die before I see that happen.'

Liantha said nothing. She listened while the others spoke, taking in their opinions before giving her own.

'And so would I,' said the Master of Law. 'You can't trust them. Yes, we had some helping us here, but they're traitors. What does that tell you?'

'I say we let them go,' said the Master of Building. 'Let them live in Liranwee. They won't be welcome back here.'

'Once the city's back in our hands, I say we reinstate our law for Northerners,' said the Master of Law. 'We won't invade them, but they're not allowed on our lands. That sounds like a reasonable decision to me. What do you think, my Lady?'

Liantha finally broke her silence. 'I'll go to Liranwee,' she said. 'And join the discussion with the other Eyrie rulers. I'll see what they think before I make any firm decisions. But,' she added, 'I agree that the law will be reinstated. This is my city, and I won't allow Northerners to live in it. Even one can bring disaster. I think all of us know that by now.'

They all nodded grimly.

'Red is a fool if he thinks he can ignore the lessons of the past,' said Liantha. 'I won't let another Arenadd come to my city.'

'None of us will,' said the Master of Law. 'You can count on it.'

*

Despite the objections that had been raised, the peace treaty between Liranwee and Malvern was signed that evening. Red, Isleen and Caradoc all signed it, with the councils of both sides there as witnesses.

Afterwards Caradoc agreed that he and his followers would go to Liranwee, and summon the other Eyrie rulers for a great council to negotiate the other peace treaties.

'Including ours,' Liantha added. 'My council and I have decided that the New Eagleholm treaty should be discussed there as well, now that Liranwee is neutral ground.'

A week later, once the dead had been burned or buried, they set out. Red, Caradoc and Teressa, all allies now, led their followers northward as one, back towards Liranwee. Liantha and Seerae came, bringing New Eagleholm's Master of Law but leaving the rest of their council behind to govern the city in their absence.

Word went ahead of them, out to the other cities, with orders from Caradoc – now acting King until he could return to Malvern to be crowned – for the Northerners to stand down and return control of the cities to their rightful leaders. He and Red sent a mutual message, inviting every Eyrie Master or Mistress in the South to come to Liranwee, and explaining why. It was unlikely that any of them would refuse.

As for Red, he travelled slowly, with Kraego, keeping pace with the armies' slow march. The Northern army carried King Caedmon's remains with them, along with Shar's ashes. When they reached Liranwee, Caedmon would go on ahead, back home to Malvern, where he would wait for his son to come and witness his funeral.

Red hardly dared to believe that it was over. The fighting was done now. The South was free. Now, all he had left to do was negotiate – but that should be simple enough. The Eyrie rulers would be so glad to have their power back, and so sick of war, that they would be more than ready to make peace treaties with the North. Perhaps if Caedmon were still alive they would have refused on principle to negotiate with him, but he was gone now. In a way, Ereska had done them all a favour.

Soon, Red told himself, soon it would be over for good. And once he had helped Isleen to make a new council and appoint a new Eyrie Master for Liranwee…once that was all done, and he was absolutely certain that Liranwee was safe, and Northerners were allowed to start living in it, then he would be ready to leave. He would stay for as long as he had to, and then go.

He wouldn't make a big fuss about it. He might not even leave a note. He would just slip away in the middle of the night, and see to it that he were never found. It shouldn't be too hard. In time, he would be forgotten.

Soon, he thought. Soon.

*

They reached Liranwee some months later, and found it in a state of confusion. The Northerners still occupying the Eyrie came out to meet their new leader, and informed him that the other Eyrie rulers had already begun to arrive.

'Good,' Caradoc said shortly. 'Now my father has to go back to Malvern, but I'm going to stay here until all the treaties have been signed. This is Captain Redguard, and he's the ruler of Liranwee now, so do what he says.'

Red listened with silent amazement mixed with admiration. The boy was already growing into his new role. He looked pale and exhausted, but his gaze and voice were steady. Now, for the first time, he reminded Red of Caedmon.

'Yes, Sire,' one of the senior griffiners said immediately.

'And I want you to send a message to Malvern,' Caradoc added. 'Tell my brother Morgan to come back. He should be here too.'

'Yes, Sire. He's been sending messages here, asking for permission to come.'

'Well he's got permission now,' said Caradoc. 'Tell him.'

'Yes, Sire.'

'I hope you don't mind,' Caradoc added solemnly to Red. 'I know you don't like Morgan.'

'No,' said Red. 'But it's not my choice. Anyway, he's a smart man, Morgan is. I think you did the right thing asking him to come back.'

Caradoc did not smile. 'He can help us,' was all he said.

Chapter Fourteen

The Night God's Punishment

The Liranwee Peace Council, as it was later called, took place a few weeks after Red and Caradoc's arrival in Liranwee. Out in the streets of the city people celebrated the end of the occupation of their home – but in a slightly subdued manner, since there were still plenty of Northerners around.

Up in the Eyrie, Red waited with Teressa and Caradoc to receive the visitors, and to his relief, they all came.

Lady Nelia, the young Eyrie Mistress of Canran, came with her partner Lessk. The oddly-named Lord Ekra, Eyrie Master of Wylam came not long after the Lords Brennin and Larkin, twins who jointly ruled Sunton with their shared partner, Yark. Penrin, the ageing Eyrie Master of Withypool, had been executed for refusing to rule his city in Caedmon's name, so his replacement Lord Fraser came instead. He had been chosen by Withypool's council, so there was no objection from them that he continue to lead them.

With Liantha they made six, and some time after this, to everybody's astonishment, they were joined by a seventh – none other than Lady Merca, Eyrie Mistress of Monag.

'I heard as there was a council-meet for Eyrie rulers happening here in Liranwee,' the old woman said by way of explanation. 'And seeing as nobody thought to be inviting me, I invited myself. Monag might be small, but we're a part of Cymria, yes?'

'Of course, and you're welcome to join us,' Liantha said smoothly.

Merca joined the group, grumbling to herself but apparently satisfied. 'We'll be wanting to be making deals with ya, Liantha,' she said. 'Trade deals. We got not much but sheep, but sheep are what ya need, yes? Yes? Very useful things, sheep.'

'They are,' said Liantha. 'And we owe you for your help. My council and I will be happy to make arrangements once this is finished.'

'Good, good,' Merca nodded happily. 'We'll see it through, so we shall. Now let's get to business, yes?'

'Good idea,' said Red, trying not to laugh at the looks on the other Eyrie rulers' faces.

With Merca's arrival there didn't seem to be any reason to delay further, so the great council went ahead that afternoon, in Liranwee's Council Chamber.

As Liranwee's temporary leaders, Red and Kraego took up the Eyrie Master's platform, with Isleen nearby as an advisor. But nobody else was allowed to attend other than the seven Eyrie rulers, who demanded the opportunity to talk the matter over amongst themselves before they started speaking to Caradoc's own councillors.

As the host, Red was allowed to speak first.

'The war's over,' he said. 'You've seen that already, and been told so, but I'll say it again now, just so you've heard it direct from me. We defeated the King's men at New Eagleholm, an' the King is dead. Now we're negotiating with Prince Caradoc, and he's agreed to sign the peace treaties we come up with here in Liranwee over the next few days, as long as we come up with reasonable terms. We'll discuss the basics of them right now, and then tomorrow and the day after that we'll meet with our Masters of Law, and with Malvern's council, to work out the details. But today is when we all agree to go ahead with it.'

'Peace treaties are the best solution now,' said Lord Fraser. He eyed all of them in turn. 'I think we've all had enough of war, on both sides. Peace is what we all need.'

Lady Nelia nodded, but the others were stone-faced.

'I saw my city overrun,' said Lord Ekra. 'I was put in chains and humiliated, and ordered to hand my Eyrie over to my enemies. There'll be no peace from me.'

'I agree with Ekra,' said Lord Brannon. 'As far as I'm concerned, this isn't a council of peace – it's a council of war. My brother and I won't be signing anything.'

'No,' said Lord Larkin. 'You make your treaty with Malvern, Lord Redguard, but we'll have nothing to do with it.'

'I see not much sense in it,' said Merca. 'The Northerners are enemies to us and have been for all time. I say ya got much persuading to do, Lord Redguard.'

'And – exactly!' said Lord Ekra. 'Why are we even speaking to you, Kearney? We all know what you are.'

'We've heard rumours,' Brannon said cautiously.

'They're true,' said Liantha. 'He's the Shadow That Walks. But he's on our side. He led us to victory.'

'Our side!' Ekra exclaimed. 'The Shadow That Walks? By Gryphus, young lady, are you insane?'

'No,' said Liantha. 'If it weren't for Lord Redguard, we would still be under the thumb of the Northerners. He saved my city and my life.'

'All right,' Red cut in. 'Thanks, Liantha. Yeah, it's true. I'm the Shadow That Walks. Not gonna lie about that. But I'm on your side, like Liantha says, and I'm not here to make war. It's time to put a stop to war. I know you've had it hard. We all have.' He held up a big, scarred hand. 'Which one of us here hasn't seen our home city in ruins? Which one of us hasn't had our freedom taken away? None of us. We've all seen it, an' we've all lost people we loved. But it was Caedmon who did that, and now he's dead. And if you all want to make sure it doesn't happen again, then you'll let go of all this and make peace with his son.'

'He's right,' said Lord Fraser.

Ekra scowled. 'Fine,' he said. 'Wylam will accept a promise from Malvern to never invade us again.'

'And you'll agree not to invade them,' Red added.

'I'll promise no such thing,' said Ekra. 'I don't owe them anything. It's them who owe me.'

'We'll do likewise,' said Brannon.

'They will leave us alone because if they do not, we will band together and destroy them,' said the fat Lessk. 'That is the agreement we will make.'

'You are right, Lessk,' said Kraego. 'And I suggest that you should make agreements not with Malvern, but with us – that if Ereska, or whatever griffin comes after her decides to invade, then every Eyrie ruler in the South will come together as one. Together, we will invade Malvern and destroy it. That will be our warning to them.'

'Yes,' said Ekra. 'That should be enough to keep the Northerners at bay.'

The others nodded and murmured their agreement – even Fraser and Nelia.

'No!' Red said sharply. 'No. We're not going to keep the peace with threats. What we need…' he hesitated. 'I have a plan for Liranwee. I'm going to let Northerners live here, and we'll be opening trade routes with the North as well. When I form the new Liranwee council, I'll be seeing to it that Northerners are on it — about half if I can manage it.'

Howls of outrage rose from the others.

'If you do that, then you can forget any help from us,' said Lord Ekra. 'As far as I'm concerned, anything you do that allows Northerners to live in our lands will make you a traitor to your race.'

'If you put Northerners on your council, that will be tantamount to an act of war,' said Lord Fraser.

'But—,' Red began, but they weren't listening any more.

'I think you should leave, Red,' said Liantha. 'Isleen can stay and represent you, but this has gone far enough.'

Red stared at her in shock. 'Liantha—!'

'That's enough,' she said sharply. 'Go on, Red. We have important things to decide here. You've led us to victory, but you're not an Eyrie Master. We'll make our agreements not to make war with Malvern again — there's no need to worry about that.'

'You cannot send us away,' Kraego snorted. 'I refuse to go.'

'Leave, brother,' Seerae hissed at him. 'You are not an Eyrie ruler.'

'He is not!' said Lessk. 'Leave, black griffin. You have no place here.'

The other griffins there started to snarl and show their talons, warning Kraego away.

Humiliated, the black griffin stepped down off the platform. 'Come, Red,' he said.

Red, though, hadn't looked away from Liantha. 'How could you do this?' he asked her in an undertone. 'I thought we were friends.'

'We are, Red,' she said. 'But you're disrupting the discussion and causing problems. This is no place for disagreement — we have to reach a decision quickly, before we're betrayed. Now go on. Isleen can give you a full report later.'

Red had no choice. He turned away and followed Kraego out — but as he left he looked back in time to see Liantha take his place on the platform.

*

In spite of everything he tried later, that marked the end of Red's involvement in the negotiations. The Eyrie rulers refused himself and Kraego entry to the meetings that followed, and Isleen took his place. She reported to him, as promised, and made it sound like everything was going smoothly, but Red didn't believe her.

'I've been brushed aside,' he told Teressa. 'An' that's all there is to it. If I'd kept my mouth shut about letting Northerners in, then maybe…'

'No,' said Teressa. 'It had to be said, and now was the only good time to say it. Ye did yer best, Red.'

Red slumped into a chair. 'It's unbelievable,' he said. 'If it weren't for me, we'd have lost the war. It would've been over months ago. I won this for them, an' this is how they repay me.'

'I wouldn't have expected them to do anything else,' said Teressa. 'Ye can't forget what they've been through, or what they were beforehand. But it doesn't matter. It really doesn't.'

'Yes it does,' said Red. 'I've failed. I wanted to bring the North and the South together, but…'

'But ye have,' said Teressa. She sat down next to him. 'Listen,' she said. 'It's going to be all right. The other Eyries will make peace with Caradoc and then go home. We'll stay here and take care of Liranwee – they don't care about that. Ye can form a new council, as planned, and do it just the way ye wanted to. Since ye signed on behalf of Liranwee, ye are its leader now. They'll elect ye Eyrie Master here for certain. And then ye can rule Liranwee however ye choose. Let Northerners live here – everything.'

'Well, maybe…,' Red mumbled.

'Lead by example,' said Teressa. 'Show the other Eyries how it can be done. A lot of things sound like madness until ye try them.'

Red started to feel better. 'Yeah,' he said. 'Maybe I was reachin' out too far. We could start with Liranwee, couldn't we?'

'We could,' Teressa agreed. 'Stand by and see what happens, but it'll be all right. Sometimes ye just have to have faith.'

*

The discussions went on for several more days after this, and by the end Teressa had been proven right. The Eyrie Masters made their agreements with Caradoc's council, and along with Alaric and Isleen, the Masters of Law drew up the treaties for each city. Red was allowed to read them, and he finally relaxed when he saw that they were all more or less the same. All of them made a mutual agreement to keep the peace, an agreement which, as each treaty said "will bind myself and all my successors until my city has fallen or until the gods strike down all of Cymria".

'That part was my idea,' Alaric said proudly.

The treaties were all signed on the same day, in the Liranwee Council Chamber, witnessed by hundreds of people who had crammed into the galleries to watch, and by all the griffiners who could fit into the space below around the Eyrie Master's platform. Once two copies of each had been signed, Red came forward to clasp hands with Caradoc.

'Sire,' he said, bowing his head briefly. 'As leader of Liranwee, I'll see to it that these treaties are kept. I may be a griffiner now, but underneath that I'm a guard, and that's what I'll be. I will guard the North. Anyone who attacks you will have to come through me.'

There was murmuring from the crowd, but when Caradoc smiled and thanked him they cheered along with most of the griffiners.

Afterwards, though, when Red had left the Council Chamber, Liantha confronted him.

'I hope you know what you just did,' she said.

Red frowned at her, shocked by the look of controlled anger on her face. 'I made a promise, Liantha,' he said. 'An' when I make a promise I keep it.'

'You've betrayed us,' she said flatly. 'You just made it completely clear whose side you're on – you're on theirs. I thought I knew you, Red.'

'I want to make sure that there's no more war,' said Red, not hiding his surprise. 'If I'm here to guard the North, that'll do it.'

'Against your own people,' said Liantha. 'You didn't say anything about protecting the South, did you?'

'Didn't have to,' said Red. 'I already protected it at New Eagleholm, didn't I?'

'No,' Liantha said quietly. 'You didn't. You only fought because you like killing. I've seen it on you. We all have.' She turned away. 'Goodbye, Red. Don't ever speak to me again.'

'I was just trying to do what was right!' Red called after her. 'Liantha, for gods' sakes—,'

But Liantha didn't turn around. She walked off after Seerae, head low. That same day she left for New Eagleholm, and Red never saw her again.

*

But the Great Peace Council had achieved its purpose, at least. The other Eyrie rulers left over the next day or so, with polite goodbyes to Red, and promises that they would be in contact again to discuss trade agreements and other matters.

'We're all allies,' Lord Fraser assured him. 'Things may have changed, but Withypool and Liranwee are sister cities, and you can rely on us to help.'

Not long after this, Caradoc left as well.

'I've got to go back to Malvern,' he said. 'I'll meet Morgan there and he can help me. I have to be crowned, so I can start ruling.'

Morgan had not come to Liranwee, in spite of the messages sent ordering him to do so. Red had been secretly glad about that.

'You're a good man, Caradoc,' he said seriously. 'I mean it. I know bad things happened to you in the South, but I hope you believe me when I say I think of you as my friend.'

'I do,' said Caradoc. 'You saved the South, and you tried to save my dad. It's not your fault what happened.'

'No.' Red reached out a hand. 'Keep in touch, Sire. And I want you to remember…' He hesitated. 'In a while you might hear something about me, and you might think you won't see me again. But if you ever need my help again, send me a message. When you need me, I'll come.'

Caradoc listened seriously. 'I'll remember,' he said. 'If you need me, I'll help you too.'

He gave Red a griffiner's handshake, and then turned away to Ereska. Now heavily pregnant, the yellow griffin lay down to let her human get onto her back.

'Goodbye, Kraego,' she said once she had stood up. 'It was good to be with you. I will raise your young well, and be proud of them.'

'Go,' said Kraego. 'Rule your lands, Ereska. You have done well.'

Ereska took off with the other griffins from the North, including the Unpartnered, who still acknowledged Kraego but wanted to go home. They formed themselves into a huge flock and flew away towards the Northgates, leaving Ereska to follow.

Red watched the yellow griffin go, with her partner perched on her back. Caradoc looked so small, but he would be all right.

'He'll be a fine King,' Red murmured. 'And a friend to the South. We'll do everything we can do make it happen.'

'Yes,' Kraego said impassively. 'But now it is our time, Red. We have fought for the South, and now it is time for us to take our place. Liranwee is ours.'

'Yeah,' said Red. 'I guess it is.'

*

Things were quiet after that in Liranwee, but not easy. But Teressa's prediction had been right, at least. In spite of the threats they had heard, Red and his friends were allowed to change things in the city as they chose, and none of the other Eyries tried to intervene.

Together, Red and Isleen formed a new council for the city. Red was on it, along with Teressa and three of her griffiner friends. Two young griffiners from Monag were appointed as well, along with three griffiners from Withypool who had decided to stay, and a local Liranwee woman who had been recently chosen by a member of the Unpartnered.

At their first meeting they discussed who would be their leader, and Eyrie Master, and the moment the question came up, everyone there turned to look at Red.

'It has to be ye,' said Teressa.

'It does, so it does,' said one of the Monag griffiners.

'You know this city better than anyone else here,' said Isleen, who had been asked to take up the role of advisor to the council. 'But more importantly, you're the natural leader here, Captain. That's why we need you to rule Liranwee now.'

Red had known this would happen, and he didn't like it. Slipping away would be much harder when he had a city to rule.

But he knew he had no other choice. If Liranwee was going to become what he wanted it to be, then he would have to be its leader. For now, at least. He thought that to reassure himself.

I'll lead them for now, he thought. *For as long as I have to.*

'I accept,' he said.

'As do I,' said Kraego. 'My human and I will be the masters of this city, and will lead this council for the rest of our lives.'

'But we'll be needing new griffiners,' Red added. 'Most of ours died in the war, or lost their partners. There's not so many griffins left here in the city either, but that'll get better. We'll sort it all out.'

'We will,' Teressa smiled. 'Together.' She bowed low. 'Eyrie Master Kearney Redguard.'

The other councillors bowed with her, and murmured as well.

'Eyrie Master.'

'Lord Redguard.'

Red smiled sadly. 'All right,' he said. 'Let's get to work.'

*

Not long after Red's ascension in Liranwee, Caradoc's coronation took place in Malvern.

Caedmon and Shar had been laid to rest in the vaults under the Eyrie, and now, with the mourning period over, it was time for a new King to take his place.

The ceremony was held in Malvern's great Moon Temple – the same one where Teressa had nearly lost her life.

As the new King's adopted brother, Morgan had a place of honour by Caradoc's side, and he stayed there in silence through the ceremony, while the new High Priestess led her fellows in prayers and songs to the Night God.

Morgan had always liked the Temple, and he looked around it now during the ceremony, resisting the temptation to shuffle awkwardly on the spot in his cumbersome ceremonial outfit.

The Temple's interior had been made to look like a forest at night, with pillars in place of trees, placed at random rather than in rows. They had been covered in tiny tiles that resembled bark, with curling silver "branches" on their sides holding blue-glass lanterns that gave the whole space a dim light, resembling night, even during the day. A mosaic of leaves, rivers and pools covered the floor, and there was no furniture anywhere to disrupt the illusion.

At the far end of the Temple, under the dome which was painted black with silver stars, a miniature stone circle had been erected. Each stone was carved with elaborate spiralling patterns, and had been arranged around the bloodstained altar where a statue of the Night God kept watch over the spot where prayers were said and sacrifices made.

Now Caradoc stood in front of the altar and bowed his head to the statue, praying silently while the High Priestess walked around him, reciting the ritual blessings over him, and asking the Night God to guide him and help him to be a great ruler.

The final words of the blessing, though, were said to Caradoc himself who stayed where he was, his head still bowed, as she said the same words to him as had been said to his father, and to the very first King of the North – Arenadd himself.

'May you be judge and warlord, master and protector; may you care for your people above all else; may you live long and shield us from misfortune.'

As she said the words, she placed Caedmon's crown on his son's head.

'Rise now,' she said. 'King Caradoc Arenadd Taranisäii the First of Malvern, ruler of the Kingdom of Tara.'

Caradoc rose and faced his people. He wore a black robe now, made especially for him, and the crown rested on his head. It was too big for him, but he would grow into it.

The crowd that filled the Temple cheered, and shouted his name.

'Caradoc! King Caradoc! Caradoc son of Caedmon!'

'Caradoc,' Morgan murmured. 'My King.'

After the shouts had died down the witnesses went quiet, waiting for Caradoc to speak.

'I'm King now,' the boy said quietly, while Ereksa left her spot over near the stone circle and came to join him. 'I know I'm only young, but I'll do my best to lead you. And I'll keep you safe. There won't be any more wars, not while I'm alive. I promise.'

It wasn't much of a speech, but the people cheered anyway.

'I will keep us strong!' Ereska added. 'And our land will be great under my rule.'

The other griffins who had come screeched her name, and she accepted it smugly.

Beside Morgan, Echo stirred. 'Ereska,' he said quietly, but with respect.

Morgan said nothing, and stayed politely out of the way, but afterwards, when the assembly had broken up, Caradoc came to talk to him.

'Did I do all right?' he asked, looking slightly embarrassed.

'You did fine,' Morgan smiled.

Caradoc smiled back. 'You're going to be my Master of Wisdom,' he said. 'Like you were for my dad. You know a lot more than I do.'

Morgan had already known about it, but he bowed anyway. 'Thank you, Sire,' he said.

'You don't have to call me that,' said Caradoc. He frowned. 'You should go back to Lady Arwydd now. I heard she was sick.'

'She is,' said Morgan. 'Thank you, Caradoc. I'll see you later.'

He left the Temple, with Echo beside him.

'We have done well,' said the spotted griffin. 'We may have failed Shar, but we have not lost our position of power here in Malvern.'

'We failed him,' said Morgan. 'I failed him. We should never have…' He trailed off. What could he have done? If he had brought Red to his King in chains, as he had been commanded to, then maybe they could have put a stop to him. But now it seemed that Red had been the one to make a treaty with Malvern on behalf of his city – one that didn't demand anything at all except peace. Another man might not have done that, and maybe would have led an invasion of the North instead.

Morgan didn't know any more. He felt he had lost sight of what was the right thing to do a long time ago. Anyway, it didn't matter any more. The war was over, and he'd played his part in it, however much he'd failed at what he had tried to do. It was still more than most men ever accomplished.

He flew back to the Eyrie with Echo, feeling pensive, and walked into the quarters he now shared with Arwydd. He had left her there, asleep in their bed. She had become ill recently and had begun spending most of her time there.

But now it was deserted.

Morgan turned around. 'Where is she?'

Echo sniffed the air. 'Someone else has been here. Other humans.'

Morgan thought quickly, wondering where she might have gone, but before he could reach a conclusion, a man came hurrying in.

'My lord,' he said, bowing hastily.

'What is it?' asked Morgan. 'Did you come from Arwydd?'

'Yes, my lord,' said the man. 'Your wife has been taken to the infirmary. She's gone into labour.'

Morgan started, and swore under his breath. It was far too early in Arwydd's pregnancy for her to deliver the child now.

'Take me there,' he said sharply. 'Now.'

He ran off through the Eyrie, following his guide, who took him straight to the set of rooms where griffiners went when they were seriously ill or wounded. Several of the beds in the main room were already occupied, mostly by men or women who had been wounded in the war and still needed time to recover.

Arwydd was in the bed at the very end, being attended to by a pair of healers while her partner Essh stood by looking agitated.

The moment Morgan laid eyes on Arwydd, it was obvious that she was in labour just as the man had said. She lay on her back, groaning softly while her lower body heaved. Her face had gone ghastly with sweat.

'How is she?' Morgan asked the moment one of the healers looked over at him.

She straightened up and came over. 'She's gone into early labour. We've been trying to stop it, but without any luck so far…'

'Is there anything I can do?'

'Stay nearby,' the woman suggested. 'She'll need your support.'

Morgan nodded, and went to Arwydd's side. 'Arwydd, it's me,' he said. 'It's all right, I'm here.'

She clutched at his hand. 'How was it?' she gasped, her body stilling. 'The…?'

'It was good,' said Morgan. 'Caradoc did well – you would have been proud of him.'

Arwydd smiled. 'Good,' she said. 'Good…' But she bit off anything else she wanted to say next, and her grip tightened on his hand as another contraction took hold of her.

Morgan hastily moved away, and let the healers come in. One of them coaxed her into drinking some medicine or other, and the other rubbed her belly and the pathetically small bulge there.

Morgan stepped back, towards Echo, and felt sick to his stomach.

'What is wrong with your mate?' the spotted griffin asked.

'The baby's coming too soon,' said Morgan. 'I…but she'll be all right. They'll find some medicine to stop it.'

Over on the bed, Arwydd screamed a weak, hopeless scream.

Morgan couldn't bear to watch. 'I'll wait outside,' he muttered, and left.

Outside in the corridor, he sat down with his back to the wall and tried to stay calm. Surely, he thought, after everything else, it couldn't come to this as well.

Morgan had never been one for praying, but he bowed his head now and whispered to the Night God.

'Please,' he said. 'I know what I did was wrong, but punish me for it. Don't punish her. Don't punish my child. Let them live. Please. Take me instead. Take me.'

There was no reply, of course.

Morgan felt as if he should say something else, but the words evaded him, so he stayed where he was instead, and waited in silence.

Time passed. He thought of going back to see what was happening, but didn't. He would only be in the way, and there was nothing he could do. After a while, two more healers arrived and went hurrying into the infirmary.

Morgan nearly followed them, but he felt paralysed. He stood where he was, mind frozen, until the healer who had spoken to him before came out.

'My Lord,' she said. 'You should come in now.'

'What is it?' asked Morgan. 'Is she…?'

'I'm sorry,' said the woman. 'We did our best, but the child…your son did not survive.'

'My wife?' Morgan asked sharply.

'She's lost a lot of blood,' said the healer. 'But she's awake. She needs you now.'

Numbly, Morgan went into the infirmary. He knew he should be thinking of Arwydd now, but the only thought that could seem to make itself heard in his head was not for her, but for the Night God.

It's the Night God's punishment, he thought, with awful certainty. She did this to us, to punish us for what we did.

In the infirmary, Arwydd lay very still in her bed. The sheets under her were sodden with blood.

Morgan went straight to her, and took her hand in both of his. 'Arwydd.'

Her face had gone as white as the pillow beneath it, and her eyes looked glazed. 'Morgan,' she whispered.

Morgan leaned down and kissed her on the forehead. 'It's all right,' he lied. 'It's all right now, Arwydd.'

'Morgan,' she whispered again. 'Listen…I have to…tell you…'

'What?' Morgan knelt, and rested his head by hers. 'What is it?'

'I love you,' she said. 'I do.'

'And I love you,' Morgan said softly.

'Morgan,' Arwydd breathed. 'Listen…'

'I'm listening.'

She whispered the words so quietly that he barely heard them, but he knew what they were, and he whispered them to himself later, just to tell himself that they were real.

'Serve the Shadow That Walks…'

Chapter Fifteen

Life

Several long months later, Red and Kraego stood together at the top of the Liranwee Eyrie, and looked down at their city.

The place had changed a lot since their arrival, and a lot since that time, years ago as it felt now, when Red had been nothing but a city guard patrolling the streets.

Of course, nobody called him "Red" any more. Nowadays even Teressa had taken to calling him Kearney, and others called him "Lord Redguard". Other people in the South probably called him "traitor" or worse, but he didn't care.

It had worked. It had all worked. Everything he had wanted to do in Liranwee had come true.

He had negotiated with King Caradoc, through letters at first, but later directly through their two Masters of Diplomacy, and had made several agreements which had benefitted the two cities. They had opened up trade through the Northgate Mountains, and Red had now passed a law that Northerners were allowed to come and settle in Liranwee as free citizens if they chose, and be treated equally under the law. Not many had taken up the offer yet, but some had, and more would follow. It wouldn't be long before all of Cymria knew what Liranwee was like. The only city in the South that had Northerners serving on its council – the only city where people of both races were allowed to live, and where the law did not favour either one. A city whose ruler was a Southerner with the power of the Shadow That Walked, partnered to a black griffin, whose closest advisor was a Northerner.

A city that Red knew he would have to leave, and soon.

He didn't want to leave it. He might be a dead man now, but Liranwee was still his home. He had grown up here, and he had wanted to grow old and die here as well. But now he knew he never would. He was immortal now; he would never age, and never die. And he couldn't live among ordinary people. Not forever.

He looked out at the roofs of the houses below, not really seeing them. There had been a council meeting earlier today. During it, while his new Master of Law was talking about something or other, his mind had wandered and he had started to look around at her and the other councillors, and imagining how they would look in fifty years' time. Even after that long he would look just the same as he did now, and they would be old and frail. Some of them would already be dead. Their grandchildren would be the same age as he would be for eternity.

He would have to watch all of them die, including Teressa.

And Kraego.

Red glanced over at his partner now. Kraego stood tall, his paws planted firmly on the stonework beneath them. He had grown over the last few months, and now looked even bigger than he had on that day when they had been reunited as adults. Kraego had the power in him too, but he was alive, and he would age too. Red would have to watch him grow old and die as well.

If he waited that long, he knew that eventually his people would start to turn away from him. For now he was a hero – the Saviour of the South, some people called him. But sooner or later that would all be forgotten. When he was surrounded by the grandchildren and great-grandchildren of the people he ruled now, they might not think of him as a hero. To them he would be an old man who looked young. They might even be afraid of him.

Red wondered if he was being cowardly to think that – assuming the worst just to make it easier for him to leave. But he knew it went deeper than that. It didn't matter so much what other people thought.

He was a monster. He knew he was. He had saved the South, but he was still the Shadow That Walked, and he had not been made to rule, but to kill. In peacetime there was no killing to be done, and that meant that he had no purpose.

There hadn't been any more visions. The Night God had left him alone – for now. But the impulses had stayed. The urge to kill still stirred and rose up in him whenever he thought there might be danger of any kind, and he felt a sickening frustration inside him every day that he didn't satisfy that urge. He felt like a drunk surrounded by wine he wasn't allowed to have, unable to ignore the voice inside, screaming at him to give into his impulses, to find something, anything, to satisfy the demand inside himself.

Red knew he couldn't lie to himself. Sooner or later he was going to lose control. He might be able to ignore it for a long time – maybe even years. But in the end it would escape, and when it did he didn't want to think about what might happen.

No. He had to leave, and tonight was the night he would do it.

He had kept to his original plan – he wouldn't tell anyone, not even Kraego, that he was leaving. But he had decided that he would leave a note for Teressa. She deserved to know the truth, and besides, there were things…

'Kearney?'

Her voice brought him out of his thoughts, and he turned. 'Yeah?'

Teressa came up through the opening that led to the Eyrie's interior, and came over to join him. 'I thought I'd find ye here,' she said. 'Watching the sunset again.'

Red shrugged. 'I like it. How's it going?'

'All right,' said Teressa. She came to his side and looked out over the city as he had been doing. 'It's beautiful,' she said. 'Our city. Who would have thought it?'

'Not me,' said Red. 'Not in a hundred years.' He looked at it properly now, with a critical eye, taking in the layout. 'Have you an' the others picked a spot yet?'

'We were thinking over there,' said Teressa, pointing. 'On the other side of the Eyrie from the Sun Temple. We'll have to take out some houses to make room for it, but Luderick says there's a patch of them over there that are in a bad way and need to be demolished anyway. We can rehouse people over near the South End.'

Red nodded. Their new Master of Building might have the eccentric speech patterns of his home territory of Monag, but he had the instincts of a city planner. 'Sounds like you've got it sorted,' he said.

'It'll make trouble in the city,' Teressa warned.

'Yeah, well, they'll just have to cope,' said Red. 'If we're gonna have Northerners living here, then we'll need a Moon Temple for them. It's no different from putting you and the others on the Council – better now than later.'

Teressa nodded. 'Aye. For now they're so glad to be free they'll do anything ye say. Later on it might not be so easy. By the way, what did King Caradoc say in his last letter?'

'It's sounding good,' said Red. 'Seems things are settling down in the North. Caradoc mentioned that Morgan's been helping him – he's Malvern's Master of Wisdom now. He probably wrote the letter we got from Malvern himself, actually.'

'Morgan!' Teressa said in disgust. 'I'll never forgive him for what he did to ye. I wish I'd had the chance to kill him.'

'I swore I'd do it myself,' said Red. 'But it doesn't matter. It's in the past now. Caradoc needs him. Oh yeah…I nearly forgot – Kraego?'

The black griffin stirred and looked enquiringly at him.

'The last letter mentioned Ereska too,' said Red. 'Says she had you chicks. Three of 'em. Caradoc says they'll probably grow to be giants like you.' He paused. 'But none of them are black like you.'

'That is good,' Kraego huffed. 'It is good to father many strong chicks, and I am glad to know that Ereska's are large and healthy.'

'Yeah.' Red looked wistfully down at his big hands. 'There's no future with no kids.'

Silence fell for a while, and though nobody spoke, Red caught Teressa looking sadly at him. He had seen her do that more than once recently, and had pretended not to notice, and she had kept quiet about it. But he guessed that she knew as well as he did what it meant.

Neither of them had said anything about what had happened in New Eagleholm, but Red hadn't forgotten it, and he knew Teressa hadn't either. She still loved him, even if she wouldn't say so again, and though she was hiding it he knew it was making her miserable. He wished he could shake her out of it – grab her by the shoulders and tell her she was being stupid. Holding out for a dead man would never bring her anything but unhappiness.

But it didn't matter. Once he had gone she would come to her senses eventually.

'Alaric and Isleen are getting married,' he remarked, not meaning to be tactless.

Teressa's face turned stony. 'Oh.'

Red silently cursed himself. 'Yeah, in the Sun Temple, of course. They've asked me to come, but I'll be unavailable. They don't want me wheezing and groaning all the way through the ceremony.'

'They want me to be the High Priestess in the new Moon Temple once it's built,' said Teressa, cutting him off. 'I've said no, but I've agreed to train some of the girls in the city. We'll have to build a new priesthood for Liranwee.'

'You'd make a great priestess,' said Red. 'But you're right; we need you here in the Eyrie. Honestly, I'd rather we built a temple to Arenadd if we built one to anyone.'

'We talked about it,' said Teressa. 'The other shadow-worshippers and I. But we agreed to leave it alone and keep on doing our worshipping in private. Maybe one day that will change, but not now. It's too soon.'

'Yeah…' Red muttered. 'Maybe.'

The sunset had ended by now, and the stars had started to come out. Soon, the moon would rise.

For some reason the thought of that bothered Red, and he turned away. 'I gotta go,' he said. 'I've got things to do.'

*

Teressa watched him go without saying anything, but she frowned to herself as Kraego walked past her to follow him.

It wasn't that he had said anything, but she had felt as if there had been something there in the way he had glanced up at the stars before he left – something sad in his face, and something final in the way he had turned away from them.

She stood still for a moment, wondering, but then shook herself out of it. Of course he was sad. This was the city where he had been alive, and she knew he must miss it.

She didn't even want to let herself hope that he was sad because of her. He had already told her how he felt about that, and he hadn't said or done anything to show that he had changed his mind. And besides, he was right. She couldn't lie to herself about that again.

But her heart ached as she stood there alone, she could still sense Red's presence beside her, where he had been just a moment before.

She knew that she loved him; she knew it with every fibre of her body, and all of her soul. She had loved him ever since that day in Amoran, when they had left on the ship together and he had stood up for her against the other Southerners who didn't want to trust her. He had given her his own trust, and he had never taken it away. He had saved her life, and he had stuck by her through thick and thin. She had begun following him because he was the Shadow That Walked, but she stayed with him now because he was Red.

Kearney. Captain Redguard. Her friend. And even though he was a Southerner, and a dead man, she had never known another man she wanted more than she wanted him, or who she had believed was more worthy of her love.

But she couldn't. She knew that now. They could never be together, and she had accepted that. The best she could hope for was to stay with him now, and help him to rule the city that had become her new home. But she had promised herself that she would never give up on him. If she couldn't be with him, then she would never be with anyone.

Teressa squared her shoulders and walked down into the Eyrie after him, promising herself that she would stay strong. She would grow old by Red's side, and maybe she would find some satisfaction from that.

She went to bed that night after saying her prayers to Arenadd, and felt sad contentment at the thought.

And then, the next morning, Red was gone.

*

The council breakfasted together, and Red didn't join them, but they were used to that. He rarely ate any more. Afterwards they went to the Council Chamber to begin their daily meeting, expecting to find him there waiting for them, as he usually was.

But he wasn't there.

They took up their usual places and waited.

Eventually, just as Teressa was starting to wonder if she should say something, Kraego came in. She relaxed at the sight of him, but then she saw that he was alone.

'Kraego,' Orak called. 'Where is your human?'

The black griffin paused in the doorway. 'Orak,' he said. 'Come to me, and bring your human with you.'

Orak obeyed, and Teressa hurried after him.

'What's wrong?' she asked Kraego. 'Where's Kearney?'

'You must come with me, Orak,' Kraego said brusquely. 'And you must bring your human. We will need her.'

Teressa looked back at the Council. 'I'll come back soon,' she told them. 'Wait here.'

Kraego had already left, with Orak following, and she followed them as quickly as she could.

'What's the matter, Kraego?' she asked as they went. 'Did something happen?'

'You must come to my nest,' was all Kraego said. 'I have found something which you must do for me, Teressa.'

Frowning and confused, Teressa followed him up the ramps to the very top of the tower, and into the Eyrie Master's quarters which Red now occupied by himself.

The room had been left more or less as it was when they had taken the Eyrie back from Caedmon's forces, but Red had removed some of the fancier decorations, leaving his new home comfortable but plain. He had left some of the tapestries on the walls, though, and added a few new ones. They helped keep the place warm, along with the thick fur rugs on the floor.

When Teressa and the two griffins entered, the room was empty.

'Here,' Kraego said immediately, padding over to the bed. 'It is here.'

Teressa followed him, and saw the roll of paper lying on the blankets. The bed itself had clearly not been slept in.

'It is a message from my human,' Kraego told her as she picked it up. 'I can smell it. You must read it for me.'

Sure enough, the paper had been sealed with wax stamped with the symbol of Liranwee's Eyrie from the ring Red had been given on the day of his official naming as Eyrie Master of the city. The ring itself lay on the blankets nearby, and Teressa's stomach twisted when she saw it.

Moving quickly, she unrolled the note.

'It's for me,' she said.

'Read it,' Kraego commanded. 'Now.'

'Teressa,' she read aloud. 'I've left Liranwee, and I'm going to leave Cymria, and I'm never coming back. I know you'll say I'm selfish for doing this, but I've done it for your own protection, and for the safety of my city. I wish I could be the man I used to be, but I'm not. I'm still the Shadow That Walks, and nothing can change that. I'm dangerous, and I don't want you or anyone else to suffer for it.

'If you're still loyal to me, Teressa, then do this one last thing for me: don't come looking for me. Stay here and look after Liranwee. I've named you temporary Eyrie Mistress in my absence, and it will be up to you to help the council choose a permanent replacement.

But if they care about my opinion any more, then tell them that I recommend you.

'Tell Kraego not to look for me either. I know he won't listen, but tell him anyway. He can't change my mind, but if he wants to follow me to whatever corner of the world I end up in, he can.

'I wish I didn't have to leave, but I know I do. Liranwee doesn't need me any more, and it's better if I disappear the way Arenadd did.

'You're the best woman I ever met. Be happy for me.

'Kearney Redguard.'

Teressa let the note crumple in her hands. 'Oh gods.'

Kraego had already turned away. 'I will find him. I will bring him back.'

Numbly, Teressa reached down and picked up the seal ring. 'He's been planning this,' she said. 'He must have been planning it for months.'

Orak moved closer to her. 'Liranwee is ours,' he said quietly.

Kraego hissed at him. 'No!' he said. 'Liranwee is mine. I will have my human back, and keep my power.'

Orak immediately backed down. 'Yes,' he said. 'My human and I will protect your territory until he has been found.'

Teressa clutched onto the note. 'We'll find him, Kraego,' she said. 'I won't rest until he's back here where he belongs.'

'I will go now,' said Kraego. 'And search for him myself. Orak, you will stay here. If I have not returned before the Day Eye is at its highest, you will leave to search as well.'

'I will,' Orak promised.

Kraego didn't waste any more time with talk. He pushed past them into his nest and beyond it to the balcony, where he took off and disappeared.

'Come,' Orak said to Teressa. 'We must go and tell the council what has happened.'

She nodded. 'Yes. But we'll have to tell them to keep this quiet for now. We don't want anyone to worry – Kearney might be back by tonight.'

But she didn't really believe that. Impulsively, she reached into her gown and brought out her prayer stone, which she carried with her every day since the end of the war. While Orak waited impatiently by the door, she cut herself and made her offering of blood, and then knelt, hands clasped around the stone.

'Arenadd,' she prayed, for once ignoring the usual opening prayer. 'Help us. Bring him back to Liranwee. We need him. I need him. Help us, Arenadd.'

*

Help us, Arenadd.

The words echoed through into the void, but they weren't heard by the Night God.

A portal opened up in the nothingness, and for an instant, light came to the place where she lived. It vanished almost at once, and there, where it had been, Arenadd appeared just in time to hear the faint whispers of Teressa's prayer.

He didn't react to them, but stepped forward to meet his master.

You were gone a long time, the Night God whispered.

Arenadd bowed briefly. 'I was enjoying the sunlight,' he said. 'But I'm back now.'

And do you have his answer? she asked.

Arenadd paused. 'He said yes. I've brought it with me.'

Then that is good, said the Night God. *You have done well. Go, Arenadd, and go at once. The Southerner has left Liranwee, and now he is alone. Go to him now. Kill him.*

Arenadd hesitated. Incredibly, he hesitated. Even now, when he had just heard the words he had hoped to hear for so long – even now, when his plan was so close to success at last, he faltered.

'Master,' he said cautiously. 'I…'

Speak.

'I don't understand,' said Arenadd. 'The war's over. The North is safe. And now – look at what he's accomplished. A temple to you, in the South! A Southerner city where Northerners are allowed to live free. He's changed things. And after he's gone, they'll go on changing. I know why you wanted to stop him before, when he was fighting our people, but why now? Why do you want to kill him now?'

He must die, the Night God said coldly. *Now, more than ever. Before now he was an enemy to my people. But now, he is an enemy to me, and to Gryphus as well. That is why you have succeeded in persuading him. He and I are enemies, but in some things, we are united.*

Arenadd stared at her. 'What are you talking about? How can this be a bad thing? If this works out, it could mean an end to it all. No more war between North and South. Surely…'

No, she said. *There must be war. There must always be war, forever, or until victory comes.*

'Victory?' said Arenadd. 'What victory? The Southerners won. That was a victory, wasn't it?'

That was not the victory that must come, said the Night God. *It is not what I wanted, or what Gryphus wanted.* Her expression did not change. *There will be war until one race, and one god, is master of the world. That is how it must be.*

Finally, the look of weary cynicism that Arenadd had worn for so long gave way to an expression of utter bewilderment and horror. 'What?' he said. 'What are you – that's insane! You can't honestly expect that to—,'

You think that I am human, she said, interrupting him. *And you judge me as if I were. But I am not human. I am a god.*

'And you want what your people want, I know,' said Arenadd. 'But this can't possibly be what they want.'

The Night God smiled pityingly at him. *You know nothing*, she said.

'Then tell me,' he said.

You will not be glad if I do, she warned.

'I haven't been glad about anything in a very long time,' said Arenadd. He shook his head slowly, and looked away from her. 'Nothing can horrify me any more, master. It really can't.'

Then listen, she said softly.

Then she told him the truth at last. All of it. And as Arenadd listened, a look of disbelief showed on his face. Slowly, it gave way to revulsion, and then despair.

'No,' he said. 'No. That can't be true. You're lying.'

Why should I lie about this? she asked. *I have told you the truth, Arenadd. You do not want to believe it, but you must. You have seen the proof of it time and time again, and you will go on seeing it for eternity.*

Arenadd looked up into her face, and knew in his heart that she was right. He had seen the proof of it again and again, just as she had said.

'But that's not how it has to be,' he said. 'Things can change. He didn't do that, did he? And his friends, they…and Kullervo…' He trailed off lamely.

There will always be some who go against it, said the Night God. *But in the end, they will always fall away. In the end, only we will remain, and we will be the truth, now and forever.*

Arenadd's expression did not change, but something died behind his eyes. 'Kill me,' he said flatly. 'Kill me, master.'

No.

Without any warning, he hurled himself at her – and for the first time in the long years he had been with her, he tried to attack her. 'Kill me!' he roared.

She threw him down without effort. *You cannot touch me, Arenadd,* she said, completely unmoved. *You cannot deny me. And nor should you try and blame me. I am not a human, to be judged as a human would be. I am only the face of the true nature of humanity, and that is something you can never destroy.*

Arenadd looked up at her in silence for a while, and then stood up. 'I'll go now,' he said quietly. 'I'll come back once I've killed him.'

Good, she said. *Go. I will wait for you.*

Arenadd felt no joy, or excitement as the mortal world opened up to him again. He barely felt even the faintest twinge of fear over what he was about to do. The Night God's words stayed in his mind, and followed him away from her, and he knew that no matter what happened they would never leave him.

I am nothing, he thought dully, and slipped away into the light, carrying death with him as his only companion.

*

Far away from Liranwee, Red walked alone through the trees. Dawn had come by now, and he had stopped running some time ago. He had used the cover of darkness to make his escape from the city, using the shadows most of the way, and now he was far enough away to feel confident that he would not be spotted from above. If he was, he would have plenty of time to slip back into the shadows.

His heart felt heavy, even though it would never beat again. Even now, when he had finally gone ahead with his plan, he couldn't stop wondering if he had done the right thing. He had spent so much time planning it, and considering the alternatives, that he had thought he was completely certain – but if he was, why did leaving make him feel so guilty? And why was it that all he could think of was Liranwee, and Kraego, and Teressa, and everyone else he had left behind?

The first rays of the sun shone through the trees and touched his face, and when he should have been thinking about where he should go, he thought about Liranwee's Sun Temple instead. Alaric and Isleen would be married there in a few days, and he had promised them that he would at least wait outside, if he didn't feel strong enough to go in. He had gone to that temple when he was alive, to pray to Gryphus, and he had hoped to be married there one day as well…

Red tried to push that thought away. He needed to plan his journey now. So far he had thought more about leaving and when and how to do it than he had devoted to deciding exactly where to go. Out of the country, definitely. Maybe the Night God wouldn't be able to reach him there. He could go to Amoran, maybe, or beyond it to the far corners of the world – Erebus, Yu Tai, Rakos, Eire – there were so many countries out there where he could go into hiding, places where he could be safe, far away from people. He could become a hunter, maybe; build a little home in the wilderness…

But before that, there was one thing he wanted to do first.

When he had returned to Cymria from Amoran all those months ago, Teressa and Orak had left him. Teressa had said she was going to Malvern to gather followers, so he had given her permission to go. But she had done something else while she was there, something she hadn't told him about until much later, in a fit of guilt.

Red knew many Northerners had gone in search of the body of Arenadd Taranisäii in the years since his disappearance. None of them had ever found it. But Teressa had. Kullervo had told her before he died, and she had gone to the cave where it lay. There, she had said, she saw it regenerate – go from bones back to a fully-formed, breathing body. But a body with no-one in it.

Red had never forgotten that strange story, and he decided now that before he left Cymria he would go North and see it for himself. If he didn't, he would always wonder.

With that in mind he changed his direction slightly and started to head northward, towards the Northgate Mountains. Any other Southerner would be unable to get through them to the North, but he would slip through without any trouble. If he was running away, at least he had the power to do it without being easily found.

He walked on steadily as the day drew on, wondering if they had realised that he was gone yet, and if Teressa had found his note. He hoped she would do as he had asked and let him go. She would be upset, but surely she would see that he had done the right thing. If not, then at least he could rely on her to look after Liranwee. She would be all right, and hopefully she would become Eyrie Mistress. She could…

As Red walked on uphill, through a stand of old spice-trees, the back of his neck started to prickle, and a strange unease twinged in him.

He slowed down slightly, uncertain, yet with a feeling that something wasn't right. He sniffed the air, but couldn't catch anything out of the ordinary. Still, the strange feeling grew and he stopped and looked around.

He couldn't see anything, but still he couldn't shake the feeling of being watched.

'Who's there?' he called.

There was no reply, but his certainty only grew.

'I know you're there,' he said. 'I can feel it. Where are you?'

Here, a voice whispered.

Instantly Red turned towards it, drawing his sword and pointing it. The voice had come from a shadow by a rock, and he took a step towards it.

'Come out and show yerself,' he growled. 'I'm warning you.'

I'm petrified, the voice said sarcastically, and then the shadow moved. It slid over the ground, away from the rock, and moved silently upward, forming the vague shape of a man.

Red froze. 'Who are you?' he asked. 'What are you?'

An evil spirit, said the voice. It was faint, but easy enough to understand, and as he listened his eyes widened.

'I know that voice,' he said. 'But…'

But what? the shadow asked. *Put the sword away, Captain. This is no way to greet an old friend.*

'Arenadd!' said Red — half relieved and half afraid. He put his sword back in his belt, and moved towards the shadow. He almost expected the shape in front of him to disappear, but it stayed just where it was, and as he got closer he could feel the chill coming off it.

That's me, said the shadow. *Hello. Where are you off to, may I ask?*

'Far away,' said Red. 'What are you doing here? How did you get here? Why are you…like that?'

I'm here because my master sent me, said Arenadd. *And I'm like this because I don't have a body any more. But what are you doing here, my lad? Running away? That's not very heroic.*

Red paused for an instant, and then decided to take this in his stride. Why not? He'd spoken to Arenadd before, after all. 'I had to leave,' he said. 'I'm the Shadow That Walks. I can't live with ordinary people. You couldn't. That's what Kullervo told me. The dead weren't meant to stay with the living.'

Arenadd shrugged. *Could be. What would I know? I might be dead and immortal, but under that I'm still just the bootmaker's son from Idun village. Now…*

'Why are you here?' asked Red.

I'm afraid my master sent me here to kill you, said Arenadd.

Red pulled back slightly, but then let himself relax. 'Fine,' he said. 'Do it.'

Arenadd's form became denser, and details appeared on it. His face became visible, then his robe, outlined in shades of grey so dark they were nearly black. *Just like that?* he said. *I thought you'd at least try and put up a fight.*

'I would've once, but what's the point?' said Red. 'I can't fight a shadow. Anyway, it's better like this. I'm leaving because I can't die.' His shoulders sagged. 'I don't want to be alone forever. I'd rather die now, so kill me.'

If you insist, said Arenadd. He smiled slyly. *You'll never guess where I've been, and who I've been speaking to.*

'Oh yeah?' said Red. 'Who?'

My master is desperate, said Arenadd. *You don't know how desperate. So desperate that she sent me to speak to Gryphus himself.*

'Gryphus?' Red repeated in disbelief.

The same. The day god. My master sent me to him to ask for his help, and he gave me…this.

Arenadd reached into his robe as he spoke, and light blazed into the clearing where they stood. Pure, white, perfect light.

Red took a step back, squinting against it. It was such a clear white that it should have been cold, but it wasn't. It was warm, and the smell it gave off…

'It smells like blood,' he said, bewildered.

No surprise, said Arenadd. The light shone through his black fingers, and when Red looked closer he saw what it was. A heart. A heart made of light, pulsating softly in Arenadd's grasp.

'What is it?' he asked, awestruck despite the sick feeling in his stomach.

Life, said Arenadd. *Pure life. Gryphus' power. The power that makes a baby grow, and flowers open. The power that drives all of nature. My master brings death, but this is what Gryphus brings. It was what you had in you once. I had it too, once upon a time. Every living thing does.*

'It's so beautiful,' Red breathed, taking a step closer – but as he did, and the light shone on his face, pain suddenly shot through him. It stabbed unbearably at his heart and he cried out and shied away.

To anyone else, this would be a gift, said Arenadd. *But as you've just found out, it's deadly to you. That's because you don't have a soul. He moved forward, gliding silently over the ground. All I have to do is put this into you, and you'll die. It'll cancel out the dark power in you, and you'll be destroyed.*

Red could feel the pain growing in him as the light came closer, but he didn't move. 'Then do it,' he gasped. 'Kill me.'

And, for a moment, it looked as if Arenadd would. He kept on coming, with a horrible smile on his face – the same smile Red himself had worn when he killed.

But then he stopped, and suddenly put the life force away – tucking it into his spectral robe as if it were a bag of money.

Oh, now, he said. *Where are my manners? I almost forgot.*

Red stayed still. 'What is it?' he said. 'What's wrong? Why—?'

Arenadd reached into the other side of his robe. *I've brought something else, he said. A little gift from me to you. Have you ever wondered*, he asked unexpectedly, keeping his hand in his robe, *why the Night God couldn't control you the way she controlled me?*

'Because I wouldn't let her,' said Red.

Because she didn't have your soul, said Arenadd. She's got mine. She keeps it with her and uses it as a… he hesitated. She hurts me with it. But she hasn't got your soul. It slipped out of her fingers on the day you died.

'It went to Gryphus?' said Red, hope rising in him.

No, said Arenadd. I'm afraid not. I'm afraid your soul did fall into the wrong hands after all. Mine.

He brought his hand out of his robe, and now it was holding something else. A tiny, glimmering light sat on his palm like a star. And the moment Red saw it he felt it calling to him – whispering his name.

He lurched towards it, reaching out. 'Give it to me! Give it back!'

No. Arenadd laughed and tucked the light back into his robe. *Not yet.* He laughed again – a cold, harsh, crazed laugh. *I've been keeping it all this time, Captain. I came for it when you died, but I didn't send it on. I hid it, and I've kept it out of her hands ever since.*

'Thank you,' said Red. 'Thank you. But…' He reached out desperately, not daring to touch the black spectre in front of him. 'Please. Give it to me.'

Very well, said Arenadd. He smiled. *But I want something from you in return, Red. Something that's mine by rights. You took it, and I want it back. And now, you're going to give it up.*

With that he reached into his robe and brought out the blazing heart, and the tiny glimmering thing that was Red's soul. With one quick movement, he brought them together, and thrust them into Red's chest.

His icy cold hands passed straight through Red's body, flesh and bone. For an instant the chill bit into him – but then the heat of the heart burst inside him like a flower opening, and the pain began.

Red screamed and convulsed, and then fell to his knees, tearing at himself while the heat rushed through his body, unbearable, sickening. It burnt at him, radiating into his limbs and up into his mind, banishing the cold. Light shone behind his eyes, blinding him for a second time, and he could hear himself screaming as if he were being burnt alive.

But then the pain started to die down, and he stayed there, shaking violently.

His sight returned and he looked up, and saw Arenadd – drifting rapidly around his head like a black cloud, and snarling at him.

Come on, come on, give it up! Give it to me!

Red opened his mouth to ask what he was talking about – and then he felt himself convulse. The scar on his throat rippled, and he started to cough and retch. Icy coldness moved up through his chest, pushed away ahead of the warmth that had started to fill him, and then, as he convulsed again, something black and cruel and misty poured out of his mouth and into the air. He watched through wide-open eyes, and the instant it was out of him he stumbled away but he saw what happened next. He couldn't look away.

The dark spirit that was Arenadd reached out with a sigh of ecstasy, and absorbed the power of the Shadow That Walked. It soaked into him, and his form darkened and became denser – almost solid.

Yes! he roared. And then when he said it again his voice lost the soft whispering edge it had had before, and became real – audible to mortal ears. 'Yes! Hahahahah! YES!'

Red didn't hear anything more. Weakness seized him, and he slumped to the ground, thinking that now it was over. He was dead.

Thud.

His entire body jerked.

Thud.

It came again.

Thud.

Red gasped and groaned.

Thud.

They came at short intervals at first, jolting through him, but as he curled up on the ground they came faster, and faster, and then settled down into a steady rhythm.

His heart was beating.

Red breathed in slowly, and let himself relax and feel it. The steady thumping from his chest, which had been cold and silent for so long. It was real. It was back.

He sat up, feeling himself. His skin was warm, and pulsated slightly with each heartbeat. The coldness was gone.

'I'm alive,' he said quietly. Then, louder. 'I'm alive!'

'Yes,' Arenadd hissed.

Red stood up, feeling the difference in his limbs – the faint tremble where there had once been unnatural stillness. But even though the power had left him, he could still see Arenadd.

The dead Northerner stood nearby, still misty around the edges, but far bolder than he had been before, his eyes two holes in his face. And, when he spoke, he sounded like an ordinary man – his voice cool and aristocratic, with a rounded Eagleholm accent not much different from Liantha's.

'You're alive, Captain,' he said. 'Alive and well, and due to stay that way for a good long while, I would think. I knew that soul would come in handy one day.'

Red could only stare at him. 'You planned this,' he said. 'Didn't you? You planned it right from the start. You kept my soul so you could give it back one day.'

'I hoped,' said Arenadd. 'Now go.' He pointed. 'Go home, Lord

Redguard. Rule. Make little Redguards. The war is over, and the Shadow That Walks isn't needed any more, and hopefully never will be again.'

Red didn't move. 'What are you going to do?' he asked.

Arenadd paused. 'I'm leaving,' he said. 'I'm taking my body back, and I'm going to go somewhere far away, where my master will never find me. My debt to the Redguards has been repaid, and there's nothing more for me to do here. Goodbye.'

He vanished.

Chapter Sixteen

A Knife in the Back

Red had meant to go straight back to Liranwee, but in the end he didn't. Not because he didn't want to, but because he got tired. Now that he had lost his power he couldn't travel tirelessly any more – and he hadn't even realised just how far he had gone before Arenadd stopped him. He was amazed by how quickly he got tired and hungry, and lost his sense of direction. Now, for the first time in months, he started to wonder how long it had been since he slept or ate. It hadn't mattered before, but now it did.

Today, though, the mundane nagging problems of hunger and tiredness made him happy. He was alive!

'I'm alive!' he laughed. He had said it several times already, just because it felt so good to say it. He was alive, and the war was over, and Arenadd was…Arenadd had gone. Red wondered where to, and whether he had been telling the truth, but for now it didn't matter. For now, all he cared about was himself. He was alive, and he could go home at last, and live.

He hummed to himself as he walked, not caring about the ache in his limbs, or the grumbling of his stomach. He would get there eventually, or someone would find him. In the meantime, he might be lucky enough to find some food.

He walked on unhurriedly, until eventually he came across a place where the trees thinned out and farmland appeared. He must have wandered into Withypool lands, or maybe this was somewhere on the outskirts of Liranwee's own lands. He wasn't sure.

He pressed on through the fields, cheerfully taking in the lush greenness of the newly growing wheat, until he found the small farming town at the centre of them, among a grove of apple trees. People were around, all peacefully getting on with the business of the day, and as he walked in among them he marvelled at how different it all was. Nobody started or looked nervous at the sight of him, nobody looked uneasy. They barely even spared him a glance. To them, he was just another man walking by.

He found a small inn by the town square and went inside.

'I'll have a beer,' he told the owner, and sat down by the cold fireplace to wait for it.

There were a few other people around – other Southerners, drinking and talking amongst themselves in the plain, low-ceilinged main room of the inn.

After a few moments the innkeeper brought Red his beer, putting it down on the table beside him.

'I'll have some food, too,' said Red, fumbling for his money bag. 'Whatever you've got. An' also…'

'Yes?' said the man.

'This might be an odd question,' said Red. 'But what colour are my eyes?'

The innkeeper gave him a funny look. 'They're brown,' he said, and walked off.

Red settled down to drink his beer, and sighed contentedly as it went down his throat. It was cheap and not very well made, but just then it could have been the finest Cymrian juice wine. When his food arrived – rough bread with cold sliced sausage – it tasted like the most delicious thing he had ever eaten in his life. He chewed each mouthful slowly, savouring it, and already thinking of all the things he would do when he got home.

He ordered another beer once he'd finished the first, and idly listened to the conversation around him.

'Unbelievable,' one man was saying. 'They've really done it?'

'Yeah, that's what I heard,' said his friend. 'I dunno what Eyrie Master Redguard's gonna do about it, but it won't be pretty.'

'What's that?' Red called over to him.

'Eh?' said the man.

'Is something up?' said Red. 'Sounded like you were talkin' about something major.'

'Oh yeah,' said the man. 'Hadn't you heard? It's all over the place. Lord Ekra's marching.'

Red started. 'What? Marching where?'

'Here,' said the man. 'The whole Wylam army's coming, an' they're saying Sunton's coming too.'

Red's heart slammed straight down into his stomach. 'They're coming to Liranwee?'

'Yeah, but they're not attacking us,' said the man. 'They're on their way to the Northgates. Sounds like they're breaking that treaty thing already.'

'Oh gods,' said Red. 'When did you hear that?'

'Just today,' said the man. He sipped reflectively at his beer. 'Shouldn't be much trouble, so long as Lord Redguard lets 'em through. Otherwise, things'll get ugly. That's what I think.'

'Gryphus' talons, I hope it doesn't come to that,' said his friend. 'I don't want to see another war, especially not with other Southerners.'

'Yeah, well, if that happens, Lord Redguard'll only have himself to blame,' the first man opined. 'Standing in Lord Ekra's way'd be suicide.'

'Let's hope he's got the sense, then,' said the other. 'What d'you reckon, carrot top?'

But Red had already run out of the room.

*

Outside, he confronted the first person he came across – a woman carrying a basket of vegetables.

'Where am I?' he shouted in her face.

She took a step back. 'Er, this is Erindale,' she said.

'I don't care what the place is called. I mean where is this?' Red snapped back. 'How far is it to Liranwee?'

The woman pointed. 'The road out of town goes there,' she said. 'It's about a three day trip if you've got a cart – probably longer on foot.'

'Damn it!' Red chewed on his knuckles while the woman beat a hasty retreat. Three days? At least? How could he have gone that far in one night, even using the shadows? More importantly, what was he going to do now? By the time he floundered his way back to the city, it might already be too late. And besides, he already knew that Liranwee wasn't strong enough to take on Wylam's entire army – especially if what he had heard was true, and Sunton was coming as well.

He stood there for a long moment, half frantic, trying to think. What was he going to do? Liranwee couldn't fight Wylam, or Sunton, or both of them together, and he didn't want it to come to that either. But he couldn't stand by and do nothing while they invaded the North.

He swore furiously under his breath.

'Those bastards. I knew they were up to something. Oh yeah, just cut old Red out while you make your secret little deals with each other behind the scenes.'

He found himself thinking back to that awful day in New Eagleholm, when he had lain helpless, his eyes burnt out and his mind half broken. But Teressa had brought Isleen to him, and made her tell him the truth about his father, and his uncle. He remembered what she had said about the infamous Branton Redguard. Bran the Betrayer, who had survived Cymrian justice, but been so disgusted by the ways of griffiners that he had chosen to disappear somewhere rather than live in an Eyrie any more.

Red's lip curled. Just then, he found himself feel the same anger and contempt that his uncle must have felt. Noble griffiners, making their plots and stabbing each other in the back, and deliberately excluding him from their dealings the moment they realised that he wasn't going to play their game.

'My gods,' he muttered to himself.

Slowly, he turned around – away from Liranwee, and looked up at the Northgate Mountains. They weren't that far away – his rapid journey the night before had brought him into the hilly country that came before them. If he went that way now, he might be able to make it in a day or so. From here, he had no idea how close Wylam's forces might be. If news of them had reached here already, they must be close. They might be within striking distance already. There was no time.

Quickly, impulsively, Red made a plan. It was an insane one, but for all he knew, it was too late to do anything else.

There was no point in going to Liranwee now. He would never get there in time, and by now they must already know about what was happening.

Moving fast, Red went to the nearest shop and bought a packet of dried food and a water bottle. He stuffed it into the small shoulder-bag he had brought.

Then, taking a deep breath first to steady himself, he turned north once again and set out for the mountains as fast as he could go.

*

Even though he had lost the endless stamina that came from being the Shadow That Walked, anger and determination gave Red the edge he needed, and he made fast progress. Not needing or wanting to hide any more, he used the road rather than sticking to the cover of the trees, deliberately walking in plain sight right in the middle so a friendly griffin flying over would be able to spot him.

He wished that Kraego was there, but knew the chances of the dark griffin coming by now were slim. And anyway, Red had no right to regret the fact that he wasn't there – after all, he'd abandoned him on purpose.

He strode on through the day, and quickly settled into a steady pace – the same one he had used back in Liranwee when he was a guard patrolling, which was just fast enough to carry him on at a reasonable rate, but not fast enough to tire him out.

Red quickly went back to marvelling at how differently he felt now. His legs ached, the sun burnt the back of his neck, and he felt the occasional impulse to stop and rest. He could feel his bag strap chafing his shoulder, and his boots rubbing his heels. All of it was so ordinary, but while he was dead, it had all left him. So many nagging little things had just vanished, and now they were back – not annoying at all now, but serving as constant, wonderful reminders.

He was alive.

If only he wasn't on his way to confront an army all by himself.

Red heaved a sigh, and wondered if this was it. One last day as an ordinary man, before he laid down his life a second time. It was all so ridiculous, in a way. The first time he'd died, he'd done it not for the South, but for Lady Ahamay. The Erebian spy who had used him as a tool in her plan for revenge on the Amorani Emperor. And now he might die a second time, for Northerners.

I'd rather die for the South, he thought – but a moment later he shook his head and half smiled. That was nonsense as well. He didn't want to die for anyone.

But if he had to, he would.

The mountains came closer, and as Red walked on towards them he guessed he would make it to them soon; possibly even that night if he pushed himself. He found himself looking ahead nervously, half expecting to see the Wylam army already. There was nothing. But then a screech came from overhead – a griffin's screech.

Red froze in panic, and then ran instinctively to the edge of the road, looking up. For an instant he imagined that he would see the thing he dreaded more than anything else: a great black cloud of riderless griffins, descending on him with their talons spread ready to kill, just as they had done in Canran, and in Liranwee, when the South fell.

But it wasn't the Unpartnered, of course. A solitary griffin circled over him, low enough for him to see that it wasn't Kraego. It was too small, and from here its feathers looked brown. It screeched again, and then came in to land.

Red kept back and let it come, his heart beating – beating! – faster with hope. It had to be a Liranwee griffin. He was saved.

But when the griffin landed, fear stabbed at him.

It wasn't a Liranwee griffin. It was another griffin, one he recognised all too well. The only griffin he had ever seen whose furred hindquarters were spotted. A griffin with a Northerner on his back, who had been the last thing Red saw in New Eagleholm, before the branding iron blinded him.

'You,' he snarled as the man jumped down and hurried towards him. 'What are you doing in my lands?'

Morgan was plainly dressed, and still walked with a limp, but he looked relieved. 'Lord Redguard!' he said. 'Thank the Night God.'

Red folded his arms. 'What do you want? Why are you here?'

'We were looking for you,' said Morgan. 'Everyone is.'

'Were you in Liranwee?' asked Red, forgetting his anger for the moment.

'We were going there,' said Morgan. 'But…'

'We have seen your partner,' said Echo, coming forward to join his human. 'He was searching for you, and he challenged us. He told us that you had disappeared, and we offered to help him find you.'

'Where is he?' asked Red.

'The last time we saw him, he was flying northwards,' said Morgan. 'Red…my Lord, please listen…'

Red sighed. 'Make it quick, I've got bigger things than you to worry about.'

Morgan looked troubled. 'I…I know you won't ever forgive me for what I did, and you shouldn't. I won't try and say that what happened in Eagleholm was an accident, because you won't believe me. You shouldn't do that either. But it doesn't matter now. I was coming to Liranwee to see you. I want to…make amends.'

Red laughed in his face. 'Oh yeah? You reckon you can get me to forget about what you did to me, do you?'

'No,' said Morgan. His shoulders sagged, and he looked at the ground. 'My wife is dead,' he said in a low voice. 'Arwydd is dead. She died along with our child. I know I'll never have a family now.'

Red frowned. 'I'm sorry for that, Morgan.'

'Don't be,' said Morgan. 'I don't deserve your sympathy. But I know why it happened.' He looked up. 'The Night God was angry with me,' he said. 'For fighting against you. Arwydd pleaded with me to see sense, back in Eagleholm. That's why I tried to let you go. You're the Shadow That Walks, and if I call myself a true Northerner, then I should have recognised that. Well, it's too late to take back what happened there, but I knew I had to do something now. So I came to see you, so I could ask you if there was anything…' he hesitated. 'I came to ask if I could serve you.'

Red blinked. 'You…want to serve me?'

'Yes,' said Morgan. He smiled bitterly. 'I've never been much of a good man, and I don't think I'll live that much longer either. I've got nothing left to live for now – I failed my King, and I lost my wife. All I can do now is try and redeem myself to the Night God, and I'll do it by working for you. If you'll let me.'

'I will not argue,' said Echo. 'My loyalty was with Shar, and Kraego defeated her. I will give my allegiance to him now, if he will accept it.'

Red nodded slowly. 'Thanks,' he said gruffly. 'But all I'll ask you to do is go back to Malvern and help Caradoc. He needs you more than I do.'

'Yes, my Lord,' said Morgan. 'But if I can do anything for you first…'

'You can,' said Red. 'You've come just when I needed help. Listen, Morgan – I don't want to trust you, but I will now, because I know you'll have every reason to help me now. The North is in danger, and I need your help to save it.'

'Danger?' said Morgan. 'From what?'

'Wylam's coming,' said Red. 'I've just heard the news. They're coming to attack. Seems they've decided to break the treaty they signed – those bastards. Their army's marching on the Northgates right now.'

Morgan swore. 'No! I have to tell the King.'

'Yeah,' said Red. 'But first – go to Liranwee. Will you do that for me?'

Morgan hesitated briefly before he nodded. 'For you.'

'Then go there right now,' said Red. 'They'll already know what's happening, but tell them from me—,' he thought fast. 'Tell Teressa to send a message to Withypool, an' one to Canran. I know Lord Fraser's on our side, and Lady Nelia might be as well. I told your king that Liranwee was his ally, an' I meant it,' he added. 'Wylam can't cross my lands without my permission, but they've done it anyway. Probably think I wouldn't dare try and stop them. But I will. As far as I'm concerned, it's an act of war. I don't want to do it, but I'll declare war on Wylam unless they turn back an' leave the North be. If I do, I'm hoping Withypool will side with me.'

'I understand,' said Morgan. 'But I still don't understand why you wouldn't let them do it. After what we did to Liranwee…'

'It's in the past,' said Red. 'We won't have peace if Wylam's so arrogant they think they can stroll across my lands an' break the treaty they made with the North like it was worthless. Go now, both of you. Go an' give Teressa my message. An' take this with you.' He pulled out his knife and cut off a lock of his hair. 'Proof you saw me. I'd write it down, but I didn't bring any paper with me.'

Morgan took it. 'What about you? They might not listen to me – they need you.'

'Maybe, but we can't both fly back,' said Red. He nodded northwards. 'I'm goin' to the mountains,' he said. 'I'm gonna head them off at the pass. I'll try an' reason with Lord Ekra. If I'm lucky, Kraego will join me if he's in the area.'

'All by yourself?' said Morgan.

'I'm the Shadow That Walks, remember?' Red lied. 'I can handle it. I'll try an' scare them if reasoning doesn't work.'

He stopped there, hoping Morgan wouldn't ask any inconvenient questions, but the Northerner must have been too agitated to think of it, because all he said was; 'Fine. I'll go to Liranwee. Echo?'

'We will carry your message,' said the spotted griffin. 'And they will believe us. We will be doing this to protect the North, and would have no reason to lie.'

'Good,' said Red. He started to walk off back up the road. 'I'll see you later.'

'Once we've given Teressa your message, we'll come and join you,' said Morgan.

'We will bring other partnered griffins,' said Echo, stooping to let Morgan climb onto his back.

'Do that,' said Red. 'Good luck.'

'And to you,' said Morgan.

*

Lord Ekra and his partner Iraka flew at the head of their forces, following the Northgate Mountains. They had gone along the border of Canran's tiny territory before joining the mountains themselves right where they became Liranwee's land, and had followed them ever since. There were very few people this far North in Liranwee territory, and they had chosen to follow this route in the hopes of going unnoticed.

Not that Ekra honestly believed that Liranwee would have the stupidity to try and stop him. Wylam might have been subjugated by the Northerners, but it was one of the few cities that had not been directly invaded, and its population had been left largely intact. The army he led now had fought at Withypool in the South's last stand against Caedmon, and had been defeated – but not slaughtered. When the King's Amorani allies arrived, Ekra had been forced to order his men to surrender. Some had been sold to the slave markets, but most had been allowed to go home.

Many of the men he was leading now had been those who had returned from Amoran. The Amoranis had taken them back to their homeland to be sold off like cattle, but after the death of their Emperor his successor had mysteriously decided to break the alliance with the Northerners, and had sent the newly-bought Southerner slaves home. Now Wylam's army was almost intact and its ranks were full of men who, like Ekra, knew the meaning of humiliation.

Ekra felt the hatred burning in him now, and he relished it. He was an Eyrie Master, but he had been put in chains after the defeat at Withypool, and so had Iraka. The two of them had stood with the other captured Eyrie rulers, and been forced to listen while their conquerer gave them his conditions. Rule in his name, or be executed.

Ekra had accepted, but he had never forgiven himself. Death

would have been better than becoming a puppet for King Caedmon. He'd accepted anyway, out of fear, but for a while his life had been more or less a life of slavery. All his decisions had to be sanctioned by the Northerners put in his Eyrie to keep an eye on him, and even though they let him pretend he was still in charge he knew, and they knew, that the moment he disobeyed them he would die for it.

And now…now that blackrobe-loving traitor Lord Redguard thought he could…

Ekra wanted to spit at the thought of him. Some people claimed that Lord Redguard was a great man, and some even said – ridiculously – that he was the Shadow That Walked. And just because he'd defeated the King at New Eagleholm, he thought that somehow made him the master of all Southerners. He'd actually tried to force Ekra and the other Eyrie rulers to make an alliance with the enemy.

Ekra had gone along with it at the time, and so had the others, but he had not for one moment intended to let it drop. He had spoken to the twins, Brennin and Larkin, and they had agreed to start preparations once they got back to their home cities. First they would repair and give everyone time to recover, and then, once they both agreed that the time had come, Wylam and Sunton would be ready to act.

Lady Liantha of New Eagleholm had been less willing; she hated the Northerners too, but didn't want to go so far as to actually attack them. Ekra forgave her for that; she was only young, and her territory was small and didn't have much of an army. Lady Nelia of Canran had stayed out of it as well, but she had always been a weak ruler, and Canran had been reduced to a tiny territory with virtually no standing army at all. But Nelia had agreed to turn a blind eye when Wylam started its march on the North. Of all the Eyrie Masters at the meeting, only Lord Fraser had outright refused to ally himself with Wylam. But he was no better than Lord Redguard – he'd been appointed as Withypool's new Eyrie Master by Caedmon, for gods' sakes.

No – Ekra knew there wouldn't be any serious opposition to him. He didn't even spare a thought for Monag at all – that territory was a joke. If Lord Redguard had the sense to stay out of it, then he would be left alone. If not, then Ekra would gladly take Liranwee as well. It was a good territory, and it was about time Wylam extended its borders.

But first…the North.

Ekra growled to himself, and watched the Northgates pass by to Iraka's left. He and the twins had agreed that his own forces would pass through the mountains into the North first. Once they had done so, they would send a message to Sunton, who would send reinforcements. For now, that city had provided a good number of fighting griffiners to join forces with those from Ekra's Eyrie.

Iraka flew at the head of the flock of other griffins, all of whom carried their partners with them. It slowed them down, but that was fine; they had to keep pace with the foot soldiers anyway. And besides, they wanted to keep their partners with them for this. A partnered griffin went into battle with his human by his side. Fly together, fight together, conquer together.

Ahead, Ekra caught a glimpse of the pass through the mountains. It was the only place where a large group on foot could get through. Once Iraka flew closer, he would be able to see the fortress called Guard's Post that protected it, but it wouldn't be much of an obstacle. A good volley of firebombs should have the men inside surrendering soon enough. Of course, it wouldn't be long after that before Malvern knew what was happening, but Ekra had no fear about that. He wasn't going up against King Caedmon this time. His enemies were led by a child now.

Idly, Ekra wondered what he would do once he had taken Malvern. He could keep the boy and force him to rule on his behalf – that would be a very fitting way to repay him for Ekra's own humiliation. But for some reason, the idea made him uneasy. It might be a good option, but the child was a Taranisäii, and Ekra hated him for it – but feared him as well. Everyone knew about the strange ability the Taranisäii family had to lead their people, and survive against all the odds.

No…it would be better to kill him. Have him publicly executed, preferably on the same day that Malvern fell. The world would be better off without that particular bloodline in it.

Ekra occupied himself with thoughts like that through the tedious journey, considering options and possibilities he should discuss with his council once they met on the ground that evening. He even enjoyed it – relishing the fact that, after so long, he was free to make his own choices again. Free to live his own life, and to rule the way he wanted to. Free to have his revenge at last.

Towards evening, Iraka flew down to the ground with most of the other griffins. She had been in the air for a long time, and needed to rest.

The army marched on. But, like all griffiner-led armies, it had brought dozens of oversized, ox-drawn wooden wagons. Some were loaded down with supplies, but a good number of them were completely empty except for some mounds of dry reeds and straw.

Iraka climbed up into one and promptly went to sleep, leaving Ekra to sit beside her and surreptitiously rub his aching backside.

His Master of War had already taken up residence in the next wagon along, and she leaned over now to speak to him. 'We're close now, Eyre Master,' she said, speaking more formally than she would in private. 'We should reach the pass tonight.'

'Good,' said Ekra. 'We'll camp there and move on towards Guard's Post in the morning.'

She nodded. 'I'll send scouts ahead, and we can make our plan of attack along the way – it'll take some time to actually reach the fort.'

Ekra nodded back. 'Excellent. For now, though, I'll get some rest. You should too.'

He lay back against Iraka's flank, and let himself relax. She might have been doing most of the work while they were in the sky, but riding a griffin in flight was hard work, and he was exhausted. He dozed off almost immediately.

Shouts woke him up.

'Eyrie Master! Ekra!'

Ekra sat up sharply. 'What? What is it?' he called out, louder than he intended, confused by the dark around him. Night had come, and torches had been lit, and their glow showed him the face of two junior griffiners.

Behind him, Iraka had already woken. 'Have we reached the pass?' she asked.

'We have,' one of the griffins there answered. 'But…'

'We think you should see this, my Lord,' said the human beside him.

Ekra jumped down off the wagon. The army had stopped its march, and around him he could see the soldiers busy setting up their tents and making camp for the night. The mountains loomed above them, black against the starlight, but as he rounded the wagon with Iraka, he saw light.

'There,' said the junior griffiner. 'In the mouth of the pass.'

The army had halted at the very edge, with its back to the mountains. The pass itself was within striking distance. Together, Ekra and Iraka walked around a small rocky outcrop to see it clearly, and both of them stopped there in surprise.

There, at the very edge of the pass through the Northgate Mountains, with a torch burning in his hand, Lord Kearney Redguard stood all alone, blocking the way through.

Chapter Seventeen

The Last Redguard

Ekra only hesitated briefly in his astonishment, before he strode forward to meet Red. Liranwee's Eyrie Master stood firm, right in the middle of the pass, flanked on either side by cliffs. He was dressed like a guard, in a leather breastplate with a red tunic underneath, but his head was bare, the rough red hair ruffled by a slight breeze. A short guard's sword hung from his hip, and he looked for all the world like a simple guardsman, protecting the entrance to an Eyrie or a prison.

Ekra approached cautiously, staying in front of Iraka and keeping his hands away from his own sword – a long, two-handed weapon made for battle, which he carried on his back.

Red tensed slightly, but said nothing, only squaring his shoulders ready for a fight.

'Lord Redguard?' said Ekra, with just a hint of disbelief.

'Yeah,' Red said roughly. 'What are you doing here?'

'What are you doing here?' said Ekra, simultaneously. 'Are you by yourself?'

'I'm guarding,' said Red. 'Everyone knows I was a guard before I was an Eyrie Master. An' I was good at it. So that's what I'm doing now.'

'You're guarding the mountains?' said Ekra.

'I'm guarding the North,' said Red. 'Like I said I would.'

'Then get out of my way,' said Ekra. 'I'm warning you.'

'You're on my lands,' said Red. 'An' you've brought an army. D'you know what that tells me?'

'We're going through those mountains, Captain,' said Ekra, emphasising the word "Captain" with as much disdain as he could put into it. 'And I'd advise you not to try and interfere.'

'This is an act of war, my Lord,' Red said stonily. 'Marching onto Liranwee's lands with an army, without our permission – that's an invasion, no matter what you want to call it. Turn back.' He held up a hand, palm-forward. 'Go back to Wylam right now, an' take your friends with you. If you do, the treaty with the North won't have been broken an' we can forget this ever happened.'

'I don't make treaties with Northerners,' said Ekra. 'And I would advise you not to get in my way. I don't wish to fight Liranwee, but if you force me to I'll be more than happy to add your territory onto my own. Considering what you've done, I doubt anyone will help you.'

'No,' said Red. 'They will. I'm warning you again, Ekra. Go back to Wylam. If you don't, Liranwee will declare war on you. If I have to I'll attack your capital myself, while you're away. But if you go past me and attack the North, we'll come at you from behind and the King and I will fight you together.'

'If you do that, it will be the end of Liranwee,' said Ekra. 'Don't make threats you can't act on, Captain. We both know your army is tiny, and you don't have any allies…'

'We've got Withypool,' said Red. 'And Malvern. Attack us, or Malvern, or Withypool, an' you attack all three. I've got messengers on their way to Withypool right now,' he added. 'Lord Fraser's already agreed to send an army to Liranwee.'

Ekra's heart skipped a beat. 'Don't be ridiculous,' he said, hiding his fear. 'You can't have had any time to do that at all. We weren't spotted until two days ago.'

'I knew you were coming weeks ago,' said Red. 'The Night God told me. I'm the Shadow That Walks.' His eyes narrowed, black in the darkness. 'And that's one other thing you should worry about, my Lord. You know what I can do. If you try and get past me – if you do anything other than turn around an' go back west, then you won't just be up against Liranwee. You'll be up against me. And I won't hesitate. If I have to, I'll kill every single one of you myself.'

Normally, such a ridiculous threat wouldn't have bothered Ekra at all. But here, in the dark, there was something in the air that made him uneasy. The man's voice was low and icy, and as he spoke, a chill prickled over Ekra's skin. Some deep instinct he didn't quite understand stirred inside him, and whispered a warning.

Even Iraka looked uncomfortable. 'You would not do that, Kraeai kran ae,' she said.

'Wouldn't I?' said Red. He pointed skywards. 'I'm not alone. Kraego's here as well. He's watching you from the shadows. Lay a hand on me, an' he'll attack.'

Ekra took a step back. 'Enough,' he said. 'I'll go and discuss this with my council. You can…you can stay here for now.'

He had said it mostly to have an excuse to think, to go somewhere he wouldn't be troubled by the strange threat in the air. But Red let him go.

'Come back at dawn,' he said. 'You've got until then before it's too late, an' even that's generous.'

Ekra said nothing. He left, trying not to make it look like he was hurrying, and Iraka followed him in silence, leaving the lone guard at his post.

*

Once Ekra had gone, Red finally let himself relax. He could hardly believe it had worked. But it had. The man hadn't called his bluff, or seen through his lie about being the Shadow That Walked. In fact he had actually looked intimidated. Maybe the mere sight of someone mad enough to try and hold back an army single-handedly was enough to unsettle most people.

In the daylight, though, it would be harder. Once there was enough light on him for people to see him clearly, it wouldn't take long for them to realise that his skin had lost the sickly paleness, and that his eyes were now warm brown instead of icy black. Everything was less intimidating in daylight. He had wanted to buy more time for Teressa to contact Withypool, but dawn was as far as he was willing to risk. With luck, the grey light then wouldn't be enough to give him away.

He glanced skywards, and wished that Kraego really was there. But there had been no sign of the black griffin. Maybe he would go back to Liranwee and find out where Red was. He would come as soon as he knew his partner's whereabouts.

For now, though, it would have to be just Red.

He chewed on a scrap of salted goat from his bag, and began his vigil. He had no power, and not enough allies. For now, appearances would have to be everything.

*

In later years, that night would become legend. All through Cymria, North and South, people would remember and tell the story as they'd heard it – of how an army marched on the Northgates and of how just one man stood in their way. One man, all alone. Lord Kearney Redguard, Eyrie Master of Liranwee, the man who had defeated King Caedmon the Conquerer, a former guardsman and the last surviving member of the Redguard family. Somehow, people said – maybe through divine intervention – he had known about Wylam's army and its plans even before it had begun its march from the West. And then – again through some kind of magic – he had run all the way from Liranwee to the Northgates, not even taking his partner with him, and put himself at the pass, where he had confronted a thousand men without a single soldier or any other ally to back him up. Some people even claimed that he actually fought them off, and somehow defended the pass alone.

Of course, nothing like that really happened. But even at the time, the men in the Wylam army whispered amongst themselves, wondering how on earth the famous Lord Redguard had managed to get here ahead of them, and why he had come alone. Plenty of them crept past their own lines to go and see for themselves, and came back to tell their friends that Lord Redguard hadn't moved since the last time someone had looked at him. He stood there in the dark, with the black shadows of the mountains behind him, and didn't falter or move a muscle.

It wasn't exactly true, but it may as well have been. Red stood there at his self-appointed post all night, and once his torch had burnt itself out he threw it away and stayed there in the darkness, feet planted well apart, arms folded. He dozed on his feet a few times, but never let himself sit down. A guard stayed at his post for as long as he had to, and that was exactly what Red did.

By the time dawn came, he was half dead with exhaustion – but the men who came to look at him didn't seem to notice. They stared at him with awestruck expressions, and went away muttering to each other, or to themselves.

'…never saw anything like it.'

'It's like he could stand there forever an' never even blink.'

'I'm telling you, I don't care what anyone says – even if the Eyrie Master tells me to, I'm not touching him. Not for all the money in Maijan.'

'Haven't you heard? They say he can't die…'

'He's killed a hundred men, all by himself.'

'He's invincible.'

Red heard them, and smiled to himself. If nothing else, at least he had them nervous. But dawn was coming now, and soon the wait would be over. Soon, his time would be up.

Sure enough, not long after the sun had begun to rise, he saw a group of people and griffins coming. Lord Ekra, and his council.

They walked up towards him in a loose group, with Ekra and Iraka at their head.

Red stood a little straighter and kept his arms folded while he waited for them to reach him. There were five of them, all armed, the griffins all angry and defensive, with their beaks raised.

Though Red was too tired and strained to feel it much, he almost savoured the realisation that, for the first time in over a year, he actually felt afraid. Now, for the first time since the fall of the South, he was facing people and griffins who might well decide to kill him and the thought scared him.

'Morning,' he said brusquely. 'Now are you gonna leave, or do we have to get rough?'

Ekra looked exhausted, but more confident than he had before. 'We're going through these mountains,' he said. 'And you're coming with us. Surrender now, and we'll take you into custody.'

Red's heart sank. 'You're gonna try and use me as a hostage, are you?' he said.

'Yes,' said Ekra. 'Liranwee won't touch us when we have their Eyrie Master. Now come quietly.'

Hesitating, Red looked up at the sky. And there, at last, he saw something that gave him hope: the dark shapes of several griffins, flying from the South.

'You sure you want to do this?' he asked, playing for time. 'D'you know what happened the last time someone tried to take me prisoner?'

'Do not be foolish,' Iraka interrupted. 'You are alone. You have lied – Kraego is not here to protect you. You will throw down your weapon and come with us, or we will fight you.'

Red drew his sword. 'Don't make me do this, Ekra!' he warned. 'I'll kill all of you if I have to. I mean it.'

Ekra gritted his teeth. 'Enough!' he said sharply. 'You don't think we seriously believe these wild stories about your supposed powers, do you?'

Red, though, had seen the hint of fear in the man's eyes, and as the griffins above grew closer, he acted fast. He grinned a horrible, savage grin and began to chant, 'I am the shadow that comes in the night…'

'Stop that!' one of the other griffiners snapped – but again, the fear showed through.

'I am the fear that lurks in your heart,' Red continued.

'Take him,' Ekra shouted at his friends. 'Now.'

Red stepped back, sword at the ready. 'I am darkness,' he snarled. 'I am death.'

Above, the griffins descended. As Ekra's fellows started forward, a screech stopped them in their tracks, and a massive griffin, black wings spread wide, beak open, screamed his name.

'Kraego!'

'I am the Shadow That Walks!' Red roared.

The griffins on the ground scattered in fright, as Kraego landed just in front of his human and rounded on them, rearing up to protect him. 'Do not touch my human!'

Around him the others landed – Orak, Echo, and every other griffin from Red's council, their partners leaping down with their weapons at the ready.

'Come to me!' Red shouted, and they obeyed at once, drawing in around him to form a tiny army at his sides, humans standing in the protection of the griffin's front legs.

But Kraego stayed at the front, with Morgan and Echo by his side. 'My human is the Shadow That Walks!' he said. 'Fight him and you fight the dark griffin. Fight us, and you will die.'

'Fight them, and you fight me,' said Echo.

'And me,' said Orak.

'And all of us!' said Teressa.

Recovering from their surprise, Ekra and Iraka's followers re-formed into a group, and for a moment the two sides confronted each other.

'Fight us and you fight the dark griffin,' Red repeated. 'You know what Kraego can do.'

'Withypool sent us a message,' Teressa said to Red, from his right-hand side, deliberately speaking loudly enough for them all to hear. 'Lord Fraser's army is in striking distance. They'll be here before noon.'

'They're bluffing!' Ekra's Master of War snapped at him. 'I sent scouts to check. Nobody's coming.'

Ekra moved back. 'Send in the army. We'll stop wasting time now. Once this lot are dead, Liranwee will be finished.'

'We don't want to fight you!' Red shouted at him. 'For the love of gods, Ekra——'

But Wylam's leaders had stopped listening. During the confrontation its army had broken camp and started to form itself into ranks, and now, as the Wylam council retreated, they advanced.

If Red had hoped that the ordinary soldiers would be too afraid to attack him, he was proven wrong now. They came forward, spears at the ready, supported from above by a flock of riderless griffins, and as Red braced himself, ready to fight, they charged.

The first line of men closed in around Kraego, and the giant griffin reared up and started to knock them back, slashing through leather armour with his talons as if it were nothing. The other griffins pushed past their partners and attacked on the ground, defending their humans.

'Charge!' Red shouted, and ran forward.

The line of griffins thinned out the ranks coming at them, but some men got through and came on to attack the humans behind them, and as Red watched them come, he found a moment to feel regret. He had fought to save the South, and now he was going to have to kill other Southerners. What a way for it all to end.

A man came at him. With a roar of mingled frustration and despair, Red dodged his spear and kicked him hard in the side, sending him to the ground. Another stabbed at his shoulder, but he turned and struck him down with a powerful sword-blow. But more were coming. A gang of men, ignoring the others around him, attacked him simultaneously, one of them shouting. 'Kill the leader! Do it!'

Red fought back. But now he had no power any more, and a long, sleepless night had sapped his energy. That wouldn't have mattered so much; he was still strong, and he still knew how to fight. But something in him made him hold back. The thought of killing honest men who were just doing what they had been ordered to sickened him. And he had killed too many people already.

As he fell back, defending himself as well as he could, he heard Teressa call his name. And she wasn't the only one.

'Don't you touch him!' a voice bellowed.

Morgan.

The Northerner shoved his way through the mess, wielding a long dagger. He thrust it into the back of a man's neck, just as Red had seen him do in Liranwee, then turned and stabbed another in the hollow just above his collarbone.

But Morgan was not a fighter, and he had never been in a real battle. One of his attackers hit him over the head, and as he staggered, a spear caught him in the stomach.

Red charged forward, killing two of the men attacking Morgan, but at the back of his mind he already knew it was hopeless. They couldn't fight an army. Not alone.

Somewhere off to his right, he heard Teressa screaming. But she wasn't screaming as though injured. Loud and frantic, but full of anger, she screamed—

'Ye can't take the North! No army will ever take it again! ARENADD!' Red saw her as she fought, sickle flashing, throwing herself at her enemies like a madwoman, her black eyes blazing as she shouted on, switching to Northern now, saying something, reciting some curse or promise or threat, where the only word he understood was a name. A name that had always been said as a curse when he had heard it as a boy, but which Teressa said as if it were a blessing that could save their lives.

And then…and then…

And then, as Red fought on, making his last stand with his friends by his side, a strange feeling came over him. Maybe it was his his imagination, or maybe it was a last, lingering touch of the power that had driven him less than a day before. Maybe it was because he was so close to death.

Coldness touched him. Not on his bloodied and sweating skin, but inside – at his heart. In his stomach, an irrational sense of dread stirred.

But he wasn't the only one who felt it. As he flinched under it, he saw the men around him do the same, and then the griffins, and one by one, everyone there faltered. Weapons lowered, faces slackened as the anger left them, and fear took its place. Even the griffins stopped fighting.

Everything else forgotten, the people in the pass turned to look northward, and then slowly backed away, pressing up against each other as if their battle had never happened at all, and they were allies now.

And there, in the pass, they all saw it.

Where the sky had been blue, tinged with hints of pink and gold as the sun rose, the light suddenly dimmed. The shadows in the pass moved, rearing up into the sky, higher and higher, blotting out all colour, and as icy terror bit into the soul of every man, every woman and every griffin, a shape formed.

A massive, black shape. The shape of a man in a robe which flapped out behind him, melding with long, curly hair. A man who grew until he was as tall as the mountains on either side, until his face became clear – scarred, bearded, and full of hate.

Everyone backed away. Humans, griffins, Northerners, Southerners, and the shape leaned forward and made a sound so loud, and so awful that everyone there heard it, and none of them ever forgot. It was half roar, half scream, and it went out over the heads of the Wylam army like a blizzard wind through sharp stones.

Then, in an instant, the sound ended and the shape disappeared.

But it had been enough. To a man, the Wylam army turned and ran – not just hurrying, but fleeing, panicking like a flock of sheep. The griffins took to the air and flew away as fast as they could go, none of them stopping to check on their human partners. None said a word, nor made a sound. Nothing mattered now but the need to run, to escape, to get as far away from the mountains and the horror that lived in them as they could.

Only Red stayed, with the others from Liranwee, but none of them dared to move at first. They flattened themselves to the ground – even Kraego, and afterwards they stumbled away, not following the men from Wylam, but starting to move in the direction of Liranwee.

Only Echo did not follow. He stayed where he was, by Morgan's side.

'Stop,' Red said sharply, waving to the others. 'Don't run. It's gone.'

The others came to a halt, all looking fearfully up at the mountains. But Red was right: there was no sign of the thing that had screamed at them. A deathly silence had fallen where it had been, and in a way that was far worse, but Red's voice had been enough to stop them panicking, and they let themselves relax.

'I think we're safe,' Liranwee's Master of Diplomacy muttered.

Slowly, feeling the sting of his wounds, Red went back to check on Morgan. But he already knew there was nothing he could do. The former spy was dead.

'He died to save you,' Kraego rumbled.

'He redeemed himself,' said Teressa.

Echo said nothing. He stared down at his human's body, and didn't even move.

'Come with us,' Red said suddenly. 'Come and live in Liranwee.'

Echo looked blankly at him, and then looked at Kraego.

'You are unpartnered now, and disgraced,' the black griffin told him. 'But you gave me your loyalty, and your human's, so you may come back to Liranwee.'

Echo stirred. 'Yes,' he muttered. 'I will come.'

Red lifted Morgan's body. 'We'll send him back to Malvern,' he said. 'To be buried.'

'No,' said Teressa. 'Bury him in Liranwee. It was where he wanted to live.' She smiled sadly. 'We're going ahead, Kearney. With the Moon Temple. The plans have been approved. To found it, we have to bury the body of a Northerner at its foundations. Morgan should be that Northerner.'

'Yeah.' Red turned away to look up at the mountains. 'He earned it in the end. I s'pose in his own way he was a hero.'

Teressa followed his gaze, and then came and touched him lightly on the arm. 'It's all right,' she said softly. 'It's over. My prayers have been answered. All of them.'

Slowly, Red turned his back on the mountains. 'All of them?' he asked.

Her grip tightened on his arm, and a look of slow surprise crossed her face. 'Yer arm…'

Red looked down at her, heart fluttering wanting to hear her say it. 'What?' he said softly.

Teressa touched him again, tentatively, and her eyes widened. She reached for his hand and grasped it. 'It's warm…'

Red smiled. 'Yeah,' he said. 'I'm all right now. It's all right…'

She stared at him in wonder. 'Truly?'

Red hugged her, chest to chest, heart to heart, warmth against warmth. 'Yeah,' he said. 'Everything's all right now. We can go home now. Together.'

Chapter Eighteen

Freedom

And it was over – truly over. Red and Kraego sent unpartnered griffins to report back on what was happening in Wylam, and the replies told them everything they needed to know. The Wylam army had managed to regroup some way west, but once it had done that it went straight back to its home city. Whatever had happened in the pass had been enough to convince them that invading the North was a bad idea.

As for whatever had happened, afterwards nobody seemed to want to discuss it. But as usual, Teressa was absolutely certain – and once Red told her about what had happened to him, she became even more certain.

'It was Arenadd,' she said. 'I know it was. I only saw him once, but I never forgot him. He saved us.'

'I think maybe he did,' said Red. 'But I know he saved me.'

'I know,' said Teressa. 'So no more running away from yer responsibilities,' she added sternly.

Red grinned at her. 'Yes, milady.'

'Don't make fun of me,' said Teressa, but without any real irritation.

Red settled himself more comfortably on the stone bench beside her. 'I'm not making fun of you,' he said. 'You're a Lady now, aren't you? Liranwee's Master of Wisdom, no less.'

'Aye, I suppose I am,' said Teressa.

They sat up on the roof of the Liranwee Eyrie together while they talked, and they were alone. Kraego and Orak had gone off by themselves. Neither of them needed to protect their partners now. The war was over, and peace had come.

Night had begun to come again, and the stars glittered above. They seemed to go on forever, horizon to horizon, mirrored by the sparks of torches and lamps down in the streets. But beyond the walls of the city, the earth was dark and still.

'Ye know,' said Teressa. 'In the North they say stars are the souls of the dead. But only the righteous dead. Sinners and blasphemers go to the void.' She paused. 'I don't know if I believe that any more, though.'

Red thought of the tiny, glimmering light that had been his own soul. 'Maybe it's kind of true,' he said. 'But I know what you mean.'

'I know,' she echoed. 'Because Arenadd was a great man, and he served the Night God faithfully, but I don't think he's up there now. He's in the void. With her.'

'He was,' said Red. 'But now I'm not so sure.'

Teressa looked up again. 'I hope yer right. I hope he's up there. If anyone deserves to be there, it's him.'

'I dunno,' said Red. 'It just looks like another void to me.' He smiled at her. 'Give me a life down here on earth any day.'

She smiled back. 'I won't argue with that.'

They sat together in companionable silence for a while, looking out over their city.

'Well,' Red said eventually. 'I suppose now I'm alive an' everything, it's probably time you and me…'

'Yes?' said Teressa.

He looked at her for a moment. She was so familiar to him now, black hair, black eyes, her face pale and narrow – serious, but with a hint of humour around the mouth. She had always looked a little fragile to him, but now he knew where her strength was and had always been: on the inside, where it mattered the most.

He smiled shyly. 'I s'pose now there's nothing in the way anymore, we should probably get married,' he said, almost casually.

Teressa started and stared at him, and then looked irritated. 'Ye know, Kearney Redguard, ye've got many good qualities,' she said. 'But ye haven't got any social grace at all, have ye?'

Red grinned roughishly at her. 'I thought you liked that about me.'

'No, I like ye because – don't change the subject!' She made an exasperated noise, and looked away.

'I know,' said Red. 'I thought about it, but in the end…I made plans an' things, but just now it suddenly felt like the right time, so I thought I might as well come out an' say it.'

She looked back. 'Do ye even have a gemstone for me? I know that's how ye do it in the South.'

Red winced. 'Uh, no. But I could get one from the treasury if you'll just give me a—'

'Oh for Arenadd's sake,' said Teressa. 'I just know yer going to drive me mad for the rest of our lives.'

'Probably, but you'll never do any better,' Red grinned. He took her by the hand. 'But look on the bright side,' he said.

Teressa put her fingers through his, and didn't let go. 'What is it?'

He pressed himself against her, feeling how the warmth of her body mingled with his now. 'At least we've got lives,' he said.

Teressa put her free hand against his chest, where his heart beat – a little faster than it needed to. 'Aye,' she said quietly. 'We do.'

Their lips met a moment later.

*

Below them, in the Eyrie, the former Lady Isleen woke up and found herself alone in bed. She lay there sleepily for a while, aware of the cold space beside her under the blankets, but when she started to wonder where her husband had gone, she heard the faint scratching of a pen.

Dim lamplight touched her eyes as she sat up. And, sure enough, she saw Alaric sitting at the table not far away, quietly hunched over an open book.

Isleen got up and padded over to him. He was so absorbed in what he was doing that he didn't seem to notice her until she put her head on his shoulder and wrapped an arm around his chest.

'What are you doing?' she asked softly.

Alaric tilted his head to the side, resting it against hers. 'Writing.'

Isleen looked down at the page, and saw what she had been half expecting to see. She smiled. 'I thought you said you were never going to do it again.'

'I know,' said Alaric. He sounded ashamed, but he didn't let go of the pen. He dipped it back into the ink, and scratched out another word. 'But I couldn't sleep, and then I just…'

Isleen waited for him to finish.

'I know it's silly,' Alaric said at last. 'But it makes me happy. I can't help it.'

'I know it does,' said Isleen. She kissed him on the cheek. 'All this time I've been hoping you would go back to it. I wanted to know what happened next.'

'Really?' Alaric asked tentatively.

'Really,' said Isleen.

*

Red and his friends weren't the only ones who had left the Northgates that day after the Wylam army had fled – though they were the only ones who went South.

In the darkness of the pass, in a shadow, something else slipped out into the light. It was man-shaped, or vaguely so, but it wasn't a man.

The black spectre that had terrified the Southerners, shrunk back to its usual size now, sped silently away over the landscape. It moved faster than a griffin could fly, not hampered by any obstacle, or by tiredness, or even by the wind. It sped through the North, towards Malvern, and then past it, on and on as the air grew colder and a second mountain range became visible in the distance.

When night fell it melted into a shadow by the trunk of a fir tree and stayed there, out of the moonlight. The mind that drove it was afraid – more afraid than any living thing could ever be. But it had learnt patience, and it did not move at all until the sun rose and the moon was gone, and its journey continued.

It went on, as fast as it could, through villages and towns, over farmland, through forests and plains and rocky outcrops, slipping through the gaps in them like water and never altering its course for a moment. It went on, past a place where a solitary tower rose up out of the ruins of a tiny village, and then up into the mountains.

These weren't mountains like the Northgates. They were bigger, taller, rougher, and much colder, snow-bound even in summer. Few people knew what they were called, and even fewer ever came here, but the shadow knew what these mountains were. They were called the First Mountains, for reasons that had been lost to history, but even so it was the right name for them – here where everything had begun.

The shadow knew the way, even after so long. It coursed up the side of one of the lower mountains and onto a plateau, where thirteen ancient standing stones made a circle.

It lingered there for a moment, keeping out of the circle itself, and then turned away and went up again – up and up, its form rippling over the stones of the mountainside that guarded the plateau and the circle, up to the place where the slope had broken and fallen away, and revealed a hole just big enough for a man to crawl through.

The shadow went through the hole, and into the cave on the other side.

It was huge – much bigger than it appeared from the outside. Big enough for a griffin. And a griffin had been here once, years ago.

In a way, it was still here.

The shadow drifted silently over the giant skeleton that lay by the cave's entrance, darkening the hollow eye-sockets with its presence. The dead griffin's beak was not pointed towards the entrance, where another griffin might have turned in its last moments. The Mighty Skandar had died as he had lived, with his back turned on the light and his head pointed towards what lay at the back of the cave. Still waiting, after all the years that had gone by, staring at what he guarded, even in death.

The shadow moved towards it, not even daring to hope. But it was there. Still there, just as Teressa had left it.

The body of Arenadd Taranisäii lay on its back, not far from Skandar's bones. Once, it too, had been nothing but a skeleton, but not anymore. Teressa had done her work well, following the instructions that the dark spectre had whispered in her dreams.

The body was naked, and even though uninhabited for ten long years before its regeneration and had since lain here like this for many months, it was intact. Perfectly preserved, without a hint of rot anywhere. The skin was clean, the hair and beard glossy. Nothing had touched it. And, as it lay there, the shadow could see it breathing. It was inert, eyes closed, but the thin chest moved up and down just slightly. The mouth was open, as if to welcome the shadow back.

The shadow hovered there for a moment, drinking in the sight, and feeling a fierce longing rise inside it. But it knew it couldn't waste any time. Time was everything now.

It poured itself in through the open mouth, down through the chest and into the silent, withered heart. It stayed there, soaking itself into the shrivelled muscle, until something locked in place, and the shadow spread. Out and through, into the bones and veins and muscle, and up into the brain. Taking back what had once belonged to it, and which it had schemed and longed for all these terrible years.

From the outside, nothing appeared to happen. But then the body moved. It jerked once, violently. The breathing grew faster. It lay still for a moment but then, inside, the heart pulsated. One hard, solid heartbeat slammed through the body. It jerked again, and the mouth opened wide to take in a great, gasping breath.

The eyes snapped open. For a moment they were blank, but then the mind behind them rebuilt itself, and they blinked, narrowed, and a look of sly cunning appeared in them.

At last, at long last, Arenadd Taranisäii sat up.

He coughed and groaned, and then started to check himself – running his hands down his body to make sure it was all there.

It was. All of it. Arms, legs, chest, face, genitals, everything.

Some things had changed. His skin was newly grown – soft and smooth like a baby's, even in the places where it had hair, and the hair itself had a touch of wispiness. The tattoos that had once covered his upper right arm were gone, and all his old scars were gone too. The one like a tear-track under his eye was gone, and the one in the middle of his chest where he had once been impaled by a sword was gone as well. The fingers of his left hand, which had been twisted and crippled, were better. They could move properly now, though they were still slightly bent where the bones had remained crooked. But the joints didn't crack or hurt anymore when he rubbed them.

His hair and beard were a mess, and his clothes had long since rotted away, but what did that matter? What did he care? He was smooth and clean and new. Reborn.

He stood up easily, trying to stay calm, and padded barefoot over to Skandar's skeleton. Despite the urgency of what he had to do next, he knew he couldn't leave just yet. Not yet.

He crouched by the griffin's huge skull, and laid his hands on it, lowering his head as if in prayer. 'Skandar,' he whispered. His voice worked, too, though it felt clumsy. He wasn't used to having a real tongue and lips. 'My Skandar. I'm so sorry. I wish…'

He trailed off and left it at that. It didn't need to be said aloud. His old partner was long dead, and his simple soul had faded away into oblivion. He would never rise again; he was gone forever.

Saying nothing now, Arenadd reached down and took hold of one of Skandar's skeletal forepaws. They were still held together with a few shreds of dried sinew, but they were no match for the strength of the Shadow That Walked. With a single, brutal wrench, Arenadd tore the longest toe away from the paw. It came free, talon and all, and he tested the point on his thumb, loving the pain it caused and the blood that followed.

'You can't come with me any more, Skandar,' he said softly. 'But part of you will. I'll keep it with me no matter what. I have to go now,' he added as he stood up. 'But I won't ever forget you. Goodbye.'

With that he turned and left the cave, climbing up over the heap of rocks that blocked the entrance, and squeezing out into the sunlight. It touched his eyes and made him wince, but he kept on, thrusting himself out and onto the mountainside.

He stood there for a moment, his hair blowing in the icy wind, and looked down at the landscape beyond, seeing it with real eyes once again.

It looked so beautiful. His old Kingdom, laid out in greens and blues, greys and browns, patched with snow in places. The North, with the River Snow winding away through it to join with the River Nive, which flowed down from Crescent Lake, where the city of Fruitsheart stood, named for the orchards which surrounded it. In time the water he could see from here would flow all the way to Malvern and beyond, into the Northgate Mountains. He imagined he could see it from here.

His heart swelled in his chest, silent but real all the same.

'Home,' he said in an undertone.

But his sadness and longing only lasted for a moment, before it twisted inside him and turned to bitterness. He couldn't go back there now, and he didn't want to either.

It was all finished for him. Too late to go back. His children were dead.

He thought of them now, while he stood there. Laela and Kullervo. The Queen and the shapeshifter. He had loved Laela, and Kullervo…he had loved him from a distance, wishing they could meet, knowing they never would.

He had stood in the void and watched both of them die, knowing all the while that there was nothing he could do to save them. His master had been right when she had promised him that. But she was nearly always right, at least when she promised death and suffering.

Pain twisted in Arenadd's chest, and suddenly he couldn't bear to look at the landscape which had seemed so wonderful a moment before. He turned away from it and started to climb down the mountainside, eyes hard, mouth set into a thin line. He went backwards, knowing that if he looked directly downward, the old fear might paralyse him to the spot.

It was hard going, even with his inexhaustible strength. He stepped carefully, not really aware of the cold. He had to get to the bottom before nightfall.

It seemed that chance still liked to toy with him though. About halfway down he put a foot wrong, and a patch of snow and loose rock slipped away from beneath him.

Clumsy in his newly rebuilt body, Arenadd lost his balance and went tumbling down the mountainside, rolling and thudding into rocks and dead shrubs, loose rubble falling with him.

He landed with an ugly crunching sound in the valley at the bottom of the mountain, and before he could get up, a large chunk of rock hit him in the back and knocked the remaining breath straight back out of him.

He lay there for a moment, winded and aching all over. Once the shock wore off he began to get angry – but then, quite suddenly, something turned itself around in him and he started to laugh.

He levered himself onto his back and lay there, laughing uproariously – a horrible, harsh, cold laugh, but a genuine one. Not a laugh at the sight of someone else's suffering, or at the joy of murder, but a laugh at life and the world. Everything was so silly and pointless. He'd come back to his body after so much effort, and now he was already trying to wreck it again.

'My gods,' he said as he stood up. 'My gods, my gods, my gods. You're hopeless, old man. Hopeless. What would your worshippers think if they saw you now?'

He groped around, found Skandar's talon, and picked it up before limping off.

The sense of absurdity that had come to him stayed, and it lifted a burden from his new shoulders.

Nothing mattered any more. It really didn't. His children were dead, Skandar was dead, everyone was dead, and none of them were coming back. But he was dead as well, and that was all right, and now…

No. He wouldn't let himself think that. Not yet. It was too soon. But he would let himself admit it later, when the time came, if it ever did.

And now that he had done the first thing, there was something else he desperately wanted to do. He'd been planning that as well.

Arenadd walked down out of the mountains without a backward glance, and went on past the tower he had built for Skandar without bothering to give it more than the briefest look. The past was falling away from him – not the memory of it, but the pain of it. He was letting it go, shedding it like an old set of clothes.

He turned away from it as he had turned away from the mountains and the tower, and looked forward instead. It was time to go and do something he had spent years wishing he could do. It wasn't much of an ambition for a man who had once ruled a country, but if he was going to leave the past behind, he should forget that as well and set his sights on smaller things. Take it one step at a time.

For now he needed clothes, and a drink – or several. He smiled to himself in pleasant anticipation, and walked on faster, holding Skandar's talon against his chest.

*

A few days after this, in a small town east of Warwick, the local guard were called out to investigate a set of crimes that quickly proved to be impossible to solve.

The night before, without leaving a trace of evidence anywhere, someone had committed a string of thefts. And they had somehow done it by breaking into people's homes while they were inside and taking things without anybody noticing, without leaving a footprint or a scuff-mark anywhere.

And the animals in the area seemed to be unsettled, though nobody could understand why. Dogs howled, chickens tried to escape from their coops, cats bristled and horses and oxen bolted.

In the end, nobody could find a likely culprit for the thefts and before long they forgot about it. It wasn't as if the thief had taken anything very valuable. Once they had made a list, the victims found that all that had vanished was a set of clothes, a knife, an old leather bag, and a small keg of wine from the local tavern.

'Very good wine, mind you,' the tavern owner grumbled.

By then the thief was long gone, knowing he wouldn't be caught. Nobody would ever be able to catch him, unless he let them do it. It was daylight now, and the moon wouldn't be in the sky for a long time, and he walked down the road heading east, unnoticed and unremarked. A raggedy looking Northerner, apparently young but with hints of grey in his long curly hair, barefoot and wearing clothes that didn't fit. He strolled along, a small barrel slung on his back, drinking from a wineskin and singing in a raucous, tuneless voice.

'I danced around the tree when you came to look for me, 'round and 'round the tree we went, 'round and back again. Won't you take my hand, and we'll dance across the land, and…damn it, why did I never bother to learn the rest of the words?' He laughed aloud and started the song again from the beginning, before slipping away into a different one, not caring one bit that people stared at him. 'Drunk,' a woman muttered.

'That's right!' he shouted back. 'I'm a drunk and a thief, and a murderer as well, and a traitor. I can do whatever I want, and I don't care. Isn't life wonderful!'

He cackled and went on his way, enjoying the disgusted look on her face. He felt as if he had never been so—

No, no, he couldn't think that yet. It was still too soon. But he felt it, even if he didn't let himself think it yet.

He travelled on, day after day, knowing the mad joy that had taken hold of him wouldn't last forever. Sooner or later he would probably go back to the way he had been before, but he didn't want to. Life was too short, and the world was too precious. He was alone and he didn't care. He was making a fool of himself and he didn't care about that either. He hid from the moon at night and drank himself to sleep to dull the terror, and that was fine. He could get drunk if he wanted to, because he was…He was something he wouldn't say or think yet, but he could feel it deep down.

He finally said the word, weeks later, when the time came that he knew it was true. He had made his way not to Abertawe, but to a smaller port town, where he wouldn't be noticed. The alliance with Amoran had been broken, but Maijan was still friendly, and trading had continued between the two countries.

In this anonymous little port town, Arenadd used his natural stealth to slip on board a ship and hide below deck. There were several Maijani ships moored in the harbour, but he had smelled something that attracted him below the deck of this one, and chose to follow his nose.

Sure enough, once he had gone down there, he saw something that made him smile. The cargo hold was full of barrels of wine, and rum, and beer. Wonderful.

By now his joy had worn off and he felt calmer, but the feeling of lightness in his body and his mind stayed. He was…

He found himself a hiding place in among the barrels, and chose one he could tap into without being noticed. There was some food down here as well, and he helped himself to that too. He didn't need to eat any more, but he wanted to now, just so he could savour the taste. After ten years in the void, everything felt so much more intense in the real world than it had before, and he loved it.

The ship set sail, and he had to spend his time hiding below deck in case somebody saw him.

But, about a week out at sea, he finally risked going up into the open air. He waited until night, and crept silently up out of his nest, up the ladder and into the smell of the ocean.

The deck wasn't deserted, of course. Three men were there as well – one holding the tiller while the other two kept watch. But he could stay out of their sight easily enough.

His breath caught in his throat when he looked up at the sky. The stars were out, and…the moon. It shone down on the black sea, and turned the shadows on deck grey. It was nearly full, and to him it looked like an eye. A great, white eye, staring down at him, full of accusation.

But Arenadd knew he couldn't hide from it forever.

Quietly, keeping out of sight of the watchmen, he stepped onto the deck, out of the shadows, and into the moonlight.

He tensed as it touched him. Ever since his return he had stayed out of sight of the moon, knowing what it could mean if he let its light touch him. If he let that eye in the sky see him, then she…

Pain rippled through him. But it wasn't her pain. Fear had taken him by the heart and begun to squeeze, and for a long, awful moment, he couldn't breathe. He stood still, arms spread, waiting for her to come. Waiting for her to drag him back into the void and torture him for eternity. His final punishment for daring to run away from her.

Nothing happened.

'I'm here,' he whispered at last. 'It's me, Arenadd. I'm here, master. Can't you see me?'

There was no reply. The moon shone down blindly. The coldness of her presence did not touch him. She wasn't here. He had left her behind in Cymria, in the North, where she would search for him but never find him. It was over. He had done it. He had escaped.

Now, at last, the word came to him. Standing there, not caring if anyone saw or heard him, he whispered it.

'Free.'

It felt like the most precious thing in the world, the most beautiful, perfect word there was.

'I'm…free.'

Up in the bows of the ship, one of the sailors on lookout turned around sharply. But he was too slow – Arenadd had already slipped back below deck.

Back in his little hideaway, he downed a cup of wine and then a second one, and said the word again, here where they wouldn't hear it.

'I'm free,' he said.

Impulsively, he put the cup down and grabbed a handful of his hair. With his other hand, he drew his knife.

'I'm free,' he said yet again. 'Arenadd is free!' He laughed wildly, joyfully, and said it again and again, singing the words to himself. 'I'm free! I'm free!' And while he sang and laughed he took his hair, his cherished hair, and began, slowly and methodically, to cut it off.

The Scholar

The traveller came to Liranwee alone, nearly eighty years after the end of the war. He entered the city with some caution, which was normal – after all, he was a Northerner, and this was the first southern city he had ever seen. He hadn't met many Southerners before, and he was almost intimidated when he walked up through the main gates of Liranwee and saw them in their dozens, some of them coming towards him as he followed the main road, as if they were on their way to challenge him.

But it wasn't long before he felt himself start to relax. There were no enemies here. The men he saw were farmers and traders, coming into the city to set up their stalls in the marketplace, or leaving to go back home. And anyway, not all of them were even Southerners.

The traveller took it all in with astonished eyes, even though he should have been prepared to see it. But it was so odd to him, so different from what he was used to, that it caught him by surprise.

A good number of the people around the gate – a minority, it was true, but still plenty of them – were Northerners. They mingled freely with the Southerners around them, neither race paying any attention to the presence of the other. And, more than that, some of them were together. The traveller saw at least three mixed-race couples, and several clear half-breeds as well. He saw Northerners chatting to Southerners and laughing freely. He saw the guards on the gate, and they were a mix of both races as well, and nobody seemed to care, or even notice.

The traveller shook his head slowly as he walked into the city itself. He had had trouble believing it but, now he could see it for himself, he understood why Liranwee had become one of the most famous cities in Cymria. The only city in the whole country where Northerners and Southerners lived together and were treated equally by the law and the Eyrie. Northerners could come and settle in Liranwee if they wanted to, and join the guard, and a few Northerner griffiners had even left Malvern and gone to work in the Liranwee Eyrie. The traveller had heard that a few Amoranis and Maijanis had emigrated from their own countries to live there too, and that they had also been made welcome.

The traveller wasn't under any illusions, though. He knew how some of the other cities in the South disliked Liranwee, and grumbled behind its Eyrie Master's back. Plenty of the people he had grown up with in Malvern had criticised the city as well, though not very loudly. It was odd, and some said it was against the gods, but Liranwee was thriving. It traded freely with the North, unlike any other city in the South, and had become rich and prosperous.

And it was all down to one family. At first just that family's founders, but their children and grandchildren had continued in their footsteps, and carried forward the plans they had made, so that when those founders were gone their dream for the city would not go with them.

The traveller smiled excitedly to himself as he walked through Liranwee's streets, taking in the sights. Northerners selling black wool, silver, and dried fruit brought from the North. Southerners selling grain and beer and cheeses. Houses built in the Southern style but with Northern touches. It was all so incredible, and so beautiful despite the strangeness of it, and even though he had travelled to stranger places in his life he felt most pleased to have come here. Here, to the city some called Mongrel City, and others simply called the home of the Redguards – the proudest and most powerful family in the South, who many people said were the southern equivalent to the Taranisäiis in the North.

The traveller had heard all that with fascination, from his own father when he was a boy. Even back then, when he was young, he had promised himself that one day he would see Liranwee for himself – and now he had done it, after so long.

He only hoped that he hadn't come too late.

He hadn't brought much with him from home, just a walking stick, and a battered leather bag which was full of books, pens, and bottles of ink. He patted it now, and pressed on, past the larger and grander buildings and towards the Eyrie itself. Now, he knew, the most difficult part would come.

The Eyrie was guarded, of course. Well before he got to the building itself he reached the wall that surrounded it, where the only open gate was watched over by a pair of armoured men.

Both of the guards were Southerners, and they held out their spears to stop him.

'No entry to the Eyrie except on official business,' one said. 'What can we do for you?'

The traveller hastily reached into the pocket of his coat, and brought out a piece of paper. 'I've come to bring a message to Lord Redguard,' he said.

The guard took it. 'Which one?' he asked with a touch of sarcasm.

The traveller felt his cheeks redden. 'The Lord Redguard,' he said. 'Kearney Redguard, the former Eyrie Master.'

'Oh, right,' the guard grinned. 'The famous one. Is that a Northern accent?'

'Er, yes,' said the traveller. 'I'm not a local. Can you make sure my message reaches Lord Redguard?'

'I'll pass it on,' said the guard.

'Thank you. I'll come back tomorrow.'

The traveller left, heart pounding with excitement.

*

He found an inn to stay in, not far from the Eyrie, and to his amazement he found that the innkeeper would accept Northern oblong. Ignoring his aching feet and sore back, he stopped there just long enough to eat a meal in the main room, and then left to explore the city.

It was everything he had hoped it would be, and more. He spent a blissful afternoon wandering through the streets with a book open in one hand, busily sketching and making notes on everything he saw. He visited the Sun Temple, and went to say a quick prayer in the Moon Temple. He went to see the prison complex, and the marketplace, and the South End, where he tried to find the place where the secret passage had once been. It was gone by now though, filled in years ago, as he had expected.

Along the way, while he explored, he stopped to talk to people as well – particularly the older ones, asking them questions and jotting down their answers with a quick but neat hand.

Once night had fallen he went back to the inn for dinner, and chatted to the people who sat by the main room's two fireplaces. He would ask different questions depending on who he spoke to, but he asked everyone two questions in particular.

'Tell me about Liranwee. Tell me about the Redguards.'

Some of them looked bemused, but all of them answered. Some of the answers they gave were short and to the point, others told stories, some jokes. But no matter what they said, the traveller wrote down every word.

'And who are you?' several people asked him.

'Nobody important,' he would answer. 'My name's Firth. I'm a scholar from Wolfton. I want to write a book about Liranwee.'

They accepted that without argument, and some of them were excited or impressed by the idea of him writing a book. More than one of them asked if he would put their names in it.

'Of course!' he told them. 'I've already written it down.'

'I wouldn't have thought I knew anything worth putting in a book,' one old man remarked. He sat back by the fire, beer in hand. 'I'm just an old man. I can't even read.'

'Everyone knows something worth putting in a book,' said the traveller. 'Everyone's seen things, and thought things, and those are the things that make a great book.' He held up the one he had been scribbling in. 'I could just fill these pages with what I see, and what I think, but it would be a poorer book if I did.'

The old man grinned toothlessly. 'I can see y'know more than most young men I've met, especially when it comes to flattery.'

The traveller shook his head. 'I only know how to tell the truth,' he said, which won approving nods from everyone listening.

He went to bed exhausted that night, but even then he wouldn't let himself sleep. He sat up in bed, with a candle still burning while he went through what he had written that day, sometimes scratching something out or adding something else while he still remembered it. It was rough, but it was a good start. He had already promised himself that he wouldn't leave Liranwee until he had finished, and the most important thing that would go in this book was still to come. Tomorrow, maybe, he would have it.

*

The next morning he went back to the Eyrie, hoping to find out that his message had been acted on and that the guards had been ordered to let him in. But the two he found on duty that day were different from the ones he had spoken to, and when he asked them about the message they said they hadn't heard anything about it.

'I'll come back tomorrow,' he promised.

'Sure, if you like,' one of the guards said dismissively.

But the traveller kept his promise. He came back the next day, and when he was disappointed then he returned the day after that, and the day after that.

In the end he stayed in Liranwee for over a week, exploring and interrogating and filling his book. Every day he went back to the Eyrie to ask about his request, and every day he was disappointed. He left other messages, in case the first one had been lost, but never got a reply.

In the end, even his normally ruthless determination started to falter, and he began to consider whether he should give up and go on his way, and maybe try again if he ever returned to Liranwee.

But then one day when he went back to check yet again, something happened.

'Oh, it's you,' said one of the guards, who recognised him very well by now. 'I was hoping you'd show up.'

The traveller stood bolt upright. 'Did he answer my message?' he asked.

'No, but someone in the Eyrie heard about you and asked us to let her know when you came back,' said the guard. 'Wait here, an' I'll go get her.'

The traveller nodded enthusiastically, and waited while the guard summoned a replacement from inside the Eyrie and hurried off to find whoever it was who wanted to meet the traveller at the gates.

When he came back, he was with not one but two others – a large sandy-coloured male griffin, and a young woman who was obviously his partner. The griffin stayed back, blinking curiously, while his human went on towards the traveller.

'Hello!' she said immediately. 'Are you this traveller I've been hearing about?'

He bowed. 'I am, my Lady,' he said.

She inspected him, not suspiciously but with open, friendly curiosity. 'You don't look like a local,' she said. 'Where are you from?'

'Wolfton, my Lady,' he said. 'My name is Firth. I'm a travelling scholar.'

'So I heard,' said the woman. She was about thirty years old, and pretty, with narrow shoulders and bright red hair. 'My name's Inge Redguard,' she said. 'And this is my partner, Thark.'

The traveller bowed again. 'It's an honour to meet you, my Lady,' he said.

She smiled. 'There's no need for that!' she said. 'I'm only a junior griffiner. Just because my Dad is the Eyrie Master, that doesn't make me special. Would you like to come inside now?'

The traveller nodded. 'Absolutely, my Lady. I've wanted nothing else since I came here.'

'Come on, then,' said Inge. 'Follow me.'

The traveller went with her into the Eyrie, scarcely able to contain his excitement. After more than a week, he had finally done it.

The Eyrie was comfortable and elegant in a homely kind of way, its oversized corridors wood-panelled for warmth and decorated with painted animal hides. Plain lamps hung from the walls, and red carpets covered the sloping floor.

'Granddad had it all redecorated,' said Inge. 'Red is his favourite colour. He says it's lucky. Here, come this way,' she added. 'We'll sit down in one of the dining rooms and we can talk.'

The traveller murmured something or other to show that he understood, but all his attention was on the walls, and the roof, and everything he could see on the way up the tower. His hands itched for his pen. He wanted to draw it all, and make notes, but he thought his guide might be offended if he did, and instead did his best to memorise it all for later.

Inge didn't seem to be bothered by him anyway and she talked cheerfully on the walk, telling him a few bits and pieces about some of the things they passed. She didn't ask him anything more about himself until they were safely up in a small dining hall, where she waved to him to sit down. Shortly afterward a servant appeared to ask her if she wanted anything.

'A drink?' she suggested, looking at the traveller.

'Yes please, if you don't mind,' he said.

'Bring us some wine,' Inge told the servant.

Once it arrived, along with a chunk of meat for Thark, Inge took a sip from her cup and looked across the table at the traveller.

'So, Firth,' she said. 'I read your note. Are you really here to write a book?'

'I am, my Lady,' he said. 'I want to record everything about Liranwee.'

'Why?' she asked.

'Because it's said to be the greatest city in the South, and it is,' the traveller said honestly. 'And because of the role it played in Cymria's recent history.'

'Not that recent!' said Inge. 'It all happened a long time before I was born – before you were born either, I think!'

The traveller smiled back at her, and smoothed down his ruffled muttonchops. 'I'm not that old!' he said. 'But it's recent in the scheme of things, and it should be written down. It all needs to be recorded, so it can be remembered. In all my studies of history, I've always been shocked by how quickly fact turns into myth and legend, and the lessons that could be learnt from the past are forgotten.'

Inge raised a carrot-coloured eyebrow. 'I can see why you kept coming back for this long,' she said. 'You're really serious, aren't you?'

'I am,' the traveller said earnestly. 'And that's why I came all the way from the North hoping to speak to your grandfather.'

Inge took a thoughtful sip of wine. 'Hmm. He doesn't see many people these days,' she said. 'Spends a lot of his time alone, up in his room.'

'But do you think he would be willing to talk to me?' the traveller asked.

'I can ask him,' said Inge. 'But what should I say?'

'Tell him…' the traveller paused. 'Tell him I've come to hear him tell his story, so it won't be forgotten. Tell him that.'

'All right, I will,' said Inge. 'I'll ask him today. Come back tomorrow, and I'll tell you if he's agreed or not.'

'Thank you, my Lady.' The traveller bowed his head politely.

Inge looked at his bag, which he had put on the table. 'Is your book in there?' she asked.

'Yes, it is.'

'Can I see it?'

'Of course!' said the traveller. He pulled it out, and passed it over the table to her, suddenly aware of how battered it looked.

Inge opened it and flipped through the pages. 'It's long,' she said eventually.

'I've already visited every important place in the North,' the traveller explained. 'I started there, naturally. Of course, it's written in my own language…'

'That's all right,' said Inge. 'I know how to read Northern. This is interesting.'

'Thank you!' said the traveller. 'I've spent half my life writing it.'

She turned a page. 'So you go to places and write about what you see, and you write down what people tell you as well,' she said.

'Yes,' said the traveller. 'And once I've finished here in Liranwee, I'm going on to the other cities in the South.'

Inge looked up at him. 'Really?'

'If I can.'

'You've got a death-wish, then,' said Inge. 'We might be open here in Liranwee, but it's not like that in the rest of the South. Down in New Eagleholm, they'll kill you on sight if you so much as set foot in their territory.'

'I know,' said the traveller. 'I intend to be very careful.'

'You'd better be,' said Inge. She turned to the later entries in the book, and flicked idly through the blank pages beyond it. 'Would you like to ask me questions as well, then?' she asked. 'So I can be in your book too?'

'If you're interested,' the traveller said, pleasantly surprised.

'I am!' said Inge. She slid the book back over the table. 'Show me how well you'll deal with old Grandfather Redguard.'

The traveller reached into his bag again, and pulled out his lucky pen and a pot full of ink. Once he had uncorked it and dipped the pen, he was ready to begin.

'Tell me about Liranwee,' he said. 'Tell me about the Redguards.'

'Sure,' said Inge.

The two of them talked for a long time after that, and the traveller asked every question he could think of. Inge answered all of them happily, and told him plenty of things he had been desperate to know, but when he moved on to asking about the war she often didn't know, and started to answer with things like, 'You'll have to ask Grandfather about that. It was all before I was born, and before my Dad was born as well.'

By the end, the traveller had filled several more pages in his book, and Inge looked satisfied. 'You're good,' she said. 'You know what to ask people to get them to tell you things. I'll tell Grandfather all about you. I think he'll be interested.'

'Thank you,' said the traveller. 'For everything.'

'It's no problem,' said Inge. 'Honestly, you're the most

interesting person to visit the Eyrie here in a long time. Grandfather's bound to like talking to you. Come back tomorrow, all right? In the morning.'

'I will,' the traveller promised.

*

The next morning he came back, just as he had every day before. He had taken special care to neaten himself up for the occasion, having carefully brushed his hair and his shaggy muttonchops, and the little patch of beard on his chin – something he often forgot to do on a normal day. He couldn't do much about the ink spots on his shirt cuffs, or the patches on the elbows of his favourite old coat, but it would have to do. Normally he wouldn't even have thought about any of that, but he felt very self-conscious that morning as he stood by the gates, waiting for Inge to come back. In spite of his age, he could feel his heart fluttering as if he were a small boy again, facing the fears that had ruined his life.

Inge took a while to arrive and well before she had, he had nearly convinced himself that she wasn't going to come at all. But she did, and looked pleased to see him.

'Good morning!' she said. 'Did you sleep well?'

'Not very,' he confessed. 'I was nervous.'

'At your age!' she laughed.

'I get nervous,' the traveller chuckled. 'Always have. I'm a naturally nervous person.'

'Well, let's hope you can contain yourself around the famous Lord Redguard,' Inge said good-naturedly.

The traveller grinned. 'He said yes?'

'He certainly did,' said Inge. 'Are you ready?'

'As ready as I'll ever be, my Lady,' said the traveller.

'Then come with me,' she said. 'He's waiting.'

This time, when he passed through the Eyrie, the traveller was far too excited to pay any attention to his surroundings at all. He plodded along after Inge and the silent Thark, feeling his own heart thudding and keeping his eyes fixed on the way ahead as if it might somehow disappear before he got there.

But it didn't, and after a slow and strenuous walk up the Eyrie's sloping corridors Inge and Thark took him to an entrance just over halfway up, which led to a large, warm room.

Inge went in first, while Thark and the traveller waited outside. The traveller heard her say something, and a faint reply, before she returned.

'You can go in now,' she said. 'And don't look so scared! He won't bite your head off. He's more than a hundred years old, for Gryphus' sake.'

But the traveller still entered with a faint buzzing in his ears, and a swelling sensation in his chest, as if he were walking into the holiest temple to the Night God.

The room he went into was a griffiner's quarters, with a bed up against one wall and a desk against another. It was surprisingly plain considering who lived in it, but cosy, with a good fire burning in the grate and thick, richly woven rugs covering the floor. As he entered, the traveller looked quickly around out of habit. He saw a short, battered old sword hanging over the bed, next to a gold medal with a broken feather strung beside it. A stack of books sat on the desk, and he saw a grubby red tunic on a hook by the door.

The room's occupants were over near the entrance to the griffin nest, and the traveller's breath caught in his throat when he saw them. He spotted the griffin first, of course – a giant even by griffin standards – lying on his belly beside the chair where his partner sat. His black feathers were greyed around his beak and eyes, but even so they were glossy, and his great thick limbs were solid with muscle. He was clearly ageing, but still strong and vigorous, and when he lifted his head to look at the traveller his blue eyes were as fierce as they must have always been.

The traveller bowed low. 'Mighty Kraego,' he said.

The black griffin huffed and looked away.

As the traveller stepped forward, he saw him – saw the man he had come so far to meet, standing up from his chair to greet him.

'Hello. You must be the scholar Inge told me about.' The voice was as rough-sounding as the traveller had been told it would be.

He stood there stupidly for a moment, not knowing what to do with himself, but then pulled himself together and bowed again. 'Lord Redguard.'

Lord Kearney Redguard stood there and regarded his visitor. He might have been more than a hundred years old, but he didn't look as old as the traveller had expected – or not as frail, anyway. His skin had gone brown and wrinkled with age, and his hair and moustache had turned pure white. A slight tremor showed in his hands. But his shoulders were still wide, his body still firm, his back still straight, and his brown eyes had not faded.

'It's an honour to meet you,' said the traveller, and he meant it. 'The greatest honour of my life, my Lord.'

Kearney pointed to a chair set up near his own. 'Nobody likes an arse-kisser, boy,' he said. 'Sit down. And call me Kearney.'

The traveller nearly laughed in his shock, but managed to contain himself, and did as he was told.

Kearney returned to his own seat, turning it around to face his visitor's without much effort at all. 'So you're here to listen to my story,' he said unceremoniously. 'Can't imagine why. Everyone else got bored with it.'

The traveller sat down with his bag in his lap, and opened it to bring out his book. 'I already know it,' he said. 'Or one version of it. My father told it to me when I was young. But I know it's not the full story. That's why I came here to see you, because there are parts of it that only you can tell me.'

'Could be,' said Kearney. 'But who are you?' He peered at the traveller. 'I'm not telling anything to a man I don't know.'

'Well, my name's Firth,' said the traveller. 'I'm a scholar from Wolfton, and—,'

'Is that so?' Kearney interrupted.

'Er, yes,' said the traveller. 'I'm writing a book—,'

Kearney kept on staring at him, unreadable.

'Er,' the traveller said again. The stare kept distracting him as he tried to speak, and he started to stumble over his words. 'Er, so, I c... I came here to write the parts about Liranwee, but everyone knows you're the most important person here. I wanted to hear your story straight from you, so I could write it down. Once my book is finished,' he added, 'I'll have it copied and send it to you. It would be an important piece of Redguard family history.'

'Was it a long journey from Malvern?' Kearney asked suddenly. 'Since you came on foot, and everything?'

'Er, yes, it took a while,' said the traveller. 'But I gathered plenty of useful material on the way.'

'I'm surprised your sister let you go,' said Kearney. 'After what happened to her, I would have thought she would be very protective of you.'

The traveller coughed. 'Er, what? My sister? What do y… ahem, I mean, how do you know I have a sister?'

Kearney sat back and smiled. 'I know who you are,' he said. 'You don't have to lie to me again.'

The traveller nearly dropped his bag. He started to lie again, trying to cover the moment, but it was too late. Nervousness ruined any chance of making himself look calm, and the dreaded stammer came back in full force.

'Er,' he said. 'I d-d-d- don't k-know wh-what you're t—,' But he couldn't say it. The more he stammered the worse his fear became, and the word broke apart in his mouth, leaving him to spit out a string of meaningless noises.

Kearney listened to him with a stony expression, and then burst out laughing. 'Hahahah! I knew it! It's all right, sonny, calm down. You're not in trouble. But for gods' sakes, what are you doing all the way down here? By yourself? You haven't run away again, have you?'

'Er…' the traveller sagged in his seat. 'I suppose so, in a way. I did come here without my sister's permission. My wife didn't want me to go either, but, well, I persuaded her. It's all I ever wanted to do with my life, you see.'

'And Inge says that once you're finished here you're going to go on to the other cities in the South,' said Kearney. 'You must be mad. They won't be happy to see a Northerner, but when they find out what else you are, it'll be your head on a spike.'

'It's all right,' said the traveller. 'I've been planning it for years, and I've learnt a few things in my time. Anyway, they would never suspect it for a moment, would they? Nobody else would have. But…' He winced. 'How did you know?'

Kearney smiled. 'You look like your father.'

The traveller smiled back, sadly. 'Yes, they do say that.'

Kearney eyed him. 'I never would've expected this, that's for sure, even after all the strange things I've seen. It's just a shame Teressa's not here to see it too. She would have been happy to meet you. But what in the world are you doing here, Cadfael?' he added. 'What brings a Taranisäii all the way to Liranwee? A prince, for gods' sakes?'

Cadfael clutched at his bag as if it were a shield. 'I already told you,' he said. 'I'm writing a book. And I don't care about what I am. I was never cut out to be a Taranisäii, or a noble either. My bbrothers were the warriors, and my sister is the leader. I'm just a scholar and an historian, and that's all I've ever wanted to be.'

'Cadfael the Disappointment,' said Kearney. 'Yeah, I've heard.'

Cadfael sighed. 'Yes, of course you've heard,' he said. 'Everyone's heard. Everybody in Cymria knows about King Caradoc's idiot stammering son. But it doesn't matter now, does it?'

Kearney sat back. 'Well, you can't be that much of a coward if you managed to get in here all by yourself,' he said. 'I'm glad to see you, you know. I've always wondered what you were really like.'

'So have I,' said Cadfael. 'I've wanted to meet you since I was a boy. I always promised myself that one day I'd come and find you.'

'And you want to hear my story,' said Kearney.

'Yes, I do,' said Cadfael. 'If you're still willing.'

'It'll take a while,' Kearney warned.

'That's all right,' said Cadfael. 'I'm not going anywhere.' He took out the book and opened it, and dipped his pen into the inkpot. Then he leaned over the open pages and waited, ready to begin.

Kearney sat in silence for a while, thinking. 'It's been a long time,' he said. 'They say I was the longest-serving Eyrie Master in history. I could've stayed even longer, but after Teressa died, well…my heart just wasn't in it any more. I retired and let my son Stirk take over. He's been doing well, but he's a clever boy. Takes after his mother, not me.' He grinned. 'Now I've got all the time in the world to do all the nothing I like. I sit up here and spend time with Kraego – we don't talk much, though. Don't need to any more, do we, Kraego?'

The black griffin opened an eye. 'You are human, and speak when there is nothing to say,' he said. 'I am a griffin and have more sense.'

'That's about right,' said Kearney. 'We don't talk. We sleep, and think. I think about the past a lot, but old men do that, since we've got nothing much to worry about in the future.'

Cadfael nodded. 'If your past had a moment when everything changed, what would you say that moment was?' he asked. 'When do you think your story began?'

Kearney rubbed his moustache thoughtfully. 'Hm. That's a hard one. Could be on the night my Dad died, or the day I met Kullervo. But after that it was all quiet for a long while. It depends, really. Did you want my story, or the story of the war?'

'Yours,' said Cadfael.

'Well then,' said Kearney. 'Well then. If that's what you want, then I know where to start, and it's not with me. It's with my uncle Bran. Yeah, that's where I'll start.'

'Then start there,' said Cadfael.

'Uncle Bran was a great man,' said Kearney. 'A hero, even if nobody thought so then. He was a griffiner later, but in the beginning, he was just a guard captain in Old Eagleholm. Until one day, he met a man named Arenadd Taranisäii…'

*

So Kearney Redguard told his story, and after his early ramblings and reluctance he quickly settled into it. In the end he talked for most of that day, while Cadfael listened, only interrupting to ask when he needed something to be clarified, making no sound other than the constant scratching of his pen.

By evening they were both tired, but Kearney hadn't finished his story.

'Come back tomorrow, eh?' he wheezed. 'We'll keep going.'

'If you feel up to it,' said Cadfael, closing the book.

'Up to it!' Kearney repeated. 'I'm not dead yet, boy. And I should know. I've been dead before. Come back tomorrow morning, and the day after that if you have to. We'll get it all down in the end.'

Cadfael did just that, returning the next day, and the day after that, and the day after that as well. Day after day he went back to the Eyrie to meet Kearney and write down more of his story. By the third day word had gotten around, and some of the Redguard children crept in to listen. Neither Cadfael nor Kearney really noticed them; by now, they were both so caught up in what they were doing that they wouldn't have cared either way.

It took five days, and by the end Kearney had started to look tired and distracted.

'Don't think I'll ever tell it again,' he rasped, putting a hand to his throat. 'There's all so much, and so much of it is hard to talk about.'

'It's all right,' said Cadfael, patting the book in his lap. 'I've got it all here now. You won't have to tell it again. The book will remember it for you.'

'Yeah.' Kearney sat back, eyes closing. 'I like that. You did the right thing, coming here. You know that? I'm glad you came.' His eyes opened partway, and he looked down at the children sitting by his chair. 'They'll be glad too one day, when they read what you've put in that book of yours. They'll know how it was, an' that way they won't forget.'

'And we won't forget either,' said Cadfael. He looked down at the pages, where he had written the last part of Kearney's story. 'So you got your life back,' he said. 'And your soul.'

'That's right,' said Kearney. 'Arenadd gave them back to me. I know most people don't believe it, but it's true.' He coughed. 'I can feel it's true, right now. Strange things happened afterwards, you know.'

'What things?' asked Cadfael, diligently writing it down.

'Teressa and I got married, of course,' said Kearney. 'And we had kids. But it was odd how they came along. There were five of them: three boys and two girls. But the boys were triplets and the girls were twins. Everyone said how unusual that was. And out of my children who had children, most of them had twins or triplets too. And look at them!' he added, looking at the rapt children. 'My great-grandkids, and you can see how many twins there are. And they're all so strong. So many children in the Redguard family, and not one single stillbirth, not one miscarriage, no deformities. Every one healthy and strong as a horse. I think that came from me.'

'How do you mean?' asked Cadfael.

'I mean there's too much life in me,' said Kearney. 'That's why I've lived so long, and never been sick a day. That's why my children were all so big and strong, right from the cradle, and they're all ageing slowly too. My Stirk is older than you, but fitter than most men half his age. It's Gryphus' power doing it. I'm sure of it.'

Cadfael nodded. 'Maybe the Redguards are a blessed family. You know they say the same about my own family. It's said we're hard to kill, and that we always lead eventful lives. We're not as lucky as your family, though.' He looked sad. 'Taranisäiis always suffer. It seems to be our lot in life.'

Kearney nodded. 'So it seems. I saw the truth in that plenty of times.'

'There's only one other thing I wanted to ask,' said Cadfael. 'It's about Arenadd.'

'Yeah?' said Kearney.

'You never saw him again, did you?' asked Cadfael, lowering his voice.

'No,' said Kearney. 'Never saw any of 'em again, and I'm damn glad about it. No more gods, no more spirits. It's a world I never wanted to see back then, and I never want to see it again now.'

'You think he's back, though, don't you?' said Cadfael.

'I do,' said Kearney. 'I'm sure of it. See, I've thought about what happened, and the things he said and did, and the more I think about it the more certain I am. I think he planned it all. All of it – the war, me, Kraego, everything. I think it was all his plan from the start. Somehow or other he was in there, making it all happen. He wanted to get away – wanted to get his body back and escape. I gave him the chance without even meaning to.' He nodded again. 'So no, I never saw him again, but I'm still sure of it. He's back.'

'I know he's back,' Cadfael said flatly.

Kearney looked at him. 'Why? What happened? Did you see something?'

'You thought he'd left the country,' said Cadfael. 'I know you did.'

'I did,' said Kearney. He sighed, and a hint of tears shone in his eyes. 'I sent my eldest daughter to look for him, but she never came back.'

Cadfael closed the book, and leaned forward. 'I've come here to tell you the truth, Kearney,' he said in an undertone, so the children wouldn't hear. 'It's been far too long. I should have come here years ago.'

Kearney looked up. 'I sent her to look for you after you ran away,' he said. 'But she was meant to look for him as well. I never found out what happened to her.'

'She found me,' said Cadfael. 'She found everything she was after.' He put the book back into his bag. 'You've told me your story, and now it's time for me to tell you one in return. I want to tell you what happened to us out there.'

Kearney stilled. 'Tell me everything.'

Cadfael freed his right arm from his coat, and rolled up his shirt sleeve. Underneath, two long, deep scars sank into his flesh, just below his elbow. 'I've never told anyone else before,' he said, touching one. 'Not even my wife. I took a vow that it would be my secret forever. But I've decided to break it now, because you deserve to know. I found answers out there, my Lord. Answers to questions I know you've asked over and over again.'

'Do you know what happened to my daughter?' asked Kearney.

'Yes,' said Cadfael. 'And to other people as well. It all happened out there, on the other side of Amoran.'

'Then tell me,' said Kearney. 'All of it.'

Cadfael nodded. He sat back in his chair and took a moment to collect his thoughts, just as Kearney had done at the beginning of his own story. And then, slowly at first, but with growing confidence, Cadfael Taranisäii began to tell the story of everything that had happened beyond the Eastern horizon.

Other Books By K.J. Taylor

The Price of Magic

Broken Prophecy

The Land of Bad Fantasy

Tales of Cymria

The Fallen Moon
The Dark Griffin
The Griffin's Flight
The Griffin's War

The Risen Sun
The Shadow's Heir
The Shadowed Throne
The Shadow's Heart

The Southern Star
The Last Guard
The Silent Guard
The Cursed Guard

The Drachengott
Wind
Earth
Fire
Water